*My Life, Starring Dara Falcon*

ALSO BY ANN BEATTIE

# MY LIFE,
# STARRING DARA
# FALCON

# Ann Beattie

HarperCollins*Publishers*Ltd

Canadian Cataloguing in Publication Data

Beattie, Ann
My life, starring Dara Falcon

ISBN 0-00-224561-2

I. Title.

PS3552.E177M92 1997    813'.54    C97-930291-9

97 98 99 AAK 10 9 8 7 6 5 4 3 2 1

Printed and bound in the United States

The quotations from Chekhov hung above my friend Lee Goerner's desk. I like to think he'd be amused that when they came to hang above my own desk, they helped inspire this book. Which is dedicated to him:

LEE GOERNER
1947–1995

*My Life, Starring Dara Falcon*

I was stretched out on a lounge by the pool at a hotel in Key West when I found out the news about Dara Falcon. A pink-faced, pink-kneed man had left *The New York Times* behind as he slipped into his flip-flops for the walk to the elevator. Before he'd gotten ten steps away, I'd pulled his newspaper out from under the mattress pad and started flipping through. I hadn't seen a newspaper since I left Connecticut four days earlier, and I wouldn't have bought one, but the temptation of an abandoned *Times* was too great. I read the beginning of several articles on page one, but didn't turn to the jump pages. I looked at the book review, but the book didn't sound interesting, even though the reviewer said it was. I was just about to tuck it back under the mattress and tilt my face toward the sun, which had come out from behind a very large cloud, when I turned through a few more pages and saw it: *Dara Falcon, Actress and Playwright*. No survivors were mentioned. There was a photograph from the early eighties, which is when she'd had her biggest success, starring opposite Viva in an Andy Warhol film, and later as Amanda Greenfield, on the soap *Time of Desire.* In the photograph, her hair was parted down the middle, and she was looking at the camera without any trace of a smile. She had on a turtleneck, and if I could have seen the rest of her, she would have been wearing her size-seven jeans and—had the photograph been taken a little earlier— the ruby-and-diamond ring Tom Van Sant had given her. It had been his mother's ring, and there had been a time when it bothered him very much that his mother had died so young, before he had any serious girlfriend. But then, what didn't make Tom Van Sant sad? His mother's death was one of the few things he hadn't orchestrated to make himself morose.

Dara Falcon had died of pancreatic cancer, according to her secretary. She hadn't written anything that had been published or, to my knowledge, performed, in fifteen years, and she had a secretary? Who could really say, I suppose: J. D. Salinger; Dara—towering piles of manuscripts might eventually materialize. But how had Dara managed to get not only an obit in the *Times,* but a photograph as well? I looked again at the photograph. This was the woman my former sister-in-law had irately described as being responsible for the end of my marriage. Before that, though, she'd gotten me to sell her my car for a dollar, and she'd let me wear Tom Van Sant's mother's ring while she wore my alpaca jacket, and then she'd given me a hundred dollars because the dry cleaner had ruined it, though I later found out they had given her one fifty.

"You blame me for *bad luck?*" she'd said, incredulously. She always made me question whether I was rational. And those times when she'd grant that I was, she'd pout because I wasn't a good sport. "Well, yes, what you say is *rational,* sweetheart, but can't you *forgive* me?" She spoke in italics. She had a way of being able to wither into a waif right in front of you, her eyes suddenly larger, the slight hunch of her shoulders reducing her instantly in size. In Tom Van Sant's presence she was often inches shorter and pounds lighter than she actually was.

After the Cafe Central days, when New York got too expensive and her career as a soap opera actress was too discouraging, she went into exile in Vermont, which was the preferred farthest edge of the world for the truly hip. She sent amusing photocopied Christmas letters (in fact, the only ones I have ever received were from Aunt Elizabeth and from her), in which she referred to herself in the third person and did an impressive job of satirizing Christmas letters, filling hers entirely with trivia. The last time I heard from her she was still the quintessential Dara, expressing her undying devotion, and cueing me that I should respond in kind, because she was gravely ill.

Above the Gulf of Mexico, a small boat pulled someone dangling from a blue-and-white parachute. Except for its bright color, the way it billowed and drifted reminded me of tropical insects that could settle so gently you'd never sense their presence until after the bite. My husband was off on a catamaran with his brother, who'd flown from a small town outside of Albany to spend a few days with us in Key West. At Christmas Jacob had found out that his wife was having an affair with their minister, so he was preoccupied and feeling sorry for himself. John thought that constant activity was the best way to distract Jacob. Panting and glazed with salt water and sweat, they would appear at periodic intervals and then rush off again. This time they had been gone for almost an hour.

A waitress in a short sarong, halter top, and high-top basketball sneakers asked if I would like anything from the bar. I ordered an iced coffee and thought about what I could do to distract myself from thinking about Dara—which really meant what I could do to distract myself from thinking about my life. A man I dated long before I met John (a man who ultimately betrayed me) had often listened in puzzled silence to my impassioned descriptions of Dara's behavior—I was even more worked up about it years ago—and then had said to me, "She sounds like my idea of hell. It makes you wonder why anyone would befriend a person when they could befriend a dog." He wasn't trying to be funny; my stories about Dara had made him doubt whether I had good sense and also inspired him to get an Irish setter.

You could ask a dozen people who knew her, and in all likelihood they would describe different Daras. The only common denominator might be that while they had first thought one thing about her, eventually they had come to think the opposite. This would not necessarily be anything negative; they might have thought her very outgoing and decided that actually she was quite a private person, or they might have thought she was a good listener and then decided that she was clever to ask leading questions and file away the answers—a writer at heart, wasn't that true? Usually men held the strongest opinions, because if men knew her for any time at all, they tended to find themselves in very deep, very fast. She was more cautious with women, and they with her. If you weren't equally pretty—though of a different type—she usually couldn't be engaged. Of course, you also had to be somebody, though I don't mean somebody in the eyes of the world: it would suffice if you were a highly recommended optometrist, or even if you could be relied on to help her. She once shared a house in Vermont with a woman who raised ladybugs. Either she raised the best ladybugs, or the biggest, or had the largest mail-order business—I can't remember. But with men or women, whatever you were—whatever you did—had to be easily paraphrasable and sound at once humorous and dramatic. If she couldn't present you in one sentence, she wasn't interested. My own sentence was: She met an actor at Cafe Central and sailed for England with him the next morning. Though she'd known me more intimately in other times, this would be the first thing she said after introducing me to someone new. No matter that the actor's name would have been unfamiliar to anyone who hadn't watched a sitcom that only lasted a dozen episodes. No description of the way this might have been a more interesting situation than it seemed (I was paid to pretend to his elderly aunt that I was his fiancée). No qualifiers or explanations were ever offered at all, except that sometimes she would digress into saying that the nightlife at Cafe Central was the most fun she had ever had in New York, and sometimes she would throw in the information that Bruce Willis tended bar. She passed over the fact that she moved away with the ladybug lady (who had tried without success to become an actress, and became, instead, a sales clerk at Macy's, before poverty drove her to Vermont) when she could no longer afford her rent. She wanted to give the impression that we—but particularly she—had been at the right place at the right time, though she didn't ever say that most of the actors who hung around Cafe Central didn't think she was a very good writer, or that, as time went on, people no longer jumped up when she walked in to invite her to join their table. Someone had found out that no one at Long Wharf had ever heard of her, so of course they were not really considering presenting her newest play. One man she'd slept with said that she'd confided in him that she was drawn increasingly to women, and a woman who'd cut her hair in exchange for a few white wines the previous night told stories behind her back, saying that Dara had picked up the cut hair and wanted her to kiss it—that what at first seemed like a joke had become frightening when Dara repeatedly kissed the hair herself, down on her knees like an animal feeding. She had risen with a whiskery mouth and tears in her eyes, looking so forlorn, the person said . . . , so desirous that someone be involved in the oddly personal ritual with her. Dara would tell you that she had spent a dreamy afternoon—"dreamy" was one of her favorite words—dancing with Patsy Cline (meaning: to Patsy Cline tapes; Dara understood she had no power to resurrect the dead), or that for breakfast she had feasted on feathers (translation: health-food-store breakfast food that looked like large, ragged asterisks; who could say what strange substances we ingested back then in the name of good health?). I let her stay at my apartment for the two weeks I was on the *QE2* and in London. She teased me by calling it my "flat" and by mock complaints that I had such a small "telly." It was necessary then, and always, to exaggerate the way someone lived so that they lived a major or a minor life. Certainly no one she would associate with could live an average life, so we were all either worse off or else really living amid opulence or, at the very least, situated in fascinatingly eclectic circumstances. I thought I had been to her New York apartment, but it turns out I had only visited a place she'd been house-sitting. At the time, though, I took careful note of the fur coat that she'd never worn, hung on a large golden hook on the back of the front door, and of a large telephone that looked like one square foot of the lighted dashboard of a superjet's cockpit. The small kitchen was painted with black lacquer, the dangling lightbulb surrounded by a large rice-paper globe, and the sleigh bed—an antique; the first sleigh bed I ever saw—doubled as a sofa, draped with worn Turkish kilims and satin pillows. The place was comfortable and eclectic, and so was Dara. I thought her apartment expressed her personality. Looking back, I suppose it certainly did, though not in the way I thought.

Dara had many good qualities, lest we forget (another of her favorite phrases, said with imploding desperation, when she, herself, was eager to temper another person's negative opinion): She was attentive; she could be kind; she was sometimes sentimental and didn't mind if you saw that she was. She was also very pretty, and petite, and you could find yourself thinking that she needed taking care of, and that you should serve as her protector. Who didn't tell a few white lies back in those days, more as a way to bolster their self-confidence than as a way to deliberately misrepresent themselves? Who was proud of where and how they lived—who had (or even aspired to) the perfect apartment? And who didn't do odd things for money, whether it was stringing along with some man's plan to get money for a nonexistent wedding from his wealthy aunt in England, or marrying someone for a fee so they could get a green card (particularly popular with homosexuals), or working the night shift somewhere you hoped against hope none of your friends would ever show up? If New Orleans was the Big Easy, New York was the Absolutely Impossible, but that was not the criterion for changing your intentions about succeeding there. You just had to be inventive. You had to play things differently. You had to realize there were no insiders—at least, no one you were likely to meet—and that everyone was an immigrant: decide on a new name and plunge right in, which Dara had taken care of long before she moved to New York.

Dara Falcon was once Darcy Fisher. She either had or hadn't been a promising young actress. She either did or did not have a baby when she was sixteen. Gossip had it that Mrs. Fisher drank, and that Mr. Fisher wanted Darcy and her sister gone so he could try to rehabilitate his wife. Other people said that simply wasn't so, but that all was not perfect in the Fisher house, because Mr. Fisher had backhanded all of them: his wife; the girls. He died prematurely, golfing. His wife sold the house and moved into an apartment and the next year took up with a younger man—a waiter. Darcy hated the man and only shook off her deep depression when she got a scholarship to Radcliffe. Franny was accepted at Williams, but dropped out after one semester and went to live with her sister in Cambridge. They shared a small efficiency apartment on Mass. Avenue for a year, or a little more than a year, and then Franny left a note saying that she had met someone interesting, and that she and he were hitching to Nantucket. She was not heard from for years. A month or so into the search, unable to sleep and frantic with worry, Darcy was hospitalized. Her mother and Ron, the waiter, went to visit her, and apparently her mother became hysterical, screaming in front of the doctors and nurses that since Darcy couldn't alienate Franny from her effectively enough, then Darcy had seen to it that Franny disappeared. She insisted that Darcy knew where Franny was. She insisted there was no boyfriend, which was something she had also insisted upon with the police, though she refused to tell anyone why she was so sure of this. When she visited McLean Hospital, Darcy's mother was in the last trimester of her pregnancy, and it was the first time Darcy knew that she had married Ron, or that she was expecting a baby. Her mother was forty-one years old. "Why couldn't you have taken my baby, if you wanted another baby?" she told me she had asked her mother. Darcy's mother visited only once, and would not return phone calls. When Darcy was discharged, it was into the care of her aunt, who had steadfastly refused to discuss anything about the past with the doctors. Years later, when Dara was telling me the story, she said she resented the way her aunt had acted; she felt that too much of a premium was put on privacy in the family, and that that had been a good part of everyone's problem. True, she hadn't levelled with the doctors entirely herself, but she had been desperate to get out of the hospital; she felt convinced that she could somehow track down her missing sister; she had hoped that once—just once—an adult could be counted on to reveal painful truths about the family, to say to the doctors those things she found so difficult to express herself. As Dara told me these things, speaking forcefully but—I now see—vaguely, she pressed to her chest a picture she managed to let me know, without words, was her beloved sister, Franny. The young woman in the photograph was attractive, and she had an open face and sincere eyes. This picture was only of her face, in a tiny silver heart-shaped frame on Dara's night table. Or on the night table in the borrowed apartment. I only went there two or three times, but even in winter, and in spite of how little money she had, there were always fresh flowers. Looking back, I must admit that while I misunderstood other things, I was not wrong in assuming that the bouquets must truly have been Dara's. So: Dara had survived her childhood, and she had either had an early pregnancy or she hadn't, and she had gotten a scholarship to Radcliffe (or so she said), and then Franny had appeared on her doorstep, there had been quite a bit of smoking dope, and both she and Franny had had sex for money a few times. . . . Then Franny had disappeared, and Dara had been hospitalized. She was treated with antidepressants; she was discharged into her aunt's care in Bronxville but soon ran away, returning to Radcliffe and living with a girlfriend who offered her her sofa and who only turned against her when the girl's boyfriend said he had fallen in love with Dara, though *("Jesus! My bad luck!")* it was nothing he'd ever said to Dara herself.

When I met her, she was phobic about Cambridge, afraid when she had nightmares that she was back there, slogging through the winter snow, high on grass or on prescription drugs, the songs of that period triggering real depression, the tastes of certain foods she'd eaten inextricable from the metallic taste in her mouth during the time she'd been hospitalized. "Promise I won't ever be back there," she would say to me—meaning all of it: on the snowy sidewalks; in the hospital; at Radcliffe; at the various grim apartments—and because it seemed very unlikely, indeed, I would promise, as if I had the power to ensure it. "One time when I disobeyed some stupid McLean rule, they cut off a bunch of my hair and stuffed it in my mouth," she told me. "They were the animals, not the patients." As she said it, she grabbed hold of both sides of her long, dark blond hair and pulled it lightly away from her face, allowing it to drift down, as if her hair were gently falling snow.

I dropped out of college in 1975, my sophomore year, and got married to a man whose family owned a nursery in Dell, New Hampshire. We moved there in 1976, after Bob graduated from the University of New Hampshire. I was twenty and Bob was twenty-one. He had a big family, most of whom lived in the area: two brothers and a sister, and also—such things were important in those days—two nephews, two nieces, and numerous cats, gerbils, and dogs. I was an only child, and I liked the idea of large family gatherings. I felt very adult taking on obligations: celebrating people's birthdays and anniversaries; going with them to the doctor if they needed moral support; offering my car, which my aunt had given me as a wedding present, if theirs was broken—which, in that climate, and given the age of the cars, happened often. We lived in the same neighborhood as Bob's brother, Frank, who had a very nice wife a few years older than he was named Janey, who was a nurse. Of all the family, we saw them the most, even using their land for a combined garden. Janey and I canned vegetables together at the end of summer and went to flea markets in the spring. The other brother, Drake, was in law school on a scholarship, and occasionally visited from Boston. He had custody of his daughter, the offspring of a brief marriage in undergraduate school. His grandmother lived with him in the Cambridge apartment and took care of the little girl, who called her Mama, though she was eighty. Then there was Bob's sister, Sandra. She was the mother of Bob's niece, Marie, a pale, gawky child who was allergic to everything and who bit her nails to the quick and who spoke out loud when she read—which was most of the time, because she didn't enjoy taking part in anything the adults did. Sandra had tried everything, and she couldn't get her daughter to stop reading aloud. Marie would make temporary progress when she saw a specialist in reading disorders after school, but inevitably she would revert to her old ways. Instead of music playing in the background—or along with music in the background—we usually did whatever we did while Marie read audibly from one book or another. She often ignored her mother and wouldn't make eye contact with the rest of us, except for those times when, unpredictably, she had talking jags. I shied away from asking her questions about school, or about what she was reading, because it obviously made her uncomfortable: she'd answer as briefly as possible and bite her fingernails until I went away. For some reason, though, she was relatively animated and available to Bob, and we all encouraged him to get her to talk, or to urge her to go along on a canoe ride because she could help him paddle, or to try petting some of the animals and seeing what happened if she did not then put her hands anywhere near her face (allergies made her prone to sneezing fits). I still remember Bob crouched on the floor with her kneeling beside him, softly stroking Jinx, the oldest and most docile of the family dogs, and afterward his picking her up and taking her to the kitchen sink to wash her hands, and his washing his hands along with her, saying, "See—I'll wash too, because that's a good idea for everyone after they've petted a dog, and then neither of us will put our hands anywhere near our faces, will we?" I also remember his playing hide-and-seek with her, pretending to have no idea she'd disappeared behind the living room curtains, or into the pantry, or whatever obvious place she'd thought to hide, asking aloud, when he got in close proximity, "Where could she be? Could Marie have disappeared like Tinker Bell, or could she have become a leaf and blown out the front door?" He would open the door, and cold air would rush in. "No Marie out there," he would say, sounding very puzzled. "Well then—could she be in the oven, baking like a cookie?" Bob and I had discussed when we would have children, and I was the one who wanted to delay it, saying—rightly enough—that I didn't know what I wanted to do with my life, and that I should decide before I became a mother. But as much as I commended him for being such a devoted soul when it came to Marie, something about the way he threw himself into the part also made me reluctant to imagine that he might be playing those same games with a child of ours. It was mean-spirited of me, and I kept my thoughts to myself, but there was something unsettling about the way his jaw would go flaccid when he spoke in such an exaggerated way. Something about the fact that at those times he looked like a snared fish. That he was trying so hard. As I watched him deliberately overlooking the black-and-white oxfords that poked out from beneath his mother's gold curtains, though, I became sure that starting our own family was a bad idea. "Methinks I spy Horatio!" I said in a loud stage whisper to Janey one time, pointing to Marie's protruding shoes. "Shh!" she said, slapping my outstretched hand. Marie's little face—her pale little face—peeked from behind the curtains: she wanted to see who, besides Bob, was playing the game. She frowned at me and withdrew. As Bob looked at me, exasperated, it seemed clear to me that something had been decided.

The first summer we lived in Dell, sales at the nursery were down because of a sluggish economy. Bob and Frank started taking bushes down to the driveway of the local library and selling them roadside. I manned the stand a couple of times while they took the opportunity of business's being so slow to supervise the building of an addition to the greenhouse. That was the way I met Tom Van Sant. He was driving a black VW bug, which chugged into the library driveway as he peered out the window to examine the flowering azaleas, rhododendrons, and spirea. "Don't have lemonade, do you?" he said. His big smile let me know he was joking. "Oh hell—no lemonade, and a wedding ring, too," he said, as I pointed out what I thought was the prettiest azalea. After standing around for a few minutes, he took out his wallet and looked inside. "As I suspected: plenty of cash, plenty of rubbers," he said. He was pleased with himself for being provocative. "Well, I might as well take two bushes," he said, handing me two twenties. Before he left, he also gave me his business card. The card did not state any occupation; there was only his name, address, and telephone number. I threw it away that night.

A month or so later, I met him again. Walking through the carnival with Janey and Bob and Bob's mother, Barbara, I saw him coming toward me, his arm around the waist of a tall redhead who wore white cowboy boots with her jeans and purple V neck.

"Hey!" he said.

"Hi," I said, raising my hand but intending to keep walking.

"Hey, what do you know?" he said. "Bob Warner, am I right?"

"Yes," Bob said, confused.

"Tom Van Sant," he said. "I was two classes ahead of you. I went to school with your brother Frank."

"Oh, Van Sant, sure," Bob said, putting out his hand. "Nice to see you."

"What a coincidence," Tom said. "I bought some things from your wife a while back. Stopped because I thought it was a lemonade stand, but decided to purchase some shrubbery."

"Nice to see you again." Bob smiled, putting his hand on my shoulder and starting to walk forward.

"Hey—I just moved back a few months ago, from Washington. We don't know many people. If you ever feel like getting together, your wife has my card." He looked at me. "You know, this is embarrassing, but I don't remember your name," he said.

"Jean Warner," I said. He didn't remember my name because I hadn't told it to him. I'd resented his flirting, and I'd deliberately not said my name.

Bob looked at me.

"I don't think I still have the card," I said. I had no idea whether Bob might really be interested in calling him.

"I've got another one," he said, pulling out his wallet. As he looked inside, he said: "Everything in here but money. Look at all this stuff . . . okay: here it is." He handed the card to Bob. Bob put it in his pocket, as I had.

"Give me a call," Tom Van Sant said.

As we walked away, Bob's mother said, "People from your generation are always moving. Young people are moving all over the place. I'm a lucky woman that my children haven't gotten too far from home."

"Are you going to call him?" I asked Bob.

"Nah," he said.

"You could be hospitable," Barbara said. "How would you like it if you just moved somewhere and hardly knew anybody?"

"If I had a dyed redhead like that hanging on my arm?" Bob said.

"Bobby! She seemed like a nice girl. You don't want to hold it against someone that she's colored her hair."

"Is there a consensus?" Bob said. "I call?"

"Not on my account," I said, shrugging. "I threw away his card."

"I say forget it," Janey said. "He's just some guy."

"But Janey, didn't he say he went to high school with Frank?"

"He worked at the gas station," Janey said. "I remember him. He was always making wisecracks."

"You two are just terrible! You should be careful about making such snap judgments."

"His mother committed suicide," Janey said. "His father sent him to Webster High because Tom had an uncle living here, and his father knew he was cracking up."

"He was cracking up? Who was cracking up?" Barbara said.

"The father. After his wife killed herself."

"How do you know this?" Barbara said. Bob and I were both listening intently.

"A girlfriend of mine went out with Tom."

"And?" Bob said.

"And nothing," Janey said. "That's how I know."

"Well, Janey, I would think that would make you all the more sympathetic—"

Janey started to say something, but stopped. We continued walking.

"Suicide," Bob's mother said in a whisper, shaking her head. Then she shook her head harder, as if to physically shake up her thoughts. "Look over there; it's a Ferris wheel. Let's take a ride."

We bought tickets, and Barbara rode with me. Bob and Janey sat in the car behind us. Several times I turned to look at them—I suppose I thought that by looking, I might also magically overhear what they were saying. It seemed certain Janey would be talking to Bob about Tom Van Sant.

"Face forward, darling!" Barbara said to me. She was gripping the bar with both hands, white-knuckled.

"Next we're going on the spider," I said.

"I'm not going on anything named that!"

"The hornet," I said.

"You're crazy if you think I'd go on anything called that!" she said, gasping as our car dipped toward the ground, then began to rise.

"The octopus," I said, wiggling my fingers toward her face.

"Be quiet!" she said. "You're making me a nervous wreck just talking about those rides!"

I was. I knew I was, and it wasn't without a slight bit of malice, because she wanted us to get together with Tom Van Sant, and I didn't like the idea of befriending anyone just because there was reason to feel sorry for him.

A s it turned out, he called us, a couple of months later. He was giving a birthday party for Dowell Churnin, the retired basketball coach. Bob's brother Frank had been Dowell's son's best friend all through school. Nelson Churnin, Dowell's only child, had been killed in Vietnam. Within a year or so of that news, Mrs. Churnin had left town, and within the next few years, Dowell took early retirement. It was generally agreed that Dowell was a tragic figure: solitary; lonely; and with a drinking problem, some said. For years after his son's death, apparently, Frank had cut his lawn every week, and he'd try to talk to him—to get Dowell to come to dinner with the family, or to go to Boston to see the Red Sox. Once Dowell came to dinner, but he said he didn't feel well and left before the food was served. He and Frank and another of Frank's friends did go to Boston, but Dowell wouldn't take them up on their offer a second time. Bob's mother maintained that Dowell had a red face because of high blood pressure, not from drinking. It was her opinion that Dowell Churnin could do no wrong. She had thought of Dowell's son, Nelson, almost as her own child, he had spent so much time at the house. If anyone had a problem, we might think about *Mrs.* Churnin's having had her demons, Barbara said cryptically.

I heard Bob asking Tom—though the night he called, I didn't at first know who the caller was—whether he thought there was a real possibility Dowell Churnin would attend a party in his honor. Our family had all but given up on seeing him, unless we ran into him and persuaded him to have a quick cup of coffee at Rick's restaurant. Bob's mother always sent a Christmas card, but she never received one in return.

"Well yeah, sure, I'm glad to know he's excited about this," Bob said hesitantly, tapping his finger on the calendar, which was hung above the phone. Only one or two boxes had anything written in them: an upcoming dentist's appointment; a notation toward the end of the month about the concert in which Marie would perform.

"It was that guy," Bob said, when he hung up.

"Who?" I said. But I knew.

"Van Sant," he said. "What is it about him that makes me uncomfortable?"

"That he flirts with women," I said.

"With you?"

"Sort of." I was stretched out in the comfortable chair, watching an old movie on TV.

"I guess the guy's just lonesome," Bob said, surprising me with his change of heart.

"You really think that's it?"

Bob shrugged. "It's nice of him to do something for Dowell," he said.

I turned through a few other stations, then returned to Fred dancing with Ginger.

"Those movies were the stuff Dowell grew up with," Bob said. "Imagine it."

"Imagine what?"

"Imagine all that silliness, all those elegant fantasy figures, and then your son gets drafted and dies in a pointless war." Bob, himself, would never have been drafted because he had flat feet and dangerously high blood pressure. His brother Frank had gotten out because a prestigious psychiatrist wrote a letter saying he was mentally ill. Before each physical, Frank had lost enormous amounts of weight by not eating and staying awake for days, taking amphetamines washed down with bottle after bottle of beer, and rehearsing long, crazy monologues about the nobility of death. Frank was quite proud of himself for what he considered a foolproof routine. I had no idea how Drake had gotten out. I don't remember its ever being discussed.

Bob sat on the footstool and untied one of my sneakers. He

dropped it on the floor. He rubbed my foot. My feet were always cold. It felt good to have my foot warmed by Bob's big hand.

"You'll like me again eventually," he said.

"Who said I don't now?"

Fred and Ginger touched the rims of their glasses together. Fred began to sing to her.

"It's not a big deal," he said. "He wants us at a party for Dowell, no reason why we shouldn't go," he said, wiggling my little toe.

"Ginger's feet must have killed her," I said. "Can you imagine women wearing high heels every day, let alone dancing in them?"

He ran his hand up my ankle, squeezing lightly. "Does it bother you that it's so provincial here? Do you wish that when we got married, we'd gone away?"

"You'd break your mother's heart," I said.

"She's adaptable."

"Well, we weren't thinking of her, anyway," I said. "You said you wanted to work in the family business. As far as I know, you're all here because you've chosen to be."

"We could have been in big-time Washington, D.C., like Van Sant."

"He's your new role model? This guy you hardly remember, that you're shamed into seeing because he's manipulative?"

"Manipulative?" he said, removing his hand. "Giving a birthday party for Dowell is manipulative?"

For some reason, the fact that the party was to celebrate Dowell's birthday—which I hadn't at first understood—made me feel small for having rushed to criticize Tom. But what would the difference be, if it was a party held for a real occasion, or just because he'd been inspired to throw a party? Why *was* I so down on Tom Van Sant? I clicked through channel after channel. Something about Tom Van Sant did seem threatening, but it wasn't because I took him for a cosmopolitan or that, even if I had, he had any power to make me question the decisions I'd made about my life. Almost all my older acquaintances from college who'd started out working in cities had migrated. Some had given up commuting entirely, deciding in favor of odd jobs and free time, instead of careers. The problem wasn't so much that Tom offended me, I decided, but that he provoked Bob in some way, which resulted in Bob's taking the long view, or his expressing attitudes I doubted he really had. After a brief phone call from Tom, Bob would become preoccupied and increasingly eager to see if he could provoke a fight with me. It perplexed me, but eventually I decided the safest thing to do would be to diffuse Tom Van Sant's power. I decided that in the future, regardless of what my intuition told me, I would indicate no skepticism about Tom Van Sant. It was not unfamiliar to me, the idea that sometimes it was easiest to be withholding, if that got you what you wanted.

The first time I met Dara Falcon was at the party, though she did not show up until the two bottles of champagne had been drunk out of plastic cups and we had already moved on to coffee. Only the tiniest sliver of cake remained. If anyone had told me that night that Dara and I would become friends, I wouldn't have believed it. She was everything I couldn't stand: self-involved; always watching other people's reactions to check how she was doing; excessive; gregarious out of a sense of greed—a need to control.

Bernie, the girl from the carnival, wearing the same white cowboy boots, opened Tom's door and looked questioningly at the small, pretty girl who stood before her, wearing a wool poncho with a fringe that dangled to her knees and a red beret. She was holding the handle of a cake carrier, but she confused Bernie by extending it and saying, "Hello. I'm tonight's mystery guest, and I've brought you a bird."

"You made it!" Tom Van Sant said. "Hey, Dowell, is this a familiar face?"

Dowell looked perplexed. He obviously didn't recognize her and wasn't quick enough to cover his confusion.

"*Sweetie!*" she exclaimed to Tom. "This is *very* cruel of you. I do not *want* to think that I look the way I looked in high school. Otherwise, what is all this hair color *for* and why have I thrown away my Doll Pink lipstick, if he's going to still *recognize* me?"

The bird/cake carrier was in Bernie's hands. It swayed slightly, like a big lantern. She stood beside Dara, her brow knitted. It was obvious Bernie had no idea who this woman was.

"And you are Bernadette," Dara said. "I've heard so much about you."

"Who is she?" I heard Osgood Smith's wife whisper.

"Hell if I know," I heard Osgood whisper back.

"Oh God, you-all, I am the only person on the planet who went to Webster High for less time than Tom! I was Nora in *A Doll's House* in my brief four months of school. I was Esther Goodall's understudy, and I finished the play when she broke her leg, and you, darling Dowell, gave me a ride home after the performance because it was snowing so hard and I lived *two minutes* from your house. You and your wife gave me a ride, and you told me I was a great actress, thereby cursing me for life!"

"I remember, vaguely," Dowell said. He was a man of few words always, but he now seemed—as had many of the rest of us—to have lost completely the ability to speak. This woman was caught in some tempest. Her energy was willed energy, not genuine. It contained an element of panic.

"Well, I guess since I didn't go to that high school—," Bernie began.

"It's not a bird, it's a *birthday cake*," Dara stage-whispered to her.

"I didn't think it was a bird," Bernie said.

"Hey, I remember that play," Lois Hightman said. "But where have you been living? You mean you've been around here all this time, and we just haven't seen you?"

"Los Angeles," Dara said. "Los Angeles, and too many places to count, but I moved back just about when Tom did, and we ran into each other at the bank."

"That ride I gave you was the night of that bad snowstorm, wasn't it?" Dowell said, thinking aloud. He spoke to Dara's back. She had pulled off her poncho and hung it on the back of the door, over someone else's coat. Underneath the poncho she had on tightly fitting jeans and, though it was autumn, a sleeveless blouse. Big amber beads hung around her neck. No one took his eyes off of her.

"Won't you sit down?" Bernie said, gesturing toward the table. There was one empty chair.

"Oh God, forgive me, but for only these few seconds I'm onstage in front of you again. I'm Nora, and you're all watching me."

I looked at Bob, who was trying to keep a neutral expression on his face. Like me, he thought that this was just too bizarre. I was convinced that she was about to cry.

"And now I am fine. I'm all grown-up. We share the stage together," she said, running her hands through her thick, highlighted hair, shaking it behind her shoulders, spreading her arms. "Happy birthday, nice man who drove me home," she said, pulling out a chair and angling it so she faced the door she had come in through, at long last becoming silent.

"Thank you," Dowell said.

I looked at the blue vase on the center of the table filled with daisies. For a brief moment, I felt like saying, *Bravo,* and handing the bunch of flowers to her and clapping until she disappeared.

But she was there for the long haul. As the young Frank Sinatra sang with Tommy Dorsey's Orchestra on the stereo Bob had so admired when he came into the kitchen, while Marie silently bit her nails, and while Frank's dog, Jinx, nosed after Larry Mazaletti's kitten, she had the attention of every person in the room.

That January, Bob started taking night classes in Boston to become a C.P.A. He thought it would help with the business, keeping expenses down by learning to do the books and taking care of the taxes himself, as well as its being a good way to earn extra money with private clients during tax season. He stayed in Boston with his brother, grandmother, and niece three nights a week. Because his brother never stopped studying after he got out of his law classes, his grandmother was particularly delighted to have another adult to talk to. At first Bob came home late Wednesday night, but after he had a bad scare skidding on black ice, he started sleeping over an extra night and returning early Thursday morning. Because of the time he took away from the nursery, he often worked both Saturdays and Sundays, quitting early only occasionally if I was clearly on the verge of blowing up at him. The business had begun to do better—especially the new greenhouse, which was filled with flowering plants—and I didn't see why another person couldn't be brought in part-time while Bob was in Boston, so Bob and I could have something resembling a life, at least on the weekends.

Bob had become infatuated with his brother Drake's daughter, Louise, whom he hadn't known as well as he knew the other children for the simple reason that Drake was so rarely around. Also, the child was shy, and it was only after he'd appeared regularly for more than a month that she began to talk to him. He brought back a snapshot of himself with his brother and Louise in front of the shark tank at the aquarium. They were all baring their teeth, and sticking out their noses. For a while this sat on the TV, framed, and then it migrated to the bookshelf. Louise and Drake occupied many of his thoughts when he was away from them: he went to used-book stores to find children's books he remembered fondly from his youth, which Drake and his grandmother hadn't been able to locate around Boston; he stocked up on the pencils Drake liked from the local stationery store. At times he talked about the two of them almost as if they were a couple, instead of father and daughter. The way he presented their relationship, they got along as perfectly as Fred and Ginger danced. I had to suggest to him, occasionally, that while he was procuring things for the two of them, he might also think about taking his grandmother a present of some sort. Of course, I wished for presents myself, but Bob had become convinced, early on, that I was like him: a practical person who didn't want a lot of silly things. And probably that had once been true, but only because I repressed my desire for beautiful things. I had never had them, and it had been communicated to me, while I was being raised and, later, by hippies I met at college who aspired to be unencumbered, free of worrisome, pointless possessions, that doing without things carried with it a certain cachet.

As he studied, Bob began to have trouble with his eyes, so I made an appointment for him with the eye doctor, where he was given a prescription for glasses. When the glasses were ready, the secretary called to say they could be picked up. They might need to be adjusted, the secretary told me, but I could come in and take them home and see how well they fit.

On Tuesday, when I was supposed to get them, it rained, and I didn't go out. I had begun typing manuscripts for people at home, and I had gotten behind in my work. But when it was still rainy the next day, I put on my raincoat and set out, convinced—as I always was—of the importance of sparing Bob errands that weren't essential. My mother-in-law had had a bad case of bronchitis, and Janey and I had taken turns doing things for her for the last two weeks. That day, I stopped at the post office to get her stamps, and I stopped at a convenience store to get her milk and coffee. If my life was as much of a grind as Bob's, that seemed only fair, but I did wonder whether there wasn't some way he could arrange things a little better. We hadn't seen a movie together for months. Except for sprawling in front of the TV, we hardly did anything. We didn't even go to the family's Sunday dinners anymore: while his mother felt under the weather, at first Janey had stepped in to cook the Sunday dinners at her house, though that had ended after only the second week. I offered to cook myself, but Janey talked me out of it. "Listen: it's just too much trouble. Let's suspend it for the winter," she said. "We don't have to do this just because it's always been done. You don't see the family helping us, do you?" The truth was, if anything touched off my hostility toward Bob these days, I could easily be persuaded not to bother doing the things I usually did. I was surprised, though, that I missed the dinners so much, and surprised, too, that Bob didn't seem to mind that they no longer took place. "Too much togetherness." He sighed. "I tell you, Drake and Louise are a breath of fresh air just because they haven't always been around. I can read everybody else's mind, by now. You may think I love all my routines, but they're pretty deadening. I hope what I'm doing is worth it." When he talked to me and was forthcoming, of course he had my immediate sympathy. It was one of the things that had first drawn me to Bob: the clarity and simplicity with which he expressed his thoughts. But I was sorry for myself: the rain; the errands; the funny feeling it gave me to miss the family more than they missed me. All those thoughts had been knocking around in my head when I went into the doctor's office to pick up the glasses. I was damp and preoccupied and I felt out of sorts. I was not in the mood to see Dara Falcon, yet there she was, the only other person in the waiting room. She looked particularly small and downcast, her hair mashed down from the rain. She was dabbing a tissue at her eyes. At first I thought she was weeping. "Sweetie, hello," she said, in a tiny voice. Compared to the way she'd been at the party for Dowell, she was downright deflated.

"Maybe your friend can take you home," the secretary said tenuously, looking from Dara to me.

"Oh God, it's not her problem," Dara said.

"What's the matter?" I said, becoming concerned.

"Somebody skidded into my car. I'm all right," she said.

"That would have shaken anyone up," the secretary said. "It's not the sort of weather any of us should be out in."

Dara's eyes were dilated from drops the doctor had put in, the secretary told me, nodding in agreement with herself, as if she were reading my mind and wanted to assure me that Dara wasn't crying. Interestingly enough, she was also having what I would soon learn was a not untypical response to Dara, as if Dara were both there and not there—someone who so clearly needed protecting that your first impulse was to do or say anything that could get it for her. She was speaking gently to me, on Dara's behalf.

"You don't have your car—is that it?" I said. I had begun speaking the way the secretary had spoken to me, as if coaxing a child.

She dabbed her eyes. "This is so embarrassing," she said.

"It isn't embarrassing," the receptionist said. "How did you know somebody was going to careen into your car? I can tell you, I wouldn't have the money on me most times for a long cab ride. Nobody would."

Dara looked at me searchingly. She had no makeup on, and she was quite pale. Her extraordinary hair seemed to be all one dull, soaked color. She had turned in such a brilliant performance at the party; this was like seeing Bette Davis scrubbing the floor.

"Oh, listen, really," I said. "I just came in to pick up some glasses for Bob. My errands are done now. I'd be happy to take you home."

*"Really?"* she said. The "really" was ever so slightly italicized, but compared to the emphatic way she usually spoke, it was the difference between a train roaring away and the slightly flapping tail of a kite.

The secretary held out an eyeglasses case to me. "Tell Bob Doctor McRae will make adjustments if these are too tight on the bridge of his nose," she said, repeating what she had told me on the phone.

I opened the case and took out the glasses. They were Buddy Holly glasses—big, dark, clunky frames; almost as bad as the rubber glasses with a nose and bushy eyebrows attached that kids wear as a joke.

Though the secretary tried to look neutral—or, for all I know, she thought the frames were perfectly nice—Dara and I gasped and burst into laughter.

That moment was the beginning of what brought us together: our realization that men's best thoughts could sometimes be absolutely, completely absurd. Another thing that brought us together was her house. The part of a clapboard house she lived in, I should say: a medium-size house in downtown Portsmouth in bad repair, with crayon-blue shutters. It was so ugly that almost nothing short of a complete renovation inside would have made it less atrocious. The shag carpeting was stained, and a white plastic sunburst clock hung over the sofa, which had a missing center cushion. The ceiling was textured with swirls of plaster and sparkle dust, and an empty aquarium on a metal stand was pushed to one side of the room. Empty cardboard boxes were piled inside it. Dara had draped a paisley scarf around a lampshade, and there was a pretty Chinese runner down the center of a 1950s coffee table with peg legs. "Don't even look at this." She sighed. "I spend as little time here as possible." She led me through the kitchen, which had cracked Formica counters along one side and a picnic table with one seat shoved against the far wall. On the other side of the kitchen, past the tiny bathroom, was another room about the size of the living room. That had been painted pale pink, and lace curtains had been hung at the windows. Under a grow light, a white orchid was blooming. The rest of the room was taken up with a bed covered with a down comforter, piled with large, square pillows in white eyelet cases and rectangular pillows covered in pale pink and green satin stripes. There were six pillows in all: three tall ones behind, two striped ones, and a deep pink rolled pillow in front. A tiny light that glowed amber was clipped to one bedpost, which she turned on as she flopped on the bed. "Isn't it dreamy? If I stay in this room, I can pretend I live in a grand house that is absolutely clean and beautiful and sunny," she said, patting the bed to indicate I should sit down. Since there was nowhere else to sit, I did. I leaned back against a bedpost, and she tossed me one of the large, square pillows. She had some beautiful things, and I found myself wanting to touch everything. I was covetous of her room. It was like a high school slumber party all over again: What would we be, when we grew up? And how had so many unexpected things happened to us so far? These things, which, as if it were night, and as if we were sixteen years old and meant the world to each other, we could suddenly talk about so easily.

It seemed that Tom Van Sant had been calling her, in spite of the fact that he was practically engaged to Big Bernie (as Dara called her). The problem with Big Bernie—and the advantage Dara was sure she had over her—was that she was not gentle. Tom Van Sant expressed this differently, but because he was honest with Dara about what he wanted that he wasn't getting from Big Bernie, she knew what he really wanted. These things included: for warm milk and honey to be brought to him in a china cup, not a mug, before bed; for his feet to be massaged with oil; for his hair to be slowly combed away from his face with a fine-tooth comb; for Dara to share hot bubble baths with him. I was a little surprised—just a little, because I didn't think I knew him well at all—that he was interested in such sybaritic experiences. I asked whether Big Bernie knew about Tom's involvement with her. "Oh, sweetie, women are never dumb. She's just playing it cool, trying to keep him," she said. She also said she felt a little bad about what was going on, though she was bemused that it was slowly changing Big Bernie into Girl Scout of the Year, as she put it. Bernie had begun to prepare dinners for Dowell; cooking for Tom and herself, then packaging portions that Tom would take to Dowell, since Tom had decided Dowell wasn't eating well. And had I noticed that Bernie had stopped wearing her cowboy boots and started wearing high heels, like (as Dara called herself, pointing to her face) *moi?* I told her that I didn't see that much of them. Since Bob had started his courses in Boston, I hadn't had much of a social life. I asked her how she saw so much of Bernie. She said she only saw her occasionally, but that Bernie was obviously going through changes. When the three of them got together for a movie, or when they picked Dara up on their way to a party, it was because Tom looked for occasions when there wouldn't have to be much one-on-one talk. She said he was in that phase where he was trying to pretend to himself that having two girlfriends was workable; he wavered in his affections toward the two of them, and he couldn't bring himself to come clean with Bernie. Dara could sympathize with that form of cowardice, she said; also, since she wasn't sure she wanted to take on Tom full-time, the arrangement was really to her benefit. "I'll tell you something about me," she said. "I'm fickle. I like the chase, but domestic tranquillity isn't something that really inspires me. I haven't liked it when I've lived in men's places. I haven't even liked sharing an apartment with another woman. I'm in this dump because I moved out of the place I was sharing with a white-trash waitress I thought would be so different from me she'd never get on my nerves, but I overestimated my capacity to see someone's ugly underwear drying all over the place. The kitchen radiator. From a hanger dangling from the lamp, for God's sake. I just can't do it. It's hard enough to live with your own clutter, let alone someone else's. Because it can be so sad, you know? The rabbit's-foot key ring that they think is their lucky charm when they go looking for love. The wedding picture of their parents, with their mother in one of those dresses that's all padded shoulders and pleats, and the father a cartoon: he's always so undistinguished; his hair is slicked down, and he's got on those sad lace-up shoes with toes as round as a half-moon . . . oh, listen to Miss Superiority. I can't even stand myself, out of this one room. When I'm in here I have on a simple white nightgown—which I wear with silk long johns in the winter—and do you know what I do? I hook up my hair dryer, and I blow the dust out of the French-lace curtains every week. I try to keep this place calm and clean and simple. Just one room. That's all I even try to triumph over."

I found this fascinating. My house was filled with hand-me-downs; it was clean, but nothing really shone. I had never given great thought to what surrounded me.

"He freaked me out," she said, lowering her voice. The sun had come out and was low in the sky, setting through the window, which faced west. She switched off the little amber light. "He was here, last week. You know, he's got a real thing about that Dowell person. He had been to see him, and he thought he might have pneumonia or TB; cancer is what he really thought. His mother died of cancer, and he's absolutely terrified of it. He had all these dire predictions about how the old guy wasn't going to make it much longer, and he was berating himself for taking him Excedrin and meatballs. Not one dish," she said, smiling. "A bottle of Excedrin because Dowell was in pain when he coughed, meatballs on the side. I said he should have taken cough syrup, and you'd have thought the Oracle had spoken."

"I think everybody likes Dowell," I said.

"Oh, I forgot. You married somebody with deep ties to the community."

"Not because of that," I said, shifting on the bed. "He was apparently always like a second father, or like an uncle, or something, to the boys. They could turn to him if they needed advice, or got in trouble. And he absolutely adored his son, who—"

"He died in that horrible war," Dara said, almost inaudibly. Tears suddenly filled her eyes. "That wasn't the white boy's war; it was the blacks who got rounded up," she said. "The blacks, and any white boys who happened not to be from affluent communities, who didn't have somebody who could help them, or who couldn't figure out some other way they could get out. That's the nasty secret we've all been let in on by now, isn't it? We had fodder to fight our battles."

"Well," I said, after a pause. "That's why people are so sympathetic to Dowell."

"He beat his son," she said, wiping the tears out of her eyes. "His son ran away to the house Tom was living in with his uncle. He stayed in the loft up above the garage for days. Tom took food to him."

"Beat him?" I said. "Beat him for what?"

"For saying he wasn't going to go."

This was perplexing. As far as I knew, Dowell had always been against the war. His wife had taken the bus to Washington, to march in protest. Dowell had hung a bull's-eye of LBJ in the school locker room that the principal had made him take down. Bob had told me about it.

"How do you know?" I said, puzzled.

"I only know what Tom told me."

"Then why would Tom be so fond of Dowell?"

"Because Dowell apologized. Tom says that Dowell knew where Nelson was hiding almost from the first. After Nelson died, he tracked Tom down in Bethesda, Maryland, where he was living, and he apologized to him. Tom said Dowell cried all weekend, and that he was skin and bones. That his wife had left him and his son was dead, and the time had come when he saw everything differently, but it was too late. Tom told me Dowell hung up a bull's-eye of LBJ in the locker room. It wasn't because he objected to the war, though. It was because Dowell thought Johnson was a hypocrite; a rich bastard from Texas, who had the worst sort of vanity: he wanted to be thought of as a redneck, when actually he was smart. Dowell thought—as many others have, lest we forget—that there was more than a grain of truth to the rumor that he'd had something to do with JFK's assassination. Dowell didn't think the war was wrong. Dowell was a patriot."

"Jesus," I said. "I don't know."

"I only know what Tom told me," she said.

Her tone of voice—the matter-of-factness with which she spoke—shook me out of the subdued, puzzled state I'd sunken into. What a thing to find out about, sprawled on a near stranger's big bed one late afternoon, when the sun had broken through rain clouds too late to cheer anyone, except as a kind of taunt.

Dara was peeking through the side of the curtain. She let the material fall free. She held out her hand to me. "Life line," she said, pointing to the palm of my hand.

I held out my hand. She took it, and shook her head. "I'm talking to someone who's going to live to be one hundred," she said, folding my fingers forward until my fingernails touched the palm of my hand. She released her grip. Her hand had been smaller and lighter than mine—smaller, yet in control. That was the thing that was so striking about Dara: that while the world she described was very problematic, she was nevertheless convincingly in control. When she curled your fingers, it felt more emphatic than it did when you curled your own. "Haven't you heard all those ways of analyzing hands?" she said, taking my hand back and opening it. "This one, here, is the life line. Some fortune-teller must have already told you you'll have a long life."

I did vaguely remember that. Some girl in fifth or sixth grade had bewitched us all with her knowledge. Now that Dara mentioned it, I did know that I was predicted to have a long life.

"What about you?" I said.

"Me?" she said. "My life line is about as long as a whiff of smoke in an enormous room. We do not have long life in Dara's cards, sweetie. We are definitely not discussing long life."

"It's hocus-pocus," I said.

"But what else is anything?" she said, snorting a little laugh. "I mean, the *Pyramids* got there by hocus-pocus. How else did they get there?"

"God," I said. "You've surprised me enough for one day. You couldn't possibly think I could explain the Pyramids."

"But you knew about Dowell, on some level, didn't you?" she said, touching my hand with her fingers. I thought my fingers would be folded forward again, but her touch was almost ephemeral. A puff of smoke from the imaginary cloud Dara had sent up earlier might have fallen on the back of my hand. The only reason I registered the feeling was because I was looking.

"That Patsy Cline song," she said suddenly. "You know the one I mean?" She didn't wait for an answer. She omitted the beginning, about the Pyramids along the Nile, and sang only, "You belong to me."

She had a beautiful voice. It was a clear soprano, muted, four sung words that dangled in the room like the crystals from a chandelier, catching the last of the day's suddenly intense light, refracting it.

A moment passed, and then I said, "It's funny you thought of that song. I thought of it myself today, when I picked up Bob's Buddy Holly glasses. Those singers were so great, and they died so young."

"Oh, my darling," she said, "what will you do with those ugly things? Can you wait for the moment when he leaves them on a seat cushion and then just sit on them?" Her expression changed, and she looked pensive. "Who was it?" she said. "The Big Bopper died, and Patsy Cline and somebody else. . . ."

"Maybe the glasses are cursed."

"Cursed glasses? Then I am *extremely* glad I have decided to wear contacts," she said.

"You wear contacts?"

"I get eyestrain," she said. "If you have any thoughts that today's accident was the result of—"

"You didn't have your glasses on?"

She threw a pillow at me. "I need them only for reading," she said. "I have an unrestricted driver's license. Would you care to see it?"

"No," I said, throwing the pillow back. "I believe you."

"You do?" she said. "You *believe* me?"

She was being mock-serious. But what did she really want to hear? The stories had registered. I would never think about Dowell the same way, whether or not what she said was true. More than that, I had subconsciously called into question many things in my own life: the ordinariness of my surroundings; my credulousness when it came to life—and people—in the town. And I also believed that she believed I'd live a long time—enough time to see what materialized and what didn't, whether it was her relationship with Tom Van Sant or how my own relationship with Bob would turn out. I looked at her, pale in the dwindling light, leaning back against the starchy white pillows. It was a moment at once casual and intimate, she propped so that she faced forward, me so that I faced backward. It made me think of magnets that would eventually connect, one magnetizing the other through some incremental advantage.

That spring, Bob and I shopped for his mother's birthday present. Barbara was going to be sixty. Frank had ordered six special French white lilac bushes: a gift from all her children, which he intended to plant in her yard under cover of darkness the night before her birthday. Because breakfast was her favorite meal, Sandra was hostessing a breakfast in Barbara's kitchen, which would feature her favorites: crepes with scallions, sour cream, and walnuts, as well as homemade biscuits with Sandra's raspberry preserves. Since Barbara had never understood her children's desire to drink Coke in the morning, they would smilingly toast and taunt her with their Coke bottles, as she drank fresh-squeezed orange juice. But what to do with the rest of the day? Some playing with Frank and Janey's children, once they returned from school, but in between breakfast and late afternoon . . . should be kite flying, Bob decided. It seemed he and Drake and Louise had been flying kites in Boston, and he thought it was wonderful fun, and that Barbara would get in the spirit of it. So we must buy kites and drive to the beach and fly them, and also take a walk up the ice-heaved cement path that curves past the big, private houses and feel torn between envy of the wealthy people who live inside (though most of them will not have arrived yet for the season) and appreciation of our own good fortune: being together, and happy, on a lovely early-spring day.

The kite shop was newly opened, on Route 1, next to a seafood place Bob and I had loved because of its delicious smoked food that had been praised in the Boston *Globe,* which meant it had been overrun by city exiles the past summer. I rarely drove Route 1, but Bob often used it to get to 95 South to Boston. He'd known that over the winter the seafood restaurant had gone out of business. As we passed it, I said, "Oh, no," seeing the bright sign in the shape of a cactus with

letters that now read, vertically, ARIZONA. The parking lot had been en-
larged; another sign advertised a newly constructed back deck. Before,
there had been a funky screened porch. There were drink specials
listed in the window. It was obviously a place I was unlikely to ever set
foot in again, and I felt saddened by the closing. It was unexpected,
since the restaurant had seemed to be doing so well, but perhaps the
owners had wanted to sell it. Perhaps they'd made a huge profit.
Things changed on Route 1 all the time, especially the part that people
just sped through; elsewhere, where outlets were springing up, there
was also turnover, but a business had to be particularly good to last on
the less popular portion of Route 1.

"Did you know the restaurant folded?" I asked Bob.

"Yeah," he said glumly. "I thought you'd find out soon enough."

"What do you think happened?"

"Maybe success went to its head," he said. "I hate the thought of a
summer without paella made with those smoked clams."

We were in the store's parking lot. Only one other car was there: a
black Volvo wagon with a FOR SALE sign in the side window. Inside the
store, a wind machine blew a cluster of kites toward the high ceiling.
The one that caught my eye was an enormous carp, its mouth gaping as
if it intended to feed on the skylight it floated toward. There was also a
long-stemmed rose with a flapping green stem, and a billowing Casper
the Ghost. There were shelves of kites, with large color photographs
tacked to the vertical two-by-fours showing them airborne. We walked
for a few moments without commenting. Bob turned and began examining the kites stacked in the next aisle, which seemed to be the snake
aisle. There was also a kite meant to be held by several strings: I stared
at the picture of a long, silver train. I reached out and lifted one of
those packages from the shelf.

"Perfect," he said.

The kites we selected wouldn't make any harmonious, peaceable
kingdom in the sky. Along with the train, and almost as tall as the train
was long, was an enormous cardinal, its yellow beak as big as Bob's
shoes. I couldn't decide between that and the carp, so we got both—
the orange-gold mottling was simply amazing—as well as a snake
shooting out its red forked tongue. "Louise loves daisies," Bob said,
putting a package with a huge white daisy under his arm. "And we
should also get at least one that isn't phallic."

I nodded. I was hoping that Barbara's birthday would be a beautiful, windy day. The family hadn't gotten together recently, and Bob's idea of buying the kites and going to the beach was excellent. I hadn't seen Janey for a month. I hadn't sat down to a meal with Barbara, even though I'd offered to cook, for longer than that. Though the truth was, it wasn't the most thrilling thing I could think of to play hostess at a family dinner. What I really wished was that Bob and I ate out more often, did more things together. I considered Janey almost a sister, but as for the others, there were no surprises. It wasn't so much that Janey did surprising things, but that she seemed open to things. She was the only person in the family who ever read a serious book, and she was always eager to talk about what she'd discovered. The less Barbara discovered, the better; she was wary and tentative—years before, she had been politely approving, not enthusiastic, about Bob's marrying me, but I knew from Janey that she worried we hadn't known each other long enough, and that we were too young. She might have been right, but it bothered me that she had always been so sweet to me, so unconditional in her acceptance, when she had not been sure the marriage was a good idea. What really troubled me was that I suspected Barbara felt sorry for me. She and I had never talked about my parents' deaths, but I knew that Bob had told her about that almost as soon as he met me, and I suspected he had told her behind my back in order to elicit her sympathy. I felt very uncomfortable with sympathy—or perhaps I was uncomfortable in direct proportion to how much I actually wanted it. At first I thought Bob must have told Barbara not to discuss the situation with me, but through the years, it seemed clear she would not have anyway. It was Barbara's way not to ask questions, and not to reveal what she knew or thought, except about the most inconsequential things. I didn't really know how disturbed she still was about her own husband's death. I intuited that she had never gotten over it, but when Janey told me that, before I joined the family, there were times when she had seen Barbara dissolve in tears for no ostensible reason, I had found it almost impossible to believe. Barbara was like my aunt Elizabeth: she liked everything to be on an even keel, and she had decided to reveal herself less, rather than more, to effect that.

Bob took his Buddy Holly glasses out of his coat pocket and put them on before opening his wallet and taking out the money to pay for the kites. They made him look very earnest, and I suddenly had to smile because it was so wonderfully ridiculous, this big man in his ugly glasses, buying kites of birds and trains and flowers with a very intent look on his face.

"Hey, man," the only other person in the store said, "look right here." He was pointing at a small ad in the newspaper. "Right here, it says they give you a giant balloon if you spend twenty-five dollars."

The woman behind the cash register muttered, "Don't blame me for not putting in the balloon before I've even collected the money."

Bob nodded, scanning the ad and turning away.

"I bought the silver-bullet train last month, and that was the coolest kite I ever flew, ever," the boy said. It was the first time I realized something was wrong with him. Just as I did, and hoped the woman behind the counter did, too, a large woman with black hair tied high on her head in a ponytail came up beside the boy. "You picked yet, or are you just bothering people?" she said.

"No bother," Bob said quickly.

"And there," the woman said, reaching under the counter and adding something to our bag. "There is your free balloon." She folded the top twice, stapled the receipt to the bag, and handed it to Bob. He thanked her.

"In Japan the bullet trains run on schedule, and if you have one of those kites, it does, too. You whistle for the wind and the train gets going, right up in the air, in exactly one point zero second."

"You were thinking about the palm tree, weren't you?" the fat woman said, as if he hadn't spoken. He didn't answer. "These people have to get on with their day," she said. "Didn't I tell you other people went into a store and proceeded with dispatch?"

The last words she spoke to him were so little what I expected that, again, I had trouble hiding a smile. I had Bob firmly by the sleeve. "Goodbye," I said, to all of them. No one answered.

In the car, Bob shook his head, took off his glasses, and folded the sides, putting them in his breast pocket.

"Poor kid," he said.

"So where are we having lunch?" I said, not wanting to get depressed because of the boy's problems.

He smiled. "Right here," he said. He was pointing to Arizona.

"There?"

"Why not?" he said. "Let's give it a try."

He turned into the large parking lot, which was apparently going to be even larger: a big patch of land at the side had been cleared, bulldozed trees lay like pick-up-sticks, and a tractor sat in the middle of the dirt.

I flipped down the visor and examined my hair: it was in need of washing, but the new eyeliner I'd bought made me look alert. Maybe my eyes would distract attention from my hair.

The inside had been painted bright yellow, and piñatas dangled from the ceiling. Where the large paintings of the quarries used to hang were tin mirrors, three in a row. Mexican fabric was draped over the tops of the windows; the places were set with plastic mats depicting the desert at twilight. There were neon-pink napkins and cactus salt and pepper shakers. The same man who seated us turned over our water glasses and poured from a big pitcher of ice water he left on the table with a pink napkin tied around the handle. "Bern will be right with you," he said, taking two menus off the table next to us and putting them on our table. Six men were in the corner; they were drinking beer with their lunch and talking animatedly. At another table, two elderly women were sharing what looked like a big taco salad. One had her napkin tucked in the neckline of her blouse.

"Oh, gosh," Bernie said, stopping short of our table once she realized it was Bob and me. "Well, hi!"

Bernie had on a purple cotton sweater with a deep V neck and tight jeans pushed into red, knee-high cowboy boots. Her red hair was tied back with a bandanna. She had on a small apron made of the same fabric that draped the windows. She was holding two menus, though we already had menus. She reached for the water pitcher, then realized our glasses were full.

"You didn't know I was a waitress, did you?" she said, bending from the waist and looking slightly mischievous as she whispered in Bob's ear loud enough for me to hear.

"No," Bob said. "We used to come here when it was the other place."

"It's nice to see you," I said.

"I don't think you're going to see much of me, unless you come to lunch here," Bernie said. "You know that Tom and I broke up?"

"No," we said, in unison. "No, I didn't know anything about that," I said.

"It was because of *her,*" Bernie said. "Theda Bara. She goes around giving me nicknames; I can think of a few that are good for her."

Bob and I both knew whom she meant.

"That's a shame," Bob said.

"I shouldn't ruin you-all's lunch," she said. "Some other time I'll cry on your shoulder."

"I'm sorry," I said, opening my menu.

"Well, to be honest, he and I still see each other every now and then, but I'm getting my own business together, and I've gone back to night school to get my high school diploma. Just call me when you're ready," Bernie said, turning to the two ladies, who were signalling for more coffee.

"It's too bad things aren't working out for them," Bob said, shrugging. "I mean, I suppose it is."

"I wouldn't want to be involved with him," I said.

He had put on the Buddy Holly glasses to read the menu. He looked up. "Why wouldn't you?" he said.

"Because he's a womanizer, that's why."

"What makes you say that? The only person you ever saw him with was Bernie, wasn't it?"

"He was hustling Janey's friend back in high school. She told us— don't you remember? He was trying to get her to run away with him. Janey told me about it later. Her friend started running around with him, and she slipped off the honor roll."

Bob looked slightly perturbed. "Oh, come on. You're talking about years ago. You were so perfectly adept at everything you did back in high school?" He looked at the menu. He was holding it so high that I couldn't see his face.

"Chicken burritos and an iced tea," Bob said, when Bernie came back to the table and opened her pad.

"I'll have chile rellenos," I said. "Coffee, I guess."

"Right away," Bernie said, and turned. She almost collided with the man who seated us, who was now heading toward the corner table with a couple following him.

"I don't want to talk about Tom Van Sant," I said.

"Fine," he said. "Let's not talk about him."

We sat in silence until Bernie brought Bob's iced tea, in an enormous glass with a slice of lime on the rim and a slice of lemon around the curve. "New pot of coffee's heating. I'll be right out with it once it's done," she said to me. She dipped sideways to hand menus to the newly seated couple.

Bob sipped the iced tea, frowned, reached for the sugar, and opened a packet. He dumped it in and stirred. He gave a self-satisfied smile when he sipped again. I reached across the table and took his hand and squeezed it. Then I studied the other couple, studying their menus. Her hair was clean. Her husband wore glasses with small metal frames. They were well dressed and had perfect posture. They were not locals.

"They put a little cinnamon in the coffee," Bernie said, putting down a big blue mug. She lowered her voice. "If you don't like cinnamon, tell me. There's an employees' pot, because we can't stand the stuff."

But it tasted good, and so did the lunch. The rellenos were thick with melted cheese, and the rice was spicy.

"I know more about Van Sant than you do," Bob said. "When he came to Webster, his mother had just killed herself. I know Janey told you that, but what she didn't tell you was that Van Sant had taken an overdose himself. He made the mistake of confiding that to one of the cheerleaders he tried to sleep with, and she told her girlfriends, and they were worse to him about being a sissy than guys are when they gossip to everybody about what girl is easy. They made his life hell, until Dowell got to the girl and made her shut up."

I was completely taken aback. There was usually nothing Bob liked more than dropping a difficult subject.

"Who told you that?" I said.

"Dowell. He told me the other day when I ran into him at Rick's. People get older and they talk about the past—what bothered them. I don't know."

I ate another bite of food. I took a sip of coffee and put the cup down.

"Well, that's definitely the sort of story that would explain why you'd feel sympathetic toward him," I said.

"Yep," he said.

Bernie reappeared, wanting to know how the food was. We told her it was very good. She nodded in a slightly distracted way. Then she went to the other couple's table and took their order. The woman was having a shrimp taco. The man ordered a taco, burrito, and cheese enchilada platter. They both ordered margaritas without salt.

"Maybe we should have a margarita," Bob said, nodding his head backward to indicate he'd overheard them.

"Not a bad idea," I said.

"Then maybe we should go home and fool around," he said, raising his eyebrows and wiggling them comically.

"Also a good idea," I said.

"Afterwards, maybe we should try out one of the kites."

"Mmm."

"Anything else today?" Bernie said, coming up behind me.

"Two margaritas on the rocks, no salt," Bob said.

"Margaritas for dessert. That shows real style," Bernie said, approvingly. Her smile was genuine, and I suddenly thought that maybe I was going to miss her. I felt sorry for her, too, because of her busted romance and because waitressing wasn't an easy job, and certainly going to night school must be tiring.

I forgot to ask her what her business was before we left. I also didn't think to question Bob's chronology once we were outside. He drove to a field to fly one of the kites before we went home and went to bed. Putting in the balsa-wood stretchers and carefully lacing the string through, Bob crouched in the field like a little boy, completely involved in what he was doing, gnawing on his bottom lip in the fear that whatever was required might be just a bit beyond him.

It wasn't. The wind took the big red cardinal and sent it soaring, and a school bus passed by, small faces dotting the windows. It was one of the images that would come back to me many times: the sunny, windy day when we'd run together, our eye on the big bird, whose own eye looked straight across the field, in the direction of the new townhouses that had been built west of town. Its black eye could have penetrated any window. Had we let it off its string, it could have drifted north and spied us in our own bedroom, not long afterward. At the moment it became airborne, it also became our bird, even though it was Bob's mother's birthday present. For fifteen minutes, until it caught a down draft and bumped to the ground and got a smudged nose, it was up there.

Barbara's birthday was overcast, with rain predicted by afternoon. It wasn't particularly warm, but it would be fine down at the beach if we put on winter jackets. By the time Bob and I arrived at her house, she'd already looked out the kitchen window and seen the lilacs. "Frank could have scared me to death, moving around the yard," Barbara kept saying, half amused, half serious about what must have been Frank's long period of nocturnal digging.

Sandra had let Marie stay home from school to celebrate her grandmother's birthday. She was stirring the mixture that would be spread gently on the crepes before they were rolled. There was a small grater and a whole nutmeg that it was Frank's job to grate over the finished crepes. He was being teased because he had played the washboards in a band in grade school. Family occasions always presented the opportunity for them to tease each other about the people they had once been, and Barbara could always be counted on to attempt reconciliations, though there were no real problems; the fact was, the family very much approved of its own oddities and excesses. Old times were talked about so often because, it seemed, everyone had been so much more colorful in the past.

"Now Bob, don't pick on Sandra about her guiches," Barbara said, sitting at the dining room table with a birthday napkin in her lap.

"What's a quiche?" Marie wanted to know, forgetting about her stirring.

"Not 'quiche,' " Bob said. " 'Guiche.' It was two little sort of spit curls that your mother had curved out on her cheeks that she kept there with enough hairspray to kill a flock of birds."

"Mama, did you?" Marie said.

"It was the style," Sandra said.

"Like if you grew your sideburns and they curled out?" Marie said to Bob.

"Just like," Bob said. "But that would be nothing, now. Men with ponytails—"

"Let us not pretend to be perfect, and above it all!" Barbara said.

"You don't even own a can of hairspray," Frank said, pointing at his mother. "You don't even wear lipstick anymore. Remember her Morticia lips? First thing in the morning, painting them on . . ."

"You are lucky that my primping was accomplished in ten seconds. That allowed me plenty of time to slave over the stove cooking your breakfasts!" Barbara said.

"I told you to stay in bed and put out a box of cereal," Grandma said. "I learned all my lessons about not doing everything for everyone too late, and then when I passed on my wisdom, your mother wouldn't listen."

"Oh, if only she'd stayed in bed," Frank said. "No criticism about mismatched socks. No questions about whether we had all our books and all our homework . . ."

"Don't forget Dad, bellowing like an elephant about how everything in the house was missing, from the toothpaste to his bathrobe to his address book."

"It all became community property. That used to drive him crazy," Barbara said. "Every one of you had a bizarre fascination with anything that was your father's. You were like squirrels, hiding nuts for the winter. You'd dart in and get what you thought you needed, and then you'd squirrel it away. You took his own personal tube of toothpaste more times than I can count, and you knew very well that the toothpaste he so loved came from England and could not be mistaken for the Pepsodent the rest of us used."

"You took his robe and rolled it up and put it inside a pillowcase, and it was missing a week!" Frank said to Sandra.

"Be nice to me, or I won't cook for you," Sandra said, lifting another crepe onto the warming plate.

"It was shameful," Barbara said. "And the poor man: he hated mornings."

"I like morning because it's my favorite time of day," Marie said.

"Well spoken, Marie," Frank said. Janey shot him a dirty look.

Janey was pregnant, and the week before, she had started to bleed. The doctor had ordered bed rest. She was cheating by attending the breakfast, though she sat in her pajamas and robe at the end of the table in a chair padded with bed pillows, with an afghan over her, and her feet elevated on a vinyl cushion.

"Take this plate to your aunt before she starts feeling sorry for herself," Sandra said. "We don't any of us want Janey to do anything against the doctor's advice, do we, honey?"

"I don't know," Marie said.

"Of course you know," Sandra said, flipping another crepe. "What a silly thing to say."

"Adults can always say they don't know," Marie said.

"I think she has a point!" Barbara said.

"But the thing is, adults can find themselves in very difficult situations," Frank said to Marie. "Adults need excuses more than people your age, I think."

"Nonsense," Janey said, frowning at Frank again.

"Oh, Janey, don't be mad at him on my birthday," Barbara said.

"Thank you," Janey said, taking the plate from Marie. "And don't listen to any of Frank's nonsense, Marie."

"Come and sit on my lap for a minute," Bob said, turning and patting his leg.

"No," Marie said. "You had Louise on your lap, and I don't want to get her cooties."

"Poor lap," Bob said, making a sad face.

"I wanted to read my book, and you said I couldn't bring it!" Marie suddenly screamed to her mother.

"Then go get a magazine and read that," Sandra said.

"No, I won't," Marie said.

Sandra tried the silent treatment. We had a rather forced conversation about the weather while Marie pouted and Sandra turned her attention to the crepes. Grandma said that the rain would hold off until late in the day. Frank said his knee was bothering him, so it wouldn't. Janey said the weather didn't affect her one way or the other, except that she wanted the sun to come out for Barbara's birthday. "Dear me," Barbara said. "Or perhaps sunny dispositions, if not the sun itself."

Louise had not slept well the night before. She had awakened many times at our house, and Grandma had gotten up every time she hollered, even though Bob or I said, as we passed her door, that we were already on our way. When we arrived at Barbara's house, Louise had suddenly begun to cry and then had conked out, in Barbara's bed. We had tiptoed up to check on her, and she had been emitting tiny snores, her arms flung open. "Baby," Marie had said, looking in on her, stating the obvious. Now Marie had climbed into a kitchen chair and

was flipping through a magazine, reading out loud: " 'Jacqueline Bouvier Kennedy Onassis was our American princess.' " She had no idea
how to pronounce the first name, or Jackie's maiden name, or the name
Onassis; only "Kennedy" came out perfectly distinct. As she droned
on, it became obvious she was reading some person's reminiscences
about going horseback riding with Jackie, back when Jackie and Lee
were little girls, and their father, Black Jack Bouvier, was absent from
their lives. No one paid any attention to Marie, hoping that reading the
magazine would calm her, but it was difficult to hear so many words
mispronounced. "Camelot" became "came a lot." Like everyone else, I
tried to tune it out.

Bob helped in the kitchen, while Frank went outside to soak the
lilacs. At one point he turned the hose on the window, and the slap it
made nearly startled Janey from her chair. We glowered at him, but he
couldn't see our faces through the water-streaked windows. "He could
get himself a new career in Boston," Grandma said to Barbara, who
apologized for the blast of water that had been trained on the windows
as if she, herself, had risen and done it.

We ate breakfast, at long last: strong French roast, with real cream,
because it was a birthday. The men had Cokes, and Janey sipped the
herbal tea I made for her. Sandra announced that more crepes were
being kept warm, and we should get up whenever we were ready and
serve ourselves. The food was warm and sweet; if it hadn't been for
Marie reading aloud in the kitchen, refusing to join us, it would have
been very pleasant, indeed—as family gatherings usually were, once
everyone had teased everybody else to blow off steam.

" 'Her stepfather was like a real father to her,' " Marie read.
" 'Hugh Ought pin close, Awk pin close was no stranger to . . .' "

"They're drowned," Frank said, coming back in, closing the door
behind him.

"Get yourself some food from the warming tray," Sandra said,
shrugging her shoulder in the direction of the kitchen.

"Gotcha," he said, picking up the plate and walking into the
kitchen.

Marie did not break stride. She read on.

"You could get yourself a lucrative new career in Boston, Frank,"
Grandma said. "People put it in the want ads that they need somebody
to clean their windows. Of course, I suppose it would help if you'd

been climbing mountains all your life, having to go up those sky-scrapers."

"I wouldn't mind a new career," Frank said.

"I see . . . motherhood in my crystal ball," Janey said, peering into her empty water glass.

"And for me, an exciting career as a certified public accountant, who also works at the local greenhouse," Bob said.

"Not going to be able to call it the local greenhouse for long," Frank said, chewing.

"Why are you not?" Barbara said.

"Why we are not is because Snell's is building next to that Mexican restaurant, and it is going to be a greenhouse *el primo,* my friends, with bargain-basement prices and great accessibility, situated conveniently on U.S. 1."

"Snell's," Barbara said, in a hushed voice. She could have been a re-ligious person receiving the news that the devil was currently standing in the adjacent room. She pressed her fingertips together and brought them to her lips. She stared at Frank.

"When did you hear about that?" Janey said.

"Last Thursday, at the Rotary Club."

"Is it definite?" Barbara whispered.

"Does a cow say moo?"

" 'Riding to the hounds was her first love,' " Marie continued.

"Wait a minute," Bob said slowly. "This is year-round? Not just a summer thing?"

"It's year-round," Frank said. "I went into the Mexican restaurant, and they knew all about it. And as coincidence would have it, do you know who one of the investors is in that Mexican restaurant?"

"What Mexican restaurant?" Barbara said.

"Where the good seafood place used to be," I said. "It's called Ari-zona now."

" 'The blare of the trumpet . . .' " Marie droned on.

"Who one of the investors is?" Bob prompted.

"Yeah. It's our old buddy Van Sant. Back in town with a vengeance. Bought up the property for a song because of an asbestos problem, knocked it down to its rafters, cleaned it all up, and acquired the plot of land next to it for a park for kids to play in. Climb the cactus, or whatever. Then he said, Oh no, maybe what we should have after all isn't a Ferris wheel with cars hanging off it that look like tacos. Maybe what we should have is a *greenhouse*—that's a logical thing to have as an extension of your Mexican restaurant, right?"

"Wait a minute, wait a minute, back up," Janey said. "You know for a fact that Tom Van Sant is an investor in this restaurant, and that he's got the land next to it and it's going to be"—she faltered—"what you say it's going to be?" she said, weakly.

"I wonder whether this wasn't inevitable," Grandma said. "So many new businesses around here, I mean. Those townhouses out in what used to be a farmer's field. I used to go there to pick my own pumpkin off the vine, not so many years ago, and now I hear it's a putting green."

"And would you like to take a guess about who another one of the investors is?" Frank said.

"I honestly don't think I would," Bob said.

"Dowell Churnin," Frank said.

We all looked up, surprised.

"You can't mean it," Barbara said.

Frank rolled his eyes toward his mother.

"Oh, dear," Barbara said.

"Fifty percent some Boston big guy. Twenty-five percent Van Sant; twenty-five percent Dowell Churnin."

"Then even if we talked to them . . ." Barbara said, not finishing her sentence.

"Even if," Frank echoed. "It's primarily bankrolled by some bastard from Boston, who's probably advertising for cheap slave labor to clean the windows of his skyscraper even as we speak."

"Watch your language," Barbara said, reflexively. There was no chance Marie had heard him, though. Her reading had become monotonous, incantatory: " 'Little sister Lee would bend over her paint-by-number painting and work feverishly, intent on finishing the leaping horse before the actual day of the hunt arrived,' " Marie read.

"I shouldn't have brought it up," Frank said.

"But there it is," Bob said. He sounded disgusted. He spoke without energy. Yet he was the only one who meant to continue the conversation. "The damn things look really good, too. We were in one a couple of summers ago, remember?" he said, turning to me. I did. The greenhouse had been airy and beautiful, with a Victorian exterior and dark green wicker furniture inside. It was more like being in someone's spacious garden than in a shop. Chamber music had been playing. I remembered how amused I had been to be lightly sprayed by the timed mist while I admired the violets and the music played. Where the ceiling was not glass, it had been painted to look as if clouds were floating over. On a day filled with real clouds, the effect had been fascinating. Snell's was a family business that had succeeded to such an extent that now there were franchises.

"Let's open some presents. What do you think?" Sandra said.

"Just one more of your perfect crepes," Bob said, rising. "You, Janey? How about one more?"

"Thank you," she said. Her small smile did not match her tone of voice, which was hushed.

Bob picked up Janey's plate and went into the kitchen.

"Lap, lap, lap," Marie said, as Bob came back into the dining room.

"You want the lap, or you renounce the lap?" Bob said.

"I want to be on it if no one else in the world can ever be," she said.

"How's that foxhunt coming?" he said, sitting and pulling Marie onto his lap.

"Who did Lee grow up to be?" she said.

"Who did she grow up to be? A woman who married a prince, I think," he said. He looked around the table for help.

"I think she married a prince who—I mean, he never presided over anything, did he?" Janey said.

"They're society people," I said.

"They say Jackie's given her money and won't leave her anything in her will," Grandma said. "In Boston, they talk about all the Kennedys as if they're going to march right into the room any minute. They lower their voices when they gossip, but gossip they do."

"Her husband is a prince? If he saw her sleeping, could he kiss her to make her wake up?" Marie said, from Bob's lap.

"Let's talk about something else now, honey," Sandra said. "It's your grandma's birthday."

"In the living room," I said, getting up and trying to act cheerful. "You hand Grandma her presents, Marie."

"You know the prince?" Marie said to me. "Wouldn't that make her a princess if she married a prince?"

"Marie, really, we aren't going to keep talking about the Kennedys," Sandra said.

"I have something to say about the Kennedys! I have something to say on Grandma's birthday about the Kennedys," Marie said.

"Then please tell us," Barbara said, sitting in her favorite chair.

"He got shot and his wife jumped out of the car," Marie said.

"Indeed," Sandra said. "Now let us turn our attention to Barbara."

"Wasn't that very sad?" Marie said.

All around, we mumbled: Yes, sad; very sad; yes it was.

Frank stood looking out the front window, his hands in his pockets. "Looks like it's clearing," he said. "Looks like it's going to be a nice day after all. Maybe it's just punishment for my malice that my knee's acting up this morning. Maybe that's all it is."

"What's malice?" Marie said.

"Having mean thoughts," Sandra said. "Now let's concentrate on watching Barbara open her presents."

Janey said, "Catch!" and threw Barbara a box to get things started. It turned out to contain three boxes of sparklers, which Barbara loved. She promised to use them long before the Fourth of July. Then Marie got in the spirit of things; she jumped off Bob's lap and began to act as present bearer. She gave Barbara the gift I had brought, edging the big box across the rug with her knee: a pillow with arms, so she could prop up while she read in bed; Drake's present, sent by way of Grandma, which was a fifty-dollar gift certificate at the local bookstore; Frank's present—a large cardboard bouquet that stood up like a vase of real flowers—was done so well that, until you were almost on top of it, you were convinced they were real; a photo album from Grandma; from Janey, a box of Estée Lauder dusting powder and cologne; from Frank and Janey's boys, Max and Pete, who were at school, a box of marzipan shaped like bananas and cherries and orange slices; from Marie, a drawing of her grandmother and herself. Marie was much more de-tailed, and Barbara was in what looked like a pink shawl—nothing I'd ever seen her wear, and probably only an invention so Marie wouldn't have to draw her customary pleated blouses or her sweaters with lace necklines. It wasn't a bad likeness. Then came the moment when the rest of the family's present was given to Barbara. I held my breath, be-cause I was afraid Frank might think kites were frivolous in the extreme. I'd told Janey what we'd gotten Barbara on the phone, and she had said what a good idea kites were, but I could never be sure what Janey did or didn't communicate to Frank. Drake no longer contributed—why, I had no idea—and Grandma never had, so really it was just a present from two of her sons, their wives, and her daughter.

"Oh, my goodness!" Barbara said. "Did you know how I was fascinated with kites when I was a little girl?"

They were a big hit. If Frank didn't approve, he didn't say so. He smiled and took credit.

"So what do you say we get a jump on the weather and go down to the beach and try them out?" Bob said.

"Take the camera and get started on filling the new photo album," I said.

"The beach? Isn't it a little early to go to the beach?"

"I wish I could go," Janey said. "Have a good time and tell me how it was."

"Oh, I don't know about the beach. . . ." Barbara said.

"Louise and I will be here," Grandma said. "If she keeps sleeping, I'll get a nap in, myself."

"Yes! I want to go to the beach!" Marie said.

"Sure, Mom," Sandra said. "It's a great idea. Get some sand between your toes."

"It's not summer, darling," Barbara said, but I could tell by the lack of hesitancy in her voice that she was wavering.

"The beach! Hooray!" Marie said.

W̲e took two cars. Sandra and Marie rode with us, and Frank rode with his mother, which we later realized wasn't a very good idea because he would probably begin talking about the new greenhouse again, but he had more or less claimed her, getting her jacket, holding it out for her to back into, taking her hat down from the shelf, and then almost pushing her out the front door. The plan was that afterward Bob and I would go back and get Grandma and Louise, who would spend another night at our house, then return to Boston with Bob in the morning. Frank would go directly from the beach to the nursery;

we would take Barbara home, and after we all had coffee she would give Janey a ride home and stay to see the boys when they returned from nursery school.

Driving to the beach, I felt sentimental: it was such a nice family; surely a new greenhouse couldn't ruin very much for such nice, hardworking people, could it? As Grandma said, it was inevitable: the new construction; the public golf course that would be going in before summer's end. Two years ago, a private club had opened just outside of town. But why had Tom Van Sant decided on a greenhouse? It wasn't a sure thing in a business sense; why not a more obvious franchise? And I certainly couldn't believe that, like Frank, whether Frank admitted it or not, he was half in love with plants. Or that, like Bob, he felt a sense of duty toward continuing something just for the sake of continuity. He hadn't been running a greenhouse in Washington, had he? It was annoying and disappointing, but some part of me took sneaky, nasty pleasure in the fact that in helping to bankroll Snell's, he had betrayed the family. They were too quick to embrace outsiders; it might teach Barbara a lesson, as well as undercut Bob's reflexive male solidarity with Tom Van Sant. I remembered the day I first met him—his getting out of his car, examining the azaleas, flirting. Was it possible that he was mulling over a greenhouse back then?

I had it in the back of my mind that if I talked to him . . . if I talked to him, what? I'd persuade him to give up a business opportunity he'd thought about carefully? Unlikely, but maybe not impossible. If he really had any of the loyalty and sentimentality about the way things were that he professed—if he really saw Dowell as something more than a fellow investor—maybe I could persuade him, in effect, to go away. This was hubris on my part, but it was also the tendency of the errand runner: Oh, sure, I'll pick up your glasses. Need something from the pharmacy—just call on me. If I'd been thinking about anything but talking Tom Van Sant out of his idea, that impulse was buried so deep I would never have been able to dredge it out. He said he was one sort of person; he'd reached out to our family; Dowell—who, Bob always maintained, was no fool when it came to judging character—had gone to Tom's house, when he wouldn't go to any other. That is, unless Dowell was a complete phony, which was exactly the way Dara had presented him.

We were at the beach, parked right in front, in one of the parking places it would be impossible to get in season. It was low tide, so the beach offered a large expanse of sand. In front of us, a man was running with his puppy, and two women walked at the edge of the water arm in arm. A few other people were in beach chairs, or on towels, wearing their wool jackets. The water was gray-blue. You could feel its iciness. I felt myself drawing inward, as the tiny white caps spilled onto shore. Though Frank had left a few moments before us, he and Barbara had not yet arrived.

"Mom, I want to see that dog!" Marie squealed.

"That simply astonishes me, that you would," Sandra said.

"Because why *can't* I have a dog?" she said.

"I don't believe I've ever once given you a reason," Sandra said. "I'm sure I've never stated any reason why you couldn't have a dog."

When she said "why *can't* I have a dog?" she reminded me of Dara. With Dara, of course, it was studied; with my niece, it was childish enthusiasm. It made me wonder what the line of demarcation was—if there was any way you could measure when overflowing emotion became calculated excess.

"I'm going to see it," Marie called over her shoulder.

"Ask the man first if it's friendly. Do you hear me?" Sandra called.

"Yes," Marie called back. She was off and running. Bob had gotten out of the car, camera in hand. He pointed it in the direction of the vanishing Marie, and took the picture.

"Youth disappearing," he said.

"Oh man." Sandra sighed. "We really got kicked in the teeth today, didn't we? What's so much fun about growing up, anyway?"

"We'll think of something," Bob said.

Frank's car pulled in, and he got out, sipping a beer.

"You talk to your brother about drinking during the day," Barbara said to Bob. "He doesn't listen to his mother."

"Relax," Frank said to Barbara.

"There's such a chilly wind," Barbara said, closing the car door and wrapping her arms around herself.

"The better to fly kites with, my dear," Sandra said.

"Then out with them!" Barbara said. "You've got them, Bob."

"So I do," Bob said, and headed for the sand, unwrapping one of the packages. He fiddled with the folded kite for a while, as Sandra hung over his shoulder, offering advice. Barbara watched Marie disappearing in the direction of the man and his dog. Then, suddenly, a kite was launched. Up it went, the long train curving through imaginary tracks, kept aloft by Barbara, Bob, and Sandra. I stood just where the rocks ended, holding the big, deflated carp. Frank stood beside me silently, drinking his beer. Finally, he said: "Son of a bitch. Guy sets up a big homecoming for himself, has us all over for champagne and cake, and what is he getting ready to do but stab us in the back?"

"I've never much liked him," I said, "but if I let on, Bob's suddenly his best buddy."

"Yeah," Frank said, drawing a cigarette out of a pack in his shirt pocket. "He was never really a friend of mine. He and I threw acid on LBJ's wrinkled old mug one time—a dartboard, down in Dowell's cellar."

"The dartboard was for real?"

"One in school, one in Dowell's cellar. We went over to the cellar, mad because the administration made Dowell take down the bull's-eye in the locker room. I don't know who had the acid—Billy Riley, or somebody. Dowell was so crazy, he let us throw it. It was gonna eat through his wall, and he didn't care." He puffed on the cigarette. "One thing I think now that I didn't think then: I think that maybe he was one of those functional drunks. He didn't slur his words or stagger around, but I think he might have had a pretty steady drip of alcohol into his system. The rumor was, anyway, that that's why his wife left him. That, and because he wouldn't put his money where his mouth was about the fuckin' war. Now I think he might have been an alkie: thought one thing one day, saw it differently the next."

"When did you start smoking again?" I said.

"Could you please do something other than mimic Janey?" he said.

"Listen, I know you're upset about the greenhouse. But I didn't think you'd smoked for years."

"Watch out, you might turn into her," he said.

"Frank, I'm going to talk to him," I blurted out.

" 'Him'?"

"To Tom Van Sant. It's worth a try."

He raised an eyebrow. "Oh?" he said.

"I can try."

"He always gets women to try with him," Frank said. "Isn't that an interesting thing. That is one thing I observe about Mr. Van Sant."

"What are you saying?"

"You hate to hold a guy accountable for rumors about him when he was seventeen or eighteen. Back then, word was that he got pretty aggressive if he didn't get his way. He pretty much ruined the would-be academic career of some girlfriend of Janey's. Either raped her or traumatized her, or whatever he did. His uncle got in the middle of it, and he got sent away."

"Sent away where?"

"The nuthouse. His uncle and the cops struck some deal with the girl's parents."

"If you hold so many things against him, why did you even go to that party?"

"Stupid," he said. "To prove to Janey I wasn't a coward, I'd go anywhere."

"Janey wanted to go?"

"She didn't want to go; he called and said Barbara was coming and all these other people, and it was a party for Dowell. Janey's not a hardass like me. She wants to think the best of people. I think she went to see if she could think more positively about him." He threw down the cigarette and ground it under the toe of his shoe.

He was probably right; like Barbara, Janey did try to see the best in people. Her similarity to Barbara—her similarity, along with the way you could sometimes see her struggling to do the right thing—was probably one of the reasons Frank had been so drawn to Janey, though Janey was much less Pollyannaish than Barbara.

Frank took the fish from me and started to run. It caught the wind on the first try, its tail snapping, and kept climbing.

"Remind you of anybody, with its mouth up to the sky?" he shouted back to me. "It reminds me of somebody who's real trusting, always ready to bite, even if all they get is a mouthful of cloud."

That spring, I began typing the autobiography of a woman who was in her seventies and lived in Dell. For ninety-five cents a page, I deciphered her handwriting, deleted most of her commas, and typed the manuscript with wide margins, as she'd requested, on the electric type-

writer Bob had given me for Christmas. The book was divided into
three sections. She had been widowed three times, and each section
was about the trips she took or the day-to-day life she'd shared with
each of her husbands. She liked to fish, and she had had little trouble
persuading husbands one and three to set off on fishing expeditions.
Her second husband seemed to like nothing: not her cooking, or her
conversation, or her friends, or even the things she chose to grow in the
vegetable garden. As I typed, I was happy to realize that he was in ill
health and would soon be gone. I'd already flipped ahead, and the
third husband was much more interesting. I had asked Barbara if she
knew Grace Aldridge, and at first she'd said no, but then she realized
whom I was talking about, and it turned out she had known her at
church during the years Grace was married to the sourpuss. She had
been Grace Dubbell then. In the second section, there was a long digression that purported to quote Mr. Dubbell's views on the garden. I
could put his opinions in quotes, or in italics, or even in capital letters,
she had told me. There were notes on the manuscript, anticipating the
questions I'd have when she switched from her customary black ink to
red. "Make husband talk with underlining or caps, if that is best," she
had written. I tried it: DO YOU THINK THAT GOOD GARDEN SOIL SHOULD
BE USED FOR THE PLANTING OF RHUBARB, WHICH WHEN COOKED HAS
THE CONSISTENCY OF SNOT?

That was a little too alarming, though it did emphasize how nasty
he was. I decided to use simple quotes, indenting each one, to make a
list, and adding an introductory sentence of my own: "He had the following views on the things I planted in the garden." I could hardly wait
to get to the section about her life with husband number three, because
I already knew they had gone hiking and fishing in Canada and taken a
ride on *Maid of the Mist* at Niagara Falls. He seemed very pleasant
compared to her second husband, and a great improvement over the
first, who suffered from asthma, so that many plans got scrapped at the
last moment. I was sitting at the kitchen table, recording Mr. Dubbell's
opinions about okra ("like dead fishes") and parsnips ("you take a
peeling of tree bark and soak it overnight, it would taste better than a
parsnip"), when the phone rang. I expected it to be Bob, asking me to
pick him up. That week, he was leaving Drake his car and taking the
bus back to Portsmouth. Though Bob had been pretty closemouthed
about it, Drake had a girlfriend. "You didn't hear it from me" was all

Bob would say. But Grandma had told Barbara, and Barbara had told me. We didn't know anything about her, though. Because he'd apparently never had her to the apartment, Grandma didn't know anything, either.

In fact, the call was from Grandma, who was calling long distance to say that Bob had asked her to tell me that it wouldn't be necessary to pick him up. A friend would be giving him a ride home, and he'd get in around eight. Grandma seemed sad to be missing spring where we lived, though she said she and Louise had been to the park, and that the tulips were beautiful. She didn't mention Drake's girlfriend, and I didn't ask, but it did seem to me that Grandma must be hoping things would go well, because if things went well with the romance, perhaps she wouldn't have to live in Boston and take care of Louise. When Drake had first gone back to school, Barbara had wanted him to leave Louise with her; she and Grandma would take care of her, and he could see her on the weekends. But he'd been bitter about his divorce, and he'd gotten custody, so he wanted to have Louise with him every minute. He was determined to show everyone what a good father he could be, though law school had been more demanding than he'd expected, and his guilt about Grandma's doing so much only made him more withdrawn. Bob had said to me that he wasn't sure that Drake wasn't just depressed—that while he had no doubt law school ate up an astonishing amount of time, Drake's constant unhappiness seemed worrisome. Bob felt more than a little strange about being at Drake's: Drake had said emphatically that he must use the apartment and not go to the expense of renting a place, yet when he was there Drake hardly spoke to him. He ate the meals Grandma prepared in silence at the desk where he worked long into the night. "I mean, he could at least sit in a comfortable chair when he reads, couldn't he?" Bob had asked me.

Grandma said, "Has Barbara gone kite flying, now that the weather's warmer?"

"I haven't asked her," I said. "I do think she had a good birthday, though, don't you?"

"One of the few more or less intact families I know of," Grandma said. "There's great value in having everybody in the same room at the same time." She cleared her throat. "Not that we expect anything of Drake anymore," she said. "Not that I do, anyway."

"Bob thinks he might be depressed," I said.

"He's never looked on the bright side. Not even as a little boy."

"Well, he'll be done with school soon," I said. "And I hope he becomes very successful and buys you—"

"He'll have to buy me a tombstone, by the time he finishes all this," Grandma said.

"Grandma, if it's too much for you in Boston, you could come back. Janey and I were talking about that a while ago. You shouldn't feel you have to be there just because—"

"Hadn't raised Barbara to be dutiful, I might have the nerve to walk out," Grandma said. "But you can't tell your children one thing, and then do an about-face."

"Barbara isn't a child anymore, Grandma. She'd understand."

"Walking out of a difficult situation Barbara would most certainly not approve of. And anyway, if I hadn't helped raise him to become the person he's become, I might be blameless, but I always encouraged his independence. I even took his side when he married Jeannette, you know. A girl from another country who was unsuited to him in every way. What did I say then but that he should follow his heart."

"Grandma, he didn't marry her because you said he should. He was in love with her."

"What I honestly felt was that she wasn't the girl for him, but no, I didn't tell him that."

"It would have just made for bad feelings. You know, when I was going to marry Bob, I felt very bad that my aunt—"

"Truth is, I thought you were both too young, but I'm happy to see that things have worked out."

"I *was* too young to marry him," I said, and was surprised to hear myself saying it so simply. There was silence on the other end. "I mean, I might have developed more interests if I'd been on my own awhile."

"Interests? Every minute of life is interesting. But so what? What's that Chinese curse? It's something like: 'May you live in interesting times.' "

"You know what I mean," I said, as if she hadn't spoken. "I mean that it's probably better to feel separate. Because I don't feel joined—I mean, we're not Siamese twins, we're not joined at the hip—but I don't feel joined to him, and I also don't feel like I have a real life of my own."

"Everybody has her own life. You can be sure of that."

"But Grandma—don't you hear the cynicism in your voice when you say that? There should be something better you could say. You should feel happier about things. It's okay if you don't want to be in Boston with Drake. Just because he made a mess of things, you aren't obliged to bail him out."

"I don't avoid things. I take responsibility. No one can fault me for not doing what I should. I'd think you'd understand because of your aunt's sacrifices. You can't say you'd be the girl you are today without her having extended herself."

"But she didn't want to."

"Nevertheless, she did."

That was irrefutable. When I had needed someone, my aunt had taken care of me. That was entirely true.

"This will make me sound like a silly old lady, which I may be," Grandma said, "but what kind of a world would it be if nobody looked out for anybody else?"

"You wouldn't not be looking out for Drake, you'd just—"

"I'd just be tending my garden and watching pretty snowflakes in the winter, and I'd be a selfish person. Though many's the time I wish I had spoken against his marriage when I should have."

"He would have done the same thing."

"Probably, but at least I would have told him what I thought."

"You know, Grandma, I've been typing a manuscript for somebody who was married three times, and that's the way she's decided to organize her life—by the husbands. And the one I'm typing the story of now was so awful that he not only wouldn't plant a garden, but he registered his disapproval of everything she planted, except maybe parsley."

"Hard to take exception to parsley," Grandma said.

"I mean, he pretty much insisted she do all the work—plant the garden; can stuff in autumn—and all he had to say was that parsnips tasted like tree bark."

"Must have eaten them when they'd gotten tough," Grandma said.

"Did you know Mrs. Aldridge?" I said. "Barbara knew her when she was named Dubbell."

"The woman who was married to Zack Dubbell? I met her once or twice. He was a religious fanatic."

"I don't think so, but I haven't gotten to the end of this section yet."

"Well, maybe his views on vegetables made more of an impression," Grandma said.

When we hung up, I went back to the typewriter and turned it on again. I liked the way it hummed. I liked the way the keys struck the paper when I turned the adjustment knob to the softest touch. It sounded a little like rain. As I typed, I kept the pages of the notebook open with a rock Marie had given to Bob for his birthday. It was a rather heavy, oval stone on which she'd painted curlicue blue eyes. The stone had a mouth with uneven lips, the top lip much fuller than the bottom. Two dots served as nostrils. A worm of a wrinkle passed across the forehead. Marie had glued curly yellow ribbon to the sides and put sequins where earrings would go. Half the ribbon/hair had fallen off one side, because of inadequate gluing. Just as I was starting to type, the phone rang. I got up to answer it.

"Oh, sweetie—can you come out and play?" the voice on the phone said pleadingly.

"Dara," I said. "I haven't heard from you in ages."

"I've got the blues," she said. "It's Tom. I've got to talk to you."

"Would you like to meet at the bakery and have coffee?" I said.

"I would like to meet there and have six chocolate éclairs," she said. "And if they served drinks, that would be much better than coffee."

"I can bring a flask," I said.

"You can?" she said. She lowered her voice to a near whisper. "Really, would you do that?"

I had been kidding, but Bob did have a flask. He took it with him sometimes when he went sailing. It was a lovely silver flask that had once belonged to Grandma's husband.

"It could be arranged," I said.

"What time can you come?"

"Right now, if that's good."

"Oh God, I am so glad to have one friend who is not subsumed by marching in step and working for the fucking *system* all day." She sighed.

I looked at the painted stone. I was certainly not working for the system.

I went into the bedroom, took off Bob's flannel work shirt, and changed into a white blouse. I kept on the black pants I was wearing, but traded my heavy socks and running shoes for thin gray socks and red suede flats. I opened Bob's bottom drawer and found the flask where I'd last seen it. It was still lying on top of a *Playboy* someone had passed on to him after a boat ride. There was also a jock strap that Bob almost never wore, and a can of foot powder. There were his hand-grips, and a metal folding cup. Bob's toy box: the bottom dresser drawer. I closed it and hung his shirt back in his closet. It smelled faintly of mothballs, and when I sniffed, I sneezed: some mothballs must have gotten onto the floor.

Corolli's bakery was the newest addition to the shopping center. It was between an AAA office and a locksmith, and even though the day was not very warm, there were three small green metal tables set up in front, and I decided to see whether it might be possible to sit outside. The flask, filled with rum—we didn't have brandy, which would have been much more elegant—was in my purse. I went inside and bought a cruller and an espresso. I also got a chocolate éclair, which I put in front of where Dara would sit. Then I got up and bought a newspaper. It was thin. As usual, nothing much was happening. I was dismayed to see an ad for Snell's, though. There was a drawing of the prospective greenhouse. "Now hiring," it said. Hiring for a greenhouse that hadn't yet been completed? I was lost in thought when Dara's old red Ford sloped into the parking lot. She coasted by, not quite sure where the bakery was, looking for the AAA office I'd told her about.

She had on a black John Wesley Harding hat and a velvet scarf wrapped around her neck. She was wearing jeans and some enormous blouse that she looked lost inside. The blouse was draped with a vest, as well as a leather jacket. It looked like she had thrown on almost everything she owned. The amber velvet contrasted nicely with the purple vest. Her hair was newly washed, a bit frizzy, but puffy and curl-ing to her shoulders. I took in all of this as she stepped out of the car, which she had left parked parallel to the curb under a big sign that said NO PARKING. She gave me a smile and rolled her eyes at the same time: an acknowledgment of her harried state. She was uncoiling the scarf petulantly, as if a big snake had curled round and round her neck, con-fining it in a most annoying way. She stilled her swinging, beaded earrings. She slumped down in a chair and leaned back, exhaling, looking at the sky. "Thank you, sweetie," she said on the exhale. "I am so glad to see you. And I see by this éclair that you have already expressed your affection for me."

"Flask in my purse," I said, patting the bag that hung off the back of my chair.

"It isn't one of those that has the devil's face on it, is it?"

I took it out. "Horseback riders," I said.

"Thank God," she said. "Do they come to the table, or do I—"

"You have to order inside," I said.

She nodded and got up, leaving the scarf draped across the chair, and her hat tossed on the tabletop. After a few seconds, I decided to follow her in and ask her to get me another espresso. Then I went back to the table. It was cool, but probably not too cold to sit there. The sky was brightening slightly.

"I have to tell you, because if I don't tell someone, I will explode," she said, returning with a tray. "I do not love Tom Van Sant," she said, pronouncing every word distinctly, removing first the saucer with my little cup on it, then her own mug, domed with frothy milk. She picked up her hat and scarf, put them on the tray, and lowered the tray to the cement. "But I do have to show you this, because I think it indicates that I may be in deep shit," she said, holding out her hand. With so many colors, and the big earrings swinging, and her windblown, excelsior-like hair, I'd missed the beautiful ring she was wearing on the first finger of her right hand. The ring was in the shape of a flower, with a diamond center surrounded by rubies. The band was either white gold or platinum. It sparkled brightly.

"It's an engagement ring?"

"I do not consider it that. I have been very straightforward about not considering it any such thing, but he says it's not proper to wear it on this finger and that we have to have it made smaller. Sweetie—*tell me:* Do you think I can get out of this?"

"Dara," I said, quite honestly, "I don't know what's been going on between you and Tom."

"He's fallen completely in love with me," she said, opening her eyes very wide.

"I didn't realize—"

"There wasn't anything *to* realize. Have you ever slept with some-body one time and known you were in love? He swears he's sure. I just thought I was rolling around in a meadow."

I shrugged, slightly perplexed: Was she bragging—more pleased than she wanted to let on—or did she really think the situation pre-sented a big problem? I took out the flask, unscrewed the top, and trickled some into her cappuccino, pouring carefully so the steamed milk wouldn't overflow the rim.

"We went out behind his house with this silly thing somebody had sent him in the mail: Instant Meadow. It's wildflowers that are sup-posed to grow when you scatter the contents in your grass, or whatever you're supposed to do. I've spent my life in cities; I don't know. We'd been drinking brandy at his kitchen table. I'd gone over there because he had a carton of books he wanted to give me. Somebody had left it to him in their will, or they'd left it behind somewhere—I don't know. I mean, I hardly know anybody here, and he's been so nice to me. He knew I liked Hardy, and Chekhov, and Dickens, and here he had all these books by these wonderful writers—hardbacks—and he said I must have them, that he'd never read them, he was trying to divest." She leaned back and looked at the sky. "By the way, darling, thank you for the loan of the John le Carré I snatched from you the second you put it down. I feel so stupid, coveting a book that way, when you were already driving me home on that god-awful day."

"I'd finished it," I said.

"Well, I know that, but it was generous." She looked at me, dewy-eyed. Tom Van Sant had given her a carton of books, and I had loaned her one. She seemed lost in thought. She took a deep breath and con-tinued: "So there we sat, having brandy, talking about what it used to be like around here and what it was like now, and then the UPS truck pulled into the driveway, and we joked that maybe it was another box of books, but it was *Instant Meadow.* Some woman had sent it to him; I could tell by the look on his face when he saw the gift card. Then, I don't know—we had some more brandy, and he was playing me the most amazing record . . . it was the music from a movie called *The Con-formist.* I have to see it. Anyway, we got up and started waltzing, except the kitchen is too small to waltz in, so he opened the French doors, and we started waltzing on the patio. He'd brought the can with him. And we just sort of started running—he did, pulling me by the hand, and we ended up in all this high, new grass which was absolutely stupefying, it was so soft and beautiful, and then we didn't have anything to open the can with, so he ran back to the house and came back with a screwdriver, and he pried the top off and he threw a handful and then I tossed some. It was like tossing rice at a wedding. And then he was behind me, and he took a step forward and put his hands on my shoulders, and he had a full erection. I mean, he was busting out of his pants. It was the sexiest thing, and I didn't expect it at all. So we did it right there, and afterwards I asked him how much land he owned, and he laughed and accused me of being materialistic, and I said that wasn't it, that I didn't want to be trampled by a fucking herd of cattle out there. I pulled the gift card out of his pants pocket, and he tried to get it away from me, but I saw that it said, 'Love, Myrtis.' " She took a sip of coffee and puckered her lips. "Strong," she said. "Tastes good." She threw her head back and considered the sky for another two seconds, then leaned forward. "The two of us got so fucking sad out there—me because I hadn't slept with anybody for so long, and there was no reason why it should have been him, and him because of Myrtis, I assume."

"And then?"

She smiled slyly. "A sequel. Some time later. In bed."

"So when did he give you the ring?"

"Because he's trying to pressure me. He wants me to be indebted to him because he bared his soul to me. Not about Myrtis—about his mother."

She'd misunderstood me. I hadn't been asking why he gave her the ring, but when. "What about his mother?" I said.

"She died young," Dara said. "It sounds like such a cliché: 'died young.' And then he started talking to me about how he didn't think anybody really liked him. That Dowell liked him, but Dowell was an old man—old people get less discriminating, don't they? Everybody they knew before is part of the past, and they romanticize it because it's gone. That's my brilliant insight for the afternoon."

"He and Dowell are going into business, I hear."

"Oh, I know," she said. "Sweetie, there have been *so many* midnight calls."

"His greenhouse is going to compete with the family's business," I said.

"It is?"

"Well, yes. It's a greenhouse, and—"

"Can I tell you something?" she said, lowering her voice. The way the light hit her earrings was hypnotic; I had leaned forward to hear what she was about to say, but my thoughts were jingling much the way her earrings did as they swayed and caught the light. She said: "I knew what he felt like, because I don't feel like I have any close friends either. When I left L.A., I let people slip away. But it's really pathetic to be liked by an orphan, just because the person's so needy, and you happened to appear." She looked at me. By this point, I was too stunned to speak. I thought about it for a few seconds. What a strange way to think of Tom Van Sant. But leaving that aside, her observation was interesting.

"He's not really an orphan if he grew up with his mother and father until she died," I said.

"But you know what I mean," she said. "After people grow up, it's all about the way they think about themselves. He all but said he felt orphaned. His mother died of cancer, he told me, though I've also heard that she committed suicide. And his father gave him away afterwards because he couldn't raise him. He said his father used to drink at night and tell him he was a ghost. 'You're not real,' he'd say. 'You're a ghost, too.' Like his wife was in the room, and Tom came in and joined her."

"That's pretty awful," I said.

"You know," she said, "at first I didn't particularly have any great feeling for him. I think, looking back, I was sort of using him. Not for nefarious purposes—just because he was needy, and I was back in town and he was so welcoming. I couldn't stand those people who were there that night—the night of Dowell's birthday party. I just wished they'd all go away. That that silly cowgirl would ride off on her horse and that it could be Tom and you and me in the kitchen."

I knew this wasn't true. She had barely noticed me. She had barely noticed anyone—nor did she seem to reflect on the fact, now, that many of the people who'd been there that night were my relatives.

"What made you decide to come back to Dell?" I said. "It doesn't seem the most likely place, after Los Angeles."

"And it's not the best place to try to establish myself as a major acting talent either. All I know is that I was drawn back. The land is so beautiful. Everything seems so open. I know it's easy to confuse opportunity with uncrowded, natural beauty, but I'm no different from any other explorer. It's just that I had a tiny peek at Dell before I arrived on its shores."

"It really seems that beautiful to you?"

"It's peaceful," she said, closing her eyes. Then just when I had begun to envision Dell the way she saw it, she said: "That night we first met, Frank was playing footsie with me. Did you know that?"

If she had told me our little table was about to burst into flames, I couldn't have been more surprised. Immediate denial set in: Frank must have brushed his foot against hers accidentally.

"It's complicated, isn't it?" she said.

"What is?"

"Getting involved with people. Because sometimes you're responding to what they want, instead of what you really want, but you don't necessarily know that right away, do you? I mean, now it's clear why I fucked Tom in the field, but at the time I thought it was my idea."

I was puzzled. She had told the story of the Instant Meadow with enthusiasm initially. With fondness for the two people involved. But now she seemed to think she had been manipulated. I had no idea whether she had been or not.

"I think I might be in love with him," she said, "but some other part of me thinks that I'm just in love with the idea of being found captivating." She pronounced "captivating" in four drawn-out syllables. "He sends me letters. We see each other all the time, and he still sends me letters. He says he can't find the right words when we're together. He thinks over our conversations and wants to let me know more clearly what he thinks. Sweetie, this man is entirely smitten."

"If you love him, what's the problem?"

"That *need*," she said. "That need. What if I gave up and was always at his side—just an appendage? He wants me there all the time. He wants me to move in with him."

"Are you going to?"

"Well, it's not like I'm living in Versailles. I mean, I could pack my pillows and be gone." She put her hands on both cheeks, fingers curled under. "Do you know," she said, lowering her voice again, "that you are the only human being who has ever once been to my secret room?" She ran her hand over her face. "Poor pitiful me," she said. "It's so perverse. Because I want you to like me, but I'm sitting here completely self-absorbed, pitying myself for all the things I don't have. That creepy, crummy little apartment: I hate it the way other people hate their enemies."

"But the bedroom is gorgeous," I said.

"I won't let him see it," she said. "It's private."

"I wasn't lobbying for him."

"No," she said quickly. "Of course you weren't."

I followed her line of vision when her attention drifted again. A woman was putting groceries in the trunk of her car. A little boy stood at her side. Beyond that was the drugstore. Painters were up on ladders, painting above the front door.

"What do you remember most about it?" she said. "What was the most gorgeous?"

I suddenly didn't want to tell her. I didn't want to be made to answer. I didn't want to state the obvious, to tell her how pretty the pillows were, how much I'd liked the lace curtains.

"You were in the spider's web," she said when I didn't answer. "I wove it together. Isn't it dreamy? It was spun out slooooowly."

"If you think of it as a spiderweb," I said, "then isn't the idea that people will come to you? What are they supposed to do if you don't let them in?"

She looked at me with a faint smile. Her eyes were level. "Maybe it would be for the best if I starved," she said.

The woman who had been putting groceries in her car picked up the little boy, who was refusing to get in the car. He kicked and cried. She continued to carry him around the front of the car, opening the door on the passenger side one-handed. His legs and arms seemed to be octopus tentacles, until she closed the door. To my surprise, he didn't open it and jump out. The woman got into the car, started it, and drove away. As she passed us, I saw the tearstained face of the boy. His mother's face registered nothing.

"I did want you to know," Dara said. "Am I correct to assume that you have at least a passing interest in what happens in my life?"

"Of course," I said. I tried to say it neutrally, but actually, I was annoyed. She had not told me much of anything, and what she said contained mixed messages. When she called me earlier, what had she wanted to talk to me about so urgently? She seemed to already have everything figured out. Also, I knew Tom less well than she did. Except for wishing his greenhouse wouldn't materialize, I didn't care what happened with him, one way or the other. Though it was pretty clear that I wasn't going to be able to enlist Dara's help in getting him to change his plans. The greenhouse's opening had been announced in the paper. What likelihood was there that he wouldn't do exactly what he intended? Still—something made me decide to try. Then, at least, I would feel that something had been accomplished by the meeting.

So I laid it out for her. I told her what problems Tom Van Sant would be presenting us with. I tried to say, without excessive pride, that there was some value in a family-owned business of long standing. I asked her, point-blank, to ask him to reconsider.

She pointed to my open purse, indicating she wanted more rum in her empty coffee cup. I poured some in her cup, then some in mine, looking around to make sure no one was watching. No one seemed to be, though the woman who'd just driven away returned to the parking lot and jumped out of her car, picking up something small—a toy?— from the asphalt. Again, we watched the woman and child drive away, but this time his eyes were bright, and he was smiling, clutching something to his cheek.

"What would it be like? What would I do? Marry Tom and have little babies and a nice little life?"

It wasn't really a question.

"You're smart not to have them," she said. "I'd never go through that again. My parents were monsters. They insisted I have the child I was carrying when I was a teenager, and then they forced me to give her away. When my mother married her second husband, she had a baby, herself. She said it was intentional, that she'd always known a woman who performed abortions. Can you imagine saying that to me?" Dara looked at the ring on her finger. "She had to show everybody how youthful she was. How *fecund*."

Dara was full of surprises. She'd had a child?

"Is it an issue with you and Bob?" she said. "Am I skating on thin ice?"

"No," I said. "It's not an issue." (Meaning: we hadn't discussed it in a while, and I realized perfectly well that motherhood would be very demanding. Still—what was I going to do? Spend my life doing errands for the family and typing manuscripts I knew would never be published?)

"It's good it isn't," she said. "It's none of my business. Though I guess you realize your family wonders what's going on. The rest of them are such breeders."

"What do you mean?"

"Frank said that, anyway. Maybe just he and his wife wonder what's going on."

"How would Frank come to tell you that?" I said.

"Frank calls me sometimes. We're sort of phone pals. I only saw Frank a few times, and I let him know very clearly that I wasn't interested." The corners of her mouth turned down, in genuine distaste. "I felt condescended to—like I was being hit on just because I was single and he assumed that therefore I was available. I reminded him that I was not the one who started the footsie game." She looked at me, and her expression lightened. "Is this something you didn't know?"

I shrugged. "I'm surprised, but I guess I shouldn't be."

"You're upset with me for telling you."

"No, I'm not."

"Just a slight bit."

"I feel bad for Janey."

"I'm sorry for her, too. Listen: I didn't try to pick up her husband; he tried to pick me up. All I did was have a cup of coffee with him and tell him it wasn't going to happen. He hasn't called for a week or so now. He did say she'd had the baby."

"She did," I said. "It was premature. A girl named Joanna."

"I don't think the baby was her idea," Dara said.

This did take me aback. I knew Janey had always wanted a girl. She had seemed happy about the pregnancy.

"He found out she was taking long walks when she was supposed to be in bed," Dara said. "Poor thing. Let's face it: for any of us who have been through it, I assure you, however she decided to deal with it was more her business than his."

"Well, the baby's beautiful," I said. I heard the quaver in my voice. Before, I'd been denying even to myself how much I was put out with her, but the information about Janey had really stung—enough so that I went on the offensive. I heard myself say: "Has your child ever looked for you?"

"How could she?" she said slowly. "She's just a little girl. But she was in the back of my mind when I decided to move back to New England. Not that she couldn't find me wherever I was living, but that it might be more fitting if she found me—you know—in the general geographic area of the scene of the crime. I was sent away to Bronxville to give birth, but my parents arranged the adoption in New England." She reached into my purse, took out the flask, and refilled her mug. She raised an eyebrow and extended the flask in my direction. I pointed to my cup. When she finished pouring this time, the rum was gone.

"To tell you the truth, I think it was one of those backdoor deals. I have no reason to believe my mother arranged for an adoption on the up and up. Straightforwardness was never her style."

I believed her and I didn't believe her. Somehow I believed that everything she said was true, but moving back to New England because she thought her child might find her there because that was where the papers had been signed for the adoption . . . it just didn't make sense. Considering the sad story I'd just been told, though, questioning her curious logic hardly seemed important. If she was overly interested in the details of Janey's pregnancy and what issues Janey and Frank might have disagreed about, or in how other people felt about babies generally, it was easy to understand why.

"Tell me the truth," she said slyly. I could tell by the way she mugged, holding her head slightly sideways, looking at me with dropped lids. "That baby you said was so beautiful. Frank says she's tiny and pink and bald. Do you think you might find her beautiful just because you're her aunt?"

"I might," I said.

"But then again, he might be describing the baby as a little tinier and a little pinker than she really is. Lest we forget, men are often embarrassed to say how much they love their babies."

"That could be, too," I said.

"I want to reassure you," Dara said. "I don't have any indication that Frank doesn't love his wife."

"Well, I don't either," I said. Not loving Janey—how could that be possible? Janey was terrific. She had always been my favorite person in the family. I had often taken my cues from Janey.

"But you know," she said, "if anyone was to talk to Tom about the greenhouse, I think Frank would have a better chance than I would.

He'd just think I was meddling in something that's really not my business, but he has a lot of respect for Frank. Maybe there's a way they could work together."

I thought about the conversation I'd had with Frank at the beach on Barbara's birthday. It didn't seem likely that Frank would do it— but maybe if I told Frank that Dara had suggested it . . . "You talk to Frank," I said. "He'd be more likely to do it if you said it made sense."

"I can mention it," she said, "but my feeling is that while he likes to cry on my shoulder, he doesn't really have any desire to have me suggest how he might live his life."

The sun had come out briefly, then gone behind a cloud. It was getting colder. Dara shivered and brushed her hair out of her face. "I've got to go," she said. "But I appreciate your listening to me. And the rum. The people around here are such stiffs"—she shivered again— "and sweetie, I really do understand that you care about me. Nobody could know what to do about Tom when I don't know myself. I have to figure out if this is something I actually *want*." She locked her eyes on me. "You like him, don't you? He thinks people don't like him, but I told him he's such a loner, he doesn't really invite other people in. That ridiculous cowgirl . . . he had her there because she was between jobs and didn't have any money or anywhere to stay. She couldn't afford to sign a new lease on the house she'd been renting, apparently. He just took pity on her."

This was clearly self-serving—Bernie did not strike me as a pathetic person—yet as Dara said it, I understood that she was trying to talk herself into Tom Van Sant. I also thought that maybe they would be fine with each other. I hardly knew him, and we had gotten off to such an odd start.

It wasn't until we'd said goodbye and hugged each other and promised to talk soon that I realized I had to see Tom Van Sant, in part because Dara was my friend; I might as well try to get to know a person who was important in her life. I turned on the radio and listened to the first few minutes of *All Things Considered.* Stopped at a light, I was amazed at how the afternoon had slipped away: no typing; no food prepared; nothing. At the same time I found much of what she'd said disturbing, I was still flattered that she'd decided to talk to me. I even thought that it must be only my own insecurity that made me so sure that she had ignored me at Tom's party for Dowell Churnin. Was it so impossible that someone might see me and want to be friends? Perhaps, like Tom Van Sant, I was too much of a loner, but I didn't always have occasion to realize that because the family was so large. Dara was my first chance at an outside friend. I admired her for being able to express herself so vividly, and, of course, no one minds having attractive friends. As I drove, I thought over our conversation and felt flattered that she trusted me. She had told me a lot of things about herself finally, and I'd really done nothing but react, except for talking briefly—and no doubt boringly and pragmatically—about Snell's greenhouse. I was faintly embarrassed to have been concerned so much with mundane problems—really, only with one—when she'd opened up so much. If she was the spider, at least she wanted me to notice that the web was flimsy.

When I got home, the red flag had been lifted again on the mailbox. Inside was an envelope containing handwritten additions to Grace Aldridge's manuscript. She had remembered several more opinions her second husband had about what grew in the garden. "Parsley is no tastier than Easter basket grass," I read. "Gelatinous parts of tomatoes are like bedsores that won't heal."

Inside, I took off my jacket and hung it up, then went into the kitchen. Almost immediately, the phone rang.

"Sweetie, you are absolutely the most wonderful friend I could have," Dara said. "Don't say a word. I just wanted to announce that I feel better about everything. Thanks for the booze and a sympathetic ear." She hung up. The one-way call from Dara was very unexpected. I looked around, as if someone might be watching. I had the strange, vague sense of some hovering presence. I put on water to make tea, and as the kettle was heating, I realized that the afternoon's conversation had left me feeling very strange. I spent too much time doing solitary things, I decided, whether those things were errands or typing or simply drifting around the house alone on the days Bob was gone. I was part of the family, yet I was detached. Apparently even more than I thought I was, if I didn't know what Janey's real thoughts about her pregnancy had been, and if I'd taken it for granted that Frank would never, ever have a woman friend who wasn't also a friend of Janey's.

As I waited for the water to boil, I took out a teacup and put loose tea in a little tea ball. Then almost without thinking, I took the phone book off the shelf and flipped through until I found Tom Van Sant's number. He picked up the phone on the third ring, and I identified my-self, adding—stupidly, I realized, the second it was out of my mouth—that I was Bob Warner's wife.

"I know who you are, Jean. What's up?" he said.

"Could we get together to talk sometime next week?"

"Well, sure," he said. "Is something wrong?"

"I'd rather talk to you in person," I said.

"You're going to keep me in suspense?" he said. "What did you have in mind?"

"Wednesday afternoon?" I said. "Maybe at"—I couldn't think where; I was drawing a blank—"the bakery," I said. "The new bakery in the shopping center." I added lamely: "We could have coffee."

"You're loyal to the bakery, I see," he said. "Dara said she was going to meet you there this afternoon. Did you two get together?"

I hadn't been expecting that. I hadn't expected any chitchat, for some reason.

"Briefly," I said.

"Good," he said. "Is she feeling better?"

"She seemed fine," I said. I could tell from the tone of his voice that he was worried. I hoped he didn't think that I was calling about his re-lationship with Dara.

"I'll find out soon enough," he said. "She's on her way over here. I've been making spaghetti sauce. You wouldn't by any chance like to join us tonight for spaghetti and meatballs?"

"Oh. Tonight. No. Thank you. Dinner's already cooking," I lied.

"Okay," he said. "So Corolli's, on Wednesday. What time?"

"Three o'clock?"

"Three o'clock. Any hint what this is about?"

"Dara will tell you," I said. I thought she would. If she was going there, I felt sure she'd be telling him everything about our conversa-tion, and it was probably best that she did. I was already convinced that I was going to plead my case—the family's case—and lose. The conver-sation would come to nothing, and all the while we were talking I would know what he and Dara had done outside his house, running hand in hand with their Instant Meadow . . . it was too intimate a thing to know. It was going to make it difficult to talk to him. I flashed on an image of Janey and Bob and Barbara and me, at the carnival. Of meeting Bernie for the first time, and how sweet she'd seemed. I remembered Barbara trying to persuade us to be nice to a newcomer, which I found I still held against her. What did she know about people? She always assumed the best, and if she could find one good attribute, she'd focus on that. Like the rest of the family, though . . . I was suddenly realizing something . . . like the rest of them, she didn't really let people in. There were certain formats for seeing other people socially, and she was always quick to do a favor, but then she retreated. She kept to herself. She belonged to no clubs. Since her husband's death so many years before, Barbara rarely went out at night, and if she did, it was with someone in the family. She barely knew other women her age in the community, though she'd lived there almost all her life.

I dunked the tea ball in the hot water and watched a brown cloud seep outward. I jiggled the ball so the water would turn uniformly bronze. On the table was the new page to add to the manuscript I was working on. I put it on top of the pile, but then wandered away. I turned on the radio above the sink and listened to the classical-music station, waiting for the tea to darken. I couldn't erase the image of Tom Van Sant and Dara running. Why did that have to stick in my mind?

When the tea was the right color, I carried the cup upstairs, sipped delicately from it, then put it on Bob's dresser and, licking my slightly scalded lips, began to take his shoes out of the closet so I could inspect for rogue mothballs. There were more shoes than I'd realized, so I got the cup and saucer and put them beside me on the floor, then sat sideways, reaching in and pulling out shoes. As I lifted one shoe a mothball rolled into the heel. I shook it out, triumphant. Then I continued to remove the rest of the shoes, tilting them, looking on the floor for mothballs. I found two more and then, tipping a slip-on black shoe Bob had worn only once that I could remember, felt something heavier than a mothball slide from toe to heel. It was a small gray cube—a box, I realized, as I lifted it out. A velvet box that contained a diamond ring. In a day of surprises, this was the most startling thing of all. I couldn't believe what I was seeing. I flicked the box closed, as if the second time I opened it, something else might be inside. But it was the ring: an antique, probably something from Grandma's era, with a circular raised diamond that sparkled in the center. I took it out and tried it on. It almost fit the ring finger of my right hand, but I didn't want to force it. It was lovely, and I could not have been more surprised if I'd found

Moses in the bulrushes. Bob was going to give it to me for . . . what? My birthday, or our anniversary? But that would be Barbaraish to think. What I really thought was that it was something intended for someone else, and that made me feel as if the floor I sat on was about as solid as a deflating raft. Carefully, I got up, leaving the box in the heel of the shoe. With my foot, I pushed the other shoes back onto the closet floor as if they were bumper cars that had been struck from behind, sending them every which way in an impossibly complicated pileup. One black shoe remained, which I picked up and tossed in the direction of its mate. Then I picked up the three mothballs and put them on the saucer. I stood, holding my tea and mothballs. Then I clumsily dropped the cup and saucer. Stupid, stupid: the liquid and the smashed pieces were all over the floor.

The ring couldn't be for me.

The whole day had been leading up to something bad. Everything Dara discussed had been a clue: that men didn't act the way you assumed they'd act; that everybody had secrets.

Downstairs, after crying for much longer than I anticipated, I made another cup of tea, but this time I used a tea bag and a mug. I dropped in two ice cubes once the tea was strong enough so I could drink it right away, stirring them into the hot water with my finger, not caring that my finger was being half scalded, half frozen.

"I found the ring," I said, the minute Bob came into the house.

"You found the ring," he repeated, slowly. "How did you happen to be reaching around in a pair of my shoes to find the ring?"

"Mothballs," I said.

"What?"

"The closet smelled like mothballs. I thought some had rolled onto the closet floor. Is this going to be one of those times where you try to turn the tables, in spite of the facts?"

"One of what times?" he said.

"You're going to pretend now that it was for me," I said.

"No, actually," he said.

I waited.

"I have to say I'm really surprised that you'd react this way, without even asking me what the ring was doing there," he said.

"You're stalling for time," I said. "Just tell the truth."

"The truth," he said, "is that Drake bought the ring to give to his girlfriend, but then he started to have second thoughts. So he gave it to me so he wouldn't impulsively give it to her. Call him, if you don't believe that," he said, taking off his coat and throwing it over the arm of the sofa. "And hello to you, too," he said. "Glad to see you, too. It's a real pleasure to be married to someone who's so trusting."

A rivulet and puddle of hot tea was ruining the finish on the upstairs floor, and I had let it stay there for the wrong reason. I had hastily accused Bob of something that was totally untrue. I had, that day, solidified a friendship and alienated my husband. It was enough to make me collapse in tears all over again.

"Since you don't mind telling me what's the case, let me caution you also," he said tersely, from the kitchen. "Drake does not want anyone in the family to know that he is serious about his girlfriend, so you shouldn't repeat anything I just told you."

I got up and said, meekly, "Can't you see why I—"

"No," he said. He was drinking a Coke. He left the unfinished bottle on the counter and went upstairs. In a few minutes, I heard him cleaning up the mess. It was not until days later, when I did the wash, that I saw he had taken one of my favorite blouses and used it to mop up, then had wadded it tightly and thrown it into the laundry hamper.

The morning of the day I was going to meet Tom, I went over to Janey's to watch Joanna for an hour or so while Janey went to the dentist. The boys were at camp for two weeks. It was their first time away from home, and Frank and Janey missed the boys and worried about them. The director of the camp had told them to stop calling. This made Frank see the light but convinced Janey that any second the boys were likely to forget that they had parents, which, in her mind, was an equal tragedy to her not having—truly not having had—sons. Frank tried to tell her that everything would be fine—that it was the perfect summer for the boys to be away for a while, because they weren't getting any sleep with the baby crying, and also because they needed some independence. The boys had been delighted to go, which led Janey to think that it was a male conspiracy. She clutched Joanna to her tightly and felt that the house was now divided into Us against Them. Then

her hormones—her much-joked-about hormones—elevated or sub-
sided or whatever they did, giving her a reprieve from the delusion that
she was living a tragic life, with Joanna her only ally. When she regained
her sanity, Frank took her out to the Italian restaurant. They laughed
about her misperceptions, and then, eating pizza, she had felt something sharp in her mouth. It was part of a tooth, and the crumbling
tooth had depressed her as much as frightened her. When she called to
ask me if I could come over the next morning, her voice was so grim
that I assumed something terrible had happened. It didn't help much
that, because I was so relieved, I dismissed the broken tooth as nothing. "If you don't care about me, at least pity Joanna for having a
mother so ancient she's likely to disintegrate," Janey said.

"Oh, Janey," I said.

" 'Oh, Janey,' nothing," she said. "My appointment is at ten-fifteen.
Frank called the dentist at home and asked him to work me in because
I was hysterical. He's so sweet sometimes. I tried to get him to call the
camp from the pay phone, since he was being so nice and so authorita-
tive, but he wouldn't do it."

It was late July. The lilacs were long gone, but the rhododendrons,
in their old-lady's-dress colors of lavender and pink, were blooming
everywhere, as were the wild roses. The day before, picking up the
newly typed pages of her manuscript, Mrs. Aldridge had brought me a
bouquet of cosmos and marigolds. They looked like Mutt and Jeff in
the jar: the tall cosmos with their feathery leaves and opalescent flowers; the solid little marigolds with their bristly blooms, their heads
barely rising above the glass. Mrs. Aldridge had a few more pages for
me, though fortunately they were not about her second husband. They
were, she said, about her third husband, but I could fit them into the
story wherever I thought best, or else I could append them to the end,
after an asterisk. She often suggested asterisks. She thought about individual asterisks with the reverence that schoolchildren had—or had
when I was a child—upon discovering that every snowflake was different. I had asked her to stay for coffee, but she said she had to be on her
way. "No more pages," she said, as she was leaving, but I knew better:
she had brought additional pages half a dozen times at least. It occurred to me that perhaps the additional writing was an attempt to
think things were still ongoing—that as long as she wrote more, the
marriages still endured.

Janey was in her nightgown when I got there. She had overslept—
something she had forgotten was possible—and was trying to do everything at once: comb her hair; sip coffee; finish writing a check. She put
the bundled Joanna into my arms and said, "Wet. She'll be crying in
two seconds," but Joanna remained silent until I took her off to change
her.

Her room was small but very pretty. It was painted light green, and
Frank had glued stars and moons that glowed at night to the ceiling
over her crib. There were two foam-rubber buffers against the crib railing, tied in place with ribbons. Several toys, all much larger than her
hands, were strewn on the mattress. As I put Joanna on the table to
change her—actually, it was a wicker table that had once been on Barbara's porch, now padded with a foam-rubber pillow zipped into a
rubber case and covered with a pillowcase; a rather strange, improvised
changing table—the top of my head set a mobile fluttering: the cow
that jumped over the moon, stars tinkling. This got Joanna's attention
and distracted her for the first few moments of the changing ritual,
which I did carefully but slowly, with no pretense that it came naturally.
I considered getting them a real changing table, but wondered if the
gift would insult them. They were taking all of this less seriously than
they had with the boys. Joanna had only been nursed for the first week
of her life. Now she was drinking formula. I tried to elicit a smile from
Joanna, but she was looking beyond me, to some mid-distance, her eyes
baby bright and blue, both hands fisted and moving through air. Was
there any chance at all that Janey, pregnant, had gone jogging? I looked
at Joanna's pink skin, and at the network of blue veins below it. My
scrutiny made her cry—or I felt as if it had—so I hurriedly finished
diapering her and wrapped her, inexpertly, in the receiving blanket
again, tugging down her little white shirt.

"Thank you, thank you," Janey said, standing in the doorway in
pants that tied at her still-vanished waist, a T-shirt tucked inside. The
nightgown dangled from her hand like a towel. She opened the hamper
beside the door and tossed it in. It was so full that the top didn't close.
I resolved to do a wash while she was gone.

"Isn't she the most adorable baby?" I said. "It has nothing to do
with my being her aunt."

"A girl," Janey said. "I must admit, I'm pleased." She came up to us
quickly, her thongs slapping, and cupped her hand around one of the

baby's fists. "Are you Mama's last baby?" she said. "Are you the third, final, forevermore last baby of your mama?" Janey no more than nodded yes and she was gone, her shoes flapping down the stairs. On my way out of the room I took the laundry bag off a hook, one-handed, baby against my left shoulder, my right upper arm bracing her head as my right hand snatched a few pieces of dirty clothing from the hamper and pushed them into the bag. This was not going to work very well. I put Joanna into her crib and had not even turned around when she began to cry. I let her cry for a few seconds before going to her, and by then the bag was half filled. Lifting her out of the crib and returning to plan 1, I dipped deeper and brought up the rest of the laundry piece by piece, while reflecting that this method would certainly not get cotton picked. I had suddenly remembered a picture from a magazine, or from an old school textbook, of women in the field, several with babies papoosed or clutched to their breast, bending, in their big skirts, to pick cotton. Joanna and I would have been whipped and gone sprawling if the hamper had been a row of cotton, and the thought of that outraged me, made my face heat up faster than it had when I'd been bending over. A world of misery and unfairness. I wondered, briefly, if Janey's raging hormones could have mysteriously set my own hormones going—if she could have communicated her absolute frustration to me as if it were airborne particles of bacteria. With those muddled thoughts, I dragged the bag to the top of the stairs and then bumped downstairs holding it by the cord, the bag as quiet as Janey's flip-flops had been loud, me following behind her as if to erase the noise. Joanna was quiet in my arm, a tiny weight against my chest. I lightly kissed the top of her head and went up to the alcove near the downstairs bathroom where the washer and dryer were. One-handed, I opened the washer top. I lifted the bag to the top of the dryer and began to pull out pieces, dropping them into the washer. "One, two, three," I said, aloud, as if giving a two-week-old baby a lesson in counting. "You're Joanna, I am me," I said, unable to resist the dual lesson: rhyming. As the washing machine did its work, she and I explored the house, looking at the pretty things (what do babies know about dust? it could be just as pretty as starlight) and returning many times to the windows. Outside, wind chimes blew in the breeze, dangling from the apple tree. There was a squirrel, which was approximately the length of Joanna, and which seemed inordinately complex, compared to the little bundled baby I held: standing on its hind legs; looking around; racing forward; jumping onto a tree. Janey kept a radio on the windowsill above the sink, which led me to think that perhaps instead of religious pictures or statues, the FM radio was the crucial item on the windowsill altars of American housewives. Also on this altar were a box of paper clips, a Brillo pad in a small dish, and a picture of the boys, with their ears cut off in order to fit both faces into the tiny frame. The younger was missing a front tooth or two—you couldn't tell, because the faces were so small. There was also a broken watchband and Janey's hospital identification bracelet. I picked it up and read the vital information: Janey's name, the date, the doctor's name, and then "7 Commercial O/P," whatever that meant. Janey had had Joanna in four hours and had left the hospital in seven. Barbara had been as upset about that as she had been excited about the birth. Who knew exactly what "something" might happen; she probably had an exact scenario too horrific to describe—but then, when Barbara had had her babies, everything had been different. She had stayed in the hospital for four days, and she had gone to Grandma's with each child for a month when she was discharged, and then Grandma had almost lived with Barbara for the first six months, after Barbara returned home.

The neighbor's boy was cutting the grass, stalling the mower every few minutes. Joanna fell asleep in my arms as I drank her mother's mug of almost-untouched coffee, after pouring in some milk. That, too, would have scandalized Barbara. You never, ever drank after anyone. Barbara never even drank after herself; she pulled a Dixie cup out of the dispenser near the sink, or else got a new glass. When I first met Barbara, I once made the mistake of rinsing her orange juice glass to put wine in it. "Oh—it's your glass," I had said, reassuringly. She had held the glass at a distance, discreetly, using only a thumb and finger, a few beads of water still adhering after my quick rinse and dry, looking at it as if I'd dug up a buried pet and reassured her that it had once belonged to her. It took me a while to understand the family, and sometimes I wished I hadn't learned so well.

The dentist managed to file Janey's tooth; she would not have to get a crown. But her head ached, and she asked me to stay for a while. On the way in, she had seen the neatly stacked laundry and almost burst into tears, she said. She was so lucky to have me. "I somehow feel Grandma and Barbara did more for each other than we do," I said.

"What? Like move in together?" Janey said, shaking Excedrin out of the bottle. "They were fixated on each other. I think it's a growth move that at least Grandma's gotten away from home and made it all the way to Boston."

What she said made me yearn to confide the news about Drake, but I knew I shouldn't. I sat on a stool and watched her look for the coffee mug, realize it was gone (who had time to think about how or why?), and take another glass out of the sink, rinse it, then fill it with water and swallow, one pill at a time. Careful Janey. Who would surely never endanger a pregnancy by walking when she'd been told to stay in bed.

"What are you looking at?" she said. "Do I look dishevelled?"

"No. Sorry," I said, self-conscious about having been caught staring.

"I'm becoming a terrible person," Janey said, turning on the water again and splashing it on her face. Dripping, she headed for the dish towel. "I feel bad about how I look, and then I accuse everyone of staring. Frank's afraid to make eye contact."

"I had an attack of paranoia about Bob a couple of days ago. He got so huffy that he wouldn't accept my apology."

"It's just too hard, being married," Janey said. Then she said: "What did you get paranoid about?"

"I found something, and I assumed it meant one thing, and really it meant another."

"What did you think was one thing that was really another?" she said.

"Oh," I said miserably, having worried as I spoke that she'd ask, "I can't tell you. It was something Bob was hiding for somebody, and I thought it was his."

"Dirty magazine?"

"No, but now that you mention it, one of the guys he went sailing with in the spring gave him a *Playboy* at the end of the sail because he didn't want to take it home and have his wife find it. I wonder whether he just sat there reading the magazine, or whether he paid attention to the scenery on the sail."

"Frank has drawers he just doesn't go into," Janey said. "I have one drawer in the refrigerator I feel basically that way about."

"I had turnips that sprouted one time, and the sprouts grew like a vine. They wrapped around the shelf above them."

"Oh, God," Janey said. "What if they really have lives? Or souls. Or whatever it was that made people think you should play music to your houseplants."

"Turnips? I don't think so," I said.

"But remember those scientists who put electrodes on houseplants, and the plants went crazy when Dizzy Gillespie was played?"

"I know, I know. But—"

"Frank believes it. That's why he's always got the stereo set up inside the big greenhouse, playing music he doesn't care anything about. They wanted to know if I wanted music in the labor room. I tried Tina Turner, but it only made it worse."

"You really did?"

"Honey—you are questioning every single thing that I say. When did I ever put you on? Doctors are music junkies. They play it while they operate. A friend of mine is married to a surgeon who learned conversational Japanese while he was taking out gall bladders. And don't say 'Reeeeally?' "

"You mean that's common knowledge?" I said.

"Probably not, but why would you think I was kidding you? You seem slightly off-kilter. Not that I'm criticizing. I mean, who got the wash done today? Who rushed over to take care of my kid?"

"That was nothing," I said.

"Listen to you. You're so self-deprecating. You're nice to everybody. You always come through, but you don't want to hear about it."

"Maybe because I still have no idea what I want to do," I said. "It's one thing to do nice things for people, but what am I going to do with my life? It's embarrassing not to have figured it out yet."

"It isn't as if you're in New York City, where so much stuff is available. I mean, what *should* you do? Go down the road and waitress? Join the nursery like the rest of the lemmings?"

"I don't even have good luck keeping houseplants alive."

"I wasn't suggesting you should be at the nursery," she said. "Far from it. But didn't Bob ever try to pressure you into it?"

"No," I said.

"Then you were luckier than me. Frank used to take it personally that I wouldn't work there. Forget my degree in nursing. When we got married, he assumed I'd work there, but I didn't find out *how* strongly he felt until I made it absolutely clear that wasn't going to happen."

"I am naive. I thought you and Frank always agreed on everything. I mean, I don't assume any married couple always agrees, but—"

"Frank? Me? He wants the kids to go to camp; I think they're too young. He wants to live in New Hampshire; I want to go live in Florida, where the winters are warm. He wants to go to his mother's to plant lilacs at night; I tell him to send somebody from the nursery, in the day. He wants to go to the Grand Canyon. I want to see Paris. You know when Ehrlichman asked Judge Sirica to send him as a volunteer to an Indian reservation, instead of to jail? Frank thought Sirica should have done it, because Ehrlichman was such a good man. Such a patriot. Frank doesn't think what Nixon did was terrible either; it's just that he got caught. You know what else Frank said? He said that he'd been reading an article in *The New York Times* about how Europeans didn't understand why there was so much fuss made over Watergate. Which he brought up to club me over the head with, as if we couldn't possibly vacation in a place where the average Frenchman didn't share my perceptions of right and wrong. He is so juvenile, sometimes. I love Frank, but he's impossible. You just have to accept that."

I nodded. I was half thinking about what Janey was telling me, half drifting off in thought about this afternoon's meeting with Tom Van Sant. I was doing anything I could not to focus on it. What would I say to him? What Janey said was true: I was not only self-deprecating, I lacked confidence. I felt sure I would be going through the motions, even saying the right things, but still there would be no chance that anything I said would result in Tom's changing his mind.

"Can I tell you two things that I want you to swear you will never, ever, under any circumstances, breathe a word of to anybody?" I said.

She looked at me wide-eyed. "Are you having an affair?" she said.

It took me so much aback that my eyes widened more than hers, which she seized upon as confirmation. She looked crestfallen when I shook my head no.

"Then it's no big deal," she said. "Don't worry about telling me."

She reached for Joanna. I handed her over. Beneath the spot she had warmed against my breast, I could feel my heart beating. As my body cooled, the heartbeat was more noticeable. I looked down to see if I could see anything. Janey took this to be shame, and urged me to speak up, saying that she was entirely trustworthy and crossing her heart, like a little girl.

"One thing isn't a big deal, but I haven't told anybody. I mean, I told Frank I intended to, but I didn't tell him I'd made the call. I'm having coffee with Tom Van Sant this afternoon, to try to talk him out of opening his business."

"And?" Janey said.

"And," I said, different words coming out of my mouth from what I'd intended, "he's going to marry that woman. Dara Falcon. She's engaged to him." What I had intended to say was that I had found an engagement ring, hidden by Bob in his shoe, that Drake was going to give his girlfriend.

Janey shrugged. "Why is that top secret?"

"Because she swore me to secrecy," I said. Which was true enough. She had.

"Well, I, for one, would be happy to have her spoken for," Janey said. "Let me also let you in on a little secret. I found a letter Frank had written to her. It wasn't romantic or anything, so at first I was consoled by that, but then I realized that they must write each other often, if he was just sending her a note about not much of anything."

"When did you find this out?"

"When I almost had the miscarriage. I told him that if he was having any sort of relationship with another woman, that I had no intention of going through with the pregnancy."

"You did?"

"Honey, really—it's getting to be a tic, your questioning everything." She reached out and put her hand on the baby's back. "Not that I was exactly reassured by his reaction, but he said there was nothing sexual between them, and that he'd already stopped seeing her. A few days after our talk, it occurred to me that it wasn't exactly great that women automatically suspect every other woman. If she was sitting in a bar and Frank started talking to her, so what, really? Maybe he just needed to talk to someone other than me, and maybe she was lonesome that night. At least, that's been the attitude I've been trying out. And every time I think that way, it becomes a little more convincing."

"I think I'd kill Bob," I said.

"Well, Bob's not Frank. I'm not trying to play one-upsmanship about husbands here, but maybe Frank did need somebody to talk to other than me. Bob at least talks to Barbara, doesn't he?"

"About what?" I said.

"About anything."

"I don't know. I don't think so."

"Frank always says Bob's the good son. That's his nickname for him, behind his back. Sandra's close to Barbara, of course, and Drake doesn't much like her, but he's at least decided to keep out of her hair—he's pretty much vanished. Maybe I'm giving Bob too much credit. Maybe it's more you than Bob. The errands, and taking Barbara on picnics and all the thoughtful things you do. Maybe that's you."

It was, I thought. Especially lately.

"So give yourself some credit," Janey said.

I nodded. This talk was making me feel better. If nothing else, it was clear how well Janey thought of me.

"So tell me about the great romance," she said.

"She's a little ambivalent," I said. "That's why she wanted to talk to me about it. We had coffee a few days ago."

"Do you like her?" Janey said.

"Do I . . . I'm not really sure. I mean, she seems nice enough. Sort of overwrought, though. I sort of feel the way Barbara felt, when we first ran into Tom Van Sant—that somebody ought to be nice. To her, I mean. Yeah, sure. I like her."

"Just remember your loyalty to your sister-in-law," Janey said.

"Oh, I *do*," I said.

"I know you do," Janey said. "I shouldn't tease you."

"I'll let you know how it turns out," I said. I had spent so much time at Janey's, it was almost time to meet Tom. As I got off the stool, I realized one of my feet had gone dead. I hobbled, but Janey didn't seem to notice. What I noticed was that she seemed tired—that circles had begun to darken under her eyes as we talked.

She waved from the back door as I started the car. On the radio, Elvis was singing "I Can't Help Falling in Love with You." What would the philodendrons do if they heard that? Aim their pointy chins down toward the floor and weep? I unrolled the windows and winced as clouds of hot air escaped past my face, waving quickly to Janey and Joanna, empowered by our discussion to try my best to prevail with Tom Van Sant. But as I drove, my certainty disappeared. As the song continued, I thought about Elvis in Memphis, at Graceland. It never occurred to me that soon he would be dead, collapsed on the bathroom floor, and all the rumors that had swirled around him would settle down into the grim realization that obese Elvis had been a drug addict, incontinent, yet still possessed of enough sense to shoot out the television every time Robert Goulet's name was mentioned. Robert Goulet was Barbara's favorite singer. Barbara this, Barbara that, which made me realize what Janey had not said, directly: too much of my life was being subsumed by Barbara.

I pulled into the shopping center and was surprised to see, again parked under a NO PARKING sign, Dara's big red wreck of a car. It never occurred to me that she, or anyone else, would be accompanying Tom, but when I saw the two of them, already at a table, I tried to persuade myself that this was for the best; together, we might talk him out of his plans.

Again, her John Wesley Harding hat sat on the table, but the rest of her clothes were different: a transparent white sleeveless blouse with a lacy bra visible underneath; denim cutoffs, scuffed red high heels with pointy toes. An ankle bracelet. Her outfit looked more like something Bernie would wear than anything Dara would put together. Her legs were quite lean and tan.

"Hello, sweetie!" she called.

I looked at them and smiled, Elvis's voice still ringing in my ears.

"Hey, I know why you're here, and I understand completely," Tom said, as I climbed up the two cement steps to where they sat.

I was flustered; I smiled insincerely. I couldn't think of any quick response, so I didn't say anything. I pulled out a chair and sat down. They had been there for a while; they both had empty coffee cups in front of them.

"Let me get you something," Tom said, rising. Every table was taken. Tourists sat at one table, discussing the route they would take to Bar Harbor. Two women sat at another table. Three teenage girls giggled at another. The ordinariness of it took all my momentum away. I felt faintly embarrassed to be there.

"I'd like an iced cappuccino," I said.

"Another espresso, please," Dara said.

The second Tom left, Dara leaned close. She smelled faintly of roses; the smell swung toward me as her hair did. "Forgive me," she said. "He was just too curious. I don't think I did your cause any harm."

"Oh, it's fine," I said.

"The situation's slightly more complicated than it seems," she said. "He'll tell you."

It was on the tip of my tongue to tell her that Janey knew about her—knew something about her—but I didn't. Beside us, one of the girls was dancing a Danish pastry through the air. Another girl almost slapped it out of her hand, but the first girl zoomed it away, like a toy plane.

"We've talked about a cooling-off period for the romance," she said. "Big Bernie," she said, but fell silent as Tom bumped open the door with one hip and came toward us, carrying a tray with cookies on a plate and three coffees. His, like mine, was iced, in a tall glass.

"Listen," he said, "I don't want you to think I'm obtuse." He put the three coffees in front of our places. He put the cookies in the center of the table. "I realize this isn't the absolute best thing that could happen for your family's business, but they're going to be such different places, it won't be as much of a problem as you think. We're going to have a lot of cut flowers, and dried flowers during the winter, which I know you don't carry. And in the greenhouse, I'm going to have a lot of gesneriads: hypocerta and columnea and things like that. The bushes and trees in the summer—to be honest with you, that's going to be somewhat competitive, but I'm limited in how many special sales I can have. Maybe there's a way we can figure out things you want to stock that aren't available to me, or that I'm not really interested in, and I could offer things you don't have." He bit into a cookie. "I'm sure there's enough demand for both of us. I think this can work out."

He was soft-pedalling. He would still have the Route 1 location. His would still be the newer greenhouse, with piped-in music and wicker furniture.

"There's no chance we could talk you into opening some other franchise?" I said. My tone of voice indicated that I knew there was no chance. His slow shake of the head from side to side let me know he had no intention of backing down.

"It was Dowell's idea, did you know that?" Dara said to me. "He has a cousin in the business, somewhere in western Massachusetts. If Dowell hadn't found Tom, he would have found someone else."

Tom shrugged, looking helpless.

"Well," I said, "I didn't think you were going to abandon the plan.

At least, as you say, we can try to have a good relationship with each other."

The teenage girls drifted away from the table, carrying knapsacks and embroidered shoulder bags heavy with possessions. Their Tampax and their cosmetics and their diaries and their mail. I had once had purses bulging with those things.

"And now for a bit of good news?" Dara said.

I looked at her. So did Tom. I was sure she was going to tell me they were getting married.

"Yours truly," she said, "has just been selected for the role of Nora, in *A Doll's House.* I have now come full circle, from high school actress to mature talent. Beginning September fifteenth, I may be viewed all nights except Tuesday and Sunday as the Star. Complimentary tickets await you."

"That's wonderful!" I said. "That's really wonderful."

"We're going to be living together," Tom said, taking her hand.

"Well—that's wonderful, too," I said.

"We're in the process of packing up that terrible dump in Portsmouth," she said. "Tom is being an absolute saint helping me."

"Too bad you can't move the bedroom intact," I said.

Tom looked at Dara. "She's seen your bedroom?"

"Only once," she said. "On a day when she absolutely saved my life."

"Consider yourself privileged," he said.

"This move does not mean I am auditioning for the role of wife," Dara said. "Someone else will do the cooking and cleaning. I will continue to act, and to function as a sex object. When I'm all set up, we'll have a feast," she said. "We're going to have a huge lobster salad and champagne."

I was wrong to have demonized Tom. He looked younger than I remembered, and, after all, he was doing everything he could to ensure we'd work things out about the businesses. They were in love, and however many qualifications Dara put on things, their happiness was contagious. I did want to go to their house. I did want to have champagne and lobster salad, and for everything to work out well.

There Dara sat: the star, with stars in her eyes. And I felt illumined, as if lit by ambient light. All at once, the day had become magical. It seemed as if, by merely being their friend, I could move at a faster speed. It was a little as if I'd already sipped several glasses of champagne. As if I could fly home, instead of sitting in traffic. I bit into a cookie, which was chocolaty and sweet, and if I could have smiled at the same time I chewed, I would have.

B︎ob had decided—quite impulsively for him—to go camping with his friends Peter, Chris, and Trenton. Chris had given him a ride back from Boston; he'd gone in to use the medical library, to research the latest article he was writing. He did the medical writing to support his poetry habit. He lived with his son, two dogs, two cats, and—until they pecked at the paint outside their cages and died—two birds, in a mixed neighborhood of blue-collar workers and hippies. Someone had dubbed his house "the Saint Christopher Menagerie." Bob reported that Chris's house was complete with the newest technology—he had an expensive word processor—but he slept on the couch, because he saw no sense in a bed that you slept in only at night and that just took up space the rest of the time. As well as his love of poetry—Gerard Manley Hopkins, in particular—he loved the outdoors. And he always packed tons of gear. Bob had once gotten furious at him because Chris had volunteered to pack everyone for a three-day hike (he was a real origami master of packing), and, at the top of the mountain the first night, Bob had discovered that one of the heavy packs he'd been hauling uphill all day contained surgical instruments. Chris was prepared to remove a burst appendix, or to tie a tourniquet around any limb that might suddenly start spouting blood.

Peter and Trenton were painters, though they painted very differently. Peter loved the Impressionists, and Trenton loved Poussin. Peter lived down a dirt road through the woods, where, in recent years, two Boston exiles had built. A wooden sign directed you to Peter's house, but instead of giving his name—Greek, and containing most letters of the alphabet—there was a hand-lettered arrow in purple Day-Glo paint tacked to a tree that said: FUN; THIS WAY. His good friend Trenton lived fifteen minutes away, in a house that had been owned by the principal of the grade school. Every door in the house was one that had been discarded during renovations at the school, and they still had graffiti on them—kids' graffiti, which doubly appealed to Trenton's sense of humor—and that institutional shellac that made everything sparkle. Trenton's studio was the only part of the big old house that wasn't an eyesore: twelve hundred square feet of attic, with a shiny new oak floor and only one chimney interrupting the clear sweep of space. He'd put in dormers, and there were skylights and big, tall windows that allowed you the tiniest peek at the river. In the fall, Trenton always had a cocktail party so his friends could see the summer's work. We'd be high up in the treetops, amid all the shocking color of the trees. Binoculars were provided so we could see the leaves more clearly, and one autumn, Peter had been looking through the binoculars when a squirrel fell from one of the highest trees at the edge of the property, hit the ground, and lay there. As Peter and Trenton ran down to inspect, the rest of us saw the squirrel get up and, doglike, shake its head. We stood there, holding our little shish-kebab skewers of marinated mushrooms, and watched as it ran into Trenton's cellar. The hors d'oeuvres were provided by the mystery woman Trenton lived with. She considered herself a writer, and wrote all the time (if you believed Trenton's reports) on her old Royal typewriter. Joyce Carol Oates could not have put in as much time as Trenton's girlfriend, but what that meant was that we never saw her.

The guys were going camping and kayaking in the White Mountains, and as Bob pulled things out of his drawers and ran in circles, forgetting one thing, overlooking another, he didn't have much interest in my report on my day, and my discussion with Tom Van Sant. He was looking for—of all things—his flask. I told him I'd borrowed it and that it was downstairs, on the shelf where the soup bowls were kept.

"Borrowed it?" he said. "Why?"

"I filled it with rum and took it to the new bakery. It improves cappuccino remarkably."

"Yeah, sure you did," he said.

"Don't you think that's a possibility?" I said, trying to continue the conversation I'd started earlier. "If they primarily sold houseplants, and things like that—"

"Van Sant is going to do whatever's required to make money," Bob said. "There's nothing we can do about it."

"He said it was Dowell's idea. Only a quarter of the money that was put up was Tom's."

"It doesn't matter where the money came from. It's going to be built, and there's nothing we can do but roll with the punches."

I didn't know whether he was resigned because he was depressed about Snell's, or because he was just pretending to have come to terms with things because he was in a hurry to leave. He was angry with me, on some level. For quite a while, he'd been absent even when he was home. He was resigned to everything: to the cancellation of the family dinners; to the new business that was about to move into town; to the routine of coming and going—endlessly packing to leave for Boston and coming back and leaving it to me to unpack: to take his shirts to the dry cleaner, and to wash his clothes. I had never in my life shined shoes—including my own—but now no one shined them, because he wore running shoes. All the shoes in his closet just sat there, useless except as a place to hide other people's love tokens.

"Did he give her the ring?" I said.

"No," Bob said. "I moved it, by the way. I thought the locked tackle box was a better place for it."

The tackle box was Bob's ultrasecret hiding place for important documents and for cash and now, apparently, for the diamond ring. Bob had glued the box to the back of the closet in a small room we never used. The winter blankets and quilts were piled on top of it.

"I'm following you around like a puppy," I said. "If you have no interest in any of this, just say so."

"I have no interest in any of this," he said.

"Do you have any interest in anything?" I said. "How your wife is doing? How your family is?"

"I hear how the family is all the time. My mother calls every day. Grandma bends my ear from the minute I get back at night until I go to bed, unless I put the TV on, and then, on top of that, she talks all through the show. Drake wears earplugs to study. He's got the right idea: if you don't want to be inundated with the fucking family, what you have to do is become a mute. Cut yourself off. Don't say anything. Don't even hear anything."

His vehemence took me aback.

"You forgot to mention your fucking wife," I said. "Is she part of the problem, too?"

"Maybe you should consider this," he said. "That there's a whole world out there, not just this little dot on the map with our teeny, tiny

little microscopic dot of a family. I mean, why couldn't you have assumed that the ring wouldn't have anything to do with you? The whole
family has become so self-referential that it would be an insult if something wasn't personal, wouldn't it? So I suddenly become the bad guy.
Whoops! There's a ring! He's leaving me for someone else. I'm probably also not going camping with Trenton and the guys. Right. I don't
think I am. I'm going around to bars, I think, and offering the engagement ring to pretty girls. That sounds right."

"I apologized," I said. "I wouldn't have been the first wife to—"

"Stop thinking of yourself vis-à-vis everybody else. Why are you a
'wife'? Why aren't you just you?"

"You are in a really horrible mood," I said.

"You know what Barbara had the nerve to say to me?" he said.
"She wanted me to come over and help pump out the septic tank. She's
hired a company to do it, but she still wanted me there. Why did she
want me there? Because I'm an expert on septic tanks? Or just to have
me by the nuts?"

"Bob, this is crazy. She probably just misses you. She knows you're
not going to go over there and drink a cup of coffee with her."

"I'm not? Why not?"

"Have you ever done that? Ever once?"

"No, because there's always something to do. She punishes all of us
because she doesn't have a husband. He dared to die on her. My God!
Something happened that wasn't in the plans! Well—just have all the
rest of them rally around forever, then. They've got the time. They've
got the obligation."

I was so taken aback that all I did was stare at the floor. It hardly
seemed the time to make more demands on him, if this was the way he
felt. It hardly seemed the time to rephrase my question in terms of
"me" instead of as "your wife." I left him in the bathroom, where he
was cursing because he couldn't find the disposable razors. He hadn't
looked far enough back in the second drawer, where they were always
kept, but he could discover that for himself. I went downstairs and
looked at the movie listing. I was happy to see there was a Bette Davis
movie on. Probably Barbara would be watching the same film, I
thought, not missing the irony. Still: I had always been a big fan of Bette
Davis's. It was a movie I hadn't seen before. I turned on the little fan by
the chair, aimed it at my face.

"I'm sorry I yelled at you," he said, standing in the doorway, holding a duffel bag and wearing a backpack. Trenton's car had just pulled up: he'd swapped the bashed-in brown Toyota he'd driven for years for a red Toyota convertible, after completing a commission for the lobby of a building in St. Louis. I turned and looked through the slightly open slats of the venetian blind; Trenton was loping up the walk in his characteristic way, his slightly bent-kneed walk making him look like a slow-motion animation of how the dinosaurs ran, drinking from a bottle of Coke.

"I think going camping will do you good," I said.

"Bette Davis, huh?" he said. It was the last thing he said before opening the screen door to let Trenton in. I never answered him. I never said anything else except to greet Trenton and to wish them both a good trip. But when they left I could have bored holes through Bette Davis. If she'd been a punching bag, I could have pushed her over. But she was only an image on a television screen, so I slumped lower in the chair and watched. Unfortunately, though, something about the way she held her head reminded me of Barbara. I'd tuned in late, and I couldn't really understand what was happening. I heard Bob and Trenton laugh, and then the car radio come on. Dionne Warwick was singing "Walk On By." Trenton's Coke had looked good. I went into the kitchen and poured some out of a big bottle into a glass. It was flat. I dropped in three ice cubes and shook the glass, making as much fizz as possible. Then I opened the cabinet door and looked on the soup-bowl shelf. Bob had left the flask, and I took it down. I opened the next cabinet door and took out the bottle of rum. I got a funnel and poured rum into the flask, then Coke. I dumped the ice cubes in the sink. I went back to the TV, this time sitting upright and concentrating on Bette Davis, as if I were about to learn a lesson. Though maybe I had already learned it, I thought sourly. Maybe the lesson was that if you cared about people, and were involved, they just left you holding the stick. I thought about that as I sipped from the flask. After half an hour, I called Tom and asked if Dara was there. She was. She was painting a room at Tom's to make it a replica of her previous bedroom. It would be painted the same color. With the same lace curtains hung. But this time, with a lock on the door. It was a condition of her moving in with him.

"You're not watching Bette Davis, are you?" I said.

"That silly cow? Of course not. Did you call to ask me that, sweetie?"

"No. I called to see if there was any leftover spaghetti sauce. I was going to come over."

"Really? Oh, that would be wonderful." She lowered her voice. "You will be doing *much* better for yourself than spaghetti sauce, my love. We have made a moussaka and we have very cold white wine and there is nothing we would like more than to have you as our dinner guest."

T he next day, the day when Bob was out on the river, Barbara called twice. Bob was supposed to be at the house to hear about a new septic system the company wanted to install, she said, puzzled that he'd never shown up. "I don't know anything about it," I said. "He went off kayaking with Trenton and the guys." Late in the afternoon she called back, to see if he was home yet. I told her he wasn't. I also said that I thought Bob needed time to be by himself and to do what he wanted to do. I was still mad at him, but I had thought about what he'd said, and I was also quite put out with Barbara.

"I see," she said. As if the problem were me. As if her son weren't doing exactly what he intended to do, with no thought of either of us.

I spent the day working on the last section of Mrs. Aldridge's manuscript. Her third husband, while quite an outdoorsman, also gambled on the horses. He put out water and cat food for the neighbors' cats, even though she snatched up the bowls as soon as she found them (alas: he was a very early riser), and soon there were numerous birds dead, or left mauled, as prizes on the Aldridges' front stoop. One summer, at Saratoga, he lost half their savings at the racetrack. A horse called Daisy Buchanan placed, but that wasn't enough to save them. They fought, and Mrs. Aldridge hit him on the head with her purse. At this point in the manuscript there was an asterisk: *I had taken one too many mint juleps.* If nothing else, Mrs. Aldridge did try to be honest. But what did she think, finally, of her three husbands? Should the reader just assume that each husband was distinct, and that nothing could be inferred by thinking of them as a trio? She had set up the book, which she called "an autobiography," in three sections, so clearly she saw herself vis-à-vis (as Bob would say; what did he read, or where did he hang out, that people said "vis-à-vis"?) her husbands.

"She sounds like a feminist's nightmare," Dara said, when I told her how the book was organized, on the phone. "But it also sounds like a laugh riot. I want to see it." Her voice changed again. "No more projects you martyr yourself over for other people," she said.

"I'm not martyring myself. It's just a boring book, and I'm just a boring typist," I said. "It's what I do to make money."

That wasn't the truth; it was what I did in order to have something to do.

The next morning, I made lemonade with fresh lemons and sugar and club soda. I wrote checks to pay bills. Frank called, wanting to know if he could borrow Bob's drill. I told him that Bob was camping, but to come over and get it. Then I squeezed one more lemon, in case Frank might like a lemonade also. The sugar was kept in what was really a small pâté pan. It was hammered tin, and it had a lid with a tin duck sitting on top. I had bought it years ago in Cambridge, at a shop that sold kitchenware imported from France. I had also bought a beautiful mold for making madeleines, which I'd never used. It might be a nice housewarming gift for Dara. It seemed like something she would like. I pulled it out from the bottom drawer of the Hoosier cabinet. It contained a button and several highway tokens. I dropped them on the counter and polished the pan with my shirttail, thinking, as I did, how odd it was: the time I'd spent living with Bob had made me think of my clothing as towels and polishing cloths. I needed some new clothes. Some pretty things.

Back at the typewriter, the lemonade on a coaster, I typed: *Each morning Mr. Aldridge would eat a big breakfast of bacon, eggs, toast, and sometimes biscuits, as well, followed by a bowl of cornflakes with whatever seasonal fruit was available. He would not eat but that one meal a day, though in the afternoon he would most often have a mint julep, followed by a late-night beer. By late night I mean only 9 o'clock, because we always turned in by 9:30.* Since the reader already knew that he had lost a considerable part of their savings the previous day, would there be any interest in knowing what he ate for breakfast? Automatically filtering out many commas, I continued: *One day Mr. Aldridge said I was bringing him bad luck and he would appreciate my not accompanying him to the racetrack. I was never as fond of the races as Mr. Aldridge and I readily agreed to stay at the motel and I was both sorry and happy that I did, because in the late morning there was banging and crashing next door which resulted in screaming and in the motel door being thrown open and my door being pulled on. A girl of about eight or nine ran in and locked the door behind her. She said her father had gone mad and indeed it turned out he had. He threw the television onto a car which was not his own which was parked outside the room, and it was the motel owner who called the police. When they came they found out that the man was down to his last dime and his wife had run away in the night, though they later found her in a bar. The poor little girl was taken by the police somewhere, but not before she said to me that it was a sin to gamble and that I should not gamble because she never would, and this was because it was a sin. I certainly could relate to what she was saying, because of Mr. A's previous bad luck, though it seemed more than a problem with gambling to me, it seemed the sad situation of being part of the human race. Here was this young girl who was frightened of her father and her mother was later to be found offering favors to men in a bar, if I believed what the motel owner later told me while urging me to stay because these people were not his usual clientele.* I skipped ahead and saw that the next day the two of them had waded into a stream and gone fishing with a temporary two-day license they'd gotten at the local store. For what it was worth, Mr. Aldridge had had better luck without his wife, though because I'd flipped ahead, I knew their losses would not be recovered.

Frank came in without knocking. He had obviously been stopped in midproject by his drill breaking. If I were Mrs. Aldridge, I would no doubt write that down: *Frank had been stopped in midproject from working because his drill had broken.* What had Frank eaten for breakfast? Would he later go fishing?

"What did you have for breakfast?" I asked him.

"Me? Breakfast?" He put his hand on his chin and rubbed it, assuming there was some telltale crumb.

"An in-joke with myself," I said. "You'll be better at finding the drill than me."

"I can do all things," Frank said. "I am Superman."

"Feeling a little overburdened?" I said.

"Yeah," he said. "How'd you know?"

"Lemonade?"

He looked at the liquid in the glass fruit juicer. "Probably a little too concentrated for my taste," he said.

"If I diluted it?"

"Ah!" he said, pulling up a stool and sitting down. He rubbed his entire face this time. His shirt was buttoned wrong. He looked like someone who needed a bath and a night's sleep.

"I had a talk with Tom the other day," I said. "Want to hear about it?"

"My, my," he said. "And did his charm rub off on you like cooties?"

I got ice cubes and put them in a glass, added club soda and sugar, then poured in the lemon juice. I stirred the mixture with what was handiest: a knife that I wiped dry on my shirt.

"Thanks," he said.

"Bob didn't want to hear about it," I said. "It's not that much of a big deal. It's not like I convinced him to pack his bags and take his business somewhere else."

"So what did he say?"

"I don't think he's trying to drive us out of business. He says he's going to have a large stock of houseplants. That he's going to do a lot with dried flowers, and with greenhouse stuff."

"So he'll have everything we have plus a dried-flower business," Frank said.

"But the lot isn't that big. I don't think he can have anything like the stock you have."

Frank thought about it. "That's true," he said. "That's the first thing anybody's said that makes me feel better." He took a long sip of lemonade. "He must have thought Bob and I really lacked *cojones,*" Frank said. "What did he think about you being the front man?"

"He didn't say anything about you," I said. I thought about mentioning Dara, but thought better of it. I wanted to give Frank the impression that Tom and I had had more or less a business meeting. And we had, I supposed—whether or not Dara had been there. Or did I just hesitate because I wasn't sure about bringing up her name? "Anyway," I said, "he didn't seem the slightest bit hostile. I realize he's still got a big advantage, being located where he is, and that it's going to be a very attractive place, but you know we're going to have a lot of loyal customers among the locals. And Warner's is a great place: people will still come."

"It's kind of touching that you've taken all this so seriously," he said. "Janey wouldn't mind if we put the business up for sale and moved to Fort Lauderdale. Or Big Pine Key. Wherever it is she wants to go." Frank shrugged. "I'm restless myself," Frank said. "I might surprise her by how far I'd go."

I considered that for a minute. "You're talking about the business, right?"

"What else would I be talking about? You think that suddenly I'm going to be like my brothers and get some new glasses and pack my lunch box and go back to school?"

"Bob's only in school to help the business," I said.

"Still," Frank said.

"Frank—you're opposed to somebody taking classes?"

"I think Drake's out of his fucking mind. I don't care about Bob taking classes if he wants to."

"Why is Drake out of his mind?"

"You're right," he said. "He's not. He's just declaring his individuality. He wants to be a high-priced lawyer and start his life over again. Why not? But think about it," Frank said. "Drake is a user. Back in the days when he did have something to do with the business, he put in six-hour days. When he brought home that bitch he married, every one of us told him to wait—at least to wait—but he didn't wait. So now he's got a kid, and Grandma has to live in Boston to keep things going, and, God knows, he's opted out of any responsibility in this part of the world. He never calls Barbara."

"Bob seems to think that Barbara's become pretty demanding."

"Oh, is that what he thinks? Is that why I had to rush over there this morning to talk to the septic tank people?" He sipped the lemonade.

"He suggested that I look at Barbara in a new light, and I'm passing on the advice."

"Okay, so we think about it, and we decide Barbara's really a harpy. Then what do we do: abandon her?" Frank said, draining the glass. "And next: Frank responsibly descends to the basement to procure a drill, to continue responsibly installing Sheetrock in the now-being-renovated basement, for whose configuration he takes full responsibility."

"Bob's kayaking," I said.

"Bully for him," Frank said, putting his hand above his head to be sure to clear the overhang.

"Bob's acting sort of like Drake himself these days," I said.

"They were always similar."

"They were?" I said. I was standing at the top of the stairs.

"You've got a dead mouse in a trap down here," he said.

"You shouldn't say that to me because I'm not supposed to know he sets traps."

"Christ. Is my brother so stupid he doesn't think women know everything?" He came upstairs. "Brrr, brrr," Frank said, pointing the drill at me. "I will go home now, and drill responsibly."

"How's the baby?" I said.

"Kept us up half the night," he said.

"Can I ask you something that's none of my business?"

"Shoot," Frank said.

"You both wanted Joanna, didn't you?"

"Sure we did. Why do you ask? Janey got a little discouraged, having to be in bed all the time, pissing in a bedpan. Who wouldn't?"

"She didn't go out for long walks when she was pregnant, did she?"

"Walking? She was in bed."

"Some woman told me she thought she saw her walking."

"That's bullshit," he said.

"It was probably somebody else the woman saw."

"Ask Janey. It'll put your mind at rest."

"That would be insulting."

"She knows you'd forgive her anything," Frank said. "Even I know that."

"You mean, you think I'd forgive anyone anything?"

"I didn't say that. I said Janey."

"How many people do you think I'd forgive?" I said.

"Is something the matter?" he said. "This is really a strange conversation."

"Tell me," I said. "Do you think I'd forgive you anything?"

He looked at me a long time. He went to the refrigerator and rum-

maged for a beer. He opened the bottle. He leaned back against the
wall and continued to look at me, his belly visible through the gap in
his badly buttoned shirt, his face streaked with sweat. He took a long
sip of beer. I thought, as he assessed me, that I probably would forgive
him anything, though I had never thought of it in the abstract.

"I guess you're saying you already have," he said.

That was the way I confirmed my suspicion that Dara had not entirely levelled with me about her involvement with Frank.

Early the following morning, the call came. Drake didn't call
himself; he left it to Barbara to tell us the bad news: Grandma had died
in her sleep; she had had a stroke. Barbara could not stop crying. Ten
minutes after she hung up, Barbara called again to say that the body
was going to be transported to Carrigan's Funeral Home, in Exeter. If
Bob ever got home (that was the way she put it), she would see us there.
I asked if she'd like me to come over and sit with her. She said she
wouldn't; Sandra had insisted on coming, and dealing with Sandra and
Marie was all she was up to. It was the first time I realized what a toll
Barbara's daughter and grandchild took on her. "I just don't know
what I'll do," Barbara added. "I don't know how I'll ever adjust."

I said what was expected: that she would adjust; that fortunately,
Grandma had not suffered.

"Oh," Barbara said, "you're such a sweet girl, Janey."

A slip of the tongue. Surely she knew to whom she was talking.

Grandma had always been very nice to me. She was one of those
dutiful New England women who'd made a religion of common sense.
She was hardworking and cryptic enough to seem wise—or perhaps
she really had been wise. Why was skepticism creeping in as I sank into
a chair and tried to think of her many good qualities? It might have
been because I was skeptical of Barbara, and because the two of them
were so similar—though Grandma had seemed almost stunningly real-
istic. Compared to her mother, Barbara was really quite neurotic.
Grandma's implicit message had always been that situations were
givens: there was not much you could do about them except to cope. I
liked the simplicity of that reasoning. While Barbara worried and

dithered, her mother had simply taken control. The afternoon she and I had had our long phone conversation I should have been more understanding: my challenging her had bordered on disrespect. The same things that were her good qualities had also been her downfall: being too accommodating; acting, always, as if freedom were irrelevant. I had been frustrated because I had really been arguing with myself. And she had touched a nerve when she mentioned my aunt. She had confronted me, just as I had confronted her. Checkmate.

The phone rang and I got up, hoping it was Bob.

"Can you believe it?" Janey said. The baby was crying in the background. I wondered if Frank had managed to get done what he'd wanted to do when he returned home with Bob's drill the day before.

"It's very sad," I said.

"Sad? It's nuts."

"What?"

"Drake wanting to ignore her wishes and have her cremated. Frank's been on the phone with him. He finally talked him into burying her. What did you think I was talking about?"

"Her death," I said.

"Oh," Janey said. Then: "Frank says Bob's on a canoe trip?"

"Yeah," I said. "There's no way to reach him, but he should be home tonight."

"So he misses a few hours of the drama," Janey said. "More power to him. Listen: I've got to go."

"Did your tooth hold up okay?"

"My tooth? Yes," she said.

"Did Frank work in the basement yesterday?"

"Is this a survey to make sure our lives are still banal?" Janey said.

"No," I said. "Honest concern."

"Oh, I know," she said. "I'm sorry. I just had to say something mean to somebody." Her voice sounded tired. "I guess we're gathering here for dinner tonight," she said. "About six-thirty."

"Let me cook," I said. "I'm not doing anything."

"I'm baking a ham," she said. "I asked Barbara to come over now, but she's too nervous to sit still, she says. What good it's going to do her to walk in circles, I don't know."

"Sandra and Marie are going over there," I said.

"That's better than her sitting there worrying all day," Janey said. "I mean, what is all this 'What am I going to do?' stuff? She's going to do what she was doing anyway."

Joanna's next wail got her off the phone. When I hung up, I didn't know what to do either. I also began walking around the house, brushing dust off a tabletop, gathering up old newspapers and magazines. An old issue of *Time* had a story about the Clamshell Alliance on the cover. Fourteen hundred people had been arrested at the Seabrook nuclear plant protest. The manager of the theater where Dara would perform had been one of them. I flipped through, stopped by a drawing of the inside of a nuclear reactor. There was a large color photograph of people being put into police wagons. I wondered what Grandma thought about Seabrook, or if she had thought much about it at all.

"Sweetie," Dara said, when I picked up the phone, sure it was Bob. "Tonight is the night. We are going to have a very large bowl of lobster salad. Can I count you in?"

"I can't," I said. "Something awful just happened."

"She married another one?"

"What?"

"Mrs. Whutzit: she married another husband, and the book is now moving into section four?"

"No, not that. A death in the family. Bob's grandmother died."

"Poor old thing," Dara said. "Did very many people love her?"

A strange question. I was not always capable of telling when Dara was being mock-serious, but I gave her the benefit of the doubt.

"We all did," I said.

"I'm sorry, sweetie. I'll call you tomorrow," she said, nearly whispering the last four words.

"How are you doing with the bedroom?" I said quickly. I wanted to have something resembling a conversation before I hung up. I felt isolated from everyone in the family—even Janey, who was more of a martyr than I was. Why couldn't she have let me cook? And where was Bob—why hadn't he at least called from a pay phone when they arrived, as he usually did?

"Almost finished with the first coat," she said. "It's going to be really fabulous." Often her voice just trailed off at the end of a phone call, but this time she blew me a kiss and said, *"Ciao."*

That seemed fitting, I thought bleakly. I might as well have been in a foreign land.

At noon I made a tuna sandwich and ate it, lamenting the loss of the lobster dinner. It was awful of me, but I regretted saying that Grandma had died; if I hadn't, I could have gone to Tom and Dara's. I could have had a pleasant evening and not thought about how difficult the coming days were going to be. I could have lied my way out of dinner at Frank and Janey's, somehow. The truth was I would much rather be with friends than with the family. It was going to be sad and awkward with the family; the only real consolation would be holding little Joanna—if I even got a chance at her, with Barbara there. Suddenly I thought about Barbara's birthday, and about Marie's obvious jealousy of Louise. Was she jealous of Joanna, or was Joanna too small to register? I doubted that Marie would have her uncle Bob's lap to crawl into after the ham dinner. I doubted whether he would be home before dark. On the rare occasions he'd gone kayaking, he'd always come home late. I would have to leave a note for him. Should I be explicit in the note, or just tell him that something had happened: to call Frank and Janey?

I forced myself to sit down and finish typing Mrs. Aldridge's manuscript. In a funny way, she did have a sense of closure, even though the book clearly concluded nothing. In the last paragraph, she quoted Mr. Aldridge: *I like fishing and I like playing the horses, because to me that's what life is: a game. If you see something for what it is, you might as well announce it, because there's a lot of billboards out there and there are a lot of TV commercials out there, and when an individual realizes something not a propos of them, it has got to be a good day for humankind. So I shout it from the roof: life is a game.*

With that, Mrs. Aldridge's book ended. Having it typed had been futile; whatever she meant to accomplish, she had accomplished nothing, and spending my time getting it in shape had been a waste of my time: it would never be published; the handwritten copy would have sufficed. What was to be learned by one random person's prosaic conclusion that life is a game? I pulled the last page out of the typewriter and added it to the pile. Then I turned the manuscript over and held it. At 172 pages, it was weighty. Feeling depressed by her life with the three husbands, I put the manuscript back on the table and got the orange binder she had left with me weeks before. I carefully centered the manuscript, clamped it in, and, as the last remaining task, put in a fresh sheet of paper and typed: *My Life, by Grace Aldridge.* Then I cut out the little rectangle of title and author's name, and slipped it in the pocket on the front of the binder. She had already paid me eighty dollars. Now she owed me eighty-three dollars and forty cents more. I felt uncomfortable about taking her money, but I had kept my part of the bargain. If she had wanted her book typed, there was nothing wrong with having typed it.

I found her number and dialed. A woman's voice answered the phone, very tentatively. "Mrs. Aldridge?" I said, though I knew it was not.

"No" was the quiet reply. "Please say who is calling."

"This is Jean Warner," I said.

"Jean Warner?" the voice repeated. There was muffled sound. "Jean Warner," I heard through the rustling.

"Hello?" A man came on the phone.

"Hello," I said. "This is Jean Warner. I'm calling for Mrs. Aldridge."

"Are you a close friend?"

"I've done some typing for her," I said.

"Oh, the lady who's typed her book," the man said. "Cora, it's the lady who has Grace's book." He put his hand over the phone. There was a longer muffled conversation. Then the man said, "This is indeed a very sad day. Grace has passed away."

"She died?"

"She fell down the stairs several days ago and broke her ribs. Before we knew it, she had pneumonia and died, right there in the hospital. This is her cousin Albert. I don't know if I figure in her book or not. This might be like my speaking to a psychic who already knows everything about me." When I was silent, he said, "Miss Warner, may I come and get Grace's book at your convenience?"

"Uh, certainly, Mr.—"

"Albert Dane," he said. "Like the dog." There was a pause, while I tried to think what to say. "The Great Dane," he said. "Of course some say the same of Hamlet!"

When I didn't laugh, he laughed himself. He continued: "We have just arrived from Athens, Ohio. Here we thought everything was going so well for Grace, and then . . . Mr. Quill is here with us," he added. "Mr. Quill," he said, somewhat louder. I waited, thinking he was calling someone to the phone. "Her intended," he said.

"I didn't know she was engaged."

"She was," her cousin said.

"I see. Well. She and I didn't know each other all that well. I was just typing the manuscript for her."

Dara's bleak joke had been right—or almost. She really had been about to marry again. Perhaps it was Dara who was psychic.

"If you would be so kind as to give me directions to your office—"

"I work at home," I said. I gave him the address. He read back what he had written. Again, there was a muffled discussion, and then he asked if he could put his wife back on. In her tiny voice, his wife slowly read my address. I told her it was written down correctly. She began to cry and handed the phone back to Albert.

"I'll be over as soon as I can, Miss Warner," he said. "Thank you very much."

I nodded, but couldn't bring forth one more word. It was just too strange: all of it.

I pulled open cabinet doors in the kitchen, exploring the possibility of eating something else, but I quickly realized that it was just nervous energy that was making me want to eat again. What was the correct thing to do about the book? I had little choice now, since I said I'd give it to them, but what if she had not wanted them to see it? Unlikely, if she told them she'd written it, I supposed. But what if they expected something good? It seemed so sad to be giving them her pointless book. Somehow, I thought, I should have done something to energize the book. I should have functioned more like a real editor, suggesting things. If I'd been at all serious, that is what I would have done. When I was a teenager, my aunt had said over and over that my passivity would be a lifelong habit, and a lifelong curse for everyone else. Had she been right after all? Were the things I did only things to fill time, easily done things that might bring me compliments? If something was difficult, didn't I shy away from it? But I *had* contacted Tom Van Sant. I *had* decided to start a business.

An hour passed. I dusted, waiting. Then I vacuumed the living room rug. Then I realized that Albert would be in the house for only a few minutes, and that whatever he thought about my housekeeping was unimportant. It was almost half an hour longer before the cab pulled up outside the house. The driver was Chris's son, who was home from Bard for the summer. He also delivered pizzas at night. He had been among the 1,400 protesters jailed in the Seabrook protest. Chris had been furious at his son for taking part in it. I waved from the doorway, and Derek waved back. Two men were coming up the walkway, the older man's expression downcast as he walked very slowly in orthopedic shoes, holding a younger man's arm by the elbow.

"Miss Warner, how do you do?" the older man said. I assumed he was Cousin Albert. He wore a canvas camouflage hat, held in place with a chin strap. The younger man looked about fifty-five. Dark circles spread under his eyes, and there was a streak of rash under one eye. His eyes were red; I could tell he had been crying.

"Pleased to meet you. Your help with such an important project meant a lot to Grace," the red-eyed man said. There it was: a compliment for a job I had only done the minimum on. I felt ashamed, but then almost immediately angry at myself for having expectations that were too high. There was every chance I had responded in terms of someone else's expectations—my aunt's. The man interrupted my ruminations when he introduced himself: "Edward Quill."

"Like the pen," Albert said.

"Please come in," I said. "I'm very sorry. I mean, I'm just shocked to hear . . ."

"I thought falling down the steps was the worst of it, but only a few days later she was dead of pneumonia," Albert said. "I thought on the way over here, I wonder if they even publish posthumous books."

"Of course they do," Edward said. His arm remained crooked for Albert to hold.

"They do?" Albert said, looking at me for confirmation.

"Yes," I said.

"Fortunately, we have a photo for the book," Albert said. "She went to the photographer's studio and had her engagement picture taken." He squeezed Edward Quill's arm. Edward Quill nodded, but said nothing. He looked down at the cracked walkway. A dandelion was growing out of a small hole.

"We mustn't keep you," Edward Quill said. "We do thank you very much, though, for all your work. For Grace, you made a dream come true."

They followed me into the house. I walked to the kitchen and took the orange folder off the table. I held it out. Edward reached for the folder, then drew back, as if it were hot.

"Thank you," Albert said, taking the manuscript. "This is such a great shock to Cora and me. Of course, it's also a devastating shock to Mr. Quill." He cleared his throat. "Do we owe you any money?" Albert said.

In the back of my mind, my desire for payment had won out over any guilt I'd been feeling. I had been hoping one of them would bring up the subject, instead of me.

"Eighty-three dollars and forty cents," I heard myself say. I was instantly ashamed that the sum was on the tip of my tongue. And also that I hadn't rounded it off.

"That much? I'm afraid I didn't bring my checkbook," Albert said. Edward reached for his wallet.

"Please," I said. "You can send me the money later."

Edward extracted his wallet and pulled four twenty-dollar bills from it. "Might that suffice?" he said.

"I'd ask you to stay for coffee, but I—"

"Our cabdriver said he knew you," Albert said. "It means a lot to me that Grace lived in a friendly community."

"A pleasure to meet you," Edward said. One arm remained crooked; his firm hand clamped on Albert's frail one.

At the doorway I waved again to Derek, but I didn't catch his eye. He was playing rock on the radio. I watched as the two men got into the backseat. Edward, helping Albert into the cab, certainly did not look like someone who thought life was a game. He was younger than Grace Aldridge by at least fifteen years, I guessed, and probably would have been able to take good care of her. The music died down; Derek leaned forward, smiled slyly, and gave me the peace sign as the men settled themselves. Squealing the tires, he pulled away so quickly it jolted all of them back against their seats.

I called Dara. "This has really been a peculiar day," I said. "Can I invite myself over for a drink before I go grieve with the family?"

"Mi casa es su casa," Dara said.

Just before I left, I decided to take the carbon copy of the book with me to Dara and Tom's. I had gotten used to the ride; I could almost do it in my sleep. When I got there, and Dara embraced me, and

Tom reached into an ice bucket for the champagne, I felt saved. Disproportionately relieved. Being with them seemed like the perfect antidote. It was exactly where I wanted to be, and as we drank, we abandoned any pretense of respect for the dead and began laughing at Grace Aldridge's book: Dara flipped through to the second husband's opinions on the garden and read aloud; Tom assumed crazed expressions and shook his finger.

"Can you imagine being married to that silly fucker?" Tom said.

"Many women choose unwisely," Dara said.

"Oh, they do? How would you know about that?"

"Tom, I don't know how to tell you this: on occasion, in my distant past, say, I have chosen men—boys—because of such attributes as curly hair, and a beautiful complexion. I, Dara Falcon, in my youth, chose on the basis of beauty."

"She had a crush on somebody named Steven Kamanski, who had dark curly hair and beautiful skin—"

Dara interrupted: "And he had hair all over his back and zits on his shoulders!"

The image was horrible. Also, we were all getting a little drunk.

"Whom did you love for all the wrong reasons?" Dara said to me.

"I didn't have a boyfriend in high school. I was a real loner."

"After high school, then," Dara said.

"Look at Jean," Tom said. "Does Jean look like the kind of person who would ever make a big mistake?"

"What do you mean?" I said.

"You look—"

"She looks stable," Dara said. "She looks, and is, wonderfully *stable.*"

I knew they were kidding, but they were making me uneasy. It made me uncomfortable to remember how little I had fit in in high school; in college I had gone on too few dates, and I had gotten together with Bob almost immediately.

"Let me see," Dara said, taking the manuscript from Tom and perusing it. "Here we have the revelation that life is a game. Do we all feel that life is a game? Do we perhaps feel it, but also feel reluctant to say it, because life is supposed to be so *serious?*"

"It's never serious when you're around," Tom said to Dara. "You're so lighthearted and easygoing."

The idea was so ridiculous that I snorted. Dara's eyes darted to me, and I took the blame: I took the blame for Tom's ostensibly harmless joke. But when she spoke, she spoke to Tom, not me. "You don't know what joy I'm capable of, my love. When I don't have to grapple with other people's insecurities, and other people's problems, I can be quite lighthearted."

Tom said nothing and poured more champagne into his glass. He did not offer any to Dara, or to me. She picked up the bottle and poured: first into her glass, then into mine.

"Where did you get these lovely glasses?" Dara said.

"You know where I got them. I got them from my mother," he said.

"A mother who had a dozen champagne glasses," Dara said. "Not everyone had a mother who was so lighthearted and easygoing that she had a dozen etched-crystal champagne glasses."

"Since she didn't break any, perhaps they were unused," Tom said.

"Oh God, when I think of the things I've left behind," Dara said. I knew that she knew she had been criticized for her cattiness about Tom's mother, and that she was intentionally ignoring his put-down. She rushed on with her conversation: "A chifforobe in Los Angeles and a black dog in Santa Monica," Dara said. "If I had a guitar, I could sing about all the things I've left behind. Maybe I had champagne glasses myself, and I've long since forgotten them."

"Dara," Tom said, "I didn't know you ever had a dog. I didn't know you ever had a chifforobe, either, but that's just a thing. A dog is a dog. What happened to your dog?"

"I only had it for a week," Dara said, matching Tom's seriousness with her tone. "It was a mutt, with a little white comet streaking across one ear. I kept it for a friend of mine who was in acting class with me. Then he got an apartment that would let him have his dog. Exit the dog."

"Did you buy the dog dog food?" Tom said. "Take it on walks? Take perfect care of it?"

Dara studied him for a few seconds. Perhaps she saw, as I did, that he was tipsy. "Yes, darling," she said evenly. "You'd be amazed at the way I can extend myself. There are depths you can't even imagine."

"Could I imagine things better if I'd been in acting classes?"

Dara cocked her head to the side. "I don't know that that helps a person to imagine," she said. "I think what it helps with is acting."

At six-thirty, being very careful not to slur my words, I called Frank and Janey's and told Frank I wasn't feeling well. It was true, in a way: the tension between Tom and Dara had not entirely dissipated even as we prepared dinner and opened another bottle of champagne, though we'd laughed together again as Tom read us parts of the manuscript.

Frank asked if there was anything he could do. "Yeah. Don't tell them it's a lie," I said. There was a slight pause. "Gotcha," he said. We hung up. That left only the problem of the unwritten note to Bob, but as it turned out, although I'd forgotten to tell him where I was, he didn't get back until dawn.

Bonnie Collingwood came to Grandma's funeral with Drake. She was young—my age, I guessed—and eager to make a good impression. I watched her making the rounds, saying solicitous things to Barbara and to the rest of the family. It wasn't the easiest of circumstances, being introduced to her boyfriend's family at a funeral. Drake, who was taciturn when he had to be with the family, was little help to her. I found myself overcompensating for his silence and for the family's distractedness by talking animatedly to her. What I knew that she didn't know, of course, was that in a fishing tackle box in our house there was an engagement ring she either would or would not get—and that how she acted at the funeral might contribute to Drake's decision. I didn't silently wish her luck because I wasn't sure whether joining the family was to anyone's benefit. Since his kayaking trip—since the night we'd had the fight about the ring, actually—Bob had been remote and withdrawn, and Frank obviously had secrets. Drake was a malcontent who managed to convey, through his imperiousness, that he disdained the family's ceremonies: the birthdays; the funerals—you name it, and Drake looked down on it.

Marie, wearing a seersucker dress and a big pink bow in her hair, clung to her mother, making herself apparent with everything she did: taking huge steps when she walked; humming; dancing in front of people. She was trying to obliterate Louise by constantly drawing as much attention to herself as possible. Frail little Louise was no match for her; she held her father's hand and looked down, as if in a trance. She was obviously hoping the big, pink-bowed whirling dervish would not spin her way.

Dowell Churnin and Tom Van Sant came to the funeral and stood side by side. It was obviously meant as a gesture of goodwill, but Frank whispered to Bob: "Vultures." There was much whispering during the funeral: Janey consoling Barbara; Marie, needing desperately to talk to her mother every thirty seconds; Bob, first whispering to me to make sure I had left the back door unlocked for the caterers, then asking me to be friendly to Bonnie, as if I hadn't already extended myself. The reception afterward was to be at our house; people from Corolli's were bringing pastries and setting up large coffee servers; they were in the house as we stood by the grave.

There were about thirty people standing around us: old ladies who had been Grandma's friends; acquaintances of Barbara's that I hardly knew. Tom caught my eye and gave me a small, sad smile. This was only the second funeral I had ever attended. The other had been when a friend of my aunt's died of liver disease. I was ten or eleven then, and I barely remembered what had happened, except that someone—the woman's husband?—had walked in widening circles around the casket as the minister read a prayer, and then eventually that person had been gone; I had stopped looking at him when my aunt turned my head back toward the minister and the casket the second time, and when I had snuck a look a few minutes later, the man was gone. It had made me afraid of vanishing, too. I was too old to have had such an irrational fear, but something in the way he circled had seemed magnetic, as if I might be pulled into his orbit, farther and farther away from the dead woman, nearer to . . . what? The park that bordered one side of the wide cemetery, or into some car, away from the place. And it hadn't seemed entirely frightening, finally: the more I believed it might be true, the more tempting it had been to think of myself vanishing.

At Grandma's funeral, I was under no delusion that I might drift away. I also wondered who would come to the funeral if I died, and quickly realized it would only be the family. My friends were gone. I was out of touch with them, because I was a lousy letter writer, and also because the place I lived in, the people I associated with, seemed so thoroughly different from them that I couldn't imagine living in a split world. It had seemed strange enough in college, the division between the straight people and the hippies: Why continue to think about peo-

ple who were different, people I didn't live among, and therefore
would never be close to? It made me slightly heady to imagine that at
my funeral there would be only the old familiars, the people guaran-
teed to show up, a small little group, but a group nonetheless.

Dowell Churnin was wiping away tears with a handkerchief. I
looked elsewhere, and saw Marie, sitting at her mother's feet, reading a
book. I could see Marie's lips moving, and I wondered if other people
could hear her. When I looked again in Tom's direction, I wondered
where Dara was. There was no reason for her to be at the funeral, but
since Tom had come, I wondered where she was. In her newly decorated room, perhaps, memorizing her lines. Or out in the meadow—
the meadow had no doubt bloomed by now. I hadn't seen her for days
because I'd been so busy helping to make funeral arrangements. I cor-
rected my thinking: She might be grocery shopping. Or at the bank. I
realized that I romanticized her life so I could wallow in feeling dowdy.
It was as if Cinderella had invented sisters, just to feel blue. The world
was not divided into happy, unconventional people like Tom and Dara
and unhappy—why pretend we were happy?—couples like Bob and
me. I was making myself feel worse by thinking in such simple black-
and-white terms. Dara had said that she and Tom were in a "cooling-
off" period that day at Corolli's, hadn't she? But what did she want, I
thought, a little angrily: he adored her; he had given her his mother's
beautiful ring; he would be opening a business that would no doubt be
very successful, even if that was accomplished at other people's expense; he lived in a charming house that was well stocked with food
and champagne, and she had her own inner chamber within it. If Dara
wasn't happy under those circumstances, how could I be happy with
my mundane life? Damn her: she had called to my attention—without
words, merely by her existence—an alternative to being enfolded into
the sameness and increasing numbness of family life.

Leaving the graveside after the minister concluded, Derek said to
me: "Those two guys I had in the cab the other day were really something, weren't they?"

"The old gentlemen are disappearing," I said. "It's true. It's going
to be a different world."

"Right. Especially if we blow it sky-high."

"I told you not to talk about politics at the funeral," Chris said,
coming up beside Derek and laying a heavy hand on his shoulder. I saw

the large shoulder pad move forward: it was Chris's too-big suit Derek was wearing; he'd been outfitted in his father's clothes for the funeral.

"Yeah, well, Dad, you might say that, but plenty of evidence suggests we might just blow."

Chris steered Derek away; Bob was approached by Dowell, walking purposefully in his direction.

"She was a wonderful lady, and I know you know how sorry we all are to lose her," Dowell said.

"Thank you, Dowell," Bob said.

"I'm very sorry," Tom Van Sant said.

Bob looked at him. "You knew her?" he said.

"No, but I wish I had."

"Jean said she was over at your place drinking champagne the other night," Bob said.

"Yes," Tom said. He didn't pick up the hostility in Bob's voice; I did, and hoped it would go away.

"We should get going, Bob," I said, hoping he'd respond to my tug on his sleeve.

"When my grandmother died, didn't Jean go over to your house for a drink? Isn't that what she told me she'd been doing when the family gathered at my brother's?"

"You mean . . . is there anything wrong with our having had a drink?" Tom said. When Bob looked at him blank-faced, he turned to me.

"If I'm restricted to quarters, it's the first I've heard about it," I said.

"Well," Tom finally said, "I really am very sorry."

"About Grandma's death, you mean?" Bob persisted.

"Yes," Tom said.

"Coffee at your place? Is that right?" Dowell said to me. He had been talking to one of the old ladies. Now he was rejoining the group.

"Amazing," Bob said. "Dowell—you're voluntarily coming to have coffee with us?"

"Bob," I said.

"I mean, I'm just confused," Bob said. "Barbara has almost—well, I think I could fairly use the word 'pursued' you for so long. We'll truly have the pleasure of your company today?"

"What's gotten into him?" Dowell said to me.

"Are you coming, Dowell? Why, that's wonderful," Barbara said, taking Dowell's arm.

"My condolences," Dowell said, patting her hand. "You know that."

"I just don't know what I'll do," Barbara said, suddenly teary.

"You'll do just fine, as we all do," Dowell said, continuing to pat her hand.

"Ain't that the truth," Bob said to me, steering me away.

"Jesus, Bob. What's gotten into you?"

"Here the two of them stand—one who never even met the old lady—they're getting ready to open their big fancy new business, and today they're standing around pretending to be brokenhearted that Barbara's mother has died? What on earth do you think Van Sant had in his head, coming to this funeral?" he said.

"Maybe he's trying to be friendly. To make it very obvious there's no ill will."

"Maybe everybody has forgotten that this is a funeral to remember a very wonderful person whose old age was spent as a servant to people who had fucked up their lives," Bob said. "Do you think anybody is having any thoughts about Grandma, or do you think they're making personal appearances to advertise themselves?"

"I'm not making an appearance to advertise myself," I said.

He looked at me. "You were fond of her," he said grudgingly.

"Maybe you should have kept it a very small, family-only funeral, if that's the way you feel," I said.

"This is Barbara's show, not mine," he said.

"I'm going home to relieve the babysitter. I'll bring Joanna over," Janey said, tapping me on the back.

"Oh, okay," I said.

"Janey—what do you think about Van Sant and Dowell turning up for this occasion?" Bob said.

"What do I think?" Janey said. "In what way?"

"Go ahead," I said. "We'll see you soon."

"I would appreciate an answer," Bob said.

Janey looked at me. She looked at Bob. "I guess I think it was a nice gesture," she said. "What should I think?"

"Just asking," Bob said.

"See you," Janey said, turning. She stopped briefly to speak to Derek, then continued quickly toward her car.

"That's really disappointing," Bob said. "Not so much the response itself—she's entitled to think whatever she thinks—but asking me what she should think. That's so typical of people in this family. They take instruction, like they're studying to convert to some religion."

"You have been in the worst mood I can ever remember you being in, Bob. Do you have any idea what you sound like?"

"You tell me what I should think," he said. "I'm with Janey. You tell me, and I'll be sure to do just what you say."

"Do you think that because Janey was polite, she's got no gumption? Is that what you're saying?"

We walked to the car. Frank was arranging for two old ladies to ride with us. They alternately thanked Frank and apologized for being a nuisance. Bob, suddenly charming again, assured them that nothing would please him more, and opened the back door of the car. They discussed among themselves who would enter first. It was decided that the smaller woman, Mrs. Bell, would precede the other, and that then she would take the other woman's handbag while she got in. Slowly, this began to happen.

"Frank," Bob said, over his shoulder, talking in small bursts so the ladies wouldn't overhear what he said: "When next you see Janey, tell her what you told me. She doesn't know there were vultures at the funeral."

Frank nodded. He turned away, distracted, to speak to the minister.

Bob winked at me. "Off we go, boss," he said.

I got into the passenger's seat.

"It was a very nice service," Mrs. Bell said.

"And a beautiful day, too," Mrs. Denton said.

Suddenly, the thought occurred to me: probably one or both of them had known Mrs. Aldridge. When I asked, Mrs. Bell immediately answered. "Gracie?" she said. "Yes, poor Gracie passed away just about the time Martha did. Did you know her yourself, Jean?"

"Not well," I said.

"Is that the woman who married Topper Moulton?" Mrs. Denton said.

"No," I said. At the same time, Mrs. Bell said, "Yes."

I turned to look at her.

"That's right, she married Topper Moulton and later she left him for another man, I do believe."

"You mean Mr. Dubbell?" I said.

"No, certainly not," Mrs. Denton said. "First was Topper, and then you can't believe all you hear, but I heard she ran off to Las Vegas to marry one man, and ended up marrying another!"

"She did, indeed," Mrs. Bell said. "My brother was the best friend of the man who thought she'd marry him in Las Vegas!"

"Irving?" Mrs. Denton said.

"Irvin," Mrs. Bell said. "All his life, everybody mispronounced my brother's name."

"Irvin," Mrs. Denton repeated.

"I just finished typing her manuscript," I said.

"Grace wrote a book?" Mrs. Bell said. "What did she write about?"

"It was about her husbands. But she only mentioned three."

"Oh, there were more than three," Mrs. Denton said. "I can remember four, and I do think there was an early marriage, but that might have been annulled."

"That's right. I believe it was," Mrs. Bell said.

This was perplexing. Why had she omitted the other husbands? At the very least, it seemed that if you were going to define your life in terms of your marriages, you should include all of them. There was a long silence.

"She made beautiful quilts," Mrs. Bell said. She touched my shoulder. "Your Grandma Martha, I mean. She had real talent."

"She did," Mrs. Denton said.

We rode in silence again. Bob hated all the chatter; I could see his hands, white-knuckled, gripping the wheel. We passed the shopping center on Route 1, and the big UPS yard. If we'd turned right, we could have wound our way to the beach. It was where I would have preferred to go, but it was not where we were headed. I remembered Barbara's birthday, and the sailing kites—finally, every one had been airborne. The birthday seemed like a long time ago, though it had only been in early spring. The time Bob and I went shopping for the kites had been one of our last enjoyable days together. That, too, seemed like long ago. I looked again at Bob. His jaw was set. The Buddy Holly glasses, with

sunglasses clipped over them, obscured his eyes. He looked thinner. I
worried—for the umpteenth time—that the commute to Boston was
taking its toll. Was it only a week until Tom's business opened? I
counted the days until Labor Day and realized there were only nine.
Then, at least, the suspense would be over. Instead of asserting that
he'd adjusted and that nothing could be done, Bob would really have
to adjust. Maybe when he did, he would get over his grudge against
Tom. It had probably been a mistake to tell him the truth about where
I'd been the night everyone else was at Frank and Janey's, but some
part of me had thought he was so frustrated with family demands that
he would approve of my having drunk champagne instead of automatically going to Frank and Janey's. Apparently, though, Bob had been
threatened by what I'd done. Or was he unhappy because of whom I'd
chosen to drink with? Maybe Tom just couldn't win with Bob. Though
Bob once claimed to feel sympathy for him, I suspected that now he
only thought Tom was a real adversary: he wasn't fond of Tom's girlfriend, and he wasn't fond of my fondness for Tom's girlfriend, and
Tom had also done the unforgivable in opening Snell's. In spite of
Bob's desire to have less family togetherness, any outsider wouldn't do.
The person would have to be . . . what? Someone hardworking. Tom
Van Sant was probably not long-suffering enough by Bob's standards
these days. Bob had a kind of reverse snobbishness about things like
that. Imagine what he'd think if he knew about Tom's scattering the
wildflower seeds, screwing Dara in the field.

When we got to the house, there was much discussion among the
two ladies about how they would disembark. They decided on exiting
through the same door. The ladies more or less bumped in unison, hats
tipping and purses raised like parasols against the sun; they were
amused at their own attempts to slide out—Mrs. Bell, in particular, getting the giggles. I found myself smiling, too, and agreeing with her that
backseats had not been designed for anyone larger than a child.

Inside the house, Bonnie and Drake stood at Frank's side, forming
a sort of unofficial receiving line. I smiled at Bonnie and she smiled
back. When Janey arrived, I knew the two of us could make Bonnie
feel more at ease. The people from Corolli's had done what they
promised: the table I'd pulled into the living room and put a white
cloth on was set up with trays of Danish pastries, and two coffee ma-
chines were on the smaller, Formica-topped table. Frank was drinking

a beer, which he must have brought with him, since we didn't have any in the refrigerator. Barbara came in and collapsed on the sofa. The minister sat next to her.

"Uncle Bob," Marie said, "did you know that Lawrence Welk was a self-made millionaire?"

"What's that?" Bob said. "A book about Lawrence Welk?"

"Yes. I want to read you something from it."

"Not right now, Marie. I have to talk to some people."

"Don't talk to Louise," Marie said.

Louise was nestled into Barbara's side. She was sucking her thumb. She had on a sundress covered with daisies. There were individual daisies surrounding the armholes and the neck. Her thin hair was pulled back with a small yellow headband.

"Lawrence Welk was a first-generation American who made good," Marie said, skipping toward her mother. On the way, she pointedly ignored Louise, even though Barbara reached out a hand, hoping to connect with Marie.

"Land of opportunity," Bob said.

"What?" I said. I was getting coffee for Mrs. Bell, who didn't know how to use the machine.

"Lawrence Welk, and his lovely Champagne Ladies. Wouldn't you love to have known what was really going on there?"

Mrs. Bell, who had heard Bob's last remark, looked confused.

"Barbara drove me nuts," Bob said. "All those nights watching Myron Floren and 'the lovely little Lennon sisters.' "

"He's having a snit with himself," I said to Mrs. Bell. It was all I could think to say.

"Watch me cause a major crisis," he said, whispering in Mrs. Bell's direction, raising and lowering his eyebrows several times. He went to the sofa and knelt by Louise, then straightened up, with her in his arms. Marie saw it within fractions of a second. She rushed to Bob's side and began to pull on his leg.

"You have to share Uncle Bob," I heard Bob say.

"Oh, please, Marie, not today," Barbara said, looking around for Sandra.

"Pick me up, too!" Marie shrieked.

"Tell me what it says about Lawrence Welk in your book," Bob said.

"Bob, please—Reverend, excuse me. . . ." Barbara was on her feet, trying to remove Louise from Bob's arms so Marie would stop shrieking.

"Quiet, Marie!" Drake hollered from across the room. "I mean it."

With that, Marie threw herself on the floor and began to cry. Everyone who had been talking began to whisper, or stopped talking entirely. As she wriggled on the floor, Marie's pink bow fell off. Louise, in Bob's arms, tried to climb higher, onto his head. "Daddy!" she called, holding out her little arms.

"Drake," Bonnie said, nodding in the direction of the chaos.

"This is perfectly ridiculous. I have no intention of intervening," Drake said. He added: "Marie's tantrums must not be indulged."

"Oh, gracious," Barbara said, trying to get Marie to stop writhing on the floor. The reverend stood slightly back, as if water were creeping in his direction.

Bonnie went to Bob and held her arms out for Louise. Something in her eyes made him relinquish the child, and Louise, of course, was happy to go, pointing, frightened, in the direction of her father. But when Bonnie reached Drake's side, Drake turned his back.

"Drake, you take Louise *now*," Bonnie hissed.

This woman was fiercer than I'd imagined. No one would have argued with anyone who used that tone of voice. And Drake did not, though he started and ended a brief conversation with the person nearest him in an attempt to save face before capitulating. At that point, both Marie and Louise were crying, and I looked across the room at Bob. What had he hoped to accomplish? Had he really wanted to cause this embarrassment and confusion and unhappiness? His look—his smirk, really—let me know he intended all of it. And then he devoted his efforts to consoling Marie, grabbing her up in his arms, waltzing her into the kitchen. For the first time, I really considered the possibility that he was a little crazy. I found myself gravitating toward Bonnie, because what she'd done made me think she was the sanest person in the room.

"I think everything's going to be all right now," Bonnie said.

"Good work," I said. Around us, other people had begun to talk again.

"When the going gets tough," Bonnie said.

"I'm really sorry," I said. In my mind, I was apologizing because

Bob was my husband, though I instantly realized that because Bonnie had no way of knowing what precipitated the problem, all she could think was that I was offering a general apology.

"Oh, I'm pretty used to the pressure cooker blowing," Bonnie said. "Don't worry." She looked at Drake, talking to some friend of Barbara's. "He does have a temper," she said quietly.

"Well, this is really a terrible way to, you know, to meet the family," I said. "I mean, under any circumstances, a funeral is—"

"He never would have introduced me." Bonnie shrugged. She motioned for me to step aside with her. "We're married," she said.

I stared at her.

"By a justice of the peace. A month ago."

"Congratulations," I said.

"Thanks," she said, and smiled. "Drake isn't exactly one for a big wedding."

"No, I guess not."

"Please don't tell anyone," she said. "I just had to have someone know. He's so peculiar. I'm sure he'll tell you in his own good time."

"Bob knows?" I said.

"No," she said. "He wasn't there that day. We just went to a justice of the peace."

I was thinking of the ring, in the fishing tackle box. She had on a silver bracelet, but no ring. She didn't even know that a ring was intended for her. She was married and she didn't have a wedding band?

"It's legal without the ring," she said, twirling her silver bracelet, as if reading my mind.

"Sure," I said, nodding agreement. "Oh, sure." I was really taken aback.

"So please don't tell," she said, and walked away. She stood by the coffee machine and flipped the black handle forward. Coffee poured into her cup. I looked around the room, not knowing where to rest my gaze. Unfortunately for both of us, my eyes briefly connected with the reverend's, and he came toward me to offer his condolences.

"As I told your husband this morning, we often think of time as our enemy, but it also allows for the healing of wounds," the reverend said, putting his big paw of a hand on my shoulder.

"This morning?" I said.

"Yes. When he came to my office. He said you were consoling Barbara." He must have seen that I knew nothing about what he was saying. "You didn't know that he and I had spoken early this morning?" he said. "Well—men sometimes think they shouldn't express sadness, which is most unfortunate."

Marie appeared at the reverend's side. "It was Myron Floren's desire to achieve success with the most successful orchestra ever to appear regularly on national television," she read. Her eyes were pink from crying. She bent over her book again, reading quietly to herself. The reverend put his hand on top of her head. He said, "It's difficult to share the affection of the person we love, isn't it, Marie?" Marie did not look up to acknowledge he'd spoken. She turned a page of her book and walked away.

"Marie, come and give your grandma a hug," Barbara said to her.

"If you and Bob would like to see me privately, I'm always available," the reverend said.

"Thank you," I said. It was an entirely perfunctory response; I didn't like the reverend much more than Marie liked Louise, but of course I had to be polite to him. He was not only by definition a good person, but one of the people ostensibly so important to Barbara. What I really thought was that Barbara was just careful to keep all the props in place: the church must be included in times of grief. Even people who actively signalled they did not want to be part of Barbara's world were still solicited, like Dowell Churnin. There was always the pretense that the door was always open, when in reality Barbara distanced herself even from the family behind that door, having to be coaxed to do simple things: go to the carnival; eat at a restaurant; do anything out of the ordinary. She and her sons and daughter were reluctant people, who masked their insecurity or their depression, or whatever it was that stopped them, by graciousness and by adhering to social conventions.

The greenhouse opened. Several days before, Dara called, saying that the family was invited to the opening festivities. Frank had already refused to go, she said; she'd sent him a note, which he'd stamped BULLSHIT with a rubber stamp and returned. She was clearly amused, telling me, "I don't know whether I should send a note and let Bob express himself also, or whether this invitation by telephone is sufficient." She quickly added: "You know, sweetie, just because they have this attitude doesn't mean you shouldn't come and have a good time."

I went. Bob was helping Trenton put a deck on his house; he wasn't there to consult one way or the other. When I'd initially mentioned Dara's invitation, he'd only sighed deeply. I called Janey before I left to see if she wanted to join me. Frank answered the phone. Janey had gone back to work a few days before. She had a private patient she was looking after. I knew that Janey had had misgivings about returning to work, but the fact was they needed the money. Frank said he was still working downstairs, creating the rec room. I could hear the boys in the background. He sounded harried, so I hung up quickly.

The greenhouse was pretty: nouveau Victorian, with a parking lot in back and large terra-cotta planters filled with bright pink flowers placed close to Route 1. A large white banner announcing the opening flapped from a pole hung out the top window of the building. There were also white balloons bobbing from the arm of a white wicker chair that sat alongside the entranceway. There were quite a few cars. As I pulled in, a woman carrying a cement rabbit with a Marie-size blue bow around its neck exited, talking animatedly to her friend. A man disembarked from his Jeep. He and his wife bent over the baby's car seat, fiddling with buckles, cooing to the baby as they began to lift him. "Mommy wants a mimosa tree, but Daddy thinks they die in this zone," the man said cheerfully to his plump, sock-footed son, as he held him aloft. "Maybe the nice man will tell Mommy the same thing." Ahead of him, Mommy stalked into the store, looking perturbed.

On Route 1, a car slammed on its brakes, narrowly avoiding hitting a black dog; other cars also slowed, allowing the frightened dog to canter back and forth. Finally, someone parked on the shoulder and called to the dog, trying to lure it to one side of the road. The dog almost crossed to the car, then turned and bolted in the other direction, causing another terrible squeal of brakes. I couldn't look any longer. I went in, braced for the final squeal of tires, and the final yelp. Dara was the first to see me, and she misunderstood my squint for trepidation.

"Come on, darling, if I can dress up like Little Miss Muffet—" she said, coming toward me in her big skirt and a low-scooped T-shirt. Everything she wore was white or blue or gray. In a way, she looked wonderful, but the clothes were so much not her style that I could hardly believe she'd dressed this way. "Wouldn't you know that the one employee Tom thought was the most reliable would be just the one to cancel at midnight? Her child has measles, or something dreadful. So I'm pinch-hitting as Miss Havisham, or whatever I am. Isn't it just too much?"

The woman who had wanted a mimosa tree was studying the selection of African violets. Her husband and son joined her, peering over her shoulder. Behind the counter, a teenage boy in a white shirt and black jacket was ringing up a sale. At first I thought he looked more sensible than Dara, but then I realized the black jacket was a morning coat. He was dressed as if he were a student at Eton. The flute music increased the feeling of otherworldliness in the place; it soothed the customers and no doubt also encouraged them to buy.

When a customer asked Dara a question, I wandered away to explore. A glass-enclosed walkway connected the front building to the greenhouse. I walked behind a mother and daughter, who were discussing the pros and cons of bangs. The little girl carried a plant. Like everything in the greenhouse, it was in a white plastic pot with tiny ladybugs painted around the border. She carried it as if it were a saucer with a very full cup of tea on it. Seeing her concentration, her mother reached out to carry the plant for her daughter. "Bangs make your eyes look bigger," the little girl announced to her mother, who did not have bangs. She did, however, have large eyes shadowed with lavender. Probably the little girl had found just the way to appeal to her mother's sense of the way things should be. "And also, Susan Davis has bangs," the little girl said. There, she probably lost a point.

I could not have been more surprised to look in front of me and see Barbara. She was standing by a large cluster of gloxinias, talking to Dowell Churnin. Dowell had on a white apron with ladybugs imprinted on the ties. Underneath, he had on his customary baggy shirt and baggy pants, though his work boots were brand-new. He was talking to Barbara at the same time he was fiddling with a nozzle that sprayed mist onto the plants from copper tubes in the ceiling.

"Oh!" Barbara said, when she saw me. "Gracious! Well—look at us both at opening day!"

I thought it was fine to be where I was, though Barbara, blushing deeply, apparently thought otherwise.

"Good day to you, Jean," Dowell said to me. He stepped back in order to avoid being misted. The little girl and her mother walked past us; unlike the Warners' greenhouse, the aisles were wide enough to allow people to pass without turning sideways and offering apologies.

"I don't know the first thing about watering systems. I only know what I studied last night from the manual. Two people couldn't make it today, and one of them was one of the most important workers we have," Dowell said.

"How are you, Jean?" Barbara said. She didn't wait for an answer. "Isn't it just lovely in here? My, my."

"I'm very glad you came because I don't want there to be any hard feelings," Dowell said.

"Oh, there aren't any. On my part," I added. "I did speak to Tom about it a while ago." I looked at Barbara. It was nasty but amusing to watch her suffering. "Did I tell you about that?"

"I don't remember that you did," Barbara said.

"Well," I said, looking around, "he represented everything correctly. Saying that he meant to emphasize the greenhouse, I mean. Not to compete with us, really, with the trees and bushes."

"I see," Barbara said gravely.

"I think Janey might be here, herself, if she hadn't gotten that gentleman patient," Dowell said. "I saw her at the post office, and I think it was her intention to come. That would have been three ladies representing the family."

Barbara nodded. She looked so questioning. She always looked so questioning. She said: "Did you know there was lemonade by the cash register? At first I didn't see it, but it's on a table just next to the checkout counter." She turned to Dowell. "Was that table of lemonade and sweets hidden on purpose?"

"I had not one thing to do with the organization of anything," Dowell said.

"I was only teasing," Barbara said.

"It really looks beautiful," I said. In another part of my mind, I was wondering several things: whether the dog on the highway had made it to safety; whether Barbara would ever tell the rest of the family that she'd come here on opening day; whether Dowell had been for, or against, the war in Vietnam—and, by extension, whether his attitude, when his son died, was newly arrived at, or if it only intensified his sense of futility about the blasphemy of that particular war.

"I should be on my way," Barbara said. "You tell Tom, if I don't see him, that this is all very lovely, and that we wish him the very best."

Dowell nodded. He had a way of standing in one place indefinitely, until someone exited. He was always the last to leave a party. The last person to determine anything, including in what direction he'd move, or when he would make the move. He truly did seem to wait for others to tell him what to do. He would decline most invitations, but if he did show up he was as immobile as one of the stone rabbits—just a big lawn ornament. In that, he seemed like quite a few other men of his generation: if he did show up, he never left until the end. Had World War II been responsible for that? For that group of men who stood like sentries in their own lives?

I said goodbye to Dowell, taking Barbara's departure as the opportunity to get away. I walked out of the greenhouse behind her. As we neared the front building, she seemed, again, a little nervous.

"I get the feeling you're not sure you should have come," I said.

"You do?" she said. "Well, I did wonder, but this morning two mourning doves landed on my windowsill, and I took it as a sign. They'd built a nest on top of my air conditioner the last two springs, but this year they just hadn't come back. Not that I couldn't do without all that noise, but heaven knows, I would never do anything to interrupt the building of a bird's nest. Oh, I'm not making much sense, I know. What I mean is that it seemed hopeful that the doves were there, even though they must have made another home. As if they wanted me to know everything was still fine, even though they hadn't been where I expected to find them." She looked at me. "It was clearer to me this morning," she said.

I walked Barbara to her car. What accounted for my sudden critical attitude toward her? She was older and a little more daffy than when we'd first met, but compared to the tales of terror I'd heard about other mothers-in-law, Barbara was easygoing and undemanding. In a burst of friendliness, I asked Barbara if she'd like to have dinner with us that night.

"That's a nice offer, but I've got some steak to cook tonight," she said. "And you two have so many things to do. We'll both be relieved when Bob's done with his course work, I know."

"Eat the steak tomorrow," I said.

"Oh, I cannot tell a lie," Barbara said. "I invited Dowell to the house just now, and he accepted. I can't even remember the last time he was there. It was years and years ago, but when I asked, he said he'd be delighted."

It began to dawn on me: It wasn't just sympathy that had made her think about him so often. Barbara liked him. She might even have a crush on him. She must have seen the surprise flicker across my face.

"You know I'd love to come otherwise," she said, unlocking the car and rolling down the windows. It was very hot inside the car. We stood back a little, retreating from the seepage of hot air. Cars were turning into the lot.

When Barbara drove away, I went back inside to say goodbye to Dara. I waited while she rang up a sale. She gave advice about watering the plants she was setting in a cardboard flat. The woman she spoke to listened intently. Dara must have been studying more than just her lines for *A Doll's House,* unless she'd always known that much about how to care for plants.

"This has been more hectic than we thought," she said, when the woman left. "Do you know, he's so crazy that he was going to call Big Bernie, to get her to help out. Her business went belly-up, you know."

"What has she been doing?" I said.

"She has been doing two things," Dara said. "She has tried to sell hummingbird feeders by mail, along with seeds to plant that attract hummingbirds, number one. And number two, she has been considering—with many midnight phone calls—whether it is the best thing, or absolutely wrong, to abort the child she is carrying." Dara reached out and smiled, taking a twenty-dollar bill from a man who had put a lipstick plant on the counter. She handed the money to the teenager in the cutaway. "But enough about that. And you didn't hear it from me," she said. She let the teenager finish the transaction.

"She's pregnant?" I said. "The last time I saw her was months ago. She was waitressing at Arizona."

"Not now," she said, coming around to my side of the counter. "She has morning sickness that goes on until midafternoon, followed by crying jags and bizarre evening car chases, racing with the wind. She ends up someplace in Maine and checks into a motel and reaches for the bedside telephone. She is entirely unhinged, and as I said to Tom: *Are you truly and absolutely sure this child is yours?* But of course he's too macho to have any doubt. If it's born, I am going to force him to find out. Isn't this all we need? Really. It's a soap opera every day, and when I have enough sanity to concentrate, I pore over *A Doll's House,* which all this has given me a decidedly odd perspective on."

"God," I said. "How awful."

"I know I should be more sympathetic," she said. "I lack courage, though. The courage to have a little baby visiting us. It's not like Tom wants it either. But life goes on, and I've got to get going," she said, looking at her watch. "I've put in my time. Now I've got to go into Portsmouth and discuss fund-raising with the theater board. Apparently I am charming and articulate. I think they want me to speak at some dinner. All in the cause of *art.*"

"This must be very rough on you," I said.

"One of the strangest things is that his anxiety over all this—" She had come out from behind the counter, ignoring two people who were trying to catch her eye, untying her apron. "Instant transformation," she said, to the people. "Can't help you anymore, but my friend behind the counter will be glad to." The teenage boy was talking on the telephone and ringing up a sale. It would be some time before they got his attention. They began to confer with each other. "Anyway," she said, "the strangest thing is that he wants to have sex all the time. He thinks sex is almost as good as leaving the phone off the hook. I have ordered an answering machine. I tell you, I am not going to be awakened every night of my life with Big Bernie's hysteria."

I followed her behind green curtains that separated a back room from the front counter. "And the goddamned *Doll's House,*" she said. "I hadn't read it since I was a girl. I remembered it so differently. I'm really having trouble getting into the role. Is it because Big Bernie's crisis has cast everything in such an odd light, or have I just changed? Have our values changed so much?"

"I barely remember the play."

"Well, you know, it's about the noble, long-suffering wife of a man named Torvald, and she'd do anything for Torvald and she *has:* she's made some terrible affiliation with some atrocious man in order to borrow money so Torvald can go away because of his *illness.*" She shrugged out of the dress. She was wearing a peach-colored slip. She reached up and took a dress from a peg and dropped it over her head. "Presto!" she said. Her hair was dishevelled. She shook it, disarranging it more. "I'll have to tell you about it, sweetie. About my big problem with thinking she never should have been so long-suffering to begin with, because who is this Torvald? She's supposed to be so self-*sacrificing.* She gets so trapped. I mean, she wasn't an animal bounding through the snow who felt something go snap on its leg, was she? Who was she *before* Torvald? I mean, it's astonishing: Ibsen doesn't think we should care."

I hardly followed her description of the plot. She'd been speaking in a rush, talking quickly as she applied fresh powder. She was looking at herself, as best she could, in the windowpane.

"That was an impassioned description, wasn't it?" she said, turning toward me. "I do that, sometimes. If I have to think about something really, really upsetting, I change the subject to something else. I even do that if I've only been thinking to myself. It's like I'm terrified to let myself really think something through. It doesn't matter about some stupid play. What's the next act for Dara and Tom? That's what I don't want to get to."

"It doesn't seem entirely within your control," I said.

She looked at me, and her eyes started to widen, but then they narrowed again. "It hurts, like a physical pain," she said. "I think I'm going to lose him."

"You won't lose him," I said, though I had nothing to base that on.

"I've set you up," Dara said. "What else can you say? 'Yes, you're sure to lose him'?"

"I don't say things because I'm set up," I said. But my voice wasn't steady. I did, indeed, say things because they were expected of me; all too often, I certainly did say whatever was expedient to reinforce the status quo. I tried to speak again, to tell her the truth. But what was the truth? Tom was going to be the one who decided their future. "I didn't say that because it was what you wanted to hear," I said, trying to sound indignant.

It only made her laugh, though that didn't even make me angry. Because it was such an honest laugh—a quick, ephemeral laugh I'd never heard before and wouldn't hear again.

"No, of course not. Forgive me," she said, joining me in my own game.

We left the room quickly after that. Finally, she broke the silence. When she did, she sounded like the old Dara: overly animated; a person who spoke like a straight shooter, hiding her indirection behind perfect eloquence, measured sentences.

We left Snell's together. "This is embarrassing," she said, "but I have to ask you, because I don't have any choice. I'm short of cash. Do you have a twenty I could borrow?"

"Of course," I said.

"Thanks," she said, pocketing the money I took out of my wallet. She waved her hand above her head to say goodbye, running to her car. Halfway there she turned and simply looked at me, hands at her sides. Her unhappy expression made her Botticelli hair seem merely dishevelled; her body slumped. Her eyes widened, but this time they widened hopefully. Expectantly. But I'd had all I could take.

"I'll call you later in the week. Maybe we can go to the beach now that the opening is over," I called to her.

"That is definitely a good idea," she said. As she turned, the words fell like Ping-Pong balls behind her.

I went back inside. The air-conditioning felt good. The music was pleasant. The plants in their white pots were nice, too. Bob and I had perennials planted around the house, but inside there were no houseplants. I picked out a purple flowering plant with long, tongue-shaped leaves. The little plastic marker said it was Streptocarpus X Hybridus. I took it to the counter. As the boy rang up the sale, I picked up a flyer advertising an orchid show in a nearby town, and thought how many things there were to see and do during the summer, and how few of them I actually did. Driving home, I decided that I would put the plant in the center of the dining room table and see how long it took Bob to notice it. He noticed every little thing when he was hiking—I couldn't believe he wouldn't now, though it had been a long time since I'd gone hiking with him—or he'd notice a new chair on a neighbor's porch, or even spy wind chimes in a tree, or ask whether so-and-so had always had an old unpowered lawnmower. He was good-natured when he was teased about not noticing people's physical appearance. He didn't even know the colors of his relatives' eyes—though he did know mine. But would he notice if I did something different with my hair? I thought about the discussion the little girl had had with her mother about bangs. Then when I got home, I washed my hair and trimmed it, lifting little strands of hair and slowly cutting bangs, which I hadn't had since college. I painted my fingernails pink, then put on a second coat of red, knowing he would never notice the pearly, subtle color. I placed the plant on the table and, as I did, I thought that maybe altering my physical appearance had been a way to divert his attention from the plant. I had become wary of Bob. His mood had been swinging between opposite poles: argumentative; silent. I wanted to shake him up—to emphasize the fact that we thought differently about things; to announce that I could purchase a plant from Tom Van Sant, and that the world wouldn't end. Bob was so territorial. So set in his ways. I had been too agreeable, rarely contradicting him, making whatever adjustments were necessary so he could proceed to do things his way. I was looking for a fight, though I didn't know it at the moment. Later, when Bob voiced his dismay about my buying a plant from the competition, I found myself asking shrilly if Warner's stocked Streptocarpus X Hybridus. I felt blood rush to my face as I bent over the marker to remind myself exactly what the plant was named. As I straightened up, I saw the look of dismay on his face.

"Well, aren't you the authority?" he said. "How unfortunate that our greenhouse is so empty of something that's momentarily struck your fancy. Maybe I need to think seriously about the significance of that, Jean: maybe it's time to admit that somebody just doesn't have what you want."


My discussion with Dara about *A Doll's House* took place in Portsmouth the following week, in Prescott Park. She had urged me to read it, and I'd found it at a used-book store, where I'd also bought some funny old cookbooks, including *The Harried Hostess,* which was about what to make in half an hour when your husband called from work to say he'd be bringing his boss home. The illustration on the front was what had gotten my attention: a stick-figure woman racing across the cover with a platter held above her head, her long, Medusa-curly hair drawn in great detail by an artist who clearly was more interested in women's hair than in what or how they cooked. I had it in my bag, along with the book containing three of Ibsen's plays and several items I'd stopped at the hardware store to get for Bob. I had packed lunch for the two of us: turkey sandwiches with no mayonnaise. In a separate little bag was sliced tomato and lettuce from the garden. I'd also brought clippings of fennel and basil. Dara sucked thoughtfully on a stalk of fennel. We each had a bottle of peach-mango juice. There were oatmeal cookies from the health-food store for dessert.

"It's one of the great roles, of course, but it can be so awkward when you have to find a new way into the character because, well, because the world has changed," Dara said.

I had read the play the night before, quickly. My question was: If a play was great, wasn't it because it said something true about human nature, rather than because it was a period piece?

Dara said that it seemed to her that while a play might present truths about human nature, unless they were completely familiar—clichés, almost—most so-called truths could be seen as a socially agreed upon morality arising out of a certain time and place. The important question would be whether, once removed from those conditions, there would still be a way to relate to a character who held particular values: to become the character without being condescending. Although she could see Nora's dilemma ("Not that I haven't found myself in a few dilemmas, also, lest we forget"), she was frustrated with Nora; she felt that she could have acted differently from the first—let her husband find his own way out of his situation—rather than assume the role of martyr. Really, her frustration was with Ibsen: he had set up Nora; he both romanticized women and then taught them a moral lesson because he wanted to punish or destroy the limited creatures he had doomed them to be.

"I can't keep thinking this way. It has nothing to do with getting into the role and making all this *live*," she said.

I wanted to say something intelligent, but when I read, I never thought to question what was there. I might not believe something, based on my experience, but I never thought about whether a character had been set up.

Two boys with long hair stood close to the water, holding their girlfriends' hands, pointing out the navy shipyard across the water. "Fuckin' militaristic morons, man," one of the boys said. The wind carried their voices back to us as if they were talking at the edge of a canyon. The girls said nothing, but both boys gave the navy shipyard the finger and spat in its direction. They talked awhile longer, then turned their backs on it.

"The important thing is to be sure not to suggest that the key to Nora is that she's neurotic," Dara said. "That's all the women's movement needs: another symbol of a self-sacrificing, frightened woman. What I have to do is make up an inner life for Nora. A life in which horrible old Torvald isn't quite as central as he seems. She has to be acting for her own reasons."

It was a gorgeous September day. The light was sharp. Everyone seemed to be pouring out of offices into the park, strolling in the gardens, finding a bench to sit on, or sitting, as we were, in the grass. It would not be beautiful much longer. Once the days shortened, the sharp light would reach an apex, and then it would quickly become weaker, barely illuminating short days that would become the quick gray slide into winter.

We were eating in silence, Dara in a funk, while I was preoccupied, wondering whether a second reading of the play would help me understand what had bothered her so much.

"Ladies," a man in a beige suit said, tipping his hat.

"How are you this fine afternoon?" Dara said, coming out of her reverie.

The man smiled, then turned to me. I had seen him somewhere before. He was elegantly dressed, with highly polished brown wing tips. He smiled, also, at me, realizing—I was sure—that I couldn't place him.

"Edward Quill," he said, extending his hand and shaking first my hand, then Dara's. Though he did not really shake Dara's: he held it and then kissed the air a foot or so above her hand. It was the man who had come to my house to pick up the manuscript. It was Mrs. Aldridge's fiancé.

"A perfect day for a picnic in the park," he said. "My mistake not to pack a lunch for myself. I ate at the new French restaurant on Bow Street. Have you been? It's quite good, but no one could prefer sitting at a table inside on a day like this to sitting on a lawn."

"It's never too late for sensual pleasures," Dara said, patting the grass beside her. Edward Quill smiled down at her, but you could see his hesitation: his pale suit; the grass that would stain. He replaced his hat on his head.

"Just what you ladies needed," he said. "Someone to tell you you were having a good time, when you knew you were having a good time."

" 'In all these eight years—longer than that—from the very beginning of our acquaintance, we have never exchanged a word on any serious subject,' " Dara said cryptically. She looked from Edward Quill to me, and I was taken aback at her bluntness.

"Nora, speaking to Torvald," Edward Quill said, cutting short my embarrassment.

I should have known Dara wouldn't be so rude, but the whole encounter had disoriented me: How would Dara know Edward Quill?

The explanation—as Dara explained, mischievously—was that Edward was on the board of trustees of the theater. "This is the gentleman responsible for adding Ibsen to the list of plays," she said. "And perhaps also the gentleman responsible, in good part, for my being cast as the complicated, conflicted Nora."

"Not at all," he said. "I merely enjoy attending auditions." He turned to me. "I had been thinking of calling you, so this is a pleasant coincidence," he said, touching his fingers slightly to the brim of his hat. "May I?" he said, gesturing toward the grass. He had decided to sit down, after all.

"Mr. Quill, we would be delighted," Dara said.

He pulled his pants up slightly at the knees and crouched, settling on one hip. "You know that your friend very kindly typed Grace's book?" Edward Quill said to Dara.

"I was very sorry to hear about her death," Dara said, deliberately sidestepping the question. "I know it must be very difficult for you." As she spoke, she sounded more mock-serious than she had when she'd been reciting Nora's line. This was the obviously false Dara. As outspoken Nora, she had totally convinced me.

"Yes," I said, finding my voice. "I had just had a death in the family myself. I'm afraid I wasn't as polite as I should have been that day." I looked at Dara. "Bob's grandmother had just died. I didn't even ask Mr. Quill and his friend to stay for coffee."

This was my performance for Edward Quill. The same day I hurried Edward Quill and Mrs. Aldridge's relative out of the house, I had recovered myself enough to go over to Dara and Tom's and show them my carbon copy of his fiancée's strange book. We had had quite a few good laughs over it.

"I was wondering," he said, "if you thought there was any dramatic potential to Grace's remembrances?"

It was the last thing I would have thought. The futility of someone's having written the book depressed me terribly. Being involved with it, even as the typist, had underscored the importance, for me, of finding something more meaningful to do with my life.

The best thing I could think to say was "I never gave it any thought."

"A one-woman piece," he said. "A commentary on marriage."

"Tell me a bit about this book," Dara said. I shot her a look, but her face betrayed nothing. She looked dewy-eyed, totally enraptured with the possibility of hearing whatever Edward Quill was about to say. This was Dara at her most insincere.

"Grace wrote her reflections on life as lived with several different husbands," Edward Quill said. "It was her misfortune to have her three husbands die, and her way of life extremely altered, of course, as she experienced three sets of marriages."

This was not what the book was like at all, and Dara knew it as well as I did. For one thing, there had been two marriages she never talked about at all, and those had not ended because the men had died. In the whole book, there were no "reflections." The reader was left with nothing that was informative or in any way illuminating. But Dara saw it differently. Or Dara meant to see it differently. I looked at her and could almost see the wheels turning.

"A kind of social history, as seen by one woman as she wed three different men in three different times," Dara said slowly.

"Exactly," Edward Quill said.

"Something that Irene Worth would perform. Or, oh, I remember the brilliance of Siobhan McKenna, doing Molly Bloom."

What was Dara trying to conjure up? Siobhan McKenna, telling us that okra tasted like snot? Was this all just something she was feigning great interest in because she truly thought that this man was responsible for her getting the role of Nora?

"I had the overwhelming sense"—he broke into his thoughts to say to me: "Please tell me if you shared this sense"—"the overwhelming sense that for Grace, as for many of us, the next possibility awaits us." He looked across the water. "Every time, she thought her life was settled," he said. "Each time, she found that she was wrong. But Grace was a woman both loyal and optimistic. A person with a will to live and to change."

A person with a will to marry, perhaps, in spite of all she should have learned.

"Marvellous," Dara said, with mock solemnity.

"I don't understand what's being written now," Edward Quill said. "A play about two people in ash cans. That play about—some long story Mr. Albee tells, about someone named Jerry. Jerry and the dog. I don't understand what nonsense like that has to say about the human condition."

"Nor do I," Dara said. She bowed her head, as if she were in church.

"So perhaps this is something to pursue," Edward Quill said, slapping his hands on his knees. I tried to look polite, but neutral. Dara's enthusiasm continued, in its dramatically understated way. When she looked up, tears glistened in her eyes.

"I am so happy to have run into you," he said, rising. He bowed slightly from the waist, hands behind his back. For a second, a bee hovered above his hat, but it flew away before he realized it was there. If it had stung him, I wondered if he would have shrieked, done something more spontaneous. He was, himself, like someone in a time warp. If Dara was having trouble connecting with Ibsen's world, how could she be so magnetized by the odd Mr. Quill?

The answer: money. He was a wealthy man. When he spoke, the theater company quickly and positively responded. At her audition, she told me, she had projected her lines to Edward Quill in the back of the auditorium. She had taken pains to make sure that what she said registered just slightly to the left of him, so that he did not feel the lines were being pitched to him. It was an old trick; when you did that, she said, it had the authority of an echo across a vast space: the person who hears it believes whatever he hears because it is overheard—it is completely convincing because it seems to have been discovered. Try it, Dara told me: Whisper barely audibly to someone at a lunch counter, for example. Tell the man next to you that he is a beast for abandoning the children, and the waitress who overhears it will instantly hate him. Much more so than if she overheard what she took to be a simple argument. "Works," Dara said brightly.

"Run through this one more time," I said. "You were being so solicitous of Quill because he controls the purse strings of the theater. I get that. But what would you do if that awful book became a play? Even Siobhan McKenna couldn't—"

"Wrong, sweetie! You play it very, very straight. For laughs."

I thought about it. It was an amusing possibility.

"Now you have absolutely *got* to help me by following up on this," she said. "This could be the great breakthrough of my career. This could really be an *amazing* performance."

"Oh, God," I said, already capitulating. "I have to call and pretend that idiotic book—"

*"Sweetie,"* she said, seizing my hand.

"All right," I said, "but one phone call. That's the limit."

"Can't you see me?" she said. "Something like this is the perfect challenge. You create a subtext. You let the audience know there's a subtext. He's crazy if he doesn't see that in Albee's *Zoo Story.* That play is nothing *but* subtext. It is simply *everything."*

I had not read the play. I could already see myself returning to the used-book store. I unscrewed the bottle cap and took another drink of juice. Being with Dara was always an adventure. I didn't believe that Edward Quill would ever have called me to ask my opinion about what I'd typed. He had only thought of that because he'd run into Dara; it had only been his way of getting into the subject—his own little fabrication.

"It's got to happen," she said, in a hushed voice. "Just knowing it would happen would make it possible to do the greatest Nora imaginable."

"What do you mean?"

"It would be such an incentive to become her. Don't you see? I could take everything that was going to come—I really mean this: I would be perfect; I would set the world on fire as Gracie—I could make Gracie the subtext for Nora. Nora would grow as big as a geyser. She'd go off like something from under the earth's surface blowing sky-high." She grabbed me by the elbow. "The phone call will be the best favor you could ever do for me," she said. It was so histrionic even she knew it was an outright lie. Dara mocking Dara was one of her favorite modes. "But one more thing I must ask of you," she said. "You said on the phone your car was for sale?"

"Yes," I said, amazed at how quickly she could change subjects.

"Because it needs so much work," she said. She was repeating what I'd told her the day we set up this lunch.

"Right. Bob insists upon being honest with whoever buys it, so they don't come back and kill us." I smiled at Bob's odd logic.

"Do you really need the money?" she said. She whispered: "Save my life."

"Dara—you want the car?"

"My car died," she said. "Here's the thing. I'm really embarrassed about this, but I don't have the money right now, and my car bit the dust. It totally bit the dust. It was towed to the car graveyard. Tom wants to get me another one, but I don't want to be any more indebted to him—particularly not while he's still entangled with Big Bernie and the Situation. Listen: let me have it, and when I get my first paycheck, I'll pay you back."

I had no idea how to say no. I didn't even think Bob would be terribly upset if I gave her the car, because he was so worried that whoever got it—in spite of the low price—would come after us, once they discovered it was in such bad shape. Someone had done that to Trenton, years ago: come after him with a tire iron, after the car he'd sold them threw a rod. Bob had always been horrified by Trenton's near brush with death. Trenton had barely made it from his front lawn into the house and closed the door when the tire iron the man was wielding split the door. If Dara had the car, it would remove his worry about violence in his future, and it would also be a good deed. Bob had already picked out a used Volvo for me; I would be getting it over the weekend.

"Take the car," I said. "Of course."

Tears overflowed her eyes. "I think the technicality is that I have to buy it from you," she said. She rushed on: "You know—something to placate Motor Vehicles. I have to buy it from you for some tiny amount."

"I'll add it to what you owe me for your share of the picnic."

"Don't tease," she said. "I've felt so awful about not having enough money to pay my share these last few weeks. Even when I get my paycheck, it's going to be nothing. Tom tries to reassure me things will change, but I don't know. I've thought about giving up acting. I've at least considered reconsidering everything." She smiled weakly. "I want to tell you about it sometime," she said. "What little money I have has been going to my sister. She's in bad shape right now, and I'm all she has. But that's another story. I want you to know something: for selling me your car, I will forever be indebted. Cross my heart and hope to die."

She reached in her bag. She took out four quarters and pressed them into my palm. She closed my hand over the money and looked at me the way I'd seen fortune-tellers overreact with clients at the carnival. It was as if she seriously believed energy from her was flowing directly into me through her fingertips. She might as well have been home sticking pins in a voodoo doll, but I didn't know that then. Her touch was at once so strong and so soft. The paradoxes Dara embodied—the equivalent of a whisper meant to be overheard—always made whatever she said both urgent and, because in those days I confused urgency with truth, true.

She had just purchased my car for one dollar.

That fall there was a combination graduation/wedding celebration: Bob's completing his course work at the end of summer school, and Drake and Bonnie Collingwood's delayed celebration of their marriage. Drake did not want a big party—he thought weddings should be "a private affair," as he told Barbara—but he did agree to be one of three guests of honor at a restaurant in the North End. The day of the party, Frank was in bed with a strep throat and a high fever. Janey almost cancelled, but once the results of Frank's throat swab came back and the doctor phoned in a prescription for antibiotics, she decided she could leave him after all. A friend of hers—a nurse—took Joanna for the day. Max decided to stay home with his father (which meant a day of watching TV); his older brother, Pete, went back and forth until it was almost time to set out, and then decided he wanted to go. He got into the backseat of my Volvo, carrying his old running shoes, in case his new ones started to hurt, and a pile of comic books. He also brought a small insulated cooler in the shape of a Pepsi bottle, in which he carried a can of Dr Pepper and a pack of M&Ms he offered to us only once, in a desultory way. Pete had shaggy bangs, which he wouldn't let Janey cut, that hung over his eyebrows. He pronounced my bangs, which I was already tired of being tickled by, "cool." He liked us both better than he let on, but we could see that he'd been truly divided about the trip: leave his brother and risk being taunted about the great shows he'd missed on TV, or go with his mother to a party in the big city and use that as a trump card? Pete was six. His brother was five.

"How old do you have to be to get married?" he wanted to know.

"Don't talk with your mouth full," Janey said to him. That was when we saw the M&Ms. That was when he poked the package vaguely in our direction and mumbled that if we wanted some, we could take them.

"Bix Hinton's parents got divorced and then got married to each other again," he said. He was pulling off his new running shoes, wiggling his toes in his socks.

"I hope they're the right size," Janey said.

"Do you know them?" Pete said.

"No," Janey said.

"Because if you did, you could tell me what they're like," Pete said. "Hey, cool, Aunt Jean. You really took that Ford."

I inclined my head to the side, acknowledging his compliment.

"Confused people," Janey said. "That's what they sound like."

"I bet you wouldn't ever divorce Dad and marry him again," Pete said, turning so his back was against the back door, his legs stretched in front of him on the seat.

"I bet I wouldn't," Janey said.

"Because it would be too much trouble," Pete said.

"Not only that, but we don't want to get divorced," Janey said.

"How do you know Dad doesn't?"

"Don't talk nonsense," Janey said.

"How do you?" he said.

I was familiar with the pattern: as soon as his mother indicated she was bored, Pete would zero in. That was all it took to make him persist.

"You can give a toast at the party," I said, hoping to distract him.

"Hey, Mom, how do you know?"

"Nobody ever knows anything for sure about relationships," Janey said. "But I want you to know, Pete, that I do not foresee a problem about our staying married." She looked at me. "Insecure," she mouthed.

"What did you say?" Pete said.

"Pete, if you're going to be a boa constrictor, I won't invite you to go with me the next time I go to Boston."

She often admonished both boys for being boa constrictors when they got in certain moods; it was the big squeeze: seizing her, in an attempt to get her undivided attention.

"What did you mean about toast?" Pete said, poking my seat from behind.

"You raise a glass after a wedding and say a few words wishing the bride and groom happiness."

"Grandma says they didn't have a real wedding."

"They did have a real wedding," Janey said. "It just wasn't in a church."

"I'm going to marry somebody rich," he said.

"That's what we all think at one time," Janey said. "Don't hold your breath, Pete."

"Isn't Dad rich?" Pete said. It was a joke question, meant to be cute. Janey harrumphed.

"Then isn't Uncle Bob rich?" he said, wiggling lower in the seat. He had our attention. That was all he wanted.

"If you're brilliant and charming and handsome and amusing and a unique person, you don't have to be rich," Janey said.

"That's me," Pete said.

"Oh, it is?" Janey said. "What's the most amusing thing about you, Pete?"

"Big feet," he said.

"That's true," she said, looking over her shoulder. "Now may I please converse with your aunt?"

"I can make you want to talk to me," Pete said.

She shook her head from side to side silently.

"Uh-huh," he said. "Do you know where these M&Ms came from? Bix Hinton stole them from CVS."

"Oh, great," Janey said.

"See?" Pete said.

"Well that's just great," she said. "And what makes you tell me that, my darling son?"

"Because I knew I could get you to talk," he said. Then, to my surprise, Pete gave up his campaign and began to read his comics, chewing audibly. In the rearview mirror, I saw him unzip the thermal bag and take out the Dr Pepper. Instead of opening the can, though, he rolled it up and down his thigh. He was still at the age where anything and everything could be a game.

I hadn't thought about Bonnie Collingwood's ring for a long time, but the night before, on the phone, I'd remembered to ask Bob if she'd received it yet. "No," he'd said. "Forget all about that. Drake asked for it back some time ago—the day of the funeral, I guess it was. He thought he'd spent too much on it."

"That's awful," I had said.

"It's not your business—or mine. Drake can make up his own mind about what he wants to do." Then he had gotten angry—probably as a preemptive strike against my continuing to question him. "Jewelry is something I don't think about," he said, "but I must say, I find it really irritating when everybody becomes so materialistic."

"Who's materialistic?"

"Oh, you didn't overhear her, I guess, but Barbara was saying at the funeral that she was going to keep Grandma's opal and wear it and then leave it to one of you in her will, even though Grandma wanted to be buried with it. I agree with Barbara: that would have been a waste. But couldn't she have just done what she was going to do without comment? Why would she think Frank and I would want to hear about all the tedious details?"

"She probably felt guilty."

"I don't care if she did, or if she didn't. If Drake had wanted to give the ring he bought to Bonnie, that would have been fine. If Dara Falcon is going to pawn her jewels to stay alive, more power to her. It's been done before."

"What are you talking about?"

"I ran into Tom a while ago at the post office—Christ, I see the guy everywhere, like he's the mayor of the goddamn town—and he was having a crisis because Dara Falcon's car had broken down, and she refused to let him loan her the money for repairs. Suddenly she's selling his mother's ring. His mother's ring! Tell me that isn't mind-fucking him."

Dara was selling the diamond-and-ruby ring? She had seriously considered that, before asking for my car?

A brief conversation between Pete and Janey:

"Are we going to a Red Sox game next summer?"

"Of course."

"Cool."

"Your parents are very cool. Remember it."

Around Newburyport, traffic picked up. A hippie in an aqua Mustang convertible passed us, his bandannaed golden retriever panting happily in the passenger seat. The music from the car was loud enough to make Pete sit up to see where it was coming from. He watched the car until it turned off at the next exit. Nothing else on the highway was as flashy: women in station wagons; men in junkers. Trucks.

Janey was wearing a short-sleeved dress with a square lace collar, patterned with tiny rainbows. She had on pink Pappagallo flats. A white plastic purse was on her lap. I was wearing a two-piece navy-blue polka-dot dress and black patent-leather high heels. That morning, I had discovered that my only stockings had a run, so I was wearing Peds, and self-conscious about them showing above the edge of my shoes. I'd pulled my hair back with plastic tortoiseshell barrettes. The night before, I had plucked my eyebrows and tried putting on two different shades of pink lipstick, to see which looked better. One was too bright, and the other too dull: I'd resolved to buy several new ones the next time I was in the drugstore. At least that would give me more imperfect possibilities.

"What do you think Bonnie's going to wear to the dinner?" I said to Janey.

"Something fashionable," Janey said. "She's very pretty, isn't she?"

"She is," I said.

"You know what?" Pete said. He had taken off his socks and was playing with them, like a cat. "Grandma's worried about Drake being married again, because she doesn't know if Louise will like her new mother."

"I'm sure Louise will," Janey said.

"Why are you?" Pete said.

"Because she seems very nice. I'm sure she'll come to love Louise, if she doesn't already."

"Do you love Louise?" Pete said.

"Yes," Janey said. "I love everyone in the family."

"Do you wish she was yours?"

"Three children are enough for me," Janey said.

"I wouldn't want her to live with us. She's no fun."

"She's had a difficult life," Janey said.

"I know she has, because her mother left Uncle Drake and because Gran'ma Martha died."

"That's right," Janey said.

"But I still don't want her to live with us," he said.

"Don't worry about it. She isn't going to."

"Who would she live with if this time Uncle Drake left Aunt . . . what's her name?"

"Pipe down," Janey said.

"I want to know!"

"Bonnie Collingwood," I said.

"Who would she?" Pete said.

"Honey, she'd live with her father."

"She wouldn't have to go back to her real mother?"

"No," Janey said. "Her mother lost custody of her."

"Then she would not live with her mother or with Bonnie Cotton-wood," Pete said. He was thinking aloud. What was he really thinking about, though? Was he worried because of his friend Bix's parents' strange exits and entrances?

"Collingwood, honey. Not Cottonwood," Janey said.

Pete was pulling the socks across his face, like a magician capturing the audience's attention with scarves. When he was finished, the rabbit that came out of the hat was: "Gran'ma says Bonnie isn't going to be around long anyway."

"What are you talking about?" Janey said. "Grandma didn't say that to you."

"She said it to a lady on the phone," Pete said.

Janey sighed. "You have a way of always being right there at inopportune times." She looked at me. She looked forward and shook her head, defeated. After a few seconds of silence, she said: "Pete, I want to make one thing very clear. Whatever you overheard Barbara saying, I do not want you to bring it up in Bonnie and Drake's presence. Is that understood?"

"Understood," he muttered.

"Now please put your socks back on and act your age."

"They itch," he said. He held them over his nose. "Phew! They stink, too."

Janey rolled her eyes. "You did understand what I just said to you, didn't you, Pete?"

"YesIheardyou," he said, in an uninflected rush.

"That'sjustgreat," she replied. Then: "That is just great."

I looked at the piece of paper on which I'd written directions to the parking garage. I turned the piece of paper over and saw that I had scribbled Bob's instructions on the back of the Snell's receipt for the purple plant. I had overwatered it, and it had yellowed and died. Every day it had not recovered had made Bob more self-satisfied. He commented on how fitting it was only once, but when I moved it from the dining room table closer to a window, he had called it right: "Still isn't going to make it," he said. If it had remained warm—if the light had still been strong, and the days long—I was sure it would have. Not willing to take all the blame, I blamed the season as well. I took it as a sign of what was to come: difficult conditions, not sun-drenched days. Like Janey, I sometimes dreamed of living in Florida.

"You know where it is?" Janey said, snapping out of her haze.

"I think so. I think it's the place we parked the time we went to Joe Tecce's."

I had gone into city-driving mode as we crossed the bridge. My driving was something I took pride in. I could also park on a dime.

"Mom, did you ever find out about the museum of kids?" Pete said.

Janey smiled. "The museum *for* kids?" she said. "No. I'm still not clear on what that is. I'll have to ask Mrs. Hinton. Remind me."

"Mom, why do you call her Mrs. instead of her name?"

"I don't know her first name," Janey said. "Do you?"

"Yeah," Pete said. "Stanley."

We both laughed. It wasn't the best joke in the world, but he said it so seriously, it cracked us up.

"Really," he said.

She turned to look at him. "Pete, think about it. How could a lady be named Stanley?"

"I don't know," he said crossly. "But that's her name."

"Maybe we're wrong. Maybe it's not Bonnie Collingwood; maybe it's *Bud* Collingwood," I said.

"That's right," Pete said, getting into the spirit of it immediately. "And I'm not Pete Warner, I'm *Petunia* Warner."

"Petunia," I said. "Whatever made you think of that name?"

"Petunia Pig," he said.

"Who shall I be?" Janey said. "Jack Warner?"

"Petunia Pig and Jack Warner and who's Aunt Jean? She's John," Pete said, in a fit of giggles.

"Petunia, you will please put on your other sock, as John has just turned into the parking garage," Janey said.

It was killing Pete. He was laughing so hard he had to wipe away tears.

"Wait, wait," he said. "Who's Bonnie? I forget."

"She's Bud," I said, taking a ticket from the machine. "Now put your other sock on."

"If I was the real Petunia Pig, I could clomp in with my hooves."

"You're not," Janey said.

"And you might have the misfortune of having someone want to pickle your feet," I said. "Terrible tragedies await pigs."

"I don't want to go," Pete said, his voice suddenly serious. He was squirming in the backseat.

"I gave you a choice," Janey said.

"Big choice, when Dad can't talk and if he was out of bed he'd just be down in the basement anyway, and Max slaps my hand when I try to change the channels."

"A life of misery," Janey said.

"You'll have fun when you get there. It's an Italian restaurant. You can get pizza," I said.

"I'm not sure," Janey said. "There might be a special menu."

"Why is there a special menu?" Pete said.

I parked on the second level of the parking garage. When I got out, I opened my arms, silently volunteering to carry Pete. In a car several spaces down, two teenage boys were inhaling deeply from their cupped hands. The car filled with smoke. One looked at us and bent lower; the other continued to sit upright, his eyes slits, his lips pursed. Janey and Pete seemed not to notice.

"I'm glad your aunt feels like carrying you, because I really don't," Janey said, more to herself than to us. I looked over my shoulder to make sure I'd locked the car. Another car came up the ramp, fast, and we moved quickly to one side. "Hold my hand when we cross streets in Boston," I said to Pete, already anticipating putting him down. Janey trailed behind us. Out of his younger brother's sphere of influence, Pete became babyish; he wrapped his arms around me at first, then draped them over my shoulders, letting his hands dangle. He turned his head to the side, finally, humming to himself. I felt as close to Pete as I had to Bob a few nights before, our heads together in the dark, pillows cushioning us. My hair touching another person's hair could make me very sentimental.

I was thinking that as we went into the restaurant and saw the sign WARNER PARTY, illustrated with a pink cupid pointing an arrow upstairs. My own wedding party had been in my aunt Elizabeth's living room, catered by a neighbor.

Janey reached around me and opened the door. Amazingly, perplexingly, Pete was sound asleep, his dead weight dangling down the front of my body. I felt the urge to protect him—though what was anyone going to do to him here, in the party room? He might be oohed and aahed over a little more, because his helpless sprawl made him seem younger. His uncle Bob, I felt sure, would have no interest in seeing him, however he appeared. Bob only liked girl children. Suddenly that was clear to me: he liked the insufferable Marie; he doted on Drake's daughter. Would Bob be cold and withholding with a son if we had children? I suspected he would be.

We were not among the first people there. In fact, champagne had already been poured, and someone was giving a toast; it was just what I'd told Pete would happen, but he'd opted out. A woman wearing a turtleneck under a sundress, with long, untrimmed hair cascading down her back, had stopped Janey to talk to her. Alone, I made my way to the table that was set up as a bar, a white sign above it saying HAPPY MARRIAGE, BON-BON AND DRAKE! with more little cupids trailing away from each side, aiming their arrows into the crowd. The bartender—a man, I thought at first, then realized it was a woman in a tuxedo—smiled at the glued-together duo approaching her and pointed to the ice bucket, in which the bottle of champagne sat. I nodded, and she poured a glass, slowly. She wrapped a white napkin around the stem and passed it to me. I would have taken one to Janey, but there was no way to carry another glass.

There were about twenty people in the room, all of them about the same age, many of them dressed more in costumes than in formal clothes: dirndls; deliberately sleazy 1940s jackets; cowboy boots. In a far corner of the room I saw Bob, talking to a man and woman who looked so alike they must be brother and sister: the same whitish-blond hair—what Bob called Mary hair, as in Peter, Paul, and. The man had on a long-sleeved shirt with the sleeves rolled up, and he wore a sparkling vest. His companion wore a long skirt that had the same, or similar, swatches puckered in panels down each side. She wore a tiny tube top and a choker on a black velvet band. She was extremely attractive, and Bob was listening to her with rapt attention. The only thing that stopped a knee-jerk jealous reaction was that, like me, Bob had a child pressed against him. Louise was sucking her thumb, eyes wide, peering at something to the side. She saw me approaching but didn't react. He was bouncing her gently. The man in the vest was laughing at whatever the woman had just said.

"Oh, here's my wife," Bob said, smiling. He continued to smile as I approached. It was a social smile.

"Is that your little boy?" the woman said, shifting her focus from me to Pete almost immediately.

"No, that's my brother's boy," Bob said. "Hi, honey," he said, leaning over to kiss my cheek.

"Hi," I said.

"Found it with no trouble?" Bob said.

"Yes. Thanks." I looked at the two people again, waiting for an introduction.

"Jason Moore and his sister, Elise," Bob said. "My wife, Jean."

I shook the man's hand with my left hand. The woman nodded pleasantly, but didn't extend her hand.

"Who came down with you?" Bob asked. He was acting so concerned. He reminded me of Barbara, asking all the perfunctory questions. He reached to his side, where his drink sat on one of the tables. Scotch? Bourbon? He rarely drank.

"Janey," I said. "Frank's throat got worse. It turned out it was strep."

"He works too hard," Bob said. "Everybody works too hard. So what's new about that." It wasn't a question, but the woman said: "Nothing that I know is new about that."

"Elise is an attorney," Bob said. "And I suppose this is as good a time as any to tell you: I'm thinking seriously about applying to law school."

Janey had made me inhibited about echoing what people said as a question. I bit my tongue and turned my head slightly, to indicate interest. Law school? Where would we get the money? How would he have the time?

"Only the first year's hell," Elise said.

"That sounds like an interesting idea. I think I might also apply to law school," I said.

I had no idea what made me say it. I wanted to say something imitating Bob's tone of voice, and I'd pulled it off perfectly. But my reaction had been so spontaneous that it made me look like an idiot. Jason frowned, his eyes darting to Bob.

"Good one," Bob said to me.

"No, I really will," I said. "I think it's a great idea."

Bob looked embarrassed. "Jean hasn't quite focused on her career yet," he said.

No one said anything.

"How's my girl?" Bob finally said quietly to Louise, bouncing her a bit on his hip. He looked at me, eyes narrowed. For a second, I was reminded of the boys smoking marijuana in the parking lot. I could almost smell it: the smell of something at once sour and sweet. The smell of something burning. My eyes must have also narrowed, concentrating on the remembered smell of grass. Years before, at the University of New Hampshire, Bob had once talked me into getting stoned and making love. It seemed like long ago.

I was rescued by Janey, who said a quick hello to the group and then wanted to know if she should take Pete. I relinquished him with misgivings, and watched Janey head off in the direction of a sofa. "I'm glad she got away from Clair," Elise said. "The fervor of the recently converted, and all that. Foot reflexology, that is. She also reads auras, says she, and if she has any reason to suspect anyone might be a receptive audience to either subject, she starts right in."

"I wonder where the bride and groom are?" Bob said. "Aren't they supposed to come on time but leave early?"

"I'm so glad they took the big step," Jason said. "Though after three failed marriages of my own, the next time around I promise to play Mother May I?"

"Don't bother to play it with me. I'm your sister, not your mother," Elise said. She had perfectly straight, white teeth. A single pearl dangled from the ribbon around her neck. It was a real pearl; there was no mistaking it.

I was taken aback that someone only slightly older than me had been married and divorced three times. It seemed excessive. Was that stranger, or less strange, than Pete's friend's parents divorcing and re-marrying?

"There was something of a problem earlier in the week, but I can't see how that would affect anything today," Bob said. "And anyway: he caved in."

"You mean about the therapist?" Elise wanted to know.

"Yeah," Bob said. To me, he said: "Louise has been losing weight for a while. The doctor called it failure to thrive. They couldn't find a medical reason, so the doctor recommended a therapist."

"A therapist?"

"Well, Jane, psychotherapy is an idea whose time has definitely come," Jason said.

"Jean," I said. Across the room, Janey was drinking champagne, cornered by the reflexologist and another woman, who was wearing a feed sack with the neck and arms cut out. You could see the printing stamped on it: it was a forty-pound feed sack, gathered at the waist with a gold metal belt.

"I went along," Bob said. "It's a woman—quite good, apparently. She wanted to meet the immediate family."

"Liz! Excuse me," Jason said, turning to grab the arm of the woman passing beside him. "Liz, have you already had the closing?"

He was gone. In a minute, his sister was also gone, lured away by a very pretty blond woman who crooked her finger and gestured that Elise was wanted elsewhere.

"Bob—what has been going on?" I said. "You didn't say anything about this on the phone last night."

"I don't think it's a good idea to talk in front of Louise," Bob said. Of course he was right, but I hadn't just meant the therapist: I meant all of it. All of it at that moment, and for the past year.

"How do you know those people?" I said.

"I know Elise because she worked on Drake's custody agreement, as did their brother Daniel, who is vacationing in Nepal and couldn't be here today. I just met Jason once before, in Harvard Square. At Brigham's, in fact, getting an ice-cream cone."

His answer made me calmer. I nodded. If we could talk, what

would I say? That I was shocked a child as young as Louise was seeing a therapist? So what if I was shocked. Was it really necessary to say I was shocked every time I was shocked? What was wrong with me, that I felt a compulsion to reveal my thoughts every second? But that was crazy. I didn't. I hadn't acted that way in the car with Janey. But maybe that was a problem, too: maybe I romanticized my great relationship with Janey, when increasingly everything between us stayed on the surface, in part because of her fatigue, in part because I had caught Barbara's reluctance to bring up anything meaningful that might lead to a real discussion, when real discussions were off-limits.

The bride and groom entered. She was wearing a short suit of satin, or some soft, shiny material: pale pink, trimmed with black lace. She had on very high heels that showed off her chorus-girl legs. She held Drake's hand and smiled nervously, surveying the room. Drake had on black pants with pleats and wide legs. He wore a white shirt and no tie. His hair had grown longer.

"Dum dum de dum," a man near the doorway sang: the beginning of the "Wedding March."

"Thank you for joining us. As you know, we got married," Drake said.

Bonnie continued to smile nervously. She towered over him in her shoes, yet she still looked like a dressed-up little girl. I had been even younger than she when I married; I must have looked almost like a child.

"We apologize for being late," Bonnie said, but she didn't project her voice, and only the people closest to the door heard her. "But today is also a party to celebrate Bob's—Drake's brother's—graduation."

"A toast!" someone called out.

"Please—after dinner," Drake said. He put his arm around Bonnie's waist and began to look at the place cards on the tables. "I know we're here. I know we exist," he said, continuing to peer at the little cards. Bonnie linked her arm with his, teetering a little awkwardly in her high heels. So this was the marriage Barbara didn't think would last. This was the bride who never knew she might have been given an antique wedding ring. But at least he was taking her on a honeymoon. I had overheard people talking beside Bob and me: Drake and Bonnie were going to some island in the Caribbean.

"Bob," I said. My voice was a little hollow. Either my ears had closed slightly, as they sometimes did at high altitudes, or the noise in the room drowned out the word the instant I spoke. I had not said his name as loud as I thought I had. I said it again. He turned, then, from having exchanged some witticism and a shoulder slug with a pink-shirted man passing by. I saw some of the man's drink slush to the floor. Bob stepped forward, into the puddle. "Yes?" he said.

The bride and groom sat down, and several people applauded. From somewhere, the lights were dimmed and raised, then dimmed again to a soft glow. Music was playing. It had been playing for some time, but only when people began to move toward the tables was it discernibly music. It had been much too loud before, contributing to the din.

"Bob, I had the weirdest feeling just now," I said. "I felt so alone."

"That's silly," he said, but I could tell from his tone of voice that I had upset him.

It was spooky. It was a feeling I couldn't shake. I had suddenly had an image of myself at my own wedding: how nervous I had felt—not because I was getting married, but because I knew I wasn't, in that one, important moment, happy enough. I had also worried that people could see my uncertainty—even my inability to let go and have fun. I had wanted to smile and laugh, but I had been stiff and self-conscious. My eyes kept darting around the room, noticing pointless things, like the dusty window ledges, ignoring the obvious: the flowers my aunt had ordered; the haze of pastel dresses, and the women with their own smiling faces. It had been such a small wedding, and I had felt so small at it. But why was that confusing day suddenly coming back to me? Would it now come back, always, if I attended any wedding? I sank down in the nearest seat to think my thoughts through. Which must have been what I was doing when Bob, in an insincere, too-polite tone of voice, said, "Jean, dear, that is someone else's chair."

A woman peered over my shoulder. "Would you like to change places?" she said.

I didn't answer. Bob was helping me up, steering me toward what he apparently already knew was our table. I caught Janey's eye. I smiled to see if she would return the smile. Of course she did.

I had started to change, but I didn't think of it that way. I thought there was something in the air, or agreed with Barbara—much as I hated to—that we were living in increasingly strange times. Twice in one week I flipped through *Passages,* by Gail Sheehy. I had seen the book around, and heard about it, but the first time I looked at it was when I found it on Janey's coffee table the night I babysat Joanna and the boys while she and Frank attended Parent-Teacher Night. It was also in the doctor's office when I went for the pregnancy test that came back negative. I had my choice of Gail Sheehy, pamphlets on diabetes, or *National Geographic.* By the time the doctor's nurse called me in, I was convinced I had more in common with midlife men than with women my own age, which, along with the strongly retained image of a wolf's eyes staring up at me, had made me happy to flee the waiting room. I accepted the news that I was not pregnant with ambivalence. I had tried to convince myself that having a baby would be an adventure, something that would in many ways at least determine what I did with my life, but in reality, I wasn't sure I wanted a baby. I knew my marriage wasn't good, though I worked hard to deny it. Since the wedding celebration and graduation party—since he'd finished up in Boston, actually—Bob and I had been getting along better, but something had happened. Somehow, before I noticed, it had not only happened, but seemed irreversible—so that Bob and I weren't close, even when we made love, even when we went to lunch, as we had at Arizona.

Bernie was long gone from her waitressing job, and she was also long gone from the area. After one particularly horrendous day and evening during which her vomiting increased so dramatically that Tom had had to take her to the emergency room, he had decided that he needed to offer her more support. (*"Sweetie, what did he think he was doing, being at her beck and call? He's entirely too critical of himself."*) He told Bernie that he would see a lawyer before the baby was born, so that financial arrangements could be made. Though Dara had constantly urged him to persuade Bernie to get an abortion, she doubted that he'd hammered away at her about it; she thought—and she might have been right—that Tom was wary of Bernie, as well as feeling great conflict about the child. Several days after the trip to the emergency room, Bernie had packed her bags and left for her best friend's house, in Chalybeate Springs, Georgia. She had decided to have the baby and give it up for adoption. (*"Imagine! She's not even going to keep it, and she's putting herself and everybody else through all this! This is a nightmare to me, because of what I went through, myself. She is absolutely, completely, making the wrong decision."*)

At a second lunch at Arizona, I had talked to Bob about the Dara-Tom-Bernie situation, making sure to keep my voice low, because I had no idea who on the waitstaff might have known her. The place seemed peculiarly empty without her, and the piñatas—the increasing kitschiness of the place—bothered me. I still missed the other restaurant, and pink and green curlicued horses dangling from the beams with their brightly painted, smirking red lips weren't helping me enjoy the new restaurant more. We had margaritas. Though I would be going to the doctor the following day because I had missed at least two periods, I hadn't said anything to Bob. I suppose I was trying to find out what he thought about babies in general, though presenting Bernie's complex situation was hardly the way to find out. He seemed to have no opinion about whether an abortion would have been better—though it was legal, he still feared it as a medical procedure—or whether she would be doing the right thing by having the baby. By the time the food was brought to the table by the too-chipper waitress, I had begun to think that it wasn't fair to Bob to always tell him about everyone's problems, or even to mull over so many vague possibilities: I might go to work more regularly as a secretary for two lawyers who had just opened an office in Cape Neddick; I thought that what I most wanted to do the following summer was see the Grand Canyon, yet some part of me also wanted to go to the Bahamas, to take advantage of the off-season rates in a luxury hotel. Christmas—I was really jumping around in terms of what I might want, when—I thought should be at our house this year, but I thought it would take Bob persuading Frank to have it happen. I had finally caught on that Janey had so many events at her house because Frank insisted on it.

I ate my chimichanga, picking out strands of shredded lettuce as if they were weeds in the garden. Then I ate the lettuce. I wanted another margarita, but thought better of it. When the waitress came to the table and asked, I ordered ginger ale. As we ate, Bob told me that he had agreed to return to Boston to see the child psychologist. Drake had phoned him the night before, though I hadn't known why. Yet again I agreed with my husband: there was so much closeness—if you could properly call it that—so much reliance by one family member on another, that it could be stifling. Though Bob had pulled back from Barbara, letting Frank pick up the slack, he seemed resigned about being part of what was now called Louise's recovery. As I had found out at the wedding, Bob was "immediate family." It crossed my mind to ask whether other family members—meaning: me—would ever be called upon, or whether for some reason the therapist thought of us as the dumb kids in the classroom.

School had just recently started, which was part of the reason I was thinking about school. Pete already hated his teacher. His younger brother had announced that the only reason he saw to go to school was that, when you graduated, you could join the marines. I couldn't imagine what Marie must be like in school. She got good grades—A's in everything except math—but I imagined she must be the sort the other kids stayed away from. An image of Marie, in mid-tantrum, with her big, silly bow shaken loose, lying on our living room rug, popped into my mind: Bob, disguising his taunt as an important life lesson, saying, "You have to share Uncle Bob."

I had been sharing Bob with everyone, and I knew how frustrating that felt. But then I began to think: What is it like to know you're being shared? He sometimes joked about people needing to stand in line to take a ticket. He might have objected more, except that it was obvious Frank was much more in demand. So many things were expected of Frank. What would Frank's ideal vacation be? Surely the Caribbean— not packing up the family and going to the Grand Canyon.

After lunch, Bob would be dropping me off in Cape Neddick. I'd agreed to return to the office to work a second half day. The lawyers wanted me to work for them. Whether I wanted them was another matter. Bob would be going to the greenhouse to see what he could do about fixing the soil-cooking machine. So far, his newly acquired accounting skills hadn't been put to much use, though at night, slowly, he'd been setting up a new system for keeping the books.

Bob had coffee, which he only drank a few sips of. It was the cinnamon-flavored coffee Bernie had told us to refuse if we didn't like it. But Bernie had left for Georgia, and Bob might have liked the coffee well enough, but just felt anxious about getting on with the day. That night, we would be going to Portsmouth. *A Doll's House* had opened to rave reviews, but we'd had various obligations—babysitting; working on the business's books—so Tuesday night was the first time we could go together. Dara was a little put out with me, I knew, because I had not come without Bob. She had put us on the list for complimentary tickets opening night. When I realized it wasn't a night we could go, I'd called Barbara. The box office didn't know one Warner from another, so Barbara and Dowell had already seen the play. Increasingly, they did things together. She must have really brought on the charm and the candlelight the night he ate with her, because since that time, every time I spoke to Barbara, Dowell was expected momentarily, or she and Dowell had plans for the weekend. Bob was simply thankful that Dowell kept his mother occupied; he must have also done odd jobs around the house, because Barbara's phone calls to Bob and Frank had dwindled.

Back at the house, we went through the mail together. My car was being serviced, so the plan was for one of the lawyers to give me a ride home. Somehow, Bob had convinced the garage to drop the car off at the end of the day, when the work was finished, so we wouldn't have to go get it. The owner of the garage was Trenton's best friend. Guys did things for other guys.

I went to the bathroom, while Bob made a quick phone call. "Oh, damn," he said, when I came out. He was looking at the calendar. "That play's tonight, isn't it?"

"What's the matter?"

"Nothing," he said. "I told Frank I'd give him a hand with the wainscoting, but I can do it another night."

"I'm sure he won't care," I said. "We have seventh row center."

"Freebies?"

"She did send us tickets, but they were for opening night, and we couldn't go. I gave them to Barbara."

"The better to entertain the charming Dowell," he said. "Dowell Churnin and my mother. Who in the world would have thought this would happen?"

"I thought you were glad she was happy."

"I'm glad that for the first time in years she's off my back. She was happy enough before she got together with him."

"I'm sure she's happier."

"Do me a favor," he said. "Don't defend Barbara. As mothers go, Barbara is fine. But she never learned to stand on her own, and Dowell isn't the solution to her perception of herself as helpless either."

"You think she sees herself as helpless?" I was putting on a sweater. My summer straw hat, on the peg, already looked dusty. The cabbage roses, faded by the sun, were droopy. It was my favorite sun hat of all time, but it would probably only last one more season.

"Sure she does. When she was raising us, we were all given to understand that everything was juuuuust beyond her grasp. She could suggest how we might do it, but it was never to be assumed that she, herself, could climb up one rung of a ladder to change a lightbulb. It made overachievers of us—of the boys, I mean. Sandra's just like Barbara. Even Marie is more on the ball than my sister."

"It must have been difficult to grow up in a house full of boys."

"Sympathy for Barbara and for Sandra as a duo is too much for me," he said. "Come on. I've got to get going."

We went out. The day was cold, bright, and breezy; it would have been a good day to go to the beach. I wondered if Barbara ever flew her kites with Dowell. Who could imagine what they did privately? I was as surprised as Bob by her relationship with him, but it seemed proper, somehow, that I take Barbara's side. I thought Bob was making fun of a loneliness he didn't understand. At the same time, I could understand that he wanted to be cut loose.

"Pete's having a bad time in school," I said, apropos of nothing, settling into the passenger seat.

"Frank told me that," he said. "I think Pete's a good kid, but all in all, I've always been more fond of his brother. Maybe that's because Max looks just like Frank, and Pete looks just like Janey."

"Who do you think the baby looks like?" I said.

"She looks like a baby," he said.

Going down Route 1, we passed Snell's without commenting. From what I'd heard, it was doing well. Tom had hired someone who'd worked at another Snell's to do the day-to-day management. By the time we got to the intersection with the blinking light, I was lost in thought, as if my thoughts could do anything to change the situation: Was Bernie right to insist upon having the baby? Should Dara have fought with Tom so much about his decision to remain loyal to Bernie?

Would Dara and Tom eventually marry? It could be preoccupying, even though it was a tempest happening elsewhere. On the radio, Debby Boone was singing "You Light Up My Life." Like me, Bob had heard it one too many times. He changed the station and stopped when he heard the Eagles. Bob tapped his thumb on the wheel. We passed the house where we sometimes bought lobsters from the fisherman. Two towheaded boys played on the front lawn. They seemed to be watched only by a Doberman on a leash. The yard was full of junk. The lobster pots were stacked neatly.

"Is this a play I'm going to understand?" Bob said.

"Sure," I said. For a minute, something in his voice reminded me of Pete's in the backseat of the car the day Janey and I had gone to Boston. I often forgot that Bob was hesitant about many things. Frank made fun of what he wasn't familiar with, but Bob approached with caution. Drake, as far as I could tell, wasn't unfamiliar with anything— only disdainful.

He dropped me off in front of the lawyers' house. Their office was in the addition. A steam room was under construction, and the kitchen was being renovated. It was a beautiful old house; I was glad they'd saved it.

"Seven o'clock?" he said.

I nodded. I leaned across the seat and gave him a quick kiss. There was zero electrical charge when our lips touched, which made me sad. I almost thought of kissing him longer, but he was in a hurry, and someone had been peeking through the curtains. I picked up my purse and got out of the car.

Inside, Nubble the cat rubbed against my leg. It was a calico that had been abandoned in the shopping center: something else the lawyers had saved.

"Hi," Gardner said to me. "Have a nice lunch?" He was always pleasant. He didn't get rattled easily. The other lawyer was his girl-friend, and she was another story: she always did at least three things at once, and everything suffered, including the two of us. She was much younger than Gardner. She had started as a legal secretary at his firm, and when she became his girlfriend, he put her through law school. She had explained the deal to me: he paid for her education; she accepted, uncomplainingly, visits from his grown sons, one of whom was in and out of rehab, addicted to both alcohol and pills, the other a lazy, unemployed "poet" who frequently visited from Dover. Both times I'd seen him he had startled me: once he'd been barefoot in clogs, wearing a kilt and a Grateful Dead T-shirt. The other time he'd had on a caftan, with metal buttons around the scooped neck. It looked a little like something Elizabeth Taylor would wear to entertain.

I sat down at my desk and put on earphones. I listened to the Dictaphone and began to type the letters they'd recorded while I was gone. The letters were dull, but the idea was not to pay attention to content. I was doing what I was doing only because it was a job, and because the opportunity had presented itself. Also, I hadn't yet agreed that it would be a permanent part-time job. They had appeared to like me immediately. They were already planning the winter break-in-the-kitchen party. They were so delighted to have fled Boston, they considered parties at every possible moment. The arrival of Nelson in his caftan had provoked a pizza party about a week ago. Things became a "party" when Penny got overly excited and jumped up and down in her chair and proclaimed the event a party. Later, I would find out that she got $B_{12}$ shots every Monday, and that she had a prescription for amphetamines, but for the longest time, I thought she was just excitable.

"I had a dream about Jimmy Hoffa last night," she said, looking up from her desk when I got up to pour myself a cup of coffee. "Can you imagine? Everybody knows he's buried in cement."

"You didn't rescue him in the dream?"

"I've tried to decondition myself from thinking about rescue—even subconsciously," she said. "Women have got to stop thinking of themselves as Saint Bernards."

I nodded. I knew, already, that she gave a great deal of thought to feminist issues. She talked about Gloria Steinem as if she were on intimate terms with her, but when I'd asked, the closest she'd gotten was to have a letter published in *Ms.* She seemed to get more wound up as the day progressed, but I was learning to adjust to that. I sipped coffee along with her, to keep myself wired; if I looked convincingly wide-eyed hunched over the transcribing machine or the typewriter she would gradually stop talking to me and concentrate on her own work. Penny reminded me, when she was in her self-deprecating mode, or her wryly witty mode, of Dara: one of the things that had drawn me to Dara was her energy. In retrospect, it seems easy to understand that anxious people are often energetic people, but in those days I wanted to think of everyone as distinct. One major difference between Penny and Dara was that Penny was oblivious to her effect on people, and Dara was not. At the same time Dara talked, she was also a good listener. To be more accurate, she wasn't *also* a good listener; she listened while she was talking, like a bird singing and simultaneously listening for a response.

Which, though I hadn't anticipated such a reaction, made it difficult for me to focus on her as Nora when we finally did get to the theater that night. I had several immediate reactions: the predictable, excited Hey-I-Know-That-Person; surprise that, although we were close to the stage, she looked smaller and thinner than I'd remembered, so that I wondered if being so upset had caused her to lose weight; and the way they had outfitted her seemed odd—the chiffon dress was so pretty and so romantic, it distracted you from focusing on Nora. It underscored the fact that Nora was ethereal, rather than offering you a way to sense the progressively more substantive person she would become. Dara's costume reminded me of my being at the opening of Snell's, when she had been outfitted in the antebellum southern lady getup—the day she had told me the news of Bernie's pregnancy. The day she had let down her defenses, but I had been too reluctant— too frightened—to come through for her.

As Nora spoke with her friend Mrs. Linde, you could sense her mounting anxiety. She was a person enthralled with another person—a missing person, a ghost for much of the play: her husband, Torvald. Dara's Nora was a caged tiger who did not quite understand the parameters of its cage. Her silly visitor, Mrs. Linde, was like a fly that has flown into a kitchen that almost instantly becomes attracted to the heat of the stove.

I snuck looks at Bob, to see his reaction to the play. Though he stared straight ahead, I thought—as I did, increasingly—that his mind was elsewhere. At intermission, he stood up quickly.

Together we went to the lobby and bought coffee. We had only been there a few minutes when Edward Quill appeared, flushed with excitement. It seemed he attended the play every night and got more out of it every time. What I really thought was that he was sweet on Dara. He gushed about her performance, saying her angelic Nora was just right: that Nora seemed only a feather until she evolved into her harder self, and then she was as hard as a nail—as hard as a nail, but not to be driven. I introduced Bob when he got back from the bathroom. Edward Quill stopped talking animatedly and became quieter; Bob said nothing about the play, except that he had never read it or seen it performed. Instead of drifting away, though, Edward Quill continued to stand at my side. I thought this was because I was a friend of Dara's.

"Who was the fruitcake?" Bob whispered, when we were back in our seats.

"The man you just met? He was engaged to Grace Aldridge. I told you about the day he and a relative—"

"Engaged to the old lady? If he was engaged to her, it was for her money."

"That's a pretty cynical way to look at the situation," I said.

"Look at the guy," he said. Bob shrugged. "Mark my words," he said. "If not money, something else."

The play began again: the final act—the act in which Nora could no longer deny the truth, and spoke it. By now, Dara's costume, which had at first seemed romantic and out of place, seemed conspicuously wrong—the dress an elegant, feminine lady would wear, not something the increasingly pragmatic Nora would have on. Her hair was dishevelled. Nora looked wrong within her own body.

NORA:   You have never loved me. You have only thought it
        pleasant to be in love with me.
HELMER: Nora, what do I hear you saying?
NORA:   It is perfectly true, Torvald. When I was at home with
        papa, he told me his opinion about everything, and
        so I had the same opinions; and if I differed from him
        I concealed the fact, because he would not have liked
        it. He called me his doll-child, and he played with me
        just as I used to play with my dolls. And when I came
        to live with you—

Dara was utterly convincing because Nora's anger at being an extension of a man happened to be the current reality of Dara's life. It was the reason she wanted her own room—and why she kept it locked. And when she spoke so sternly to Tom, it was her desperate attempt to influence things. Her wildness was a way to temper her anger. Her ambivalence about her engagement was because she was in conflict with herself, not with Tom Van Sant: she wanted her own career, her own space, yet she couldn't bring herself to leave Tom's house. She couldn't make a break, so she was letting the situation in Georgia play itself out. His devotion to Bernie meant she might ultimately lose him. And if that was the case—I had long ago stopped listening to Nora and Torvald's exchange—playing the role of the newly self-righteous Nora must be a catharsis for Dara. Acting the part of a woman who took a stand must seem inspirational. As the play concluded, Nora's power was palpable. The curtain closed. When Edward Quill jumped to his feet and shouted "Bravo!" it was well deserved: Dara, in all her complexity, and Nora, with her hard-won new resolve, had merged, resulting in a weird hybrid, a creature larger than life.

I wanted to wait to see Dara after the play, but Bob said he'd had a long day. I knew he hadn't liked it. Torvald's role hardly presented men in a good light. I imagined there might be quite a few couples who would quarrel on the way home after such a charged performance by Dara and the other actor. I didn't see Edward Quill in the lobby, or anyone else I knew. I held Bob's hand, and he walked us quickly toward the exit. A sharp breeze was blowing as we went through the door.

"She really got off on that role," Bob said. We were walking down Bow Street to the street where the car was parked.

"She was amazing," I said.

"I wouldn't say she was amazing," Bob said. "She was good. She's just an averagely talented actress performing in a small theater in New Hampshire, you know."

"What does the location of a theater have to do with a person's talent? It would be a pretty sad comment on the way things are if excellence can only be perceived in sophisticated places. By sophisticated people," I added.

"For Christ's sake, that wasn't a criticism of you," he said. "I just have a different opinion. If you think she was amazing, then you think she was amazing."

"You're biased against her, Bob, to state the obvious."

"Did you know that one time she slept with Frank?" Bob said, turning the key to open the car door.

It was the last thing I'd expected him to say. I knew it was true, but it surprised me that Bob knew about it.

"Oh?" I said.

"Actually," Bob said, getting in his side, starting the car, and pulling out of the parking place, "I already know that you know that, because Frank told me you did."

He said nothing else. It was as if he'd said it was a nice night. We drove in silence for a minute or two. "Then why do you bring it up?" I said.

"She scared the hell out of Frank," Bob said. "Enough so that he told me about it, and we don't exactly confide in each other. Maybe because there's usually not that much to confide," he said. "Does Janey know?"

"You're asking so you can tell Frank?"

"Actually, yes," he said.

"I think she assumes it. Yes."

"It's over," Bob said. "For what it's worth, you can pass on the word to Janey that it's kaput."

We drove past the enormous pile of salt behind the brick walls on our right—the mountain of salt that would be spread on the roads when the snows began. It was surreal: a white mountain banked on asphalt.

"What did she do that scared Frank?" I said.

He looked at me. "I know you think she's quite something," he said. "But I'd be careful, if I were you."

"Stop acting so superior," I said.

"Big bad Torvald," Bob said.

"You know what I mean," I said. "Come on—it's not fair to bring up something like that and then not tell me what happened."

"She wanted to have a suicide pact with him."

I had imagined something kinky; something not quite imaginable— at least to me—that would also have flipped out Frank. I thought back to the day Frank borrowed the drill, saying, "I am Superman." I remembered the moment in which he knew that I knew. But what did I know?

"She's depressed. You have to worry about what people who are that depressed might do," Bob said.

"She's depressed?" I was doing it again: my old habit of echoing.

"I don't remember the details," he said. "Something about checking into some hotel by a bridge. Fucking, and then going off the bridge together." He looked at me. "I take it she hasn't indicated great despair to you."

"No," I said.

"She won't sit in a restaurant with her back to the door," he said. "Have you noticed that?"

"No," I said again.

"And the reason she won't is because all her life she's been afraid of being taken from behind. Does that sound normal to you?"

I didn't answer the question.

"Frank told me that, in case you were wondering. Must have been pretty comical: pulling out the chair for the lady and her having an anxiety attack at the mere thought she'd have her back to the room."

"If he was so afraid, why did Frank continue to correspond with her?"

"He stopped," Bob said. "It wasn't exactly blackmail—he thought, at first, that there was no harm in it. She told him she was desperate—that if she had notes from him, letters, whatever, she could use them to calm down. She acted like his letters were some sort of mantra she could repeat to herself, and maybe they were, but she also wrote back, and he didn't know how to respond to what she wrote him. She sort of entrapped him, I think."

"But she didn't do anything when he stopped writing, did she?"

"No. By then she was involved with Van Sant. Messing up his life with Bernadette."

"Why are you telling me this now?"

"I don't know," he said. "She was a little more frightening than she needed to be in that role, didn't you think? I know you like her, and I don't want you to get hurt."

I thought about it. Jealousy, on Bob's part? An overreaction, because he loved Frank, and Frank had been hurt? Or simply the truth—at least, the truth as he saw it.

Everything he said had been so disquieting that, although I would never have admitted it to Bob, I was glad I had a protector from the shadows, from the dark. I wanted to be convinced that what he was saying was untrue, but Bob was a straightforward person: he had only been telling me what Frank had told him.

Naturally, when I saw her next, I would observe her more carefully. She had, indeed, been extremely impassioned onstage. In the role of Nora, she had given the impression of being truly uncontainable.

Edward Quill's courtship of Dara began in earnest halfway through the run. He had arranged for a producer friend from Newburyport to see her performance, and the man had liked her so well he had immediately suggested a second production with his company the following summer.

That same week, Edward Quill invited Dara to Blue Strawbery for dinner. Tom had returned from Georgia, and things seemed better between Dara and Tom since a lawyer had been brought in to set up financial arrangements for the unborn child; unlike most people I knew, the two of them had only praise for the lawyer, in spite of his fees. Dara tried to make the dinner a foursome, with Tom and James Kames, the lawyer, joining them, but Edward Quill made it clear that although he could change his plans from dinner to drinks, he would appreciate her undivided attention. She met him alone at eight o'clock, driving my car—what had been my car—and wearing my alpaca jacket that she often borrowed.

What Quill proposed, during the dinner, was that Grace Aldridge's book be adapted for a one-woman show—with Dara, of course, playing Grace Aldridge. He and his friend the producer would collaborate on the adaptation, he said, though nothing would be done without Dara's approval. He was considering the possibility that it might be interesting to add some other voices: some people who had known Grace well might speak to one another briefly before the monologue began— or perhaps someone should take the various roles of her husbands . . . he himself might possibly, if he could overcome his misgivings that it would be immodest, say a few words about how he and Grace had once planned a life together. This might happen near, or at, the end. He saw it primarily as a one-woman show, and he was so sure Dara would be perfect that he was about to propose it to the board on the weekend, when they had their first planning meeting for the next season. If Dara was willing, she might record just a bit of the text—read something from the as-yet nonexistent script: a sort of auditory aid to help him make the best pitch possible.

Naturally she was flattered. Naturally she said yes. Naturally she also had to protest a bit first, though, and naturally she could also not laugh and say that she'd seen the book, and that if something captivating emerged from that text, it would, indeed, be a credit to her abilities as an actress.

She and I walked along the beach the day after her dinner with Quill. She'd asked to borrow my carbon copy, and I'd brought it to her during my lunch hour. It was one of the three days a week I was working in Cape Neddick. The lawyers didn't care how long I took for lunch, but I didn't tell her that.

The beach was almost empty, except for two women and their small children. The women sat in folding chairs and talked while the children played with buckets and shovels. An elderly man walked quickly through the surf, blue weights fastened around his ankles. Beside him, a cocker spaniel raced ahead, then circled back, jumping slightly in the air in an attempt to get the man's attention.

"You seem subdued, sweetie," Dara said. The canvas bag containing the script dangled from one shoulder. Her elbow held it tightly clamped to her side.

"I'll be honest with you," I said. "Frank told Bob that you two had had an affair. I don't care if you did or you didn't, but that wasn't the way you presented it to me."

Almost nothing I said was as true as it might have been: I did care; I'd omitted mention of how offended I'd been when Bob had attempted to sound me out so he could tell Frank how things were going; I said nothing about her ostensible thoughts of suicide, which was the part that bothered me most.

"Oh," she said, kicking a little sand. "You've got every right to be put out with me. I misled you. I know I did. I was more lonesome than I knew for a while before moving in with Tom—and so Frank played footsie with me, and he and I had a very unremarkable one-night stand, and that was it." She kicked more sand. "Except for the letters," she said. "And in fact, I'd like to give him back his letters. It was stupid of both of us, but it didn't really mean anything."

"You don't have to explain anything to me," I said. "It was just that you presented it differently."

"Well," she said, "I didn't lie a second time, did I?"

In fact, she hadn't. It really wasn't any of my business. And I had started to feel uncomfortable about having put her on the spot.

We walked awhile in silence. Finally, Dara said: "I'm so excited about next summer. I'm not too excited about making a silk purse out of a sow's ear, but after all, what was my training for? It's a challenge. To become Grace is definitely a challenge."

We turned around and began walking the other way, going in the direction of Pogg's Neck Inn, on the cliffs above the beach.

"What do you say to my buying us coffee at the Inn?" I said.

"I never decline caffeine," she said. "But isn't the Inn a little chichi?"

I shrugged. "I'm a working woman now," I said. "Of sorts."

"I'll bet Bob is glad you've got a job," she said. "I'm living in fear of the same idea dawning on Tom. I've been so happy in my little nest, reading plays all day, taking notes, dreaming of how I'd play the parts. If I didn't need money, I would be an absolute layabout. With not the slightest sense of shame about it either."

"Do I dare ask if the situation has quieted down with Bernie?"

"Poor Bernie. You'd think she was the first woman who had ever gotten pregnant. There is a woman who's played it for all it's worth."

"She still doesn't feel better physically?"

"It's all in her head. Maybe a little morning sickness truly crept in, but the blacking out is pure hysteria."

"How's Tom?"

"Oh, you know, Tom is a very *busy* man. Tom is racing around doing things at his business, and he's having tête-à-têtes with the lawyer, and then he's digging in the yard to plant bulbs the squirrels will dig up. He's been buzzing around my door like a fly. I just turn off the ringer the second he goes out and return to my own room, where I guess I'll now try to project myself into the rather unfathomable mind of Grace Aldridge."

She walked up the steps ahead of me, hands plunged into the pockets of the alpaca jacket. It was unbuttoned. The walk had made us warm. What a notion: Grace Aldridge, played by stylish Dara.

The hotel bar overlooked the beach. We took a table by the window. A few people were finishing lunch at a table nearby, but it was two-thirty, and no one else was in the restaurant.

"Two coffees," I told the waitress. "Pastry?" I said to Dara.

"As long as you're buying," she said.

The waitress recited the desserts. Dara chose bread pudding with currants. I ordered strawberry sherbet.

"You know why I'm not sympathetic? Because I went through it once. I told you about that. Big Bernie's a grown-up. She's up to it. I wasn't. I didn't know what hit me when those labor pains started. My prenatal care hadn't been the best either. I'd—." She looked at me. "Don't be so shocked, darling. I survived." She fiddled with the sugar packets, flipping through them, tilting them forward and backward. "The worst of it was living in this awful house I'd been sent to—my aunt's house. I'm surprised they didn't march her into the delivery room with me. Lest we forget, such things were unheard of in those days, or my aunt would have seen to it."

"My God," I said.

"God wasn't anywhere near the delivery room sparing me any pain, I can tell you that. Or I should say: she was otherwise occupied, watching over her fellow Chinese."

"You started to tell me about this once before," I said.

"It was back in the days when I was still little Darcy Fisher," she said. "Before I legally changed my name as a further way of distancing myself from them. It happened when I was too young, and poor little Franny who was never up to much—they lectured us both and punished us both. If someone in our family had been a soldier, my parents would have taken that opportunity to have Franny go off and witness a war. My mother didn't love me, but at least she admired me for having a will of my own. She hated Franny. I think she tried to abort her, and it didn't work. I think that she was so crazy she was punishing Franny for that in some way when she made her go with me to my aunt's."

I shuddered. I knew what she must have felt like, because I, too, had had to go somewhere by default. But Dara and Franny's case was different than mine; at least, Dara had put herself at risk, while my parents had put me at risk so they could go to a wedding.

"Parents get overwhelmed," I said. "I've always been afraid I would. Get in over my head, I mean. Want to ditch the kid."

She looked at me. "It was only for a while," she said. "I could have gone back afterwards, but I was too proud. Maybe it didn't have that much to do with me. Maybe any child could put any parent in that state."

"I wasn't trying to say that what happened to you wasn't awful," I said.

"Don't be so quick to placate," Dara said. She spoke quickly; her words were at once kind and emphatic. I felt sure that when she spoke again, there would be no italics—that her voice would continue with the same strangely un-Daraesque tone with which she'd first spoken. "It probably was the way you say," she said. "I might have been the one who was so unforgiving."

The waitress returned and took two desserts off the tray, then placed a pot of coffee on the table. She took a dish of unwrapped sugar cubes off the tray, and a little pitcher of milk. "There you are, ladies. Anything else?" she said.

"This is fine. Thank you," I said.

"It's more than fine. And I offer a toast to telling the truth," she said, raising her empty cup.

I thought nothing, at that moment, about the cup's being empty. I had no reason to think she was at all peculiar about how she sat in the restaurant, because all the tables for two were parallel to the windows. What I did wonder was who else knew this—whether she had confided in Tom, as well as Frank. If she had, that would certainly explain why they treated her gingerly. Perhaps why Tom quickly accepted the fact that she needed her own room. I looked at Dara, who was fighting back tears. A person didn't stop distrusting adults just because that person became one, I thought.

"All in the past," Dara said. "Forget it."

She reached across the table and took my hand. It was the gesture of someone desperate to make up. Or was she apologizing for misleading me about Frank, or was it sadness that she'd provoked sadness in telling me about her teenage pregnancy? I squeezed her hand and nodded; if she wanted me to forget it, I would. "You Light Up My Life" had already been turned into Muzak. It played in the bar, slushy and up-tempo, as we slowly spooned up our desserts.

"You remind me of Franny," Dara said. "Not that that would make your heart leap, since you don't know Franny. But when you tilt your head a certain way, sometimes it makes me remember her. What breaks my heart is that what they put her through did something terrible to her. She ran away, and for the longest time, even I didn't know where she was. She's in Oregon now, working as a nurse's aide. She had a drug habit she kicked years ago. She said when she gained more weight and could afford something beautiful to wear, maybe she'd come see me. She might be moving East with her new husband. What I wonder is how much she holds against me. She had some boyfriend who turned her against me years ago, but maybe she thinks differently now. I'd love to have her forgiveness."

"Forgiveness for what?"

"I was the only one in the family who focused on her, and when I was pregnant, I let her vanish. Living right there in the same room with me, I made her disappear."

"She was old enough to know you were going through something, wasn't she? At least she must realize by now."

"Maybe she does," Dara said, spooning pudding into her mouth. I could tell she wanted to end the discussion. Out the window, I saw a woman in a red parka walking toward us, her little black dog on a leash. Dara saw her, too.

"What is it that happens to Little Red Riding Hood?" she said. "She gets eaten by the wolf, but what happens before that?"

"She takes Grandma a picnic basket, doesn't she?"

"That's right. She's in charge of the groceries, and then she dies."

We both laughed. When the waitress brought our bill, we had been sitting at the table for an hour. We'd talked about inconsequential things: the beach; summer memories. I had almost forgotten the present, in which I was obliged to return to work. If Dara herself wasn't always mesmerizing, being with her still was: sitting in the sunny room, having coffee. Having a friend who always seemed able to suspend time to be with you. Dara's focus on you, and on the moment, was beamed so directly that you took center stage. Even if the talk was about her life, you were the central focus. I could understand why her sister might have suffered terribly if that attention had been withdrawn. Dara was like a light, and once switched on, she was constant.

On January 20, 1978, two days after Tom Van Sant flew from Boston to Georgia in order to be with Bernie when their child was born, twenty-three inches of snow fell on Boston. During the next few days, people began cross-country skiing on Mass. Avenue. Bob, who had gone for his monthly meeting with Louise's therapist, was snowed in with his brother's family. The meteorologists all sounded alarmed. There were constant bulletins on the radio. Snow broke the roof of Snell's, and before Dowell could get there to repair it, more than three thousand dollars of damage was done. My Volvo was almost buried in the driveway. The plows and sand trucks couldn't keep up with the incessant snowfall. "I don't know if even Norman Rockwell could present this in a cheerful way," Barbara said to me on the phone. Norman Rockwell was her favorite artist. She fantasized that he would do a painting of her marriage to Dowell Churnin. As she'd said to Janey, "I do hope that my dreaming that doesn't send the poor man to an early grave!" It wasn't exactly sending Bob and Frank to an early grave, but they were both dismayed. If Drake thought anything at all, I wasn't aware of it. I had hoped that his wife would urge him to take more of an interest in the family, but it hadn't happened. I had not seen Bonnie since the wedding party in the North End, and on the rare occasions I phoned, she was subdued and distant. It was as if she'd never confided in me that they'd married. Perhaps it was because I was housebound because of the snowstorm, but when I look back, I realize that that January was the beginning of a period in which I became much more introspective. Left alone, I began to really think about what it would be like to be alone—its advantages, as well as its disadvantages. At the same time, I wouldn't have traded lives with anyone. Certainly not with Tom or Bernie or Dara, who seemed suddenly to be blown around in a storm they had more or less created. In my case, I was still wondering how many things I was responsible for, or even had a part in. I was admitting to myself that in spite of the family, and in spite of Dara's friendship, I was lonely. Yet it also began to seem like a pattern, that someone would come into my life who had the potential of being a real friend, someone I could really talk to, and then that person would change, put distance, or formality, between us. I was convinced that Janey was saying less and less to me. That earlier, she might have said more about Dara, more about Frank—more about whatever problems she had. Was it Barbara's consistent, covert message that one should always be discreet that was gradually changing the family dynamic? I felt that I could still say anything to Janey, but I hesitated to do it, because it had begun to seem that she didn't feel that way about me—that she had decided, consciously or unconsciously, that our relationship had changed. I tried to rationalize, telling myself that she was overwhelmed by the new baby, that her immediate family probably took all her time and energy, but I didn't quite believe it. What I really thought was that she had retreated, and I didn't know why. Of course I wondered if it was something I had done (was it possible that she resented my friendship with Dara more than she let on?), or if I had changed myself in some way I didn't realize. And I suppose I had, a little: I had picked up Bob's skepticism about Barbara; it was clear that I had long ago abandoned the idea of having any real relationship with Drake—because if truth be told, in spite of his more obvious quirks and limitations, I thought he was a terrible snob. And Bob: Bob seemed to be fighting his own demons; I had done nothing to provoke him, unless having one friend who was outside the family constituted some bizarre disloyalty. It had gotten to the point where Dara was the only person I ever saw who had any spontaneity. She was the only person I would consider pouring my heart out to, though it frightened me that I thought of that so often, yet I thought of it in the abstract. Troubling as it was for me to realize, I couldn't think what a heart-to-heart discussion with Dara would even consist of. But those few times she had let her guard down with me—the times she had talked about her teenage pregnancy; the time she had admitted that she feared she was losing Tom—I had felt needed, important. Even though, through time, I would come to understand that Dara only infused me with the illusion of importance and power, I might not have articulated that such feelings were important if not for her. Everyone around me, in those years, radiated complacency, or at the very least let it be known that they were coping with things, rather than making any substantive changes. Bob's sister, Sandra, kept her distance from the family, yet never went far from home; she relied on the fact that while they saw her for the limited, self-pitying person she was, they wouldn't risk criticism about themselves, so they wouldn't expect her to do anything about her situation. Drake, who I think basically disliked himself more than anyone else, simply used the family for his convenience. Bob dug his heels in deeper, doggedly determined to persevere in the family business; Frank hid behind his identity as the solid family man, even as he mocked his own seriousness with ironic statements that let you know he was on to his own game. That was what I came to see over time. At first, because they discussed things more—because they were simply younger, and more talkative, and not quite worn out with each other's routines, I suppose—I had mistaken them for being flexible, and their interaction with one another had seemed, to an outsider, both genuine and admirable. It took me a long while to see that they created a sort of claustrophobic world in which they kept each other contained—that Barbara's unspoken fear of the outside world was the guiding spirit.

At the beginning of the storm, many of the phones weren't working in our part of New Hampshire, Dara and Tom's among them. Tom called me from Georgia on the twenty-first, to have me relay the information that the child—a boy, born by cesarean—was six pounds, one ounce, his head covered with dark brown hair, and healthy. If I was able to reach Dara before he could, he wanted her to know that. "Am I doing the right thing?" he asked me. "We didn't exactly discuss what I'd do when the baby was born. I'm—tell her I'm only staying because there's no way I can get back. Logan's closed, as I'm sure you know."

"Yeah," I said, choosing to respond only to what he said last. "Bob went to his brother's in Cambridge. He's snowed in."

"This is setting a record," Tom said.

"It's amazing," I said. As soon as I spoke, I remembered, for some reason, having used the word "amazing" about Dara's performance to Bob. And it was not, he had insisted: it was not amazing. Though even Bob could not argue with me about the astonishing amount of snow.

"You take care," he said. Our connection wasn't good; there was crackling over the telephone line, but if we spoke loud enough, we could hear each other. We both said goodbye quickly. I tried to call Dara, right away, before I lost my courage, but got only a beep-buzz. Though I meant to keep trying, I hoped Tom would reach her before I did. I didn't want to be the first to give her the news.

There was no way I could get to work, which pleased me. Penny called and told me not to come in, and I thanked her earnestly, though

I'd never had any intention of trying to go. Barbara called to make sure we were all right, and I didn't tell her Bob was away. I said we were fine. Janey called and said that the boys were cavorting in the snow and that Frank, whose truck wouldn't start, was laying linoleum downstairs. She and Joanna were rocking by the fireplace, and she said she wished I could be with them. The hospital was trying to send someone to get her in a four-wheel drive, but she was hoping the person wouldn't be able to make it. Everybody wanted time out; also, the snow was beautiful. I put Chopin's études on the stereo and flopped down on the sofa to read the adaptation Edward Quill had done of Grace Aldridge's book that I'd typed what now seemed a lifetime ago. No cars were moving. No one else called. It didn't take long to read. By the time I'd listened to Chopin and one side of Bach, I had finished. Much of the manuscript I had typed had been omitted. The characters, besides Grace, were "The Suitor" (Edward Quill had created a role for himself) and "Lady 1" and "Lady 2." Quill's dialogue appeared, but there were only two empty pages where the ladies would apparently have lines that would be written in later. What Quill said interested me, because I knew nothing about his relationship with Grace, but it also disappointed me. Quill wrote:

> *Grace was kind enough to make a provision in her will for money to be allocated for a dramatic performance, as well as a gala celebration in her honor. I can think of no finer celebration than to offer some of her own thoughts as she proceeded through a life that demanded of her new responses, new responsibilities, new respites from life's challenges. She was a woman of her time in each time she lived. She was an artist who recorded the day's subtle nuances as they gradually devolved into the pattern that would determine her future. As wife, as widow, as a celebrant of life, Grace's verve and veracity will be portrayed for you tonight by Miss Dara Falcon, who appeared last season, triumphantly, as Nora, in Ibsen's masterpiece, A DOLL'S HOUSE.*

So Bob had been right; Edward Quill's association with Grace Aldridge had resulted in his being able to find a vehicle, already funded, for Dara, with whom he was clearly infatuated. Though it couldn't cost a fortune to put on a play that would require little scenery and few actors, I imagined he could, nevertheless, withdraw whatever he wanted from her estate to boost the career of the next woman with whom he hoped to insinuate himself. This didn't take into account the obvious, though: Grace Aldridge was in her seventies, and rather plain, while Dara was in her twenties, and gorgeous. How could he possibly assume Dara would be interested in him beyond being interested in what he could do for her?

I made tea—an entire pot of tea, just for myself—cut lemon, and took out my favorite cup and saucer. I put everything on a little tray. When the water boiled, I dropped in three tea bags and carried the tray to the table by the living room sofa. Wind blew snow against the picture window, and I got up on my knees to watch the storm. On the windowsill was a pet rock Bob's nephews had given him years before, now forgotten and covered with dust. I watched the snow for a while, though the wet, streaked windows made it difficult to see much of anything. I was glad to be safe inside the house, dry, smelling the pleasant aroma of the tea. Yet something was bothering me. It was that I remembered my aunt, my mother's only sister, Elizabeth, kneeling on the sofa, looking out the window at what she already knew would be emptiness. My parents were not going to return. An unmarried, childless woman herself, she had just inherited me, aged six, after an American Airlines Boeing 707 crashed in New York, in Jamaica Bay, shortly after takeoff. My parents had been to a wedding. They were to have been gone twenty-four hours. Twenty-four hours, plus forever. It was only the second time my aunt had ever stayed with me. I knew she didn't particularly like me, but as my mother had explained when I voiced my concern, she didn't dislike me either: she just wasn't familiar with children. She got very familiar with me. When she was not looking out the window for what would never arrive, and when she was not staring into space, she was focused on me—a Dara-like focus. She seemed to think so thoroughly about me that she missed nothing: that it would be good to paint my fingernails pink for my friend's birthday party; that fabric-covered rubber bands would not break off my hair when the rubber band was removed. When she tucked me in bed, she looked so deep into my eyes, it was as if a myopic person were searching in a mirror for a single hair. She could make fun of her own ineptitude, but if she overlooked a detail—if I had a slightly unravelled hem, or if a minuscule fleck of lint was in my hair—she would become almost frantic. After my parents' death, I would silently repeat to myself my mother's words: She just isn't familiar with children. I thought that by letting her examine me, she would quickly become more familiar. When I finally began to accept the fact that my parents weren't returning, I wanted desperately for her to like me. Little did I know that she wanted the same thing: she wanted to be on friendly terms with the person she would be living with, unexpectedly, for the next dozen years. She was as willing to spend time with me, to stare at me, as I was to stay close to her side.

The way Dara paid attention to me reminded me of Elizabeth. When Dara had told me that I reminded her of her sister at times, I had thought, for a split second, that that was interesting, because she, too, reminded me of someone. But then I had looked out the window and seen the empty beach, and decided not to tell her my own long, sad story. And then Little Red Riding Hood had come along. And then, and then. My life was as the daughter of my parents, and then.

I had married the first man I ever slept with. Not the only man I ever dated, but the first man I ever slept with, sleeping with only two others before Bob also became the last. I believed strongly in first impressions. Bob maintained that I relied on my intuition, but there was nothing intuitive about it: I understood people in terms of their gestures, how much space they took up, how relaxed they were in their body, as well as whether I could see their soul in their eyes. I would never, ever, verbalize those things to anyone, including Bob, because I thought I would sound conceited: Who was I to see their soul? I had learned the manner of looking from my aunt Elizabeth, but I was different: while her close observations left her still obviously perplexed, some inner desperation had allowed me to actually see clear through to something.

Drinking my tea, the steam rising from the cup, the wind lashing wet snow against the window, I could see through to nothing, but that didn't bother me. It only bothered me if it was a person. Janey believed in auras, that there was an aura of illness or health surrounding everyone. I believed in the depth of the eyes. Together, we could have set off for Taos or Topanga Canyon and been a forceful spiritual duo. But I had never said anything to Janey about the way I could look into people's eyes. I picked up the dusty pet rock. The card with its name lay underneath it, but I left it there. I looked at the small black disks that rolled around its flat, clear plastic eyes: of course the rock's eyes were dead.

Poor Elizabeth, not marrying until she was forty-four, and then having another man's half-grown children to bring up. She had moved all the way to Montana. It had been a long time since I'd last seen her. She looked less and less like my mother. From a photograph she sent with her Christmas letter, I saw that she had become pudgy and a little red in the face—high blood pressure, or the Montana weather?— though perhaps she did look like my mother, or at least what my mother would have looked like if she'd lived.

Families. The pathos of families. What I could have told Dara, if I'd decided to open that can of worms.

Bob was very fond of his I SURVIVED THE BLIZZARD OF '78 sweat-shirt. He sometimes slept in it, bare assed, which I found hard to un-derstand, because if you were cold enough at night to wear something on top, why would you want to be naked from the waist down? He had always worn inventive things to bed: a terry-cloth robe, minus the sash; cutoff khakis. Though Barbara had given him several pairs of pajamas, he had only worn one set, once or twice, and then had tossed them all, the other two packages unopened, into the bottom drawer, where the *Playboy* languished and, again, the flask.

In the aftermath of the storm, Frank had gotten his truck going. He and Max had come to pick me up. The wild, destructive, but always beautiful storm caused no damage to the business or to any of our houses, but it had provoked a new sense of solidarity. We had all been invited to Barbara's for the first time in as long as I could remember. I let Frank come for me without telling him that I was the only one he'd be picking up. Bob had been back for one day—a day spent checking things at the greenhouse with Frank and then crawling into bed, ex-hausted, in his new sweatshirt—but then he'd returned to Drake's. He'd gotten embroiled in some fight Bonnie and Drake were having; he was going for Louise's sake, he said, and for the first time since I'd found myself thinking that things were not good between us, I wondered if his brother and sister-in-law were a smoke screen for his seeing someone else.

Frank was surprised Bob had returned to Boston. He also seemed to think that Bob was taking everything in Drake's household too much to heart. He told me—as if I didn't know—that Bob had a wife of his own, and a business he was responsible for, and that it might be a good idea to grow up and start functioning again in that context. "He bought a ticket for this ride" was the way Frank put it. I looked at him behind the wheel: he didn't know anything, I decided; he was as perplexed—maybe more perplexed—than I was. Frank's idea of Bob's retreat as a display of immaturity was worth thinking about. Maybe it wasn't anything personal: maybe this was a form of adolescent rebellion. He'd been made to be responsible all his life.

"I built six snowmen and dressed them in two tons of clothes," Max informed me as we passed a snow fort on someone's front lawn. "This whole blizzard was completely cool."

Max had no idea he'd made a pun. I could see from the flicker of Frank's smile, though, that he was amused.

"If your uncle Bob was here, maybe he could have contributed his new shirt that says I SURVIVED THE BLIZZARD OF '78."

Sand on the roads had turned the white snow to grainy brown slush. Frank was driving carefully, with both hands on the wheel. "Over the river and through the woods, to Grandmother's house we go," he sang, drowning out the Bee Gees on the radio, singing, "How Deep Is Your Love?"

"You promise that if I go I can see *Fantasy Island*?" Max said.

"You can get up from the table without even asking permission, and you can race into the TV room and take control of the set, no matter who else might be there. I'll come and fight for you if necessary," Frank said.

"Yeah, sure you will," Max said.

"Janey is trying to teach Max and Pete manners," Frank said to me. "Notice that in overstating the opposite of what is expected, I am trying to tactfully instill the proper virtues that Janey so applauds."

"You said I could see it," Max said. His father's outburst had confused him.

"You will see it if I personally have to slay a dragon breathing fire in front of the set." Frank picked up a bottle of Budweiser that was wedged between his seat and the emergency brake. "Sip?" Frank said to me.

"No thanks," I said.

"Mom wouldn't like it if she knew you were drinking in the truck," Max said.

"Your mom thinks *Fantasy Island* is dumb," Frank said. "So that goes to show that Mom doesn't know everything."

When we got to Barbara's house, Frank hopped out and opened the passenger door. Max pushed past me and ran toward the house. Frank said to me: "Why he's got such a hard-on for that midget is beyond me." He pushed his bottle into the snow. "When it melts, Dowell can complain about how much this neighborhood has declined," Frank said. "Jesus: Barbara and Dowell. Do you think they do it?"

I put my hand over my face, not wanting to think about it.

"I can envision it better between Ricardo Montalban and pip-squeak, there. Toto, or whatever the hell he's called."

Inside, a fire was going. Janey had come directly from work. She'd been at the hospital, where they'd set up a makeshift day-care center during the storm. Joanna was sleeping on the sofa. "Hi, honey," Janey said to Frank.

"Max gets to watch *Fantasy Island.* He does, he does!" Frank said, going toward his wife's open arms.

Max had run into the kitchen without stopping to say hello to his mother. There was some chance, though, that he'd been moving so fast, he hadn't even seen her. Pete imitated his mother's behavior and ran to hug me around the knees. Then I hugged Janey. She said: "Sandra and Marie are coming, and she's bringing her new beau. Can you believe it?"

"I want beer!" Frank said, still imitating Max, as he walked toward the kitchen. "I want beer and TV, and I want to do anything I want to do always!"

Janey rolled her eyes as he disappeared. "Barbara had some near disaster with string beans," she said. "She told me my help wasn't needed, and I'm taking her at her word."

I sat with her, in front of the fire. Pete had also run off to the kitchen. "Sandra called us last night to inform us that we were expected to be on best behavior with the beau," Janey said. "I guess she meant she didn't want any bedpan stories from me."

"Who is he?" I said.

"Where's Bob?" she said.

"He's around so seldom, it even takes a while to do a double-take, doesn't it?" I said. "Bob's become the constant companion of Drake and Bonnie, as far as I know. There's one compelling reason after another why he has to rush to Cambridge at every opportunity."

She looked at me. "What do you make of it?"

"When I've been snowed in for a while and I'm paranoid, or when I'm rational?"

The question hung there. In the fireplace, a glowing ember split in two, sending sparks up the chimney. The airplane, I thought instantly. I thought as little as possible about the airplane. Years ago, I had forced the image of the plane, burning, plunging into the water, from my mind. Elizabeth had bought a book about how to banish thoughts. It sometimes worked, which I had been very grateful for when I was young. The book advised that in place of allowing something unpleasant or anxiety provoking to take hold, you train yourself to immediately substitute another song, or place, or image. If you didn't want to see a dead seagull, you moved your eyes to the waves; if you did not want to see a plume of fire, you looked at the blue sky above it.

I said to Janey: "I wonder if I find it hard to connect with anybody because I always think I have to look to the next thing."

"What?" she said.

"Because of the plane crash, Janey. Because back then, when I couldn't get the image of the burning plane out of my mind, I trained myself to look beyond things, and around things. You can condition yourself to shift your focus. But lately I've been thinking that when you're never directly seeing what's upsetting, the big shadow of that thing spreads over everything. It's likely to black out everything, eventually."

"What got you thinking about that?" she said. "Feeling helpless, because you were snowed in?"

She was talking to me! Even if she was playing armchair shrink, Janey had heard what I'd said. Why was it, then, that I couldn't answer her—that I couldn't hazard a guess, or say something else, almost anything else, to keep talking about the crash?

She was looking at me intently. As if one question hadn't already gone unanswered, she said, "You think Bob has a girlfriend?"

The front door opened and Sandra walked in, holding Marie. The man who had pushed the door open entered quickly, stopping at the edge of the large mat inside the door and removing his boots. He was tall and thin, a blond man in a camel's hair coat. He seemed to take in everything all at once. His gaze was so riveting I could almost believe he saw the burning plane in the rectangle of the fireplace. Janey jumped up to greet them. The noise awakened Joanna, who started to cry. I went to Joanna. Janey went up to Sandra and her friend. She was trying to take their coats, to say hello to Marie, who had mashed her face into her mother's coat, to assure the man that the little snow his boots had tracked onto the mat was nothing to worry about. "I'm Janey Warner," I heard her say. Then something about snow, and the kitchen. People were already coming out of the kitchen. Marie began to cry. Still in her hat and coat, she turned her head sideways and screamed out a long protest when Barbara reached for her. When the man reached for her, she slapped his hand. This provoked a stern rebuke from her mother, who put her on the floor with a quick thump. Marie looked around quickly, then ran upstairs, taking them two at a time.

"How do you do?" the man said to Barbara, looking nervously after Marie. "I'm Jasper Cismont."

"How do you do?" Barbara said. "Oh, this snowstorm has gone on so long it's put everyone's nerves on edge. Won't you let Janey have your coats, and she can put them—Janey, dear, can you just put them on the sofa in the TV room?"

Frank switched his beer bottle to his left hand and shook Jasper Cismont's hand with his right. I came into the hallway, carrying the quieted Joanna. She was wet; she wouldn't be quiet long.

"Nice to meet you," I said. "I'm Jean."

Everyone was clustered around the newcomers, except Dowell, who had stayed in the kitchen. "Dowell!" Barbara called over her shoulder, but his response was barely audible. He did not appear. "My fiancé is basting the lamb," Barbara said. Her formal tone, for some reason, struck me as the funniest thing I had ever heard. Clutching

Joanna, I made a run for the TV room, and Janey. " 'My fiancé is basting the lamb,' " I repeated to Janey, handing her her wet child, and
then threw myself on the coats and buried my face in their scratchy,
woolly coldness, laughing.

"Shhh!" Janey said. "She'll hear you." She wiggled her finger
around inside the baby's diaper. "Ugh," Janey said, extracting her finger. "Here—give me the changing bag. Do something useful."

I stood up and made my eyes bug-eyed, like Barbara's, imitating the
way she stood with her hands crossed.

Janey shook her head and squatted on the floor, laying Joanna out.
"Be useful. Unzip the bag, will you?" she said.

"I don't think I'm a very useful person," I said. "I mean, think
about it: I work a few days a week. My husband avoids me. I don't cook
anymore; I run frozen macaroni in the oven—"

"Ugh," Janey said, folding the diaper and putting it in another com-
partment of the changing bag. "Ugh, yuck, phew," she said. "I need a
vacation. If we're not moving to Florida, I really need a vacation." She
sat on the rug. Joanna raised her legs over her head and smiled.

" 'Oh, my goodness,' " I said, again imitating Barbara.

Janey finally started to laugh. Frank came in while we were sitting
on the floor laughing. He had a beer can in his hand.

"What's funny?" he said.

Barbara came into the room. She was carrying a scarf, which she
placed on top of the pile of coats. "What are you doing in here?" she
said. "My gracious, come into the living room where the fire is so nice.
Sandra's gentleman friend is building the fire again. Do go in there
while I see what's keeping Dowell."

Frank was helping Janey up. Then he reached down for me. We
stood there in front of Frank as if we were dolls he'd dressed and put
on a shelf. He bent over again, and scooped up Joanna. "Hello, little
person who makes baby poo," he said. He headed off with her toward
the kitchen.

"I can't face it," Janey said. She sounded utterly exhausted.

"Sandra's boyfriend looks too serious," I said. "What are we going
to talk to him about?"

We talked to him about computers. Actually, since we knew nothing about them, we listened, and from time to time asked a question.
Sandra hung on his every word. She was drinking her favorite drink, a

mixture of club soda and orange juice. She sat sideways, looking not at Janey, in the chair, or at me, on the sofa, playing with the repossessed Joanna. Dowell had never come out of the kitchen. Frank had retreated. Bob was smart enough not to have been available for this evening in the first place.

"By the way," Janey said to me, when Jasper left to get Sandra another orange juice and club soda, "that woman Pete was talking about. You know the woman I told him couldn't have a man's name?"

"There are names like Sydney that could be either a man's or a woman's name," Sandra said.

Janey looked at her briefly, then decided to ignore the comment. She said: "Well, it turns out this woman is Southern, and that her name is Staley Hinton. So he was almost right when he said she was named Stanley. You've got to be careful when you correct children." Janey was prattling on because she didn't know what to say to Sandra. "Sandra," Janey said, suddenly, "don't you want to know what we think of him?"

Sandra looked shocked. "Actually, I don't," she said.

"Is it serious?" Janey persisted.

"Janey, really," Sandra said. She looked at the doorway, nervously. "We haven't slept together yet," Sandra finally said.

"Do it tonight!" Janey said.

"Well, I don't know that that's solved all your problems, Janey," Sandra said.

"Solved all what problems?"

"Quite frankly, it concerns me that you've had a third child," Sandra said. "I worry that they won't get the attention they need if you have so many, and if you continue to work."

"Who are you to talk to me like that?" Janey said.

"If you don't mind overstepping your bounds, I don't mind—"

Jasper came into the room. "Do you know that great line from Richard Brautigan?" he said. " 'There is some of each of us in the fire.' " He handed Sandra her drink. He was drinking a glass of wine.

"I think Brautigan meant that as a joke," Janey said.

"You've read Brautigan?" Sandra said.

"Oh, stop trying to put me in my place," Janey said. "I have three great kids, and you have one daughter who's bounded upstairs like a dog."

"Bitch!" Sandra said.

It was another half hour before we were called to the table. When we did sit down, I felt sure this was one of the last times we would gather this way—that the storm had brought us together, but that it was not really uniting us. So much of what went on seemed wearisome. Dowell didn't know what to say to anyone, and Barbara, I finally realized, would have been just as nervous whoever sat at her table. She was accustomed to her nervousness; she fretted about whether Dowell was enjoying his food, worried that the candle wax would drip on the tablecloth. I had never had an adolescent rebellion—I knew better; I had seen what a huge task my aunt had taken on when she took me into her home, and I knew I should be grateful—but sitting at the table that night, I felt peevish and petulant. I was mad at Bob for not being there. I thought Frank was taciturn, and that he rarely did his share to make conversation. Frank was fine one-on-one, but he hated gatherings and let everyone know he was present, but absent. I had given up trying to like Sandra. She was uptight and unpleasant, and I distrusted her boyfriend simply because he liked her. Or maybe he wasn't that wild about her, if they hadn't even slept together. I found myself thinking mean things about them, and I also felt mean-spirited toward Marie, who seemed to exist to cause problems, and toward Louise, too, because she had someone to mother her now, yet she'd still taken Bob away from me. I saw the family through the haze of my disappointment. I had glommed on to them because of what they represented, but as time went by it would have been fine with me if all of them except Janey, and maybe Frank, had disappeared, the baby crying and the boys pummelling each other in front of the TV, Marie no doubt hiding under a bed upstairs, as she often did, turned into a big dustball. I was pouting. But so were the others: Frank, going through the motions; Bob, spending his time with the people he chose, rather than suffering through evenings with his family; Sandra, wanting approval, but trying to get it by testing—by being absolutely unlovable. They were all as much cases of arrested development as I was. I looked around, glowering at them. Barbara was talking about a book she'd just finished: *Angels: God's Secret Agents,* by Billy Graham. Dowell alternated between polite attention and slowly deepening frowns. Frank drank. Sandra chimed in, changing the subject from angels to (surprise) herself. In the kitchen, the boys were at war. In the background, from the TV in the kitchen, Herve Villechaize screamed over and over again that a plane was coming. The dustball sulked upstairs. Barbara wondered aloud whether it might not be true that each of us had his or her own guardian angel.

Dara's performance as Grace Aldridge happened earlier than expected, at a different theater. Edward Quill resigned from the theater in Portsmouth over a dispute with the board, and in late April opened a theater in a converted barn in Exeter. As master of ceremonies of his own show, he was obviously in seventh heaven. He wore long capes lined in bright colors never found in nature, and glasses with enormous tortoiseshell frames. He wore black cowboy boots and rings on many fingers. He had been well provided for in Grace Aldridge's will, it turned out. She had inherited stock from her first marriage—stock she might have cashed in and led a different life, though apparently she'd enjoyed being a beetle riding downstream on a leaf (Dara's image; not mine).

I went alone to opening night. I had gotten my hair done, and wore a new wool-crepe navy-blue dress that cost more than anything I had ever bought. I was being brave. I was the Woman Rejected. In the first big fight Bob and I had after the blizzard, he announced that he wanted children, and complained that I had taken the occasion of my part-time job to distance myself from the family. It didn't matter that he also had distanced himself. He, at least, had not bought what he called "a flower" from Snell's greenhouse. He, unlike me, grieved for his dead grandmother—he had just that day placed flowers on her grave *and there were no other flowers there* and was commuting regularly to Boston, trying to help Louise overcome her anxiety. As he presented himself, he was so chivalrous he might as well have been doing those things while riding a white horse. Perhaps dramatically wearing a long, Edward Quillish cape lined in green velvet, charging forward with his sword (or snow shovel?). He spoke of the maturity that was a necessary prerequisite for parenthood. Of the need to be vigilant about the path one chose in life. It seemed I was a monster not only for not wanting children but for never having suggested we get a dog. In the second fight, he most certainly did not want to find himself married to a wife who was a reluctant mother, and he wondered whether my having suggested we go together to the SPCA, if it was so important to him, was not an indication of where my heart was truly inclined: toward four paws instead of his projected four children.

"Maybe he's trying to outdo Frank," Janey said with consternation when I told her about Bob's recriminations. The night *Grace: A Graceful Life* was to premiere, Bob informed me that I was a sycophant, a person who lived vicariously through the dubious accomplishments of a woman who sponged off men, tried her best to wreck marriages, and who was conceited enough to think that her paltry performances in vastly overrated dramatic productions would add up to a meaningful life, while in reality she was a liar, a home wrecker, and an opportunist.

This despicable creature had given me her ring. She had tried to return it to Tom Van Sant weeks before, and he had taunted her about how willing she was to just give up on their relationship the minute the going got tough. Bernie had decided it would be best to give the baby up for adoption to a couple in Georgia; he was not in favor of the plan, and was always on the phone with her, or with his lawyer, and when he was not communicating with them, he was trying to change Dara's mind about how nice it would be to have a baby in the house. (*"Sweetie: Can he possibly, possibly, have misunderstood what is already my complete and absolute misery at being dragged even this far into this mess?"*) She had flung the ring at him, and it had taken him an hour, on his hands and knees, to find it, and as he searched, he had begun to cry. His crying had become contagious, and then Dara had wept half the night, and she had told me on the phone the morning she asked me to take the ring for safekeeping that no amount of makeup was going to disguise her swollen eyes. She told him she had no intention of marrying him, in large part because he had never banished Bernie from his life, and she had come to doubt he ever would, if he sought custody of the child. She reiterated that she would not consider having children— not her own, and certainly not anyone else's—before she had a career. She gave him a book by Germaine Greer. She said his anguish was manipulative—that he was torturing Bernie, as well as her. He had insisted on too many things, she had come to see: he had pressured her to move in; he had tried to control her financially, even if he manipulated through generosity. She wanted him to take the ring back. She would offer it calmly, and if he truly had her best interests at heart, he would take it back. He had said to her: "It would break my heart if I had to put it back in that little box. It would be like burying my mother a second time." She had suggested he put it in a dish. He had said he hated her. She had said she knew that. It turned into quite a fight, she told me, but in the end, when he had begun to weep again, she had been so drained that she stopped defending her rights. So much anger and bitterness. She would have to be glad she had something to command her attention. She would have to be happy that now, rather than being so unhappy at home and then playing trapped, miserable Nora, she could at least portray a woman whose life had not been lived in extremis.

There were not many people in the theater. Edward Quill made the rounds in the lobby, and two pretty high school students offered cups of tea. One was the daughter of the architect who had renovated the barn; the other was a foreign exchange student from Bolivia, who lived with the first girl's family. Placing a sugar cube in my cup, the Bolivian girl had giggled when the sugar cube began to bubble. They were charming, dressed in crushed-velvet dresses, slightly elegant and slightly awkward in the way they served tea. They both wanted to be actresses, Dara had told me. Outside, about fifty people were noisily chanting, "Seabrook no, Seabrook no, save our earth, Seabrook no." The demonstrators were waving signs. Some carried dolls painted black. In the distance, I could hear the wail of sirens. "Seabrook no," the voices continued.

"Ghastly riffraff," Edward Quill said to a man standing near me. He was becoming more and more nervous that the protesters, who were mistaken about the governor's being at the play, would discourage people from coming in. I gave an usher my ticket, got a program, and walked behind the usher to my seat. More people arrived in the five minutes before the curtain rose, but the crowd was still disappointing for opening night. One of them was Tom Van Sant. Wouldn't you know it: just when Dara had given me the ring because she feared she might do something impulsive with it, like throw it out the car window, Tom came in and sat down in an aisle seat two seats away. He must have suspected he was out of favor with a close friend of Dara's, because he only nodded hello and then quickly looked away. I twirled the ring so the band was on top of my hand. I said what I hoped was a polite hello. He nodded. His eyes were quite red. I knew Dara had asked him not to attend the performance, but he'd gone back on his word.

When the lights dimmed, Edward Quill walked from behind the dark brown curtain. Vaguely, faintly, the protesters could still be heard. At first I assumed he would be welcoming the crowd, but instead, he began to recite his preface: *"She was a woman of her time in each time she lived,"* Quill said. He had memorized the lines. Looking at some distant point, he said: *"She was an artist who recorded the day's subtle nuances as . . ."* Everyone sat listening attentively, though as he continued to talk, Tom eventually slid forward in his seat and covered his eyes with one hand. The preface was short, but the audience's attention span was even shorter. Quill was the warm-up act keeping them from the main event. He was a curiosity they would have been just as happy to dispense with. I think I was reading minds correctly: the longer Edward Quill stood there in his cowboy boots and Count Dracula cape, the itchier the men in the audience became. Men began to whisper to their wives. In my peripheral vision, I was watching Tom Van Sant, and wondering if he was crying. When he lowered his hand I looked quickly at him. He did not seem to have been crying, but he did say, quite conversationally, as though there were no space between us, "The poor bastard's hanging himself."

"Shh," I said, but many people overheard him.

*". . . Nora, in Ibsen's masterpiece,* A Doll's House," Edward Quill said, then clasped his hands like the good student who has finished his formal recitation, and exited stage left.

To my surprise, when the curtain rose, I saw the enormous faces of Mrs. Bell and Mrs. Denton projected onto a screen at the back of the stage. Dara had told me nothing about the production, because she wanted it to be a complete surprise. It certainly was: their faces were so alarming I jumped back in my chair. I felt like an ant, staring up at a skyscraper. They had been filmed talking about their friend Grace. But what the purpose could have been—why they had been filmed in such extreme close-up—was a mystery. Instead of revealing character, the closeness of the lens tended, rather, to impart an abstract quality to what we looked at. The enormous faces crowding the screen made me so uncomfortable—who wanted to see craterous moon chins, the worms of wavily pencilled eyebrows?—that I wanted to look anywhere but at the screen. My eyes darted around, and finally locked with Tom Van Sant's. He shook his head slowly from side to side. I looked away quickly, afraid that he would start talking again. The only talk, though, except for a few whispers, a few initial gasps, was coming from the two old women on the screen, who were chattering away the same way they had in our car after the funeral. They were discussing Grace Aldridge's various marriages, and they must have been excited to be filmed, because instead of one waiting for the other to finish, each chimed in with asides and contradictions. They were having a great time, but the size of their faces, and the rush of their words, became increasingly surreal. Finally, someone decided that whatever was going on was meant to be humorous, and laughed. No one else laughed, but people began to whisper. By then, though, I was trying hard to concentrate on what the two women were saying: it was something about quickie divorces and marriages in Reno—or was it Las Vegas? Mrs. Bell wanted to know. It was essentially a rundown of Grace Aldridge's early marriages, but I only followed what was being talked about because the two women had discussed the same things riding in the backseat of our car. They were so animated, and their mouths so fun house large, that you tended to divide your attention between listening and staring. It was going on much too long. It was gossip, only gossip, in extreme close-up.

As the old women's voices gradually became fainter, the audience began to realize there was a person onstage. I suppose because she was dressed all in black she looked even smaller, but below the enormity of Mrs. Bell's and Mrs. Denton's faces anyone would have looked tiny. Their faces, with mouths gaping, were frozen on the screen. They had become silent. Below, as if taking a casual stroll, Dara walked slowly for a few paces, then turned and glanced in the direction of the audience, though it was clear that really she was looking into the distance. She was like a person sleepwalking, and everyone became hushed, observing her. Every motion was almost Kabuki slow. I began to think that she might never speak, and it made me—as was no doubt intended— terribly anxious. I was used to Dara's asking a probing question looking deep into my eyes, as if she were trying to see the answer appear on the back of my skull.

"You," she finally said, in a small voice. Again, she was looking somewhere, and nowhere. "Have you been married? Were you a bride at nineteen?"

In fact, I had been. I had married Bob near the end of my sophomore year at the University of New Hampshire, against the advice of Aunt Elizabeth, my guidance counsellor, and my best friend. There was nothing wrong with Bob; I was just too young. They all said that, in various ways. I had thought: I wasn't too young to handle everything else that happened. Maybe by choosing something, I'd get the upper hand with fate. I didn't really believe it, but at the time it had seemed important to have instigated a plan. Not to wait for something to happen. My master plan had been: sex; more sex; engagement; marriage. Joining a ready-made family had been a bonus.

Dara was narrating the story of Grace Aldridge's unhappy first marriage. That had not been part of the manuscript. Edward Quill must have learned about it from the old ladies. Dara moved around the stage looking like a totemic bird: lean, and darkly elegant; you wondered what its wing span would be. There was that possibility: that out of her smallness, something expansive would eventually emerge. As Grace, she spoke quietly, her tone of voice underscoring the unremarkability of her life. The cumulative effect, however, was quite different: as Dara moved, standing in one quadrant to narrate her first marriage, moving elsewhere for the continuation of the monologue, I began to perceive of her as a chess piece that could miraculously move itself, and as the husbands died, or as the marriages were annulled, and the men never seen again, it was as if Grace Aldridge—self-propelled—was winning a game of chess; after much consideration, Dara would move in a way that seemed very deliberate, and then the conjured-up person whom she had convinced you all the while she talked was so real would vanish, as if plucked from the game by invisible fingers. Between each marriage, Dara would stand immobile as the sound track of Mrs. Bell and Mrs. Denton's chatter resumed, and the screen revealed the old ladies' faces reanimated from the freeze-frame. "I suppose we've all heard of Our Lady of the Flowers," Mrs. Denton said, "but what you have to know about Mr. Dubbell is that he was Our Tyrant of the Vegetable Patch." They chortled and sighed and banished people with a blink. Were they the stand-ins for God, the way Fitzgerald, in *The Great Gatsby,* had made T. J. Eckleburg a haunting visage that presided over a godless world? I was thinking back to my classes at the University of New Hampshire. About meeting Bob, becoming determined to marry him. No, I didn't want an engagement ring—a simple wedding band would be fine. I had promised Aunt Elizabeth I would finish college, but then I had quit. I thought Bob and I needed more money, and I was willing to work for it. Bob was the good student. Bob was the one who would really need a college degree, I had thought. Underneath my finger, I felt the tiny bulge of Dara's ring: the rubies and diamonds. The person who had given it to her was sitting two seats away, and he had no idea I was wearing it.

There was no intermission. After half an hour, a man and woman sitting in front of me whispered urgently for a few seconds, then got up and walked up the aisle. During the next half hour, several other couples left. I began to be extremely annoyed. Dara was mesmerizing as she recited the story of Grace Aldridge's life, and I saw for the first time, in the way Dara moved, in the way she softened her voice to inaudible whispers so that connecting sentences elided, that Grace Aldridge did, after all, have some personal sense of culpability. In the manuscript, she had seemed only to have been acted upon, but Dara's performance gave you the sense that Grace realized she bore responsibility for the deterioration of so many unions. How could Dara herself, that night she and Tom and I had sat in the kitchen looking at the carbon copy, have ever laughed, if now she could see such inherent power and tragedy—such dimension—in Grace's life? I felt envious of Dara's power. She really had made a silk purse. That people were walking away from it was as unbelievable to me as people not chasing money blowing around in a windstorm. They didn't get it: they didn't see the pathos; they couldn't see their narrow, monogamous lives as having anything in common with a woman who had married and divorced and married again—they didn't see that having taken the first step themselves implied that they, too, might become habituated to marriage.

I thought it was an inspiring performance. I liked it so much, while almost everyone else apparently liked it so little, that I wrote a piece for the local paper, explaining the play. The paper printed it. Among people who knew me, it was taken as a position paper: a quite unexpected feminist stance—which elicited from my former employer, Penny, at least, an approving letter. Edward Quill later carried a copy with him when he talked to off-Broadway producers. Dara was grateful that I had validated her as much as she had validated Grace Aldridge. Angry theatergoers wrote letters to the newspaper, refuting my essay, but I was convinced I was right. What Bob, chagrined, called "the tempest in the teapot" was really the beginning of the whirlwind of self-confidence that picked me up and took me away from him.

At the end of August, Bob and I separated. He acted as if, by leaving, I were betraying him. Suddenly Dell was no longer a meaningless small town, as he'd chosen to portray it the night he'd said I overestimated Dara Falcon's talent, but a quintessentially advantageous place to be. I was turning my back not only on Bob and the family, but also on Dell's advantages, pretending there was nothing I could do there, as if Dell were so different from any other place. Even the great Dara Falcon had moved back to Dell, hadn't she? He urged me to move in with Frank and Janey for a while if I was so dissatisfied living with him. When I insisted I was leaving and was going to get a college degree, he wouldn't talk about school at all and insisted upon seeing my unwillingness to intrude on Frank and Janey as my dislike of his family. "Frank and Janey would be a dead end for me," I said. "Sure, they'd have me, but what would I have? I have to get an education. Quitting school was a big mistake, but it's not too late to go back."

"Then go stay with your great friends Tom and Dara until you get over your snit," he said. "Go drink champagne and think everything they do is amazing. Maybe he'll flirt with you again, or you and Dara can lock yourselves up in the room he gave her the money to decorate and despise men together. She can read her stupid scripts, and you can continue to hide your face in every book you can find. Or maybe you'd like to work at Snell's. Why don't you go ahead and join the competition? Give Barbara the big test: see if she's able to find a way to think that's perfectly wonderful, the way it's suddenly so wonderful to be with that robot, Churnin—the way opening day at the competition's just another occasion for a lovely party."

"Bob, listen to yourself: first Dell is a great place, and then when you start talking about who lives there, it's hell. A place *is* who lives in it. That's what a place is."

"And a place is also what you choose to make it," Bob said. "I admit that the wrong sort of people are doing the wrong thing here now. It's getting built-up; people are taking advantage of the place; they're living on the fringe, and not contributing anything. Does Van

Sant ever show up at a town meeting? In fact, did you ever consider going to a meeting?"

"Oh, stop trying to force small-town life down my throat. I read *Main Street* in school."

"You quit school," Bob said. "I don't know why you did, but you did. And now you don't know what to do, and I'm to blame, and the only solution is to go running back to school because Dell is a nowhere place that offers you nothing."

"I'm going to get a degree," I said. "I'm going to learn things and I'm going to meet people. People who'll actually talk about things that matter."

"Well, aren't you self-righteous. Should I have interrupted you while you sat around all summer, keeping your nose in a book? Were there things you were dying to talk to me about? Excuse me, but I was *working.*" He glared at me. "You know, Jean, you intend to do whatever pleases you. And I think you always have," Bob said. "I look back, and I think I fell for the oldest trick in the book. I thought that because you couldn't keep your hands off of me, you were in love with me. What was that about—all that sex? You don't have any interest in sex. And God forbid if it might lead to pregnancy. God forbid if we were like Frank and Janey, instead of angst-ridden like Van Sant and his ménage à trois. Ask Dara whether she doesn't have to put out to continue sponging off Van Sant. Ask her if she's really getting a free ride. Learn some lessons from your great friend about how to pretend, why don't you? Maybe we could be very modern and settle for pretending—if you come to your senses and want to come back, that is."

That same day, I withdrew money from the secret savings account that I had let sit in the bank ever since I learned of the payment that had been made to the families of the victims of the plane crash—what little was left after Elizabeth gambled it away. I had already applied to the University of Connecticut without telling anyone in the family I'd applied, and been accepted. I intended to study literature. A few days after Bob's nasty outburst, I was there. I drove to the university alone. On a bulletin board, I discovered the ad that led to my sharing a house with four other students, in Eastford, Connecticut.

I only saw it briefly before I decided it would be a perfect place to live. Like the pared-down set of *A Doll's House,* there was little furniture to distract you, and it was old—consolingly old—with sloping floors and brass hardware and prints of birds framed and hung on the walls. Only one of the people who lived there was at home to show me around, but he had lived there the previous year and said it didn't cost as much to heat as I might expect, and that they were desperate to find another roommate before school started. I could have my choice of rooms, including his, which he would move out of, if I liked that best. I followed him around, noticing the nice light, the bare floors.

Janey helped me move, in Frank's truck. Barbara wept and said her "oh my" mantra a thousand times. Janey also cried, but only because she couldn't believe I would be living so far away. She said she envied me for breaking away. I think she found it so frightening to consider the possibility that someone could take a stand and leave the family that she immediately became pregnant again as a way of restraining herself. All the way to Connecticut, Janey engaged in double-talk: I was doing the correct thing—the only thing I could do. I might be doing the wrong thing, judging Bob too severely; I might be frustrated with the whole family, and I might have just made Bob the fall guy. We both agreed, though, that Frank and Bob were conservative, rigid people. She told me that in the spring of 1977, when Nixon was on *David Frost,* Frank had stood and cheered when Nixon uttered his infamous "When the President does it, that means it is not illegal." She shook her head sadly. "You wonder what Pat Nixon thought, hearing that," she said.

"If he even told her it was on," I said.

"She tried everything to avoid marrying him," Janey said. "You know, when she was dating other men, Nixon used to drive her wherever she was going and wait for her. He proposed more than once, and she said no. Then she must have been worn down. She'd had a very sad life. She must have thought that, at some point, marrying Nixon was inevitable."

"She could have resisted him. Why couldn't she?" I said to Janey.

"Not everybody has it in them," Janey said. "And also, he's sort of a malevolent force, don't you think? God help me if I ever expressed that opinion in front of Frank, but that's what I think."

"What does Frank think about my leaving?"

"He thinks that for some reason you've decided you're too good for us. He's not angry at you. He's confused. He thinks it has to do with Dara. Bob thinks that, too; that's what he told Frank."

The implied question reverberated. She already knew I thought that was nonsense—that it was an easy way for Bob not to be account-able for his own lack of interest in the marriage. Who could believe that a husband who wanted to keep his wife would urge her to pretend to passion she didn't feel? I told Janey about Bob's outburst. She asked me to consider the possibility that my walking out on him had made him so frightened, he'd become vicious. "Maybe it's because of their fa-ther's death. His dying so young. So unexpectedly. If any of them think they're being left, they sort of go crazy. I think Drake went crazy when his first wife went back to her country for a visit, and he ruined the marriage by insisting she'd deserted him and refusing to have her back. And Frank: Frank would have you think that I'm about to throw it all up and walk out the front door and disappear just because I think it might be nice to live in a milder climate. Sometimes when he drinks, he gets morose about it: how I'm going to be gone tomorrow. Bob proba-bly came unhinged because he was being abandoned. Don't you think that's a possibility?"

"Janey—you're giving me Introduction to Psychology."

"Even so," she said, "does that mean that because it's obvious, it can't be right?"

I didn't answer her. I didn't want to fight with Janey.


In spite of his best efforts Edward Quill could not convince any-one in New York to produce the play. This was difficult enough for Dara—she'd had to take a job at the checkout desk of the Portsmouth library to make ends meet when she left Tom's—but she had also be-come Quill's confidante, and he was a demanding confessor; when she called me, she reported that he had begun to call at least twice a day from New York, in at least two wildly different moods. He was not in-dependently wealthy, as she had once assumed. Recently, he had told her about his bisexuality. He was having trouble finding what he called "a life partner," but increasingly, Dara began to suspect that what was really troubling him was that he could not meet anyone of either sex who was suitably rich in New York. She got angry at him for confusing business with pleasure—he had slept with a man, a would-be producer, but the next morning the possibility of putting on the play had disappeared as quickly as the breakfast dishes—and, although Dara did not say it to me, she seemed slightly offended that while he professed undying love for her, it was platonic and, clearly, even at that, a masquerade. What did he want? she began to wonder increasingly, and her best guess was disheartening: that in being fixated on her, he was gaily buzzing around the Diva—that they were all a bunch of losers, and she was the best leading lady he could find to worship. *("I mean, sweetie, we have to remember that this is the man who was engaged to Grace Aldridge.")* What was disheartening to me was that while I had changed my mind about Grace Aldridge, Dara had explained to me that her portrayal of her had been a put-on: she hadn't, in her heart of hearts, reinterpreted Grace—she had just decided that she could fool some of the people some of the time by unblinkingly transforming herself into a phoenix to rise out of the ashes of mediocrity. She had presented Grace Aldridge as the woman Edward Quill wished she had been. And now she had come to think, increasingly, that Quill was a foolish man. As she became more and more disillusioned with his inability to take their show on the road, she began to admit that he was not the person he claimed to be. Productions in converted barns in New Hampshire were one thing, but that would never sustain them, she said, making me uncomfortable by unintentionally echoing Bob. What was wrong with so many men? she wondered: Quill, deluded into thinking he had mercurial powers; Tom, bouncing like a ball between his house and the life he had once chosen with the woman he supposedly loved in New Hampshire, and his role as Sometimes Daddy in Chalybeate Springs, which she'd renamed Chilly Feet Springs because of his inability, even after so much time had passed, to decide between Big Bernie and the baby or her. She thought Bob was a simple coward for not having chased after me. In the end, in spite of my protests to Janey, I'd felt bad about leaving and tended to reflexively defend him when anyone said he sounded like a Mama's Boy, or a self-absorbed jerk, or whatever people came up with by way of response on the rare occasions I found myself describing the husband I had left.

Talking long distance, Dara and I would confer late at night. I had the smallest room in the house, with the largest fireplace, on the first floor. People coming and going with girlfriends and boyfriends, letting the dog, Sparkle, in and out, disturbed me early in the morning, but I stayed up later than anyone else, and from midnight on the house was quiet and seemed like mine alone. That was when the rates were low, and I would call Dara, who had become disgusted with Tom's indecisiveness and moved back to Portsmouth on a month-to-month basis, and into a tiny garret apartment above a florist's. She had left many of her things behind in the locked room at Tom's, just in case he came to his senses; the apartment was sparsely furnished with whatever the previous tenant had left behind. In our late-night calls, though, we would inevitably imagine living in more wonderful and exotic places where we would be surrounded by beautiful objects and be perfectly appreciated. I was going to work my way to the top; Dara was going to persevere until her talent was suitably recognized. In my first two months of school I had impressed my professors, or imagined I had, but I'd made no real friends. I was older than most of my classmates; this was not true at the house I lived in, but in class I didn't quite look or act like everybody else. The last time I'd been in college, although I hadn't been a hippie myself, the diverse people, the freewheeling style, must have put me at ease, I now realized; at the University of Connecticut, many of my classmates struck me as ultraconservative, relentlessly pleasant: they were paler, younger versions of Barbara, minus her dither and her maternal solicitousness. Dara assured me that it was never a virtue to fit in. I thought about Janey as an example of someone who had wanted to fit and who had—narrowly.

I still had Dara's ring. I wore it every day, even though the expensive ring was another thing that set me apart from the other students. Dara still had the alpaca jacket I had bought myself on impulse shopping one day with Janey in Boston, but I had decided not to mention it, assuming that if I didn't, she might not mention the ring. It didn't occur to me that it was actually Tom Van Sant's ring—or, at least, that it probably should have been. While her relationship with him remained in limbo, the ring remained on my finger, and I didn't give the slightest thought to who its real owner was. When anyone admired it, I said only, "Thank you." Wearing it also underscored the fact that Bob had never even given me an engagement ring—or much of anything else by way of a present, when I thought about it.

At night, I did think about it. I was rationalizing ending the marriage. I wallowed in self-pity because Bob had never given any thought to special days, or special songs, or meaningful trinkets or gifts. Would it have been futile to have tried to compensate, late, for my rather spartan upbringing? I had told him about it: he couldn't have thought I'd had love lavished on me, let alone tokens of affection. It was only much later, long after childhood, long past my adolescence, shortly before she married, that I discovered Elizabeth had gambled away most of the money I'd inherited during the time she was my legal guardian. Aunt Elizabeth, who'd looked dazedly out the front window, as if my parents hadn't died in the plane crash, as if, like the mysteriously disappearing and reappearing Mary Poppins, my mother, at least, might have bailed out to come drifting down with her special umbrella—Elizabeth had gone every year, on her birthday, to Las Vegas, until less than a quarter of my inheritance remained. She had told me this the summer before I went to the University of New Hampshire while we were eating hamburgers at a drive-in restaurant. I could never order Coke; she always brought a Coke from home, to save money. A milk shake was out of the question. Drinking my Coke, having asked her about setting up a checking account before I started college, I had somehow elicited that information. Living with her, I had just assumed that there had not been much money. I didn't know about insurance payouts. And because I had tried so hard to put the tragedy out of my mind, I certainly did not give any thought to what survivors got when their parents died in a crash. I had assumed that she had always done her best—she had certainly insisted that she was always doing her best—but there we sat, in her old Chevy, eating our hamburgers, and something had made her confess.

"What did you gamble on?" I finally asked her.

"Blackjack," she had said. She looked me right in the eye, her glistening eyes widening the way they did those times she meant to almost hypnotize me with the intensity of what she felt. The tip of her nose had wiggled slightly. It was as if she could sniff the money. But actually it had wiggled because she'd been about to cry. She had bent her head and let the tears fall, and even if I might have said something critical, that had stopped me cold. As she drove home, though, my half-uneaten hamburger still sitting on the paper wrap . . . I could remember pushing my finger around inside the bun, drawing out my finger red with ketchup and holding it up—holding up my finger and then pressing it to the windshield, drawing it down until the smear of ketchup paled and disappeared. She did not say a thing. She cleaned it off the window, also without comment. She must have, because the next day the smear had not been there. And that was one of the most distinct memories of my time with her: the smear on the glass. Many nights, the image still comes to me of Elizabeth at the window, the intensity of her gaze, the slump of her shoulders letting me know that nothing was out there: not my parents, not some storybook lady about to save people from their own helplessness.

"That was so cruel," Dara breathed into the phone, when I told her. "So cruel, to be a thief of your own loved one's money."

With distance between us, it was easier to say things to Dara. Since moving, I had told her more about my childhood than I'd told Bob in all the time we were together. He and I had talked and talked when we first met, though even in the beginning I had been restrained: something had made me want to say only so much, to ensure that he didn't pity me. Then years later, when I would have welcomed sympathy, I'd had no idea how to reopen such a discussion. He was my family, then, and—as he had said several times, when I'd brought up my odd, unhappy childhood—the past must be put behind me. The longer we were married, the more I resented his failure to make everything better. So out of some misplaced sense of propriety I had retreated. Like the runoff from a stream, though, my thoughts had eventually overflowed and trickled off—in the direction of Dara. She had a very literary bent; that analogy was the way she chose to express it. Because she gave me so much attention, and because she did not hesitate to express herself, I perceived in her the openness I hadn't experienced in Bob's family. They rarely discussed anything; they just acted, after they had determined what was best. Had Grandma ever talked to Barbara about her thoughts on being recruited, as such an old lady, as a replacement mother for Louise? Did Barbara ever confide to any of her children her thoughts about the pros and cons of marrying Dowell? Dowell fit right in: he was not so much an enigma as he was simply reluctant. They were all reluctant. When Bob and I separated, I got a note from Trenton saying that he hoped I would still consider him my friend. He said he understood that it must be very difficult to be married to someone who never asked questions, who didn't even seem to question himself. I was taken aback by the note, because I had never thought Trenton gave me a second's thought, much less that he had reservations about Bob. How interesting that one of Bob's friends had misgivings similar to mine, though I was sure I would never have known that if Bob and I had stayed together. Everyone—me included—was complicitous in letting the family remain isolated. When Pete was a little boy he had once approached a snowman on the front lawn and said, "When it warms up, you know, you'll melt." Though Janey had been greatly amused when she heard Pete's remark, his confronting the obvious was more than anyone else in the family ever managed.

Pete, Janey, Barbara—I thought of them often when I was away. Dara wanted me to drive back to see her new apartment. Eventually, I did. Driving up, I'd debated whether to call Janey and see if I could drop by, but that day happened to be Janey's birthday, and I thought that seeing me might make her sad. It was an odd experience, going back; I felt that at that period in both our lives, Dara and I were free floating, attached to no one, but too preoccupied to really be attached to each other either. The new apartment was a real step down from the unattractive apartment I'd seen that had once contained her wonderful inner chamber. She had not decorated it. There was only an alcove she used as a bedroom, with a cot set up to sleep on. Of course, there was no champagne. She made green tea, and we sat on Marimekko-covered cushions on the floor and sipped it, listening to the classical-music station on the radio, both of us feeling slightly martyred. I didn't want to go out, because I didn't want to meet anyone on the street I might know. I suppose I did feel ashamed, but I also felt angry: Dara and I had worked hard to attain something, then suddenly—because Tom had wanted a child, and in part because Bob had been so angry I had not wanted a child—our worlds had come unravelled. In Connecticut I had just begun to feel truly independent. Although I would have been able to be solvent even without Bob's help, once back in New Hampshire I began to feel that my independence was real only to the extent that I kept away from the place; I feared that my will might vanish if I spent any more time in or near Dell. Both Dara's solution and mine had been to throw ourselves into work; she had borrowed money and was taking voice lessons, as well as taking an acting class once a week with a man who had been her teacher in Los Angeles. In fact, the teacher had "floated her a loan," as she put it. He had also said she could stay overnight at his apartment near Copley Square if she wanted to, but she was afraid that what that meant was that she would have to have sex with him. "Lest we forget," Dara said, "men are not to be depended on—except, perhaps, for the uniformity of certain desires."

"Are you sorry you moved to New Hampshire?" I blurted out. Because I was obviously sorry I ever had. "You could get out if you wanted to, couldn't you?"

"Tomorrow," she said, "with my vast reserves of cash. And with the nation clamoring for my unique talents."

"But you do have that," I said. "All I have is the ability to study something and eventually know more about the subject. But I'm not creative. Nothing I've ever done has been creative."

"It's overestimated," Dara said. "Creativity only takes you so far."

"Don't talk like you've hit a dead end," I said. "You haven't."

"No?" she said. "I'm glad you don't think so. Lately I've been thinking back to certain discussions I had with Frank about how inescapable places become if you stay long enough. He thinks he hit a dead end, speaking of dead ends. So what does he do but procreate. I guess it's his version of having a big party at the end of the road."

"They all like to talk about how noble their suffering is," I said. But I meant Bob; I didn't really mean Frank. Frank always sounded more honest than Bob because he spoke more dispassionately. That was it: Frank seemed to be detached enough from his problems to sound like an authority.

Dara took my hand, the way she had at the Inn overlooking the beach. The way she had when she'd first examined my life line. "Tell me again that I haven't hit a brick wall," she said.

"You're between acting jobs," I said, holding her hand for a few more seconds before I let go. "This happens in your profession."

"You sound so sure," she said. "Maybe you're the proof that the opposite of what you say is true: get out of town, and the world will become more manageable."

"You've never had any trouble managing," I said.

"Are you joking? I'm in debt. I don't have a job. The man I might have married is shacked up with somebody else."

"You weren't really going to marry Tom, were you? I always thought"—what had I always thought?—"didn't you sort of fall in together when you were both on the rebound? You as much as said that."

Dara looked at me. "You listen too carefully," she said. "How about giving me sympathy just because I'm asking for it?"

"You wouldn't want that."

"I wouldn't?"

"No," I said. "You're always the one who wants to get on with things. When things aren't going right, you do something: You take classes; you move from Los Angeles to a place you'll be happier. You figure out how to get things done. You don't sit around waiting for sympathy."

"You're confusing movement with progress," she said.

"If that's the confusion, I'm still glad it's what I believe. I was stifled as a child, and as soon as I stopped being stifled, I stifled myself. I got married when I was nineteen. You always got out there and did things."

She looked at me. "Maybe this is my fault," she said. "Maybe when you've acted long enough, it gets ingrained, and people believe what they see."

"Why do you want to make me doubt myself because I think you've got volition?"

"Volition," she said. "Volition. That isn't a word I've heard in a very long time. My mother used to accuse me of having too much volition. It sounds vaguely clinical, like some part of the body timid people would immediately give a nickname to."

The phone rang. As she talked, I had the feeling that Dara was playing to two audiences—that she was playing to me, her visible audience, as well as playing to whoever was on the other end. "I'm so down in the dumps I haven't been practicing," Dara said. To me, she mouthed: *"Lex."* It was the man from Boston—the drama teacher. "Well, maybe I will," she said. "Maybe I will drive down the day before the class. It's not as if my presence is needed elsewhere." She listened for a few seconds, then spoke quietly into the phone, turning away so it was hard for me to hear. "I do remember," she said, just before she hung up. "Why would you think I'd forget?" When she put the phone down, she looked at me. "Why would you think I'd forget?" she said again, with exactly the same incredulous inflection, but when she locked her eyes on me, I froze; it was as if something in the past that had happened between us was being alluded to, and I searched my mind for what, exactly, she had in mind. My discomfort made her smile. "Poor Lex," she said. "All that matters to him anymore is that he was once the very best."

She left it that way; she left me assuming that she was speaking of sex.

Ly next visit with Dara was a little before Thanksgiving, when she drove to Eastford in what she had come to call the Brown Bomb. She had no idea what she would do to get around if my/her car quit on her, and she was worried because the mechanic had made it sound like it was a ticking time bomb. She got a tune-up and two used tires and made the trip anyway, claiming to be worried about my isolation.

I didn't think of it that way, though my initial elation about being on my own had dissipated. It was true that I had come to like the dog more than the other people in the house and saved my best rhetorical questions for the dog. That made me no stranger than a lot of people, I felt sure. I had had coffee twice with my favorite professor, but she managed to subtly communicate how busy she was; I also wasn't about to sit around the ugly, depressing student union assuming I might meet someone interesting. So I had been working harder, staying up late reading supplementary texts, rereading things I had already as-similated. How could Dara pretend to be so upset with my single-mindedness when she herself had spent days shut in her room, reading and taking notes, which was exactly what I now chose to do with my days? I had asked her that on the phone, but I knew I wouldn't get an answer. It was important to Dara to think we were soul mates, but any-time I compared our similarities, she either disagreed or changed the subject. If we were alike, Dara wanted us to be alike only in the ways she chose. The idea that I was a separate entity was ultimately no more pleasing a notion to her than it had been to Bob. Both of them had al-ways given me the covert message that they liked me just the way I was, though I began to realize what they really meant was that I should not change, because the things I did were a convenience for them. If I was lulled into a sense of false security, I would not question them as much as I might otherwise. A Billy Joel song that was popular then had seemed at first to express a lovely sentiment—that the singer loved the person he sang to "just the way you are." But they didn't know—or care—what way I was, and for the longest time, I didn't either. I had continued to hold on tenaciously to those things—okay: people—I had first latched onto for security. These truths had become apparent to me almost as soon as I left Dell, and I was so grateful to have realized them that by the time Dara visited, I was wary of falling under her influence again. She was right that I had hero-worshipped her. That had become apparent to me the moment I left New Hampshire, though I hadn't told her that for fear it might seem unnecessarily insulting. My new awareness made me guarded. Her own guardedness only took a different, more flamboyant form: she appeared to be always involved, engrossed, performing in one capacity or another, more than living up to my previous expectations of her, whether or not a real stage was involved. She took more than her share of a room's air is the way I think of it now. I think that for a long time I had been breathing shallowly, resisting the impulse to compete for air, even, when the person next to me was—I suppose I intuited this long before it came to me clearly—fighting for her life.

When she arrived on her self-proclaimed mercy mission, ostensibly rejuvenated by her acting teacher's fucking and enthralled again with the world of possibility, she sat on the side of my bed, staring. She had gotten her hair cut, and the thick bangs and the evenness of the cut had the odd effect of making her look a little like a blond Louise Brooks. She had on jeans and a jade-green sweater with an enormous turtleneck she said Lex had bought for her at a shop in Back Bay. She also was wearing the alpaca jacket, which I didn't comment on. I had on the ring, which she looked at briefly, taking hold of my fingers and saying "pretty" in a faraway little voice before she let go of my hand. She sat amid the tangle of covers, and I stretched back, leaning on my elbows. A fire was going in the fireplace. The dog was curled up beside me. Upstairs, somebody was knocking around. Soon we heard the Bee Gees, then the bedsprings creaking. Dara rolled her eyes. "I don't know about this," she said. "This big old dilapidated house in the middle of nowhere with people you don't really—"

"But Dara," I said, "it's not as if you're living in such a wonderful place yourself."

"But darling, this isn't temporary."

"You don't understand," I said. "That's the point. There's no way anyone who wasn't rich could begin to restore this house. I don't have to run errands or cook or celebrate their birthdays or even encounter them much. It's nice, actually. I read all the time. I take Sparkle for long walks. I listen to music." I nodded in the direction of the stereo with one speaker I'd inherited with the room—an exchange for taking the draftiest room in the house.

"But this place is creepy," she said. She looked at the paint-chipped ceiling. At the masking tape over the cracked window next to the bed. At the furniture with peeling veneer.

"I like it," I said.

She considered this. I'd indicated the coat hook when she came in, but she'd perched on the bed without taking off her coat. She was like someone nervously visiting a patient in a hospital. Finally, she got up and examined the books in the bookcase. "I'm going to take your *Godot,*" she said. "Then I can write you something intelligent about it." She put it in her purse and sat again on the bed. "You know, Edward has just sublet an apartment in the Village," she said. "He says I can use it whenever I want. I think maybe I should go to New York and make the scene, if you know what I mean. If I did that, would you want to come with me?"

"I'm in school," I said.

"On the weekend," she said. "I am a person who greatly admires our educational system—having achieved the rank of Phi Beta Kappa in college, back in those days when I could focus my attention on *anything* I thought could give me the answer to life's mysteries."

"He makes me nervous," I said.

"Edward? I can understand that," she said. She shifted farther back on the bed. She picked up my pillow and folded it, putting it behind her. She leaned back. She placed her hands across her stomach. I was being appraised. My living inelegantly clearly perplexed her.

"When he goes to London at the end of the month, maybe you can join me at the New York apartment."

"What about your job?"

"Oh, that," she said. "To be honest with you, I've quit. I borrowed a little money and I'm commuting to Newburyport to take an acting class with one of Lex's old rivals, one night a week. It's a lot closer than Boston. I've also started the Alexander Technique, which gives me the dreamy feeling that I am floating through life—at least, for the first hour after the lesson."

In the old days, I would have said, *You quit your job?*

"Sweetie," she said, "don't you miss people? I mean, are you suffering and too proud to admit it? About Bob, and everything?"

"It was a mistake, trying to fit into that world," I said. "I'm glad I realized it before it was too late."

"He had dinner with me last night," she said. "He says you won't return his calls."

"You had dinner with him?"

"At Trenton's," she said. "I didn't have dinner with just *him.*"

"And?"

"He seems very sad. He called Trenton wanting to get together and have a barbecue Trenton had promised him, out on the back deck. Never mind that it's November, and not exactly the time to have a cookout. But Bob always did want to collect his due, didn't he? Those errands he kept you doing constantly, I mean. Things are always pretty quid pro quo with Bob. But anyway: I got the benefit of having a very good grilled steak. I think he was surprised when he showed up and I was there."

"I'm sure he was."

"Aren't you curious about what I was doing there?"

"Dell's a very small place. Everybody knows everybody else. I presume you met Trenton, and the two of you hit it off."

She frowned slightly. "Are you angry at me about something?" she said.

"No," I said. It was a disingenuous answer. I was put out with her—not angry, just put out—because her presence reminded me of what I'd left behind. And also because she disapproved of what I was doing.

"Well, I'm modelling for him," she said. "He saw me in *A Doll's House* and wrote me a fan letter, and eventually we had a drink, and he asked if I wanted to model. He said he'd thought of the idea long ago, but that strange girlfriend was apparently very territorial. She had to approve all his models! Can you believe that? I mean, even Trenton finally wised up about how possessive she was. He compared her to Jo Hopper—you know: the painter's wife. Who apparently insisted she be in all his paintings, she was so jealous of other women. But don't you think that at some point, even poor old Jo Hopper must have sat on the side of their tacky bed or slumped at some table in her god-awful clothes for the umpteenth time and figured, *Fuck this.* Anyway: she went to the Iowa Writers' Workshop. The mystery girlfriend, I mean."

"Trenton's a good painter," I said.

"Sweetie, you seem so distant. It isn't anything I've done, is it?"

"Do you want your ring back?" I blurted out. She was obviously surprised. So was I. My words hung in the air.

"You only left your husband. You're not trying to leave me too, are you?" she said.

That was the moment when I could have said that I was. But it wasn't at all clear to me that day that I wanted to leave her. Even though the ring was spoken of in the context of marriage, it didn't come clear to me that it had become her love token to me, as well as Tom's love token to her. There was the moment I could have disengaged; there was the opportunity to break off with her, however precipitous it might have been. That day, seeing her in person after I'd realized she'd levelled with me when she'd insisted she wasn't living a unique, exemplary life, the spell had been broken, though what I said was a reflection of my own surprise at what I had almost set in motion. I said that of course I wasn't trying to sever my ties with her. The second I spoke, her relief was instantaneous. "Thank God," was all she said.

We took the dog for a walk, down past the farm at the end of the road. We talked about meaningless things: the weather; the area; the fact that she had recently begun to play indoor tennis. She had sorted out her confusion and decided to be quietly angry at me. I'd forced her to admit that I mattered to her. That had always been our implicit understanding, of course, but before she had always had the upper hand: we met to talk about her problems; she was the self-dramatizing, eccentric femme fatale, I was the dutiful little housewife; I was the audience, she the star; for too long, while I had gone on under the delusion that I had been the principal actor in the play that was my life, that play could more properly have been called *My Life, Starring Dara Falcon.* Then the balance of power had shifted, and as we walked, we both sensed it. But leaving Bob had made me—at least temporarily—more callous than I would have expected. I liked my newfound power, and I also didn't mind her discomfort. For a long while I had been attached to people who had their own trajectory, in which I figured only when it was convenient. They didn't bear me any malice, but the family—most of the family—was impervious to what I really thought or felt. Being away from them, I had begun to realize how they cued me to keep my distance: all Barbara's sighs, letting the listener know she already felt overburdened; Bob's remoteness, which he masked by presenting himself as a practical, plainspoken fellow; Frank's immediate self-deprecation ("I am Superman") to dissuade you from being the first to judge him insufficient. His drinking wasn't to be spoken of. His affair with Dara. Maybe he'd let himself appear vulnerable to Bob, but he would never have said anything to me about his relationship with Dara, or have told me about the letters, or about how she frightened him suggesting a suicide pact. The guys: the brothers were the guys, with their own secret codes, their own rules of behavior.

"You know," I said, deciding to be provocative myself for once, "Frank said something a while back to Bob that I've never gotten out of my mind. It was the strangest thing, and to tell you the truth, I have trouble believing it. What he said was that you had written him some letter proposing love and death. Suicide, I mean. Having sex in some hotel. And then you'd drive off a bridge."

She stood stock-still. I also stopped walking. Standing in the middle of the road, I turned to look straight at her. The dog sat down and, when no one moved for a few seconds, or spoke, whined. I patted the dog, then straightened up and gave Dara a look every bit as searching as the looks she'd given me so many times.

"Frank said *what?*" she said.

"That's what he told Bob."

"Then that would explain why Bob thinks I'm a nutcase," she said.

"He does, actually," I said. "You knew that?"

"My darling, I am not insensitive," she said. "At dinner at Trenton's last night, he looked at me like I was something in a petri dish."

"He was always worried you'd do something that would—oh, what did he think?—he thought I should watch out," I said.

"Amazing," she said, slowly. "I wonder why Frank would invent something like that?" And then, with perfect timing: "And also, if Bob believed it, and if he tried to spook you about me, why do you think he would try to kiss me goodnight in Trenton's driveway?"

"I don't know," I said, in the only quick comeback I could ever remember making. "Do you think he was drunk?"

The lines were drawn. I'd confronted her, and she'd confronted me. I don't think she thought I had it in me—and probably back in New Hampshire, I wouldn't have. There seemed every possibility that at the end of the walk she'd get in her car and drive away, and that would be the end of it. Which was suddenly confusing to me, because at the edge of my consciousness, I realized I wasn't as angry at her as it seemed: that she'd caught the blame for what other people had done to me, for the way other people had acted.

"Let's drive into Ashford. There's a good coffee shop there," I said. "I'll buy us coffees." It came out fine. Neutral. I felt the malice receding.

"Sounds nice," she said, as if I hadn't recently insulted her.

"It's really not the boonies here," I said. "There are some very nice places. I've been on some beautiful hikes, too."

"Maybe sometime we could go walking in the woods," she said.

Point registered: she wanted there to be a next time.

"Not in hunting season," I said.

Meaning: not soon. Certainly not today. Let's not prolong today any longer than necessary.

Back at the driveway, the dog hopped in the car, and we took him with us. He stood between the seats, with two paws on Dara's lap, and sniffed the air through the inch of open window. Dara patted him. She also looked out the window, deliberately distancing herself.

At the coffee shop, we ordered coffee at the counter. I deliberately did not ask if she wanted dessert. She didn't mention it. We looked around for a table. There was a table for six, which was too large, and one for two. It was not until we approached it and she overtook me that I realized what she was doing. She was taking the inside seat, so her back wouldn't be to the room.

On the way back to New Hampshire for a pre-Christmas visit, I stopped at a craft shop and bought a foot-high upright mouse, dressed in white, its gray tail sticking out from a hole in its skirt, a little white nurse's cap perched on its head. I paid cash, though I had recently applied for and received my first credit card. It had a seven-hundred-and-fifty-dollar limit, which I thought I might need if I decided to visit Dara in New York. She had expressed her frustration that the second time I'd returned to New Hampshire, she was gone, staying in Edward Quill's apartment while he was in London. She had told me that he slept on red satin bedding and had velvet thongs that matched his sheets. She gave me an inventory of the things she'd found in his apartment, from the spotlit shell sitting on a Lucite cube on top of the toilet tank underneath an Edward Weston photograph of a similar shell, to a rhinestone-encrusted riding crop, found in with the umbrellas. She thought that Edward Quill was, as she put it, "just too far gone" to be able to help her; how—if it was true—he managed to have meetings with producers and directors, she couldn't imagine. She thought he might be delusional or, at the very least, a consummate liar. He was living off the money Grace Aldridge had left him. Grace's engagement photograph was on his bedside table, along with a photograph of a young man Dara described as looking like the bird in "Peanuts." She wore his bangles and used his hairspray. And she wondered aloud what could possibly have been going on between him and Grace Aldridge, whom she called "that little blue-haired lady," although Grace's hair had been white, not blue. I was tempted to go visit his apartment. It had really begun to sink in with me that people lived very differently from one another. (Gail Jason, my favorite professor, lived with a black futon on a black frame and two black metal chairs with fake-leopard cushions, a kitchen table with four more chairs padded with black cushions, and little else except books, books, books.)

Going back to visit Janey and Barbara—even going back to the house I had shared with Bob (though I still wasn't sure I wasn't going to ask him to meet me in some neutral place)—was sure to be daunting. While my room in Eastford was hardly fascinating, I had come to like its shabbiness. I thought the cracks in the wall and the shavings of paint gave the room character. It was totally my environment, shared only with the dog, for whom I'd laid a pallet, the walls newly hung with a series of paint-by-number landscapes I'd bought at a junk store. I congratulated myself for having a sense of humor. Perhaps it had been liberated because of the books I was reading, or because of the underground movies I'd come to love, screened on campus in the auditorium of the Physics Building every Friday night. Gail Jason's favorite mode was the ironic, which, while it did not exactly constitute a sense of humor, still persuaded me that detachment could be amusing, rather than just a cover-up, as it was with Bob. I was discovering who I was slightly late, but at least I had begun to think about myself, instead of about everyone else, and I had also thrown off my Republican cloth coat. On cold days, I wore a purple poncho over a fisherman's knit sweater, well-worn jeans, and men's size-six hiking boots. In October I'd written a long letter to Aunt Elizabeth, asking her whether she didn't feel guilty for what she'd done. I asked if she had gambled because of an irresistible urge (I said that that seemed unlikely to me, since she'd felt the urge on schedule, once a year, year after year) or to punish me. I asked her to explain herself, either by letter or by phone. By December, she still had not responded. As I drove, I listened to "Sweet Baby James": James Taylor, singing about "the turnpike from Stockbridge to Boston." It was good driving music: appropriate to where I was; elegiac—appropriate to my state of mind.

Naturally, I went first to Janey's. She ran out without a coat and hugged me as I got out of the car. I was so thickly padded, I could hardly feel her embrace. She had on tennis shoes and plaid slacks and a blouse made of material that looked like autumn leaves. It wasn't just her maternity clothes; she dressed like an older person, I realized: ill-fitting slacks; an ugly blouse that had no style. But I was happy to see her, and my impulse was to try to pull her into the car and drive away with her, just steal her away, make her sit through the same classes I sat through, read *Rosencrantz and Guildenstern Are Dead,* see *Blowup,* read the same "Zap" comics.

"So you're doing really well in school?" she said. She was like the proud, solicitous parent I'd never had. She was beaming at me. I could do no wrong.

The baby was crawling. Pete was at a friend's house. Max was accompanying his father on a ride to the dump. She expected them back any minute.

I picked up the baby, and her face clouded over. I gave her to Janey before she actually began to cry. Jinx the dog sniffed my leg intently, no doubt smelling my dog, who was not really my dog, but whom I thought of that way. Janey wanted to do everything at once: give me coffee; show me the completed downstairs; urge Joanna on me a second time. She was four months pregnant, but already looked quite large. She held Joanna in one arm and gently clasped her own belly, rolling her eyes upward as if the pregnancy were some strange, momentary digression in which her body was participating—something slightly amusing that didn't need to be apologized for, but that wasn't exactly correct either, like Joanna's teetering walk.

I went outside and found the bag with the nurse mouse and brought it in to Joanna. She hesitated to take it, but Janey peered in the bag and exclaimed, and then Joanna reached in. She lifted the mouse by one ear and immediately dropped it on the floor, then stared at it. I picked it up and rocked it in my arms, pronouncing it a "nice mousey." She reached for it. Again, I gave it to her, and she tossed it on the floor, then reared back in her mother's arms. Janey sat her down. She started to walk, fell, then crawled to the mouse. When she reached it, she held it by one ear and raised her other hand, to suck her thumb.

"Pick her up," Janey said. I did, and Joanna accepted it. She reached out and pinched my nose. I removed her hand. She reared back again, but I reached out and braced her. "Do you remember your aunt Jean?" I said. "Do you remember me?"

"She'd better remember," Janey said. "The girls have got to stick together."

We went into the kitchen. She offered me soup or a sandwich or both or neither: I could have a Snickers bar that she kept hidden from the boys, or I could have . . . she was looking through the cupboard.

I told her I wasn't hungry.

"I'm hungry all the time," she said. She opened a jar and dug around in it. She lifted out the Snickers. She unwrapped it, put it on the counter, and cut it in two pieces. "Save me from myself," she said. I reached out and took a bite of the other half. Joanna reached for it and began to bounce in my arms. I chewed quickly, then put the remaining piece in my mouth. Joanna looked at me, wide-eyed. Then she frowned and wailed.

"At least, we have to stick together except where sharing candy is involved," Janey said.

I jostled the baby. It was hard to stop smacking my lips, the sweetness lingered so long.

"Sit down," Janey said. "Tell me everything."

"How are you?" I said. Joanna leaned toward the floor. I placed her on it. "How's everybody? How's—"

"I mean, it's not as if we never talk on the phone," Janey said. "But that's so different, isn't it?"

I nodded yes. I began to think that if something meaningful wasn't said soon, it never would be. But what meaningful thing was there to say? Should I tell her, again, that I was sure I'd made the right decision to leave? I worried that if I said that, I might be talking more to myself than to her. Still, it was all I could think to say.

She listened. She said: "You do seem happier."

"What about you?" I said. "Are you feeling okay?"

"I'm fine," she said. "I won't be working again until after the baby's born. I was bleeding a little. Same problem every time. I've been off already for a couple of weeks."

"And Frank and the kids are fine?"

"Frank's got more of a nesting urge than I do," Janey said. "He's excited about the new baby. He's going to turn the porch into a nursery. We're waiting for the building permit."

"I guess you need the space," I said. I liked their porch the way it had always been, with the blowsy screens and the hydrangeas outside. I hated to see their porch disappear.

"I don't know. I don't see why every child has to have a separate bedroom, when the littlest are so, you know, little."

"Maybe he should have become an architect," I said.

"He really thinks more is better. He told me last night that if we had another boy, he'd still like to try for a second girl."

"You wouldn't, would you?"

"You sound so horrified," she said. "Really: What's the difference between four and five?"

"Janey!"

"I know," she said, the bubble bursting. "But he sounded sincere. Maybe this is the big new thing. Fatherhood, I mean. Maybe it's because he was so close to his own father. I don't know."

"Have him visit the grave, instead of having a fifth child," I said.

She laughed. She said: "You always make me laugh."

"I suppose I'm not the one to give advice," I said. "You and Frank have always worked things out. I just worry for you, that you—"

"I know you do," she said. "I appreciate it."

"Would you do it over again?" I said.

"Are you kidding? Of course I would." She got a glass of water. "I mean, everybody has bad days," she said.

"You don't think I've just been having a bad day, do you, Janey?"

"No," she said, frowning. "No—I assume you thought long and hard about it, and—"

"I didn't. It just struck me that everything was wrong. That the only way to fix anything was to leave."

"I'm sure you thought about it more than that," she said. She examined her fingernails. "Well, I guess if I had it to do over, I wouldn't have moved to Dell," she said. "Frank would have done fine somewhere else. Frank can do all sorts of things. We could have . . . I don't know. We could have moved away and done something. I know he could have."

"Do you ever talk about it with him?"

"Oh, in a way. I guess it's become something of a joke. He always answers me as if I'm a broken record, saying we should go to Florida. He knows it wouldn't have to be Florida. And that if it was, I'm not talking about Miami Beach. You know Frank: he likes to kid me, and he also doesn't like to focus on what he doesn't want to focus on."

"Maybe I could talk to him."

"Don't," she said. "I've got cold feet now, myself. If things don't start going better with the business, we're going to be in trouble."

"Has Tom's greenhouse cut into business a lot?"

"This is a small place, and in my opinion, which I wouldn't say to anyone but you, Frank and Bob have always had small aspirations. See? I'm more like you than you think. I think they should have thought about updating, or really expanding, long before Snell's moved here. Boy—I really sound like Grandma today, don't I? Saying that if it hadn't been that, it would have been something else." She picked at a cuticle. She looked at the baby. The baby liked her nurse mouse; she was waving it in her arms, like someone waving a flag at a parade.

"How's everybody else?" I said.

"Actually, the good news—at least, I consider it the good news—doesn't have anything to do with the family, but it's made me happy. Tom brought Bernie and the baby back from Georgia last week. It seems she never did give it up for adoption and was living with her friends all this time. She called me to come over and see the baby. She was absolutely delighted to be back, and of course I didn't let on that I knew anything about her having considered giving up the baby. For all I know, her hormones were just on a roller-coaster ride. Anyway, it's a sweet baby, and the two of them seem very happy."

"Wow," I said. "Has that news caught up with Dara?"

"How would I know?" Janey said. She dropped her hands in her lap. Then deliberately changing the subject, she pointed to the ring on my finger. "Don't you think you ought to return that to him?" she said. "It's weird that you took it in the first place. Don't look at me that way: I have good instincts, and I sense that your wearing that ring that strange woman gave you is going to cause nothing but trouble."

"What do you think? That it's casting a spell?"

"Don't be mad," she said. "I hate to state the family motto, but okay: It's None of My Business."

"No," I said. "It's good that we discuss it. Bob and I never really discussed anything, and look where it got us."

"That's something else entirely," she said.

"So how is he?" I said.

"He's sulking. He hangs out a lot with Trenton these days, from what I've heard. Trenton's blue because the great writer left him. The two of them have tried to recruit Frank for various things—trekking up mountains, or whatever it is they do. Trenton bought an iceboat."

"I heard that Dara was modelling for him," I said.

"I wouldn't know."

"Janey," I said, softening, "I agree that if she'd set her sights on my husband, I wouldn't like her."

"I don't like her," Janey said. "Frank swears that's all in the past, though, and I believe him. They're not the most sophisticated men, you know? I mean, I don't think that being raised by Barbara exactly taught them how to understand women. They always think that at any moment the helpless woman is going to simply tell them what's needed. She killed their intuition, in my opinion."

I was surprised that Janey had given such thought to the way Barbara had brought up her family. I probably shouldn't have been surprised, because as a mother, Janey would have more reason to think about those things than I would. Still, I was taken aback.

"Bob and Frank and I all think you should dump her," Janey said. "Though I'm sure that's just going to reinforce your loyalty."

"Dump Barbara?"

"No. Dara."

"The three of you talk about who should be my friend?"

"Don't make it sound like a witches' cabal," she said. "Frank really cares about you. And Bob's told you what he thinks—don't pretend you're hearing it from me for the first time."

"Stop lecturing me, Janey. This isn't like you at all."

"I don't care what's like me and what isn't," she said. "It may surprise you to know that I'm every bit as fed up with the way I'm supposed to be as you were. I only bite my tongue with the family. I talk straight to my patients. I talk straight to everybody else. Since you decided to step out of context, how about rethinking sweet, proper Janey."

"I don't think you're sweet and proper," I said. "I mean, you're one of the nicest people I've ever met, but that's a lot different from being sweet and proper."

She looked at me. When she spoke again, her voice was lower. Almost a whisper. "Tom told me she's written Bernie very disturbing letters, Jean. Threatening letters. If Dara thought that was the way to win him back, what she did had the exact opposite effect."

I was surprised, but I didn't want to be sucked into the family's paranoia. "People think about her too much," I said. "When relationships break up, people do crazy things. Do you know what he's written Dara, or said to her? She's everybody's scapegoat."

"I really doubt whether you would have left Bob if it hadn't been for her," Janey burst out.

"Janey, that's nuts. And also, think about it: this is a place that isn't friendly to outsiders. It's a small town, and people have ways of protecting themselves, by not letting anyone or anything new in."

"Snell's was built," she said.

"Nobody had any control over that. You know what I mean. If you know so much about what Bob and Frank think, you must realize they feel stifled."

"I realize that more and more every day," she said bitterly. "Next he'll build a wall around his expanding fortress. We're here for the long haul, Jean. Just do me a favor: Don't drop me. Don't stop talking to me, or visiting me. I married into the family. I am not this family."

She burst into tears. Joanna looked at her mother and reached out. I saw her out of the corner of my eye and ignored her, as I stood and swooped down on Janey, awkwardly hugging her, kissing her cheek. "Janey, Janey, I don't think you're them," I said.

Frank came in the front door, whistling. Max stood beside him. A draft of cold air blew in.

"Tell her, Frank," Janey said, wiping tears away, as if Frank had been in the room all along. "Tell her that she should give Tom the goddamn ring. Tell her we don't want to be in the middle of this. Why should Tom think we'd want to be the ones to sort everything out between him and the great Dara Falcon?"

We were both stunned, but Frank knew less than I how to respond. He stood in the entranceway, squinting. He looked as puzzled as I'd ever seen him look. He did not say anything, including hello, to me. I finally said, quite hollowly, "Hi, Frank."

"Jesus fucking Christ," Frank said. He turned on his heel and steered Max back through the door.

"Why did you do that?" I said. "Why did you do that, when you'd already talked to me?"

Frank's car started. We heard two car doors slam shut, then the squeal of brakes, as he backed out of the drive.

"Look at how bent out of shape you are because I said something honest in front of Frank," she said. "Barbara's the one who thinks everyone's feelings always have to be spared. What do you think about him sleeping with your friend? Just one of those things?"

"I think it was wrong. I'm sorry he did it," I said.

"Did you ever tell him that? He thinks you're his big buddy, I'm sure. You act like one of the guys with Frank. If you're going to change your life, maybe you need to know that all too often you don't back up the people who matter. Like me, for instance. Right now."

"Janey—you want me to censure him for getting involved with Dara? That's what it will take for you to feel better?"

"Don't you see what you're doing, Jean? When I tell you you haven't put anything on the line for me, you react like I'm irrational. Like you should humor me, the way parents plop a pacifier in the baby's mouth."

"Okay," I said. "I'll say something to him."

"Not to humor me. Because you *should* say something," she said. When she spoke, she sounded, for an instant, like Dara, underscoring her words, pressing you to believe what she believed. How had it ever happened that Dara had come between me and Janey?

"Janey—Tom asked you to have me return the ring?"

"Let's drop it," she said. "I've got a headache."

"Please just answer that one question, and I'll drop it."

She folded her hands on her lap. "It's more complicated than that," she said. "Bob got into some fight with Tom. I think that's it—he ran into him over at Trenton's. And he pretty much told him what a sonofabitch he was for everything: for sucking up to us—Frank told me Bob said that—and then sabotaging us with Snell's. And apparently he also blamed Tom, which I admit is irrational, for introducing Dara into our midst, as if he'd brought in plutonium, or something. It ended up, somehow, with Frank stepping in, and then Tom said to Bob that if everyone wanted to set things straight, one way would be to have you return his mother's ring, which he'd given to Dara. So of course Frank came home and reported this to me. For all I know, Bob's already discussed it with you."

I shook my head no. The baby was sucking a red rubber ball. Children's voices screamed, then faded away. For a minute I thought a voice might belong to one of my nephews, but it didn't.

"Just give the damn ring back," Janey said. "It will earn me points with everyone. And it isn't yours. It isn't yours, Jean. It belongs to Tom. Tell her you had to return it. You're not afraid of her, are you?"

I hated fighting with Janey. I got up and took a coffee mug off the shelf, filled it first with water and took a long drink, then poured coffee into it. I had gotten used to cappuccino; the coffee tasted bitter.

"Tell me about life in Connecticut," Janey said, letting me off the hook. "Talk to me about something else."

"I feel like a trained seal," I said. "You clap your hands, and I—"

"I honestly want to hear about your life," she said. "If that makes you feel like you're some creature in a zoo, that's your problem."

"Okay," I said. "You're right. The truth is I've been feeling unsocial for quite a while. Come to think of it, that's why I even avoid my roommates. I don't want them to ask me questions."

"Because you're uncertain about the future?" she said.

"Because I'm uncertain about the past," I answered.

After a few sips of coffee, I asked to see the renovated basement. Janey raised an eyebrow, then decided I was serious. She got up and picked up Joanna on her way to the basement stairs. She handed

Joanna back to me and, flipping on the light, walked slowly to the bottom, holding the railing. At the base of the stairs she turned on another switch, and the recessed lighting began to glow. There was a dropped ceiling. There were bookcases with baskets and boxes on them—very few books. The old dining room rug was on the floor, and there was a large desk for bill paying, covered with framed pictures of the family. Around the corner, covered with indoor-outdoor brown-and-russet carpeting, was a bar with two bar stools. Behind it was an aquarium, but as Janey turned on another light, I saw that the fish were plastic, sunk on transparent line with sinkers. A plastic fern stood in the center. A Farrah Fawcett poster was tacked up on one wall. On the other was a large blowup of Frank, Bob, Drake, and Sandra, the year Frank graduated from high school. Frank was standing in his cap and gown, and Sandra sat on the arm of the sofa, to his right. Next to her, in front of the sofa, stood Drake, the shortest, and Bob, who was almost as tall as Frank. He was holding a beret. When I'd seen the photograph before, I'd taken it to be a Frisbee, but then I saw the little nub on top, and knew it must be a hat Bob had once been fond of. I found it hard to imagine Bob—plain, always-simply-dressed Bob—in such a hat. Bob was smiling, but Drake was poker-faced. Everyone had been cut off at the ankles. They looked so young: so round-faced; their hair so fussed over, and so wrong.

"He loves to be down here," Janey said. "Around the corner it's still the same. Just the washtubs, and the tool bench. Five million jars."

I pushed the door open. Joanna did not like this tour of the basement, and tried to climb down. I lowered her to the floor, but then she wanted to be picked up by Janey. I picked her up again. The rest of the basement did look exactly the same, and it smelled vaguely of wetness and of Tide. Broken toys waited for Frank to fix them. A sunburst clock ticked on the far wall.

"Frank's inner sanctum," Janey said.

Which made Dara's room—her room in Portsmouth I'd seen once and the re-creation of that room at Tom's, which she'd said was an exact replica—leap to mind. Now she'd moved to a one-room apartment. All she'd taken was books and clothes. How difficult it must be to have a private place disappear. I wondered why she hadn't said anything about it. Having purposefully retreated to my own odd quarters,

I knew how vulnerable I would feel if I had to move around the larger house. I could also understand how Frank would want to leave some of the basement just the way it had always been.

"What are you looking at?" she said. "The heart of the heart of the chaos?"

"It's nice," I said. "I find it reassuring, somehow."

"You and Frank," Janey said. "Come on upstairs. I'll make fresh coffee."

We did go upstairs, but I already felt jittery and decided against more caffeine. The more of the house Janey showed me, the more deserted it seemed. Probably it was the quiet—the unusual silence in the house—but the clutter made the rooms seem emptier, rather than fuller. I noticed the things that were thrown here and there: toys; clothes; shoes; magazines. They seemed more conspicuous than the furniture. More real. They were in transition, I supposed—on their way to the garbage can, or the recycling bin, or downstairs to be repaired, or upstairs to be put in toy boxes or mounded in the corners of the children's rooms. I realized that the thought was melodramatic, but I identified with the pacifiers, and balls, and Magic Slates, and *Life* magazines. I'd pretty much thrown myself somewhere, when I thought about it. I'd flung myself away, and then I'd carved out a little nook. I could imagine reading about it in one of Joanna's storybooks: the tale of the hoop that rolled all the way to a new life. A little songbird perched on the hoop on the last page, its musical notes floating over the pretty landscape, where the hoop leaned against a flowering dogwood.

When I left Janey's, however, after many hugs, our eyes brimming with tears, I was just a body in a car. There was nothing magical about it: I had put my sweater and poncho back on, and I was back behind the steering wheel, no pretty birdie chirping, but some nice enough music on the radio, on my way to see Barbara and Dowell. I really intended to go there. Instead, I pulled onto the shoulder and looked into the distance and quite simply could not imagine walking through Barbara's front door, sitting in the living room, saying polite things. It was asking too much of myself. What I would do was tell Bob that I had visited, and let him find out later that I hadn't. If he thought I was crazy, so what? Maybe it would be a good example to him about non-compliance.

I went to a pay phone to call Bob. The phone was in front of the convenience store I had often stopped at to buy things for Bob and me, or for Barbara. The phone booth looked uninviting: people's names had been sprayed on the outside, with lopsided black hearts adorning them, and a bag spilling garbage leaned against one side. It was getting cold, and what I really wanted was to be back in the car, with the heater turned up high. Still, I felt guilty—it would be one thing to skip out on Barbara, another entirely to postpone, yet again, a discussion with my husband . . . so I turned back to the car, intending to find another phone booth and, on the way there, to calm down and to think things over.

Instead, I drove all the way to the beach. It was the beach where Barbara's kites had flown. Where I had walked with Dara the day we ended up at the Inn having coffee and talking. I had once been under the delusion that I would work part-time, doing clerical work for lawyers, which now seemed absurd. There had been the Red Riding Hood woman, but the beach had been pretty much deserted, as I saw it was again today when I parked the car and walked to the edge of the rocks. The water was slate gray. Only two figures in the distance, walking a dog, leaned into the wind. From the other direction, a man in a wet suit jogged through the wet sand, working his arms as he ran. How dare Bob have wanted so little for us, I thought. How embarrassed he should be—though I felt sure he was not—to have capitulated to what was easiest. Had he been genetically encoded to become dutiful, vigilant, unadventurous? In college, he had told me that Dell made him feel at peace with himself and with the world. Just a short drive away from the place where he'd grown up, he often became so nostalgic for Dell that I'd had to remind him we could easily drive there if he needed to reimmerse himself. But after he moved back he hardly used the region. He occasionally went kayaking, or hiking, but most of the time he devoted himself to work and assumed the world was there to be used by other people, and I had almost fallen into that pattern, too. Connecticut was the first place I'd lived where I thought the terrain was neutral, and therefore, possibly, mine: it wasn't my aunt's world; it wasn't Bob's. For the first time in years, I went out every day and looked at things. I went out for the purpose of looking. It was not true any longer that I might settle for catching a glimpse of something while I was getting groceries, or picking up my husband's eyeglasses, or any of the other numbing activities I'd programmed myself to do. Now I went out with the dog to observe: frozen twigs; clouds; cows in a field.

The people coming toward me had picked up their pace. It was Chris's son, Derek, I saw, and another boy who held a stick that a black dog constantly jumped for.

"Hey, Jean, how are you?" Derek said.

"I'm fine. I moved, you know."

"Yeah. I did hear that," he said.

I bent to pat the dog.

"This is my friend Steve," Derek said. "This is Jean Warner," he said to the boy.

The boy shook my hand. He looked like Bob had when he was in college. He had on the same sort of corduroy shirt Bob used to wear, and his longish hair was the same color as Bob's. His hand was the same size, and when he shook my hand, he had Bob's firm grip. It made me uncomfortable at the same time it interested me. Here I was avoiding my husband, and suddenly it was as if I were in a time warp.

Derek was talking to me. "Did you ever get the lowdown on those guys I had in my cab that day?" he said. "Those guys I brought over to get that lady's book?"

"What makes you ask that?" I said.

"Because I ran into that friend of yours—the one who acted. And she said one of those guys was in love with her or something. Do you know what I'm talking about?"

"Edward Quill," I said. "He's a producer. A would-be producer, maybe. Did they really strike you as that odd?"

"Oh, yeah, absolutely," Derek said. "I had the older guy and his wife in my cab the next day, and they were saying awful things about Edward Quill—that he was a con man and that what's her name—"

"Grace Aldridge," I said.

"That she'd been hoodwinked. That guy, Quill, had apparently gone into a rage with them about something in her will. They were all buddy-buddy in my cab, but not the next day." He turned to his friend. "I tell you about that couple?" he said.

"You tell me about so many people I don't remember."

Just then, a black Ford coasted to a stop near where we stood. A pretty girl rolled down her window and said hello. "Hey—got to go," Steve said. "See you later."

The girl's sudden appearance took me aback. I had been listening to Derek with interest, but I had been distracted by the Bob look-alike. Bob, as he'd been years before: my walking across a college campus with him. And then the car had pulled up and he was gone. It made me think that fate could always have intervened. Bob might have gotten into another girl's car, fallen in love with someone else instead of falling in love with me. Then I would have no doubt met someone else, had a different life. While hardly profound, it was enough, on a day fueled only by coffee, to make me wonder whether, back then, that would have been lucky or unlucky.

"Quill had a big fight with them?" I said, trying to bring myself back to the moment.

"Yeah. The woman really hated him. She didn't buy it that he was going to marry that woman—don't tell me again: I'll never remember her name. I guess the old guy was afraid of that Quill guy all along. That's the way he talked, anyway. It was really odd stuff. I don't get duos like that very often. Most of it's pretty run-of-the-mill: take old so-and-so to the doctor; pick up somebody at Logan if I'm superlucky." He ran his hand through his hair. "I've been doing work with Amnesty," he said. "Amnesty is the hope of the future, I kid you not. I'll do whatever's necessary to have time to work with that organization. Listen, if you've got a minute, I've got a few photocopies in my car of some things you should read about political prisoners."

I walked to his car with him. I didn't see what else I could do. There was no point in being impolite, and running into Derek had been a good thing. Because of his friend's being with him, it had been a good thing: now, I was thinking of Bob more fondly.

Derek gave me several pieces of paper, and an application to join Amnesty International. "Please think seriously about it. There are enormous injustices," he said.

"I will," I said, my serious tone matching his serious expression.

"Don't take any Canadian nickels," he said.

"No," I said. "Give my best to your father."

"Will do," he said.

"Bye," I said.

"Take care," he said.

I walked to my car. I was thinking about a million things at once: the necessity of calling Bob; how our meeting might go; how wrong it was of me to have seduced him years ago, how needy I had been, how random I'd been in whom I'd selected. If I'd been Grace Aldridge, I would simply have taken who came along, but instead, I'd orchestrated things. Though how did I know she hadn't? Maybe she had wanted people to think she simply moved from man to man, like someone dancing her way through a waltz. Maybe she had been angling as well as, say, Edward Quill. Maybe she had wanted his youth, and he had wanted her money. It wasn't romantic, but then again, the statistics tell us that romance doesn't carry much weight. Unlike Grace, though, I intended to have no more husbands. It was going to be painful enough to extricate myself from the one I had. I was so upset at the prospect that I preferred to stand and stare at the ocean in the middle of winter rather than phone Bob and begin to unravel our lives.

I would have called him immediately when I left the beach, except that Derek's car wouldn't start. I heard the ignition grinding as I pulled out and made a U-turn and headed up the hill. Halfway to the top, I stopped. I listened to him trying to start the car. Then I put the car in reverse and coasted back, my foot on the brake.

"Goddamn," Derek said. "I just got this back from the shop. They told me they fixed it."

"Do you want to call somebody, or—"

"You don't have jumper cables, do you?" he said.

I shook my head no.

"Would you mind giving me a lift to my dad's?"

"No," I said, because there was nothing else I could say. It was getting late. I had already kept Bob waiting too long. Though maybe I could explain skipping Barbara's by telling him what had happened at the beach. Right. That's what I would do.

Derek got into the car, clearly dismayed. The Amnesty information slid off the dashboard. He put it between the seats.

"Thanks," he said. "If this really takes you out of your way—"

"It's fine," I said. "You'll just have to tell me where to turn."

"Yeah," he said, dejectedly. "I guess he assembled a nice zoo for himself, but my dad doesn't exactly have people over. I think the day my mom left was the last time I ever saw anybody in the house except our shadows."

"I didn't know him in those days," I said.

"Those days," Derek said. "That's what they were, all right: those days. Now suddenly he's got himself a girlfriend after—what? Fifteen years."

"That's good," I said.

"Yeah. Terrific. Except that she drinks, and now she's got him started again."

We drove in silence for a few minutes. "Left at the store," he said.

"Did your mother just leave?" I said.

"Just left. Yup."

"That must have been pretty awful."

"Yeah. Suddenly there you are with the old man, and he's blotto."

"My parents died," I said. "My aunt raised me."

"Yeah?"

I nodded yes. "She was good to me in some ways, but she had a gambling problem. I would have had some money, but she gambled it away."

"Oh, man," he said. "That must make you mad."

"It used to. What I've wanted lately is for her to explain herself, but she won't answer my letters. I used to visit her, but I've stopped. If she can't even write back, now that we're both adults, and—" I stopped talking. My voice was too high.

"That's a real bitch," he said. Then he said: "Left then right. First house on the corner."

I turned left onto Dial Street, then right onto a street whose sign was missing. Chris's house was a split-level, brown with white shutters. Two of the shutters had fallen off. There were several small dead trees on the front lawn.

"Not home," Derek said. "Let me just see if he's got cables in the garage."

He was gone awhile. After a few minutes of sitting in the gradually cooling car I got out and stretched. Then I followed him into the garage. Instead of looking for jumper cables, Derek was sitting on a mattress on top of wooden crates. Beer bottles were at his feet. A car was on the far side of the garage, on blocks. He looked up when I came in, kicked a beer bottle, and sent it spinning.

I watched it roll. There was broken glass on the garage floor. Also, a gin bottle.

"Just great," Derek said. "Just absolutely fucking great." He picked up a beer bottle. "Just great," Derek repeated. "Some woman who's nothing but a cow to begin with, and now he's back to communing with a beer bottle. It looks like he has them right here, too. Nice and secretive—no having a drink in, maybe, the living room."

I sat on the mattress beside him.

"Beer?" he said, holding out the empty bottle.

I reached for it, but wrapped my fingers around his wrist, instead. "Talk to him," I said. "He stopped before."

"Stop, start. Stop, start," Derek said. "Bad on the transmission."

I let go of his wrist. He looked at it. He reached out and took my hand. We sat there like that for a few seconds, before I leaned back and he leaned with me. He tossed the bottle over his shoulder onto the cement floor. By the time it stopped rolling, he was kissing me. He got up after a few minutes and closed the garage door.

"What if he comes home?" I said.

"You don't know drunks very well," he said. "This is happy hour."

"How do you know what he'll do today?" I said, but that was my last protest. We would hear the car. We could jump up. My clothes were still on, except for my pants, around my ankles. He was kissing my thighs. I kicked my feet free, because that would make it easier to cover up, if Chris came back. What was I doing? What could I possibly be doing, with my pants on the garage floor? But I found it difficult to concentrate on that question. My other questions were: Will the mattress flip over, since it's only stretched across a bunch of old crates? Will Chris return? Derek stepped out of his pants. He wasn't wearing underwear. He knelt between my legs and ran his hands up under my sweater, cupping both breasts. I arched higher, into his hands.

"This isn't happening," I said. "Don't worry."

"I'm afraid it's going to happen very fast," he said. He kissed up my stomach to my breasts, burrowing under my sweater. He put my hand on his penis. He kissed my hair, my eyelids. When I stroked him, he wrapped his hand around mine, to still it. Finally, I guided him inside me. It was freezing in the garage, but our bodies were hot. We had orgasms as quickly as a car ignition starts. Then we did it one more time before we put on our clothes and he walked me back to my car.

"I really like things that never happened," he said, leaning forward to kiss my neck. He was red-faced, tousle haired. This was Chris's son, who had been at Grandma's funeral not so long ago in his outlandishly oversize suit. Years later, when I saw David Byrne in one of his famous suits, doing a crazy dance with a weighted microphone that bent deeply left, then right, the memory of Derek would come back to me instantly, making it impossible to concentrate on the rest of the film. At that moment, though, I hardly believed the present was happening, let alone that there would be a future. I squeezed his hand, but I got into the car before he could kiss me, afraid that someone might be looking out a window, afraid, all over again, that Chris might pull up. I looked in the side mirror and saw him waving from inside the garage. Below his image were the words: NEAR, FAR. Halfway down the street, I rummaged in my purse for a tissue, but couldn't find one. I raised myself enough off the seat to pull a mitten out of my pocket and push it into my crotch. Then I looked at the remaining mitten and felt myself blush. Could I really have done that? And next, could I really be about to stop at a pay phone to call my husband?

Instead, I went directly to the house, the folded mitten chafing me as I went up the front walkway, reminding me of my embarrassment, when I'd been a teenager, those days I'd had to wear a sanitary napkin to school, sure everyone would see the bulge, sure the blood would overflow.

When the door opened, Bob took me aback by reaching out and hugging me. It was a weird continuation of sorts, a further caress. I could return it because it was easy to pretend I was still hugging Derek. The harder I hugged, the easier it was to be transported.

Bob and I went out. We went to Corolli's and drank coffee, talking quietly to each other. I was relieved that there were not going to be recriminations. I wasn't sure exactly what I had expected, but he was matter-of-fact, almost detached. He surprised me by saying that he'd suspected at Drake's wedding party in Boston that I was going to tell him I wanted to end the marriage. He admitted that he'd spent more time with Drake than necessary, partly as a way to avoid the long talks with me we should have had. He said there was no one else. He surprised me again by saying that marriage was more difficult than he'd realized when we first started out: Drake's marriage was already in trouble. Though everyone's relationship seemed problematic, didn't it? It was a rhetorical question. "One small confession," Bob said. "I asked Grace Aldridge to get in touch with you about that manuscript. I thought you'd be happier if you had something to work on, because you'd typed something else, and then it didn't seem like anything was coming your way. It was stupid of me not to realize that it would just be a lot of crap. Her godson was working at the greenhouse for a while, cooking soil. Turned out to be a real pothead. He lasted about a week, and then he was getting dry heaves every afternoon, because he couldn't smoke enough grass on his half-hour lunch break to keep going. Imagine that? Anyway: he'd been asked to type the thing, but he only knew how to hunt-'n'-peck."

I shrugged. It didn't bother me; it hadn't been a bad impulse. "Nothing to worry about," I said.

"There might be," Bob said. "Recently, I ran into Mr. Dry Heaves, and he said there had been some section about Quill that Quill made her leave out. He thought things had gotten pretty ugly between them."

I shrugged again. "I don't know anything about it," I said.

"There's more," Bob said. "Which is that Dara was at one point going to type it. She thought she'd have more time on her hands, I guess, but Van Sant put her to work at Snell's once he found out she was going to freeload off of him."

"He wanted her to move in. I was with the two of them when they announced it. He was very excited about it, Bob."

"She told him she had all these plays she was writing. Like Trenton's mystery woman: just one more day, just one more week, then the million-dollar sale. But what it turned out to be was that she holed up in her room and read Ibsen all day."

"She's an actress," I said.

"Yeah, and I work at a greenhouse," Bob said. "But I don't freeload off of anybody."

"I already know you don't like her," I said.

"I'm making this too long. The point is, when the kid gave the manuscript to Dara, it had the Quill stuff in it. The old lady had pointed it out to him—shown him that was what some drag-out fight had been about, or something. He didn't really read it; he just transported it to Van Sant, because he was switching over to Snell's. Van Sant didn't care who was a pothead and who wasn't. Anyway: Van Sant gave the manuscript to Dara."

"What about it?" I said. "What's the point?"

"Jean—I'm trying to talk to you. Why are you so impatient?"

"It's difficult to be here," I said. He was acting like we were having a business meeting. He was the boss, I was the employee.

"Well, later Dara swore him to secrecy that she'd ever seen the manuscript, because she wasn't about to type it, but the point is—don't jump down my throat about this—possibly she read all about Quill and she was blackmailing him. Because when Grace farmed it out again, to you, the Quill stuff was gone. Then she fell down the stairs and very conveniently died, didn't she? What I'm saying is that Quill might have quite a temper. He gave the kid a shiner before he found out the kid knew absolutely zip."

"Bob—that's crazy. You want me to think—"

"I don't like, or trust, Edward Quill. You already know what I think of Dara Falcon. But notice that she's there, in the background, or on the sidelines, a lot of the time. A lot of the time, Jean. And that her presence is always in situations that are problematic. Think about it. Dell's not that small a place. What things are all muddled up that don't involve her? Okay—I'm not a saint. I asked her not to tell you she'd ever been asked to type the stupid manuscript because I didn't want you to think you were getting sloppy seconds. But if she tells you . . . whatever she tells you about the two of us being complicitous about finding you a little cottage industry, I want you to know it's not true. That's not the way it happened."

"Okay," I said. "Fine."

I looked at a woman getting a real estate guide out of a holder. She went to her table and pored over it, pen in hand.

"Van Sant finally decided to live with Bernie and the baby," Bob said. "Did you know that?"

I waited for Bob to also ask me for Dara's ring, but he didn't. He looked at the woman reading the real estate guide, and then he looked at everything on our little table—the salt and pepper shakers; the ashtray; my hand—but he said nothing about the ring. He began to talk about Barbara and Dowell's plans to get married aboard a cruise ship to Bermuda in the spring. He shook his head and wondered again why his mother was marrying Dowell Churnin. "Maybe because she sees the lemmings all going over the cliff," he said. "Frank's taken something of a stand against Barbara's endless requests and hoked-up crises himself. With a fourth kid on the way, I think he got forced into choosing between being the perfect son or the perfect father."

We seemed like two people who had drifted so far apart that even other driftwood had become more interesting. I kept looking at the young woman behind the counter: her earrings; her bright lipstick; her tired eyes. For a few seconds, I was reminded of the way I had felt as a girl when Elizabeth had turned her back on me and stared out the picture window. Not daring to distract her, I had noticed, instead, every detail of her appearance from behind. I did the same thing now: Bob's bitten cuticles revealed that he was nervous, even if he seemed unusually placid; his bad haircut let you know he took little pride in his appearance.

"I didn't go to see your mother," I said.

He shrugged. "I didn't ask you to," he said. "You came up with the idea of seeing everybody." He fiddled with the salt shaker. "The other night I had an awful dream," he said. "I always hesitated to tell you when I had a bad dream, but this one keeps coming back to me: We were on a mountain. The sort you ski down, but nobody had on skis. I went before you, and it was sort of thrilling, but it was also sort of scary. No trouble interpreting that, I guess. But then you didn't come down, and finally I tried to look for you, but it was a foreign country, and I had a lot of trouble making myself understood. Then all the lights went off, and I was the only one there. I had to break into some fenced-in area and, when I did, I saw a little body curled up on the mountain, and I started sobbing, because I knew it was you. There was nobody to talk to, nobody to help me, and I was so scared I could hardly go toward you, because from the way you were curled up, I knew you weren't just hurt. And I couldn't stop sobbing."

I looked at him. "Do you see what you're doing?" I said.

"Doing? In the dream?"

"What you're doing right now. You're using a dream to try to manipulate me."

Behind the counter, a plate clattered to the floor. The salesgirl cursed as she bent to pick it up. When I looked back at Bob, he was resting his cheek on his hand.

"What exactly did you come back for?" Bob said.

"To reassure you that I'm just fine," I said. "That I haven't fallen on my face and died, on a mountain or anywhere else. And also to say that I'd like some of the furniture. When I finish school, I mean."

"The furniture," he echoed.

"You know, for what it's worth, Bob, I think you made a mistake by taking me for granted."

"I took you for granted," he said. He said it as if by repeating, he was testing something: water temperature; the sweetness or sourness of some unfamiliar food.

"You didn't quite accept that I wouldn't just go into the family business. Be a worker bee at the nursery. No matter how well I did with being dutiful, there was always the outstanding example of Janey, who ran in circles getting all the errands done while Frank had drinks with his buddies down at Rick's, plus she had her patients, plus she had children. Didn't you think I was inferior to Janey?"

"Not at all," he said. He said it so immediately that it took me aback.

"Why didn't I want those things?" I said. "Do you understand?"

He was quiet for a few moments. "Probably because you had a difficult childhood, and you were married to a man who was ambivalent about having children himself. I don't think it was unique to our marriage that we didn't discuss every disagreement all the time. At some point, all couples seem to have unspoken agreements about what's negotiable and what isn't."

"Doesn't your damnable sanity ever drive you crazy?" I said.

"What did you want, a husband who was insane?"

"Someone freer," I said.

He laughed. "Forgive me," he said, "but can you understand why I'd have trouble taking that seriously? You always let me know in no uncertain terms that I should do whatever Barbara wanted. That I should be at her beck and call. You got depressed when we couldn't have dinner over there every week, for God's sake. You never sympathized when I put in more and more time at the greenhouse. Even Janey nagged Frank about getting more help."

I didn't know what to say. When he put it that way, I could see why he felt the way he felt.

"I've started to meditate in the morning, before I go to work. It's about pulling body and soul together, I guess you'd say. And I've begun to think about the importance of really connecting with nature. I've been hiking a lot. Next spring, I'm going to go camping more. The other thing I've decided to do is see a little of the world. I'm going to go to Europe at Christmas with a friend of mine. London, for the theater and all the sightseeing, and then Paris."

"Really?" I said. "Who's the friend?"

"Jason Moore," he said. I could tell that he took great pleasure in being able to surprise me twice: that he was going to London and Paris, and that his friend was not a woman.

"Why do you think we never went to Europe?" I said.

"Where did you want to go?" he said. He said it pleasantly, with slight curiosity. He had me: I'd never seriously considered going.

"The same places," I said.

He looked at me. "This isn't like your saying you might go to law school because I thought about going to law school, is it?"

"No," I said, immediately. The volley had begun. "I always wanted to go to the Tate."

"I'd invite you," he said, "but we don't seem to get along anymore."

Bam: his comment registered. It was gone. The marriage was gone. I had half expected he'd plead with me to come back. I had thought, at the very least, that I would be gratified by his anger in the face of my calm assertiveness. Had I just recently had sex with Chris's son?

"We're starting to get sad," Bob said. "There's no point in that, because we both deserve to be happy. Let's go."

"Are you sad?" I said. "You don't seem sad."

"It would do me no good to try to persuade you I'm not some unfeeling automaton," he said. "Maybe you'll eventually think more kindly about me. Come on, Jean: let's go."

Light-headed from confusion and caffeine and simple tiredness, I kept my distance from Bob, because I feared that otherwise I might lean on him on the way to the car.

"Send me a picture of yourself in front of the Eiffel Tower," I said.

He looked at me. "I'll try to be photographed somewhere that's not that predictable," he said.


I did well in my courses. I got a B-plus in history, an A in art history, and A's in both my literature courses. Gail Jason decided to bump me up to a graduate-level course in Modern British Lit the following semester. She and I drank Constant Comment tea, sitting in her apartment, talking about what odd turns our lives had taken before we decided what our focus should be. She was divorced. She, too, had a dog she loved. It was named Winnie, after a character in Beckett's *Happy Days*. She quoted Willie, from the same play: "Life without win a mock." She said this while rubbing the dog's ears and nodding to the dog that this was true. She wrote poetry that she wouldn't show anybody, including me. It was important, she thought, to have things in one's life that were private. She kept a journal and suggested I do the same, but after a few weeks of trying to infuse days with the extraordinary, I stopped keeping the journal and immediately stopped feeling so deficient. I wrote a few letters: to Bob, telling him that I was proud of him for taking charge of his life (I didn't mail the letter, though, because I wasn't sure myself whether I sincerely felt that); to Dara, telling her about what I was reading and thinking; to Elizabeth, saying that it had finally come clear to me that on some level she hated me. I wrote Derek, in response to two notes, telling him as kindly as possible that I didn't want to continue seeing him—"seeing" being a euphemism for having sex. From Dara, in New York, I got a note that gave me no news, but said, simply: *Write me a letter, my dear. I love your writing: when I see it, I grow cheerful. Besides, I shall not hide it from you. My correspondence with you flatters me.* She thought it was corresponding to say nothing in reaction to what I'd written her about Samuel Beckett, to tell me nothing at all about what she was doing in New York? Still, having failed with my journal, I didn't want to force her to write if she didn't have the inclination. I also waited in vain for a response to my letter to Elizabeth. She was obviously glad to finally be rid of me, with miles between us.

I had written the first letter to her in the fall, sitting near the low, square table I had taken from the living room and put under the window in my room. I couldn't remember my exact words (they had been temperate, though), but I could remember the front door slamming just after I had finished writing the letter, and how I had felt that something peculiar and haunting—some essence of Elizabeth—had responded immediately, floating into the room with an unpleasant draft that came under the door. It was actually one of the people I shared the house with, I quickly found out: one of the men, bringing some girl home, but the slammed door reverberated as if Elizabeth had flown in to word-lessly haunt me for a few seconds. I do not believe in ghosts, or have any tendency to personify the wind, but when my heart began to beat wildly in my chest, it clarified what I really did fear: a vulnerability I always tried to deny. What if Bob simply came for me and took me back to Dell? What if Bob someday walked through the front door and—since physical force would have been unthinkable—argued me back? This could all be a dream, I thought. Simple freedom might be a dream. But then the autumn leaves had caught my attention, and they were more real—more consoling—than any salve. It was fall. I was in Connecticut.

When first semester classes were over, everyone left the house for the holidays except meepy Megan McCall, who drove me crazy by sleeping all day and prowling the house all night. Sometimes, around midnight, she would practice playing "A Whiter Shade of Pale" on the pump organ in the living room, which would result in another longer walk for Sparkle, who also avoided Megan like an imperious cat. I would see boxes of Super Tampax in the bathroom and worry about her—there were three large boxes of forty each per period, I guessed. Only years later would she tell me that she plunged the plastic Tampax tubes into dirt to provide support for the fragile marijuana seedlings she grew in trays in her bedroom, under a grow light. But all I knew back in Eastford was that one of the housemates was quite possibly bleeding to death, which made me anxious because I might be the only person there to save her.

Shortly after my visit to Dell, I had called Tom and told him that I understood he wanted the ring back, and he had been delighted to get the call. I said I would insure it and mail it, but he said he would be driving to New York with Bernie and the baby to spend Bernie's birth-day at the Plaza with her friends from Georgia; if it would be all the same to me, he'd like to stop and get the ring. He didn't ask whether this was all right with Dara, and I wouldn't have lied if he'd asked. She didn't know anything about it; I'd thought over what Janey had said, and I'd decided she was right.

So he had come to the house in Eastford on an unusually mild De-cember day, pulling into the driveway in a new blue van. Megan had been asleep, because it was only noon. From the front lawn, I could look back at the house and see the relentless purple glow of her grow light.

Bernie greeted me warmly and couldn't wait to show me the baby. The baby was asleep in a car seat, and she pushed the material of his little shirt down so I could see his mouth and chin. I lightly touched the edge of the baby's blanket, but I didn't want to wake him up. I had on the ring, and I looked at it for a second—looked at my finger, instead of at the baby, as I ducked my head into the car—and I thought how pretty it looked, how wrong Bob was never to have bought me any pretty jewelry, and also that I was doing the right thing: the ring should be Tom's to give to Bernie. They seemed like a happy family. If he seemed slightly more ill at ease than she was, that was only natural. I took off the ring and pressed it into his palm, saying that they must come in and have coffee.

"Honey, that's lovely. That really is a beautiful ring your mother had," Bernie said.

Was he going to slip it on her finger? Was I going to be the third wheel in a romantic moment? Apparently not. Tom nodded, but he did not give Bernie the ring. Instead, he reached into the car and got Dara's John Wesley Harding hat from the backseat. "You can tell Dara that whatever she left in the room is still locked up there," he said, handing me the hat. "Since I can't open the door, I couldn't toss this in."

Later, the hat sat in the middle of the table. Bernie sat down in one of the oak chairs surrounding the oval table. The cloth was covered with crumbs. A prism in the window sent a jagged rainbow bouncing across the cloth. The dog came over and made friends. Tom crouched to stroke the dog's head. The ring was on his pinkie. It sparkled in the afternoon light. The baby was sleeping in an armchair in the corner.

"I guess we've both been through a lot of changes since the last time we met," Bernie said. Her accent sounded even more Southern. Her hair was in a French twist: it made her look elegant, but older. She had her figure back: tight jeans; a beige sweater; a poodle pin, with a rhinestone eye, just below the V neck.

"Your ex-husband's taken quite a dislike to me," Tom said. "Just out of curiosity: You don't think I came back to Dell with any idea of opening a greenhouse, do you?"

"I don't think they think it matters what you intended. They're mad because it's what you did," I said.

"Please let's not talk about things we can't fix," Bernie said.

"I understand that," Tom said to me. "If I had it to do over again, I wouldn't do it."

They stayed in the dining area when I went into the kitchen. The dog came in and got its rawhide bone and curled up at my feet, chewing. I had to constantly step around the dog as I found the coffee filters, put the kettle on to boil. I was rarely in the kitchen. I'd gotten a toaster oven and fixed things for myself at odd hours, bringing frozen food from the kitchen to the bedroom and putting it in the little oven that sat where the TV used to sit. I washed my plate in the kitchen, but that was about all I did there. I even had a small refrigerator in my room.

"It's awfully nice to see you again," Bernie said. She leaned against the door frame. "Just in case you think I have bad feelings of any sort myself, I don't. I know Dara is your friend, and I respect friendship."

I nodded. Dara was going to be furious when I told her I'd returned the ring.

"When you come back to Dell, you come see us," Bernie said.

"I will," I said. "Thank you."

"Tom said you helped him to have some nice times in his house. He always enjoyed having you there."

"It helped keep me sane," I said.

"That room he was telling you about isn't really locked anymore," Bernie said quietly. "It's the strangest thing. Really downright scary. I don't go in there. Did you ever see it? Tom says he never went in when she lived there."

"What about the room?" I said.

"Well, she did this silly artwork on the wall, over all her perfect coats of paint. Just a little thing, about the size of a pie plate, but it is about as weird as anything I've ever seen. It's like something a teenager would do. I mean, it's this silly spider's web, painted in dark brown paint, and in the center is a picture of her face, cut out of some photograph—it sounds more funny than awful, now that I hear myself telling you about it. Anyway, she put herself right there in the center of the spider's web, and then she took the paintbrush and she drew a big X through it. It's like some awful, ugly tattoo. It scared Tom half to death. He thought about its being the baby's room, but when he took the door off the hinges and saw that, he just leaned the door up against a wall, and neither of us ever goes in there. Imagine putting graffiti up on walls. There it is, in that room with the lace curtains and all the antique linen."

I didn't know what to say. It was the single craziest thing I had ever heard about Dara, and Bernie had described it graphically. So Dara was serious about despising herself: about being the spider who should starve. Or was it that, by X-ing it out, she had decided to leave that concept of herself behind?

"Forgive me if I shouldn't have told you," Bernie said.

"Oh," I said lamely, "it's fine." What did I mean? What should I say?

"It's just that I know she's your friend, and I thought maybe somebody should know."

"Yes," I said. Still, I had no idea what I should say. "Bernie," I said, shaking my head, "I hope you don't think that whatever Dara does, I automatically defend her. I don't have any idea why she did what she did. But I appreciate your telling me, and I'm really glad that things are working out with you and Tom." I looked at her, and said something else I had suddenly realized was true. "You know, you're inherently nice," I said.

"What does 'inherently' mean?" she said.

She looked so young when she asked the question. Her body looked more like an adolescent's body than a woman's. When Tom came up behind her, he overwhelmed her. It seemed almost sinister when he clamped a hand on her shoulder. For a dizzying second, I saw Dara, not Bernie—Dara, standing outside with Tom coming up behind her, as she'd described it to me—Dara, about to lie down in the scattered meadow. The image was as vivid as if I'd been there. Dara was as powerful a storyteller as any of my favorite writers. She had superimposed herself on Bernie, on the present, with a greater reality. Except that I was the only one who saw her. Then she wavered and went away, and Bernie stood there again. She was still waiting for an answer to her question.

" 'Inherently' means something that's intrinsic."

Bernie's eyebrows came closer together. She shrugged.

"It means sort of naturally. I meant that you were naturally nice."

"You two forming a mutual admiration society?" Tom said.

"I wouldn't mind that," Bernie said.

The kettle whistled, and I took it off the burner, measuring coffee into the filter, picking up the kettle and slowly pouring.

"I want our baby to go to college," Bernie said.

"I'd settle for not having to change his diaper until we got to New York," Tom said.

"I also want him to be president," Bernie said.

"And no more wake-ups at four a.m.," Tom said.

"He's embarrassed to say how many hopes he has for him," Bernie said.

"Excuse me while I go sit down and die of embarrassment," Tom said.

"It's true," Bernie said, picking up two of the mugs I'd filled with coffee. "He adores his son. It's why we're together."

"He's certainly beautiful," I said.

She put the mugs back on the counter. "If you truly think the three of us belong together, make an exception," she said quietly. "Tell her to stop writing Tom and me. Tell her to clean out that goddamn room. She's haunting us," Bernie said. "You said that you were glad that Tom and I could have a chance."

She left the kitchen. I heard her cooing to the baby, who was still sleeping soundly. For a few seconds, I stared at the empty doorway. Then I put the things on a tray and left the kitchen also.

Dara's black hat sat on the table. It looked like an unetched tombstone.

Tom held Bernie's hand. When I came toward them, Bernie looked at me and smiled.

I had begun to spend time with an assistant professor in the psychology department. He, like me, loved Maria Muldaur music, and the two of us once slow-danced around his living room, he in pajama bottoms, me in pajama top, to "Midnight at the Oasis" and to Bob Dylan, singing the dirge-like "Sad Eyed Lady of the Lowlands," which Dylan explained, in the song, had been written at the Chelsea Hotel for the Sad Eyed Lady—his then wife, Sarah. The assistant professor's name was Liam Cagerton, and the rest of his family was in England, where his brother was a composer and his sister a dancer and his father an accountant for a Greek shipping company. His mother sewed hats for the royal family and raised corgis, like the queen. We pretended that I would meet his family, or perhaps he did think that I would meet them, which was about as likely as my accompanying Bob on his European trip, or—years later, when I finally did see London—my really being the fiancée of a man I had met the previous night in a bar.

I met Liam at Rein's deli, when he sideswiped my table and knocked over the bright green kosher pickles. What was a ploy to say hello became an occasion of misery for the busboy, who slipped in a rivulet of pickle juice as he ran to mop it up. Liam had only meant to jostle the pickle dish, as he later put it. He said that he had not assumed I was a university person (he had hoped I wasn't), and he was disappointed when I told him that, the minute he began to apologize, I assumed he was a professor. That day, I'd had on Dara's John Wesley Harding hat that Tom had left behind. I'd called Dara in New York several times after Christmas, thinking it would be easier to tell her what I'd done than to write her a letter, but each time the answering machine at Edward Quill's had emitted a long beep, signalling that the tape had run out.

Finally, just before Christmas I had gotten a note from her, postmarked Provincetown. She said that she was having a reunion with her sister and her sister's new husband. She said her Christmas would be magical, walking around the deserted beach and climbing sand dunes, staying in the grand house that her sister had rented for the winter, where there would be a huge Christmas tree with a ton of tinsel and a hundred strings of lights. She would call when she was leaving the Cape, she said, and try to rendezvous with me in Connecticut. The Brown Bomb was still ticking. She ended by using the same line she'd written me once before: "Write me a letter, my dear." Little did she know how little she would like to hear what I had to say; until I told her about returning the ring, though, I was sure I was going to continue to feel queasy. I'd told Janey, and she had applauded my decision. I had thought about dropping Frank a note and telling him, too—letting him know I'd decided to allow myself to be caught in the middle, after all—but it didn't seem fair to Dara that everyone should know before she did.

Just before Christmas, I had been invited to dinner at Gail Jason's.

She was having a dozen people, she had told me on the phone; she hoped I'd come if I didn't have anything else to do. I'd had coffee or dinner at Gail's apartment several times, and I thought I'd figured something out about her: I thought she kept her own loneliness at bay by becoming a sort of protector of others. I was doing as much for her by going to her home as she was doing for me by issuing an invitation. Gail's invitation to Christmas surprised me, though. Didn't she want to be with her family—or at least with close friends? I'd been considering the possibility that at the last minute I'd cave in and go to Frank and Janey's, because according to her, the children would otherwise die of heartbreak, but I really didn't want to return to Dell. The last trip had been too emotionally exhausting, too bizarre. So I accepted Gail's invitation and then, that same afternoon, Liam called to say that his brother in Bath had come down with terrible flu, and all his children were ill, too, so he would not be taking his trip to England after all. He asked whether I'd like to get together on Christmas Day. I told him about Gail's invitation. He sounded disappointed, and also said that he knew her.

"Why don't I call and see if we can't both go there?" I said.

"She'll try to spook you about what a bad boy I am," he said.

"I'll tell her I already know," I said. He was flirting by reminding me; I was reciprocating by alluding to our previous encounter.

I called Gail and asked if I could bring Liam Cagerton.

"Liam?" she said. "I didn't know you knew him. He has quite a reputation for loving and leaving, which I guess you know."

Liam had told me about this—about his peculiarly bad luck, and the mistakes he'd made in getting involved with unstable women.

"It's fine, if that's who you want to bring," she said, when I didn't respond, proving that I was right: she did really want me to be there. We were to bring two pies and whatever we wanted to drink.

I called Liam. He was obviously relieved to have somewhere to go. It was December 23. He suggested we have dinner in Hartford that night, at an Italian restaurant. After which we returned to his house and made love. After which we danced in the living room.

In bed, I told him about having returned what Janey had described as the magic ring. It was meant as a good deed, to atone for the mistakes I'd made in the past year—a preemptive strike against having to make remorseful New Year's resolutions, I supposed. From the ring I backtracked to the cast of characters: Tom and Bernie; Bob and his family; Dara; the people whom I'd lived among in Dell. It was difficult to know where to begin, but he seemed to find everything I said fascinating. "You know so many people," he said over and over. "No, please go on," he said, whenever I stopped talking and asked whether he hadn't heard enough. We were in bed—the first time I had ever been in a king-size bed—drinking brandy. I remembered hoping to find brandy to put in the flask the day, early on, when I'd met Dara at Corolli's. Then I remembered being inside Corolli's in the late afternoon, and Bob's saying to me that we both deserved to be happier. Here's to you, Bob, I thought; here's to you.

"You were selling azaleas near the side of the road," Liam prompted. "What exactly are azaleas?" Liam had made me back up and explain how I had first met Tom Van Sant. But every time I tried not to digress, he had another question. I described azaleas as best I could, only to realize that when I had finished, he had them confused with rhododendrons. "The leaves aren't waxy," I said. "They're paler green than rhododendron leaves. Some are rather large, but usually when you see an azalea, the leaves are quite small. The flowers can be a lot of colors, but the pink and red ones are the most prevalent. They could also be lavender, or white, or peach colored, and every shade of pink and red, really."

"How on earth does anyone recognize one?" he wondered aloud. "Most confusing plant I've ever heard of."

I skipped from the day Tom had bought the azaleas to the story Dara had told me about the Instant Meadow. "Doesn't it all just blow away?" he said. "You can't mean it really makes a flower meadow." I had told him the story to see how he would react to Dara and Tom's impulsiveness. He seemed to take it for granted, wondering only whether scattered seeds wouldn't blow away before taking root. When I tried to tell him more about Dara and Tom, he interrupted me. He wanted to talk about what he wanted to talk about, and he was enjoying interrupting me. He was pretending to be preoccupied with what he called "the Rousseauish forest" that surrounded us up in New Hampshire. He was teasing, a little bit: "So then, with all these flowers and bushes and trees—I can only imagine the number of trees—people still open nurseries to sell even more trees and bushes to each other?"

"What about English gardens?" I said. "It's no different from England, is it?"

"I suppose not," he said. "But now, topiary. Do you have privet sheared to look like jumping rabbits, or deer standing on the front lawn?"

The image made me laugh. "Of course not," I said.

"Very important to have your bushes do double time as bunny rabbits, or whatever," he said. "And you absolutely must have a maze, with your birdbath in the center. Very important to make it almost impossible to get to the birdbath unless you fly in."

"I don't think Americans are very interested in obstacle courses," I said.

"But everything you've described makes it seem like they are. No one seems to find the right person, or if they do, they muck it up. Everybody running all over the place."

"No, no," I said. "What I've been trying to explain is that they're rooted to the spot. Nobody looks far afield—like my mother-in-law, marrying a man she's known almost all her life, just because he's there. And my sister-in-law, who's given up her dream of living in Florida, and who tolerates anything, just to stay married."

"Well, yes, but it strikes me that your husband was always off in Boston, was it? And then your friend, she sounds downright peripatetic, being in this man Tom's house and then in her own apartment somewhere else, and then leaving there for some man's apartment in New York, but then she's away on the Cape for the holidays. It sounds like quite a bit of coming and going. Like a perpetual holiday."

"It frightens me that I might be like Bob's family," I said. "I thought about that the other day—that I've been shut up in my room in Eastford for so long."

"Yes, well, now you've come out to play with me," Liam said.

"Liam, I'm serious. I was feeling so good about my independence, but since I've met you, I realize I'd begun to vanish. I was living like a hermit."

"Oh, nonsense. You moved, didn't you? And you tell me you're going to be visiting your friend in New York, and until just recently you thought you were going to New Hampshire for Christmas, and when I mentioned our going to England together, you seemed quite excited about the possibility. I mean, one has to sit still sometime."

At first what he said made me feel better, but slowly I began to realize that it bothered me that we all paled in comparison to Dara. She was living her life at least—following her instincts. Putting herself in New York to try to meet theater people, racing to her sister's side in Provincetown—it seemed impulsive. She hadn't even mentioned to me that her sister was back on the East Coast. One of the things I liked about her was that her life wasn't a process of trying to restrain herself. She found a way to do what she wanted to do. She was out there, pursuing. . . .

I drew a blank. Well, an acting career, of course. A relationship. She must want a new relationship, now that things had so clearly concluded with Tom. She was taking acting classes and playing indoor tennis, refusing to stay put in dead-end jobs. She borrowed money if she needed money; she found a way to keep moving—she'd gotten my car, which was not much of a car, but still: it was a car. I admired her. In a minor way, I was imitating her. Seeing her refuse to capitulate to difficult circumstances had inspired me, made me realize that I should go back to school, find out what I loved—to find out whether something couldn't be my passion, the way acting was hers.

But then I thought of what Frank had said to Bob: that she had proposed grand passion, followed by extinction. And then Bernie's words came back to me: Bernie, telling me Dara sent them hate mail. Dara kept moving, but she didn't disengage from the past, or from the people she'd left behind, even when they wanted her to.

I had thought about her often during December. I was preoccupied, though, with the feeling that I was falling in love with Liam, with his gentle kidding, with the good sex, with his devotion to me. What would it be like to tell Dara not only that I had given back the ring, but also that another person had become important in my life? When Janey had asked me if I was afraid of Dara, the question had hit the mark. I wasn't afraid in the sense that I thought she might strike out, or say terrible things—though there was certainly the possibility that if she was as volatile as people thought, she might. It was more the fear of disappointing someone who was already terribly disappointed. Though I had looked at her as an inspiration, another way of seeing her might be that she was barely holding on: she had no job; she was not getting acting parts; she was living in a borrowed apartment, and when (if?) she left there, where would she go?

She called me in January. She didn't suggest a rendezvous. She was back at Edward Quill's, and there was good news: he had found a performance space on lower Broadway. Someone—"a Wall Street type," Dara said—had agreed to bankroll it. The one-woman show would be performed at the end of a brief rehearsal period, which was why she was going to be unable to pay me a visit. Between seeing Liam and trying to get a jump on the new semester's reading, I was relieved to hear that the idea had been ruled out. She was so elated when she called that I decided against mentioning having returned the ring to Tom. I doubted that he would be calling her, or that she would be contacting him. Her talk was all about the coming performance, except for the few times that she told me—vaguely, but enthusiastically—about how wonderful it had been to be reunited with her sister for the holidays. "You haven't been a bookworm, have you?" she said, near the end of the call.

"No," I said. "Actually, I've been dating someone. He's here now, in fact."

"What's his name?" she said.

"Liam Cagerton."

For a few seconds, she said nothing. Then she said: "Well, darling: Is he wonderful?"

"He is," I said. "We spent Christmas together."

"Sounds serious," she said.

"Might be," I said.

"Well," she said. "Leaving your old stomping grounds has worked out for you."

She didn't sound happy. She just sounded appraising. I was a little offended by her assumption that I had left my husband, moved, and enrolled in school again only to find a man.

"February twentieth," she said. "Mark it in your book. But now I've got to run, sweetie. Edward is waiting for me downtown."

"He's back from London?"

"Yes, yes. Of all ironies, he met the man who's bankrolling this over there. They had dinner at Mr. Chow's, and by the time they finished, it was a done deal."

"That makes me feel good," I said. "You know why? Because in New Hampshire too much seems to happen because of claustrophobia. I'm very glad that Edward found someone on another continent who wants to do the play."

"Thank you, darling," she said. "Spoken from the heart."

When we said goodbye, I turned to Liam, stretched out on my bed. "You're going to get to see her perform," I said. "The one-woman show's going to happen."

"I'd rather see you perform," he said.

His new mood was raunchy. He thought about sex a lot, and didn't hide the fact that he did.

"I thought we were going out for pizza," I said.

"But then the phone rang, and I stretched out on your bed, and when I'm in bed, I get horny."

"Get up," I said, taking his hand and trying to pull him up. "Come on—you said we'd get pizza."

"But then you answered the phone," he said.

"I hung up," I said. He was tugging me down. The dog thought we were playing a game and jumped on the bed. The telephone rang again: two short rings, then silence. I couldn't get to it in time, because Liam was wrestling me onto the bed.

"That's it," he said. "Two rings is the signal from God to have sex."

"It's Dara calling back," I said. I felt sure that it was. That she was calling back because my news had surprised her, and because she wanted to ask more questions.

"What kind of a name is Falcon?" he said, pinning my arms to my sides.

"I don't know," I said. "And anyway, it's a stage name."

"A stage name? I thought those days were over. I thought that nowadays Norma Jean Baker would be Norma Jean Baker."

"If she calls back, you have to let me get it," I said, succumbing to a kiss.

"Yes indeed," he said. "We must most certainly wait here and see if she calls again."

"Come on," I said. "Pizza?"

"I'm very worried about her," he said. "I think we must stay put. Wait for the call."

"You are? You're worried about her?"

He drew back. "Why would I be worried about her?" he said.

"Liam—do you think she was calling back because something was wrong?"

"Use your amazing powers to examine my soul," he said. "What do you intuit?"

"That you want to fuck," I said. He had broken the spell.

I heard nothing from her for days. Several times I almost brought myself to call, feeling a mounting urge to confess that I had given back the ring, but I always found an excuse not to: my premonition that she would call that night; the necessity to study. Finally, I wrote her a note. In the note, I pretended she would be happy the ring was back with Tom. I didn't mention his visit with Bernie or the baby. I told her only that he had asked for it, and that I had thought it was the correct thing to do to return it. I apologized for returning the ring without asking her, but pretended that it was no doubt what she would have wanted done. I decided against saying anything else of substance. At first I had thought to put the information about the ring somewhere in the middle, but starting out by telling her how wonderful and interesting and funny Liam was set the wrong tone, and chitchat about the weather seemed pointless. I didn't want to tell her about what I was reading, because it hurt my feelings that she never responded. I had gotten used to the classroom discussions: I wanted, and expected, people to be serious about what I was serious about. But she never asked questions or commented on what I thought.

Her response came about a week later. It was typed in script on lavender paper that said "Edward Quill Productions" on the top. She, too, avoided bracketing what she had to say. The note read:

*My Darling, my darling, I have just learned that my pretty bauble is gone. If I had given you my word, would you have erased it? If my heart, might you have squeezed hard to test its durability until it burst, and would you then have fed it to your dog, your much beloved dog—a treat for sitting up, or rolling over? Oh, but the forces of righteousness are on your side. Surely the ring was only*

*a loan, a token of something vanished. What a silly romantic I
am, trusting that trust was the scaffolding of friendship. My dear,
the ring was not yours to give away, and with it has gone my
trust. Will I recover it? One day, will we again be what we were
to one another?*

*In general, I am finding life tedious and, at times, I begin to
hate it—something that never happened to me before. Lengthy,
stupid conversations, guests, people asking me for favors . . .*

*Dara*

I was so upset by the letter that I called Liam and told him I could
not spend the weekend with him after all. We had intended to visit
Stonington: my first coming out; my first introduction to his friends. I
knew he had been looking forward to the trip, but the letter had made
me feel so horrible that I knew I couldn't face anyone. I left a message
on his answering machine, saying nothing about receiving the letter,
but saying, emphatically, that I could not make the trip, and also that I
needed time alone. I thought, nastily, of calling Janey and reading the
letter to her, letting her hear the reaction to what she had wanted. I also
thought furiously of calling Elizabeth and demanding an answer to my
still-unanswered letter. Who did she think she was that she could avoid
a discussion? But I did not make either call. It became increasingly
clear to me that it was Dara I was angry with—Dara, with her flourishes
of recriminations, her display of fragility. In her insular world, people
existed only to serve her, whether it be me, or Edward Quill, or all the
nicknamed, expendable people—expendable if they thwarted her, or
didn't cave in and do what she wanted: she made them caricatures
then, and shrunk them with her scorn. In my mind, I wrote her half a
dozen letters that night, all intemperate, all as succinct as hers were
flowery. I had been her friend and loyal supporter. When I dared to do
the correct thing though, she, thinking first and only of Dara, had tried
to make me feel miserable and guilty.

Liam called and urged me to tell him what was wrong. He offered
to delay the trip for a day. He begged me to talk to him: Was it something he had done? A problem with Bob? Something at the university?
I told him I just didn't want to talk, and that it was better to hang up,
which I did.

My anger was diffuse: even Sparkle became dull: a creature of habit, curled up on the only comfortable bed that had been provided for him. In my new life, I had become a recluse. My liberation was nothing but a new set of patterns that had replaced the old: study; walks; coffee. It was sort of like: get the groceries; babysit for Janey; clean the house. Tom Van Sant: Why couldn't he have stayed where he was, not tipping the balance of life in Dell so that he ascended on the seesaw while we bumped to the bottom? Why had he given away his mother's ring if he hadn't been sure the recipient was the right person? It was a valuable antique, not some varsity jacket. He acted like he was back in high school—which was probably the context in which he still saw everyone: date the prettiest girl; be a nice guy, then do whatever was expedient; get sympathy by invoking your troubled past. And Dara was every girl's high school nightmare years later: didn't run with the crowd; dressed with flair; flirtatious; artistic; able to attract any boy she wanted. It was a sign of my own arrested development that I had felt so privileged, so special: that the coolest girl liked me. But my real fear was that in leaving Dell, and in being separate from Dara, something disastrous might happen. More accurately, what I thought was that altering any pattern might make me like an airplane out of control. In a matter of seconds, there might be blackness; then nothing but fire. Or water.

I bottomed out. I sat on my bed and cried. I recast history so that I had always been intimidated: the scared, grateful little orphan in childhood; then, as a young married woman, a servant—what else was really meant by "domestic partner," as Gail Jason had witheringly asked me the day we had sipped tea and she had talked about her own divorce—and then, making progress, I crumpled at the first sign that someone did not approve of me, further punishing myself by staying away from the man who did love me.

The next day, a much more temperate note arrived from Dara. They had both been postmarked on the same day, but the accusatory note had arrived first. There was also a postcard from Derek: the famous photo of Marilyn Monroe with her skirt blowing up. The postcard had been doctored, though, so that Goofy stood below the billowing fabric, staring up with his big, popped eyes. The message said that he would be happy to simply be my friend. He had moved. He gave me his new phone number. In another envelope was a picture of Janey, pregnant, surrounded by the three children, who all had clothes stuffed under their clothes, imitating Mom. Everybody but Joanna was smiling hugely. I rummaged in my desk drawer and took out scissors. I cut Goofy off Derek's postcard and dropped him in an envelope. Then I wrote a brief note to Derek and addressed the envelope: "You're officially out of the picture," I wrote. "What happened between us meant nothing. Although you might like to think so, we have nothing in common. Find somebody else to get interested in." Like Dara, I omitted a closing and simply signed my name.

The house was empty. I had retreated so completely that no one called goodbye as they went out the door anymore. For a while, Megan had pushed notes under my door, inviting me to "family spaghetti feasts," but I never went, no matter how loud the polka music played on the stereo, or how amused everyone seemed with everyone else's conversation. They weren't my real family, so they had no way to coerce me. I also didn't care at all what they thought of me. I knew that keeping my distance was peculiar, but I didn't care. I was trying it as the flip side of having volunteered to do so many things for Bob's family. All I felt that day was disappointment in myself for my cavalier treatment of Liam, but that, I hoped, could be remedied with a phone call. Yet I didn't make the call. I walked the dog quickly, throwing only three sticks, not leaving the vicinity of the house. Anything that I was more or less required to do made me resist. Inside again, with the dog visibly disappointed, I tore up Derek's postcard. I also tore up Dara's second note, but as much as I wanted to, I couldn't bring myself to destroy the first. I sat in the living room, which in itself was an adventure, because it was something I hardly ever did, and began to read *Mrs. Dalloway.*

By noon, it seemed strange to me that Liam hadn't called. By midafternoon, I convinced myself that something had happened to him: he had fallen, painting his bedroom ceiling (the New Year's project); his car had skidded off the road. Still, I didn't call. Instead, I became maudlin, thinking that it was foolish to go to such lengths to keep my distance from people when they didn't care about me or want to be around me in the first place. My cynicism from the night before returned: by late afternoon, it was clear to me that my husband was relieved that I was gone, that Dara was only smoothing over her true dislike of me for her own purposes, and that everyone from my lover to my housemates thought I was a dark cloud it was best simply to ignore. Eventually, I put the dog in the car—a way of apologizing to someone, at least, for my endless inadequacies—and began to drive. I turned into the parking lot of the tiny white clapboard liquor store in Ashford and bought a bottle of Beaujolais Nouveau, which was one of the few wines I knew, because a hand-lettered banner was stretched above an opened case, saying that it had just arrived. The owner was pleasant. I had been told that he was always pleasant if anyone bought a bottle of wine that cost more than three dollars. I put the bag in the backseat.

Driving aimlessly, I wondered what I would do with a degree in English. I also felt that I would never be able to live without the dog—his head was in my lap; all was forgiven—and convinced myself that the people in the house would never relinquish him. That would be the custody battle I had avoided with Bob; it would still happen, only it would be about Sparkle the dog.

I turned off the highway and parked, briefly attaching the leash to the dog's collar as we walked at the side of the road, until we reached a dirt path where I felt the dog could safely run free. It would be all I needed, to have a car strike the dog.

It didn't happen. We walked and walked. At the end of the road was an outcropping of houses with the foundations poured and some framed in, and then the houses seemed to have been abandoned. A bulldozer leaned crookedly into the frozen muck. Had the people run out of money? Or was I looking at something abandoned for no good reason—an idea people had simply lost interest in. Perhaps work would start again in the spring. I made a mental note to check then, but not to return to this site during the winter.

It occurred to me that the world was pretty much divided into people who constantly moved, and those who stayed put. When I was younger, I had never known anyone who moved. Aunt Elizabeth never moved; my parents never had. But when they died, there had been some talk of Elizabeth's moving into that house, because it was bigger, and because people had suggested to her that it might be better for me if I didn't have to leave. She had asked me whether I wanted to stay, or to move in with her, but I had understood from the tentative way she phrased the question that she hoped I would be willing to move. I had been. Instead of thinking the house would hold pleasant memories, I had felt sure I would feel my parents' presence everywhere and I would be tortured by not being able to actually see them. When I married Bob, there had been some talk of Barbara's moving out of her house, because it was so difficult to keep up, and because she could use a smaller place, and letting us rent the house from her very reasonably. But Bob hadn't wanted that; like me, he hadn't wanted to have memories surrounding him. For the first time, I wondered if he had had any trouble staying on in our house when I left. I thought that I might have been the lucky one, moving into a place I felt no responsibility toward—a house that held no memories, good or bad. It allowed me to be a little like an amnesiac. With nothing to remember, more seemed possible.

That night, I accepted a last-minute invitation to Gail Jason's for dinner. Like everyone else I knew in Connecticut—not that there were that many—she lived in temporary quarters. Something about her house, and Liam's—though not so much the house I lived in, because I had not decorated at all—was at once permanent and impermanent. Both serious, and not serious. Unlike the people in Dell, the people in Connecticut were concerned about their careers, about themselves— about where they would eventually go, and what they would do in the world—not about their houses where they would live day after day. And frankly, I liked the unfinished, extemporized environments; I liked them because they reflected the unfinished aspects of the people who lived in them.

I went back to the car with the dog, thinking vaguely of the many places Dara had lived since I'd met her—or the many places she'd stayed, with no pretense of really living there. If I hadn't seen how grim some of them were, it would be easier to romanticize her moving from place to place. As I looked at a big, leafy squirrel's nest high up in a tree, I thought of her spiderweb—the web I had thought of as metaphorical; the web Bernie had vividly described as real. I felt sure it was meant as a joke—a nasty joke, as if Tom Van Sant shared, or should be expected to share, Dara's concept of herself. Or maybe he did. Maybe that was one of the reasons he had decided to stay with Bernie. Maybe he had come to think that Dara was trying to entrap him. Maybe Bernie should give thanks that Dara had made literal her metaphorical spider's web.

Driving home, I felt tired and cold. The initial excitement about being in school was being eroded by the amount of studying I had to do, and my gradual realization that it was going to take quite a bit of time to accomplish what I needed to accomplish. I was upset—why not admit it—that Dara was angry with me, and upset with myself that I had been so angry with Liam. I couldn't always account for my moods; like an adolescent, sometimes I overreacted, and other times I probably underreacted. But then I had been so intimidated, always the grateful little orphan, that I hadn't enacted the throes of adolescence when everybody else had, so maybe I was just coming to all that very late.

At the house, I hugged the dog and explained that he could not come with me. He understood from my tone of voice, not from my words. It reminded me of how much I always knew by looking at someone, even before the person began to speak. I patted Sparkle, reassuringly telling him a lie: that he wouldn't want to come with me, anyway. At the last minute, when I decided to wear a scarf and went back into the room for it, I also decided to put Dara's letter in my pocket.

There was a stream of cars on the highway, once I got off the back roads. I only had to drive a short distance, though, because Gail lived between my house and the university. She lived on the second floor of a turn-of-the-century house that was occupied downstairs only in the spring, when the retired professor who owned it returned with his son for a two-month vacation. The rest of the time Gail was there alone: no music she didn't turn on herself; no people banging around in the morning to wake her up. There was a back staircase that led into her kitchen. On her porch were frozen geraniums and other flowering plants from the summer, still in their pots. There were also dusty brown bags stacked under two brick weights, and lawn chairs, folded and leaning against a wall, an old shower curtain wrapped around them. The porch was a mess. It was hard to believe it was the same clean, airy, flowery place I'd first seen only a few months before.

Gail already had wine, it turned out: a gallon of Gallo Hearty Burgundy, which she and another woman had been drinking before I got there. I was surprised to see another person in Gail's apartment; I thought she must have invited me over, as she usually did, because she was lonesome, but she and the woman seemed to be having a good time. Jazz was playing quietly. The bag of groceries sat on the table. I liked the fact that she and her friend had had a drink before she'd even put the groceries away. Gail introduced me and then seized my bottle and pronounced it much better than hers. She handed her friend the corkscrew as she took my coat.

The other woman was named Joyce. She worked for an architect in New York. She and Gail had been friends since high school, when they had both been cheerleaders. I was amazed at this information. Every-thing Gail did was done slowly. I couldn't imagine her holding pom-poms and jumping in the air. She held out the possibility that after a bit more wine, though, she might show me.

"Come on, tell us," Joyce said. "What were you like in high school?"

"I was just—I didn't do anything," I said. "I didn't even go to the senior prom."

"I'll bet you were one of the smart girls," Gail said.

"I wasn't particularly smart. I was a B student. I wasn't in any clubs, or anything."

"Oh, a lot of people who are smart don't show their intelligence in high school."

"No, really," I said, sitting down next to Joyce at the kitchen table. "I lived with my aunt, who hardly even spoke, and at school I was very shy. Nobody paid any attention to me in high school."

"And then you were very young when you got married, like me, weren't you?" Gail said.

"I was nineteen."

"I beat you by a year," Gail said.

"And I stayed an old maid," Joyce said.

"Stop it. She had a lover for five years who set her up in an apart-ment and paid all her bills. She was the happiest kept woman in New York, and she didn't have to worry about marrying him, because he was already married."

"Then he was hit by a truck," Joyce said.

The way she said it made me laugh. I didn't doubt that she was se-rious, but it was so unexpected, and she said it so drolly, that I couldn't help laughing.

"It's the truth," Gail said. "We went to the funeral, all dressed in black, pretending we knew him from work. I don't know what the peo-ple he worked with thought, but maybe they thought we were friends of the family."

"I was crying that day," Joyce said.

"No wonder," Gail said.

"So how come you lived with your aunt?" Joyce said.

"My parents died in a plane crash."

"Oh my God!" Joyce said.

"And her aunt gambled away her inheritance," Gail said.

"She did *not!*" Joyce said.

"As you always say to me, Joyce, who doesn't surprise you?"

"But how could she get away with that?" Joyce said.

"Because when it was happening, I didn't know."

"Don't the courts protect children?"

"Apparently not," Gail said. She said to me: "If I give you these garlic cloves, could you pretend they're your aunt's jugular vein?" She handed me a large knife and a chopping board. I was taken aback by what she'd said but didn't want to seem humorless. Also, Joyce reacted for me. "Gail!" she said.

"I've been trying to get her to explain herself," I said. "She got married when I went to school. But since I've started asking for an explanation, she won't answer my letters."

"Couldn't you sue her?" Joyce said.

"Letter writing. A lost art," Gail said.

I realized for the first time that Gail was a little drunk. She was examining the lettuce as if it were an unfamiliar substance. "Why did I buy this? It's wilted," she said.

"Because you don't live where there are the finest supermarkets," Joyce said.

"She wants me to live in New York and be miserable along with her," Gail said.

"When you leave here," Joyce said. "You won't be here forever."

"I won't be here past next year," Gail said glumly, pouring more wine.

"Maybe we should live in Wellfleet, where my parents are, if you don't want to live in the city. They have that house they always rent out."

"And just sit there, stringing beads?"

"My parents like you," Joyce said.

"They say they do," Gail said.

"My best friend has been living in New York," I said.

"Does she like it?" Joyce said.

"She's an actress," I said. "It's either there or L.A."

"An actress? What's her name?" Joyce said.

"Dara Falcon," I said.

Joyce shrugged. "Don't know her," she said.

"She did an amazing job acting the role of Nora in *A Doll's House,*" I said.

"Off Broadway?"

"In New Hampshire, actually."

"That's definitely off Broadway," Gail said. She was rinsing lettuce leaves.

"In fact," I said, rushing on without being entirely conscious of what I was about to blurt out. "In fact, I'm not so sure that she's still my friend, because I got caught in the middle of a situation that involved Dara and another person, and she ended up thinking I betrayed her."

"Did you?" Gail said.

"I don't know," I said. "I don't think so. At least, I felt like I had to do something, and I tried to do what I thought was right."

"The other person was your friend, too?" Joyce said.

"Not really," I said.

"Couldn't you have let them work it out?" Gail said.

"Go ahead and tell us," Joyce said, pouring wine. "We're not going to know what you're talking about unless you tell us the story."

I didn't know where to begin. While I was thinking, Gail shook the lettuce and droplets of water rained down on us. "You have to suffer for your dinner," she said.

"Well, Dara and Tom used to be a couple. And then it turned out that a woman he'd dated before he got together with Dara became pregnant with his child. And he went back and forth, not knowing what to do. Dara was living in his house. He'd given Dara a ring that had been his mother's. And somehow—I can't remember exactly how it happened, but she'd flung the ring across a room one time, and I think she was afraid she'd throw it into a field, or something—"

"Don't tell me she gave you the ring," Gail said.

I nodded.

"Naturally," Gail said. "People love to involve other people in their pain."

"There's also the fact . . . my sister-in-law thought the ring was bad luck. She got involved in this situation, too, but that's too much to go into. What she thought was that I should give the ring back to Tom, and that would be that."

"Tell us what was really going on," Joyce said.

"What was really going on? Well, I guess Dara did want to involve me, but she missed her guess about my just doing what she wanted," I said to Gail. "I suppose in a way the ring was a symbol of something that had happened in my other life . . . I mean, when I left Dell and came here, I wanted to extricate myself. And Tom decided to remain loyal to Bernie—that's the other woman, the one who had his child—he wanted the ring back, I heard, and I gave it to him."

"Why didn't you give it back to Dara?" Gail said.

"I guess because I believed she'd throw it away."

"That would have been between her and Tom," Gail said.

"But Gail—Jean had taken the ring. She was the one who actually had it."

"I don't understand why you didn't give it back to Dara," Gail said again.

"Because Gail—she would have felt responsible if Dara had thrown it out the window, or whatever she was going to do."

"That still wouldn't have been her problem."

"You can't just detach yourself that way," Joyce said. "You know it's not that easy."

"Then look at it another way," Gail said. "You're acting like her having a fit and hurling the ring into space was an inevitability. You might have given it to Dara, and Dara might have returned it to Tom." She looked at me again. "Did you ever ask her whether she didn't think it was right to return it?"

"No," I said. If she asked, it was going to be very difficult to explain why I had not.

"Why not?" she said.

"Well, because I know Dara. She didn't—she doesn't—change her mind. If she said she was afraid of what she'd do with the ring, there is every reason to be afraid of what she'd do."

"Worst scenario," Gail said. "The two of them aren't getting back together anyway. The ring is gone. So what?"

"It was his mother's."

"The thing does sound cursed," Joyce said. "Now Gail—stop questioning her!"

Gail frowned. "He'd given it to Dara as an engagement ring?"

"Well, I think—I think he might have, but she said she didn't mean to marry him, although I'm not one hundred percent sure that was true."

"Say," Gail said, "I've got a suitcase some stranger left on my porch. It's making a weird ticking noise, like a clock's inside, or something. Do you think you could take it home with you?"

"You are so nasty!" Joyce said to Gail.

"And also, I think I might kill myself if you don't cook the dinner instead of me, so could you make the meatloaf?"

"She is *nasty!*" Joyce said to me.

"You think I was really stupid to get involved," I said to Gail.

She nodded. "But do you understand now why you wanted to?"

I held the knife and didn't chop. I felt a strand of hair tickling my eye, but didn't brush it away. Finally, Joyce poked the side of my hand with another garlic clove. I responded by jumping slightly.

"She's wickedly good at getting people to confront themselves," Joyce said. She sounded quite sympathetic. She spoke as if Gail weren't in the room. Gail was drying the lettuce. She had begun to dry it leaf by leaf.

I got up and took the note out of my coat pocket. "Here," I said to Gail. "Read this. Tell me if she's right." I looked down at the floor. "I guess I already know that she was right," I said.

"What is it?" Joyce said.

Gail took the note out of the envelope. She began to read, frowned, then frowned deeply. She reached for her glass and drank the last of the wine. Then she did the last thing I would have expected. She burst into laughter. She held the letter in her left hand and slapped her hand over her heart. "Oh, Jesus!" she gasped. "I don't totally get the joke, but is this what you've been worrying about? This is a put-on."

"It's not a joke," I said angrily. "She's taking me to task. Worse than you did."

"Jean—do you know what this is?" She held the note out to me. "This is Chekhov, writing to some friend of his."

"What?"

"Is this woman so histrionic that you took these for her words? I suppose that says something in itself."

She got up and went to the bookcase. She found the book she was

looking for. She began to flip through it. Joyce poured more wine in
everybody's glass, and I sipped mine quickly, utterly confused. Gail did
not touch her glass until she found the page she was looking for, put
the book in my hand, then pounced on her wineglass triumphantly.
I read

> In general, I am finding life tedious and, at times, I begin to hate it—
> something that never happened to me before. Lengthy, stupid conver-
> sations, guests, people asking me for favors, handouts of a ruble or
> two rubles, or three, having to pay cabbies for patients who don't give
> me a cent—in a word, everything is so balled up that one might as well
> run out of the house. People borrow money from me and don't pay it
> back, walk off with my books and don't consider my time of any value.
> The only thing lacking is an unrequited love.

I was completely speechless. It might have been odd—it might even
have been some in-joke I couldn't possibly have knowledge of—except
that the last line rang so true that I finally understood what had been
the issue all along. I was the unrequited love. She might even interpret
that love as being far from sexual, but still: her bitterness was because I
was not what she wanted me to be. I had loaned the money. I had lent
the books. I was more in the position of the letter writer, more in
Chekhov's position, than Dara—except that she was the only one who
bore a grudge. She was also the only one who thought in terms of unrequited love.

It was ironic, of course. I couldn't have invented a stranger context
in which to have come to the realization: the minute Gail handed the
letter and book to Joyce, holding out her offering with one hand and
clasping Joyce's free hand in her other hand, I realized they were lovers.

"I don't understand what's so terrible," Joyce said. "If painters steal
from one another, it's called appropriation."

"Joyce, look at the whole picture: the histrionics; the grandiosity of
choosing a famous person's voice instead of her own; the unkindness of
playing a sort of in-joke on a person who was obviously already in a
state of conflict. I don't like her, sight unseen."

Joyce eventually became quiet, deferring to Gail. She also let Gail
have the last of the wine, and the last word: "Keep your distance," Gail
said to me. "Not from us—from you know who."

Liam and I made up. In Liam's house, I baked pork chops while he was teaching his night class. I had all but moved in, taking Sparkle with me. My housemates had been very generous in agreeing to let the dog go, but I suspected that some of their reaction had to do with their relief in getting me out of the house; I hadn't really understood how much they had worried about me, always shut up in the room. When we finally did have a long talk, the more I tried to reassure them I was fine, the more doubtful they had seemed. But the truth was, for a long while I hadn't been able to socialize with anyone: a combination of guilt, fear about whether I'd made the right decision, or perhaps even simple relief had nevertheless depleted all my reserves. I was spooky to them, the ghost of the house, who could be easily appeased by letting it drift off with the already vanished dog—Sparkle had been my unfailing companion since the first day I laid his pallet and began to feed him the same turkey potpies I ate for dinner.

As Liam and I ate dinner at the big rectory table that had been shipped over from his father's house in England, I decided it was time to tell him about Dara's letters. He was tired from having taught his class, and tired, too, from having fought his way home in the snow. He wasn't completely concentrating, which, surprisingly, didn't bother me: I both wanted to tell him, and I also wanted him not to question me, because I didn't have any good answers about why Dara had done what she'd done. Dara, also, was not Liam's favorite subject. He had told me more than once that I thought about her too much. In a way, I think he thought she was my scapegoat, the way I thought—still did think—she was everyone else's. In his mind, she tied me to Dell—and therefore to my unhappiness. No matter that she was gone from Dell herself; to Liam—and possibly to me—she typified much of what was wrong with a dull small town. In stirring things up, she had called our attention to the fact that there was little to stir. Everyone who knew her had ended up realizing more intensely what his or her boundaries were. Everyone who knew her had ended up, for one reason or another, more disappointed.

" 'Turning and turning in the widening gyre . . .' " Liam intoned portentously, when I mentioned Dara's name.

"Stop trying to sidetrack me before I've begun," I said. "This is not about William Butler Yeats. It is about a friend of mine."

"Yes," he said. "She wrote you letters, one of which—the more pleasant—you ripped up. Go on."

"Liam—do you think I'm the sort of person who puts out signals that she's, I don't know, naive? Easily co-opted?"

"No," he said. "I can't make you do anything. You're hardly easily co-opted."

"But I didn't know that Gail was gay."

"Who goes about wondering all the time? Something of a surprise to find out, but ultimately, so what?"

"Liam—it worries me that I don't see things as they really are."

"Much debate about that 'actually are.' Not a concept anyone buys anymore."

"You're just defending me because you like me."

"First you were worried about being a hermit. Now you think you're a functional idiot. I think you have many peculiarities, your willingness to see yourself as a naïf every time anything unexpected happens among them." He put his cutlery down. "Let's say you're a naive person. What things might you do to function better? We all try to grow and change. You're studying literature. That can't hurt. You've left the shelter of your former life. That's a big move. Why should you expect instant improvement?"

"Then you do think it," I said.

"In fact, I don't. I fail to understand your relationship with the self-named bird of prey, but I do acknowledge that this is a relationship you're struggling with. I personally wish that she would just leave you alone, but that's neither here nor there, because you, yourself, do not wish it. And tomorrow we will be driving to New York so that I can see this strange creature. Almost worth it, snow and all." He cut into his pork chop. "You do cook wonderfully well," he said.

"You don't have to listen to the story," I said.

"I will listen to the story. Continue."

"Well—she wrote me two letters after I wrote to tell her I'd given the ring back. And one of them, maybe both of them, for all I know, were lifted from Chekhov. Gail knew it the minute she read the letter."

"How would anyone know that who hadn't studied Chekhov?" he said. "Is that the problem?"

"Aren't you even surprised that she'd do something like that?"

"Well, I don't know. Was it apt?"

"Was it apt? Was it *apt?* Are you trying to out-English yourself, Liam?"

"I have great patience," he said. "I feel sure that, in time, you will stop ascribing every speech pattern that is not your own to the fact that I am English, which you equate with being humorous."

"Liam. Answer me."

"Answer me," he said. "What did she pilfer from Chekhov? I don't see it as the end of the world, if that's what you're getting at. If she had put quotation marks around it, would you be so upset?"

"But she didn't. She pretended they were her thoughts."

"Being . . . ?"

"That, well, in one letter she said, 'My correspondence with you flatters me.' "

"Most apt," he said. "She seems to do nothing that doesn't flatter her. Buying hats and scarves all the time, according to you. Always dressed up for a different party. Going after everybody's husbands, or leading on homosexuals who she thinks can make her famous."

He was confusing me. He was trying to defuse the power of Dara, as he always did, but he seemed sincere in not thinking her letter was as weird as Gail had. Maybe I had overreacted. Maybe the letter was not so insidious; maybe Gail had really just wanted to gloat about her knowledge and sophistication.

"But at the end of the letter there's a line she didn't include, and the minute Gail gave it to me to read, I knew why she had left it out. Can I get the letter?"

He shrugged. "You are obviously intent upon convincing me," he said. "What does it matter what I think, if you're so convinced?"

I went into the bedroom and dug around in my bag. I found the letter and went back to the table. I handed it to him. He read it.

"Whether it's Chekhov or not, it's a letter from an actress, capital *A,*" he said.

"But at the close of Chekhov's letter, there's a sentence that sent chills up my spine. Liam, you know about my lending her that money? And the books? That's all there, in Chekhov's letter—he's complaining the way I might have reason to complain. It's almost as if she got inside my head and then sent the letter to make a preemptive strike. But the last sentence is—" I flipped the letter over. On the back, I had copied down Chekhov's words from Gail's book. "His last sentence is: 'The only thing lacking is an unrequited love.' "

"What of it?" he said.

"If you read the letter the way I just said—if you read it as her cueing me about what I should complain about . . ."

He continued to eat. I watched him delicately lift applesauce to his lips. "What are you asking me? Whether she's trying to plant the idea in your mind that you're in love with her? Really, it's too absurd. You're overthinking this."

"You think I'm crazy," I said.

"I think that the woman baffles you, and probably she would baffle anyone. But how you make the leap to thinking that some hitherto unspoken love is the issue between you, I don't quite understand."

"Because she selected that particular letter. And she's always been so seductive. Part of the thrill has always been to be observed. She dresses to attract attention. She told me things about Tom and her that I wouldn't have known. She said that Bob tried to kiss her, which I now think was a lie. Liam—I think all along it's been a seduction."

"Well, it certainly seems to have worked. Every time she drops you a note, she has your undivided attention. I really do think that whatever's going on, you could use a cooling-off period. Both of you." He looked at me. "She's quite indiscreet, at the very least," he said.

"But I think if you knew Dara—"

"She sounds like my idea of hell. It makes you wonder why anyone would befriend a person when they could befriend a dog."

"Tomorrow night, I don't want you to say anything that would embarrass me. Will you promise not to do that?"

"When have I ever embarrassed you?"

"You haven't," I said, halfheartedly.

"Why we have to go to New York to see this woman perform is beyond me. Why we couldn't at least wait for the roads to clear . . ."

"Because I have this odd premonition that there might not be a second performance."

"What a tragedy that would be, I'm sure."

"I'll go alone if you don't want to go," I said.

"Don't be silly. If you're going, I'm going. I've got to meet this seductress." He smiled tiredly. "This does occupy much of our conversation. We've had very little time together lately. Couldn't we talk about something else?"

"I'm sorry," I said.

"It bothers me when you jump to conclusions and think I find you crazy. I happen to have been involved with one or two women who were really quite crazy, and it bothers me when people use the term loosely. Please give me credit for realizing that you've been going through a difficult period. I care for you. I don't rush to pass judgment on your every action."

"You were angry that I didn't come to Stonington," I said.

"We'll stop and see my friends another time."

"We could see them on the way back from New York."

"I just saw them."

"You could see them again."

"Jean—you have nothing to atone for. You were upset, and you didn't want to socialize. That's fine. I accept that, and you should, too."

"You're still angry."

"This is most certainly the way to fan the flames, if that's what you intend. I would suggest that we watch a movie on the television, or that we draw a bath and sink into some bubbles. Would you like that?"

"No," I said.

"You're not that easy to seduce," he said. "Don't worry about yourself."

I picked up our plates and took them to the kitchen. He walked behind me, stopping first to put music on the stereo. In the kitchen, he ignored me as he rinsed our glasses in hot water and put them upside down in the dish drainer to dry. I decided that I was a monster. He was a very nice man who had agreed to go to New York with me, and I was sulking over something that no longer seemed as apparent as it once had. I was withdrawing from him because of my insecurity, pure and simple: I couldn't shake his equilibrium, and that shook mine. Ever since Dara berated me for returning the ring, I had alternated between anger at her and anger at myself. I probably wanted Liam to decide for me: bad Dara, or bad Jean.

I drew a bath and went to get him in the kitchen when it was half filled. He was still washing dishes in the small trickle of water that came out of the tap.

"You're perfectly fine, except for the times when you're upset by this so-called friend of yours. It's like Superman getting hit with Kryptonite," he said.

"I'm not Superman," I said, squeezing between him and the sink, leaning into his chest. "I'm Lois Lane, and I just don't get it. Something is right in front of me, and I just don't get it."

"I'm right in front of you," he said, unbuttoning his shirt. "You get me."

Later that night, wearing Liam's pajamas and watching an old movie on TV, doubt began to creep in again about Dara. Maybe all the times she'd called me darling and sweetie she hadn't been speaking loosely, or histrionically, which was a quality both Liam and Gail had noticed. But that made no sense, really; she'd never put a hand on me, never suggested in anything she said or did that she was desirous of anything more than she was already getting. Maybe she didn't realize it herself, I thought; maybe she would have been as surprised to articulate her desire to herself as I was when I felt I was the recipient of that desire. I shrugged lower in the bed, throwing my arm over Liam, as if to weigh him down. I felt better when he was near me; it was almost as if—even though she was miles away—I did fear her on some level. It was her caginess that troubled me: her poker face; her perfect timing. Like any good gambler, she was good at playing her cards close to her chest. It was my sense that however much she said, she was still always withholding something that bothered me most—not the idea that in much she'd said and done she had been obliquely making a proposition. I didn't think she liked it that I had gone away. Of course, people were always sad when their friends left, yet even if I had stayed, she would still be in New York, while I was in Dell. She would have gone, just as I had. Or would she? Was it possible that if I had stayed, she would have? They were unanswerable questions, but because it was late at night, I fixated on them, wondering and wondering about the answers, which receded farther and farther each time I tried to arrive at some conclusion. I rubbed my hands on Liam's chest, as if I were trying to pin down the truth. That he took it as an invitation for lovemaking was only logical, yet I was amused that something I'd been doing with my mind elsewhere had provoked his lust. We were so much in our own worlds. Perhaps Dara was only in her own world, too. Perhaps everything meant much less than it seemed—which was either a relief or, sadly, something that presented its own set of problems. In my literature

classes, I was being trained to look for connections. Searching for sub-
tleties was sometimes exhausting; it was tempting to throw up my hands
(now linked with Liam's) and say that things meant less, rather than
more, than they seemed. If I was really going to become a different person, though, I felt sure that it would help me to be able to decipher
Dara. It was just that I couldn't turn to anyone for help; people were biased against her, or knew her only in passing, or they'd quickly made up
their mind when they'd seen she was a person who stole words from
someone else. I still thought that I was the person who might be capable
of seeing her most objectively, yet the more I knew, the more confused I
felt. I could understand that my vanity had been flattered because
someone so mercurial had chosen me to be her friend. I could even understand that I had been easy prey (okay, Liam) because I had been in
an unhappy marriage, lonely, looking for a way to escape. She was outgoing—intoxicated with her high regard for herself, really—while I was
introverted. She was always steps ahead of me, though it was also
slightly interesting that often we had found ourselves on the same path.
I had done as much to establish the relationship as she had: I had been
available; I had taken pride in being useful; I had been needy, too. But
now I no longer felt I needed what she had to offer. Liam had changed
that, with his obvious devotion to me. Being involved at the university
had given me confidence. Escaping Bob, and his unarticulated despair,
had freed me to have my own thoughts and perceptions. I even felt a little sorry for Dara, because her power was dwindling, through no fault
of her own. No one could be larger than life unless you let them occupy
that position, and Dara—whatever and whoever she was—had been cut
down to size as soon as I began to assert myself. That was the way I congratulated myself the night before we went to New York, silently,
proudly. I had seen, when she visited, that I could have power over her,
too. I was eager for her to see me with my lover. I wanted her to see I
had something she did not. It was not a kind impulse, but I did not want
my own version of success to be lost on Dara.

The loft was above a framer's shop on Greene Street. My instructions were to press the buzzer of 4F: Grandin. Liam dragged behind;

he had had to put the car in an expensive garage because there were no parking places. I tried to tell him it was better that way; at least we'd come out and still have the radio. He wasn't to be consoled; the roads had been slushy and narrow laned, and because he had to teach the next morning, we couldn't stay overnight. With his downcast eyes and pursed lips, he was letting me know he was doing me a favor.

There were instructions inside about buzzing again if the elevator wasn't on the ground floor. Liam reached around me and hit the buzzer. I was usually the one a step or two behind him: if he lagged behind, it was because he was perturbed; it always took me a while to react, but Liam took in many things at once, and reacted quickly.

The elevator descended, with four people inside. I didn't know three of them, but unexpectedly, Trenton was in the elevator. He smiled. It took me a minute to realize whom I was looking at, partly because I didn't expect to see him, and partly because he had a bright green wool hat pulled down over his eyebrows. "I'm not a ghost," Trenton said.

I wasn't worried about that; I was wondering who else from New Hampshire might be at the play if Trenton was. I felt suddenly shaky, seeing him. "Hi," I said, finally recovering myself.

"Hello," he said. "I'm Trenton," he said, extending his hand to Liam. "And these people and I were apparently buzzed back before we got to the fourth floor."

"Terribly sorry," Liam said. "We saw that the lift had disappeared and read the sign saying we should ring for it."

"Same thing happened the last time I saw a performance here," a man in a down vest said. The thin woman at his side said nothing. Neither did the other woman. We began to slowly rise. This time, the elevator bumped to a stop in front of a fire door. Someone inside the loft pushed back the door.

"Are you just in town for the play?" I said.

"I dropped a couple of paintings off at the gallery. But I'm here to see Dara. Yeah."

"I never thanked you for writing me that note, back in September. It was nice of you."

What I really wanted was to move away from him. I did regret that I hadn't responded, but the note hadn't really required a response. Seeing Trenton was reminding me of other people in Dell, and I didn't want to be reminded.

The girl who had opened the door gave us programs. They were photocopies, on lavender Edward Quill Productions paper. Gold sealing wax, with an intertwined *E* and *Q*, had been applied to the front. I glanced inside and saw his preface. On the opposite page was a small photograph of Dara and information about other plays she had acted in. We sat halfway down the rows of card chairs: there were ten or twelve rows of about ten seats each, all covered with bright red cushions. So far, only a few people were sitting down. I caught a faint smell of incense, and also cooking grease; above us, it sounded like someone was moving furniture. Liam busied himself, taking off his coat and scarf and draping them over the back of his chair. I could sense that he wanted to know more about Trenton. I was hoping Trenton would sit away from us, but instead, he sat directly behind me.

"Did you know I'd been painting Dara?" Trenton said.

"Trenton is a painter," I said to Liam.

"I gathered," he said.

"I guess you and Bob did some hiking in the fall," I said, reluctantly drawn into conversing with Trenton, but not wanting to talk about Dara.

"Yeah, Bob really got into it. We took a trip to L. L. Bean and got some gear."

"Camping, you say?" Liam said. "I used to love it. Haven't done it in years."

"Liam teaches at the university," I said.

"That doesn't preclude my camping, I hope," Liam said. It was not likely I could say or do anything now to get on his good side. He seemed as annoyed with me as I was with Trenton.

"You're looking great," Trenton said, touching me on the shoulder. "It's good to see you."

He was a nice person; it was just that I didn't want to talk to him. I was also afraid that unless we stopped talking, Trenton would start giving me news of people in Dell. The sharp odor of onion began to suffuse the room. Upstairs, people were dragging things across the floor. Furniture had also been pushed back against the far wall of the loft we sat in: sofas; chairs; torchères; marble tables.

"Who is our host?" Trenton said.

"I don't know," Liam said. He looked at me. "A friend of hers, is it?"

"He's somebody who works on Wall Street. I'm not sure exactly what he has to do with the theater. He's a friend of Quill's, I think. They met in London."

It was a full recitation of everything I could remember about the man in whose loft we sat. I had no idea what he looked like, or what, exactly, he did; I only knew that he had made the evening possible.

"I forgot to ask Dara what he looked like," Trenton said. He got up. "Maybe he's in that group over there," he said, and walked down the aisle, to a group of four men talking.

"Quite nice of him, wanting to introduce himself to our host," Liam said.

"Why are you so mad at me?" I said.

"Well, to tell you the truth, I felt like you were embarrassed to be seen with me, you were so reluctant to introduce me. I mean, you do have your moods, you know. I frankly think that it was folly to drive to New York on this particular night. If it's on all week, I don't see why some premonition of yours needs to be heeded."

"I'm sorry I made you come," I said.

"Oh, I'm probably making too much of it. My own nervousness about driving in bad weather." He took my hand. "Sorry," he said.

"We're both moody," I said.

More people entered the loft. Every face that was unfamiliar put me more at ease. A tall girl in a long brown monk's coat came in, holding a little dog. Two men dressed in suits and overcoats came in behind her. Their eyes scanned the crowd. They went to the first row and took a long time taking off their coats, folding them, and putting them on a chair. Then they sat down, with the coats stacked between them, one seat apart. Every time the elevator went down and came up again, more people entered the room. They all looked striking; it was clear that we were attending a performance in New York. Trenton came back, saying that he had just met Andre Gregory, who told him our host was flying in from the West Coast, but probably would not make the beginning of the performance. The man's wife was here, though—or at least she was rumored to be here.

Edward Quill came down the aisle, striding purposefully in a black suit and black-and-white saddle shoes. His shirt was tangerine, his tie imprinted with crossed-out squiggles that looked like a very impatient person's telephone-pad doodlings.

"Face-lift," Trenton whispered, as Edward Quill passed.

"You mean *Quill?*" I whispered back.

"You sounded just like Dara then," Trenton said. "Yeah. Apparently this was supposed to happen a week or so later, but it had to be bumped up because it was the only time our hostess could be in town. Dara told me Quill was in a dither. He's got on some sort of makeup because his face is still purple."

"Indeed," Liam said. The increasing strangeness was putting Liam at ease. He was looking around, taking it all in. "No stage," he said, more to himself than to me.

There also seemed to be no special lighting. In the twilight, the tall, dirty windows looked as if algae had grown on them.

"Good evening, ladies and gentlemen," Edward Quill said. When everyone did not become quiet, he clapped his hands. He stood with his feet turned out, like a ballerina. His suit jacket was tightly tapered, and the pants flared at the ankles. He unbuttoned the single button of his jacket. "The audience is asked to be silent," Edward Quill said. I was examining his face; it looked at once taut and puffy. I thought that he had on eyeliner. I squinted, trying to see.

"Our performance this evening will be a one-woman monologue. Your program notes will give you information about Miss Dara Falcon's previous acting endeavors. Let me say only that you will soon agree with me that the range of her talent is spectacular. Tonight, we are privileged to see her interpretation of one humble woman's thought-provoking life. As a personal note, may I add that Grace Aldridge was a wonderful writer and a generous, spirited woman: poetry was inherent in her prose, and grace—for she was aptly named—abundant in her too-short life. We are indebted to our host and hostess for the evening, Mr. Jeffrey and Mrs. Constance Grandin. After the performance champagne will be served. Miss Falcon has graciously agreed to circulate to discuss the performance. Please stay to share your thoughts." Edward Quill unclasped his hands and gripped them together again, behind his back. He bowed slightly and walked quickly to an Eames chair to the side of the open area.

For a full minute, nothing happened. It was enough time to register the movement upstairs, the honking of horns on the street. People shifted in their seats. I was distracted when Dara appeared, coming through a swinging door from the kitchen. Behind her, I saw a butcher-block cutting board and a row of cabinets. Then the door vibrated closed, and Dara stood alone, tinier than I remembered her, in the calf-length black dress. She did such a good job of acting disoriented that I fell for it: I thought something was wrong; I thought she could not remember her lines.

"You," she said suddenly, pointing to a person a few rows back. When the woman did not respond, she continued to stare. The person misunderstood, just as I had: Dara was acting, but the woman she had pointed to didn't realize it. "Yes," the woman said, hesitantly. This provoked a ripple of nervous laughter from her companions. They understood she should not have spoken. Dara continued to stare at her, hard. The woman sensed, correctly, and too late, that her one word had been one word too many, but her friends were not easy to quiet down. "What about me, instead of her?" the man next to the woman she had initially spoken to called out. Dara's momentum was dissipating. A shadow of worry crossed her face. "Shhh!" a woman sitting near them said. I looked at Edward Quill, sitting to the side. He was rigid. Dara whirled away from the people she had been facing, pointing again into the audience. "You," she said again. "Have you been married? Were you a bride at nineteen?" The second woman sat taller and looked around, not sure how to respond. Dara's pauses were so long that the audience thought the play was participatory.

Then Edward Quill raised a mask to his face. It was flat, like a fan, and both sides—as we soon saw—depicted two different faces: the gossiping old ladies, Mrs. Bell and Mrs. Denton. It was incredibly odd, but also mesmerizing: as Quill took both parts, he alternated between a silly falsetto and a convincing, slightly Southern accented voice just slightly higher than his real voice. In the high-pitched voice, he made some observation; then, with the Southern accent, he interrupted. It was more jarring than someone singing lead and also singing backup. Then Dara's voice began, and Quill's two personas dwindled, though they were not entirely quiet: the gossip continued; the chaos was intentional.

The fight that broke out upstairs, though, was not. A piece of furniture was dragged across the floor and rumbled like thunder; then a woman, her voice sharp and angry, began to scream. The people were fighting about where the dishwasher should be installed. Everyone in the audience looked at the ceiling. For a second we all considered the possibility that this, too, was part of the performance.

"Carry on!" Edward Quill called to Dara, putting the mask on his lap and clapping his hands, but she, too, now looked at the ceiling. "The gods are angry. They are angry about the dishwasher," she said, turning toward the audience. She shrugged: What could be done? Many people laughed at what Dara said, Liam among them. For a few seconds there was quiet, and then the dragging and scraping began again. "You would think this was a fucking tenement!" a woman in a blue fishnet dress said, jumping to her feet. "Those people upstairs are animals. Nothing but pigs. This is what happens when the co-op decides to admit tenants in the entertainment business."

Someone tried to get her to sit down, but instead she ran up the aisle and threw open the door, muttering to herself.

"Our hostess?" Trenton whispered.

"This is part of the play," a man behind us said.

Dara looked at me. Was it the pale, pale makeup that made her look so haggard?

"People in the entertainment industry," she said. "What the hell does she think yours truly does for a living?"

Again, a few people laughed.

The mask was at Edward Quill's side, discarded like a handkerchief that had been used for waving once the person had departed.

"You can back up to the dishwasher, and I'll shove it up your ass!" the man upstairs hollered. Plates began breaking.

"Ladies and gentlemen," Dara said, with perfect composure, "Theater of the Absurd has infiltrated tonight's performance. Mr. Quill and I shall regroup behind the scenes and prepare to continue, after a brief intermission."

"I think it's one of the Beach Boys," someone said to someone else. "I can't remember which one. The one that left his wife and moved in with some belly dancer."

Everything was breaking upstairs. Everything. People stood and said the police should be called. Many people had run out behind the woman in the fishnet dress. She was screaming outside the elevator, trying to push them away so she could go upstairs if what she called "the fucking piece of shit" ever arrived. Someone tried to reason with her. Soon there was a small fight going on outside the elevator. While I looked away, both Dara and Edward Quill had disappeared.

"Jesus Christ," Liam said. "If this isn't the most preposterous—"

"She must be devastated," Trenton said. "I can't believe she walked off like that."

"Should I go backstage?" I said, but when I turned to get his answer, I saw that he had gotten up and was walking in the direction of the elevator.

"I should think you ought to keep out of it," Liam said.

"I thought Brian Wilson moved in upstairs," someone else said.

"This is really quite wonderful in its own way," Liam said. "If someone filmed and recorded the audience, this could be fed into the mix on the next go-round."

"Liam, this is *terrible.*"

"Well, of course I see that, but in another way, it really isn't so terrible. I mean, we're all going to be on her side once she comes out again. You know she's going to get a terrific round of applause now, regardless of what the performance might have been." He looked self-satisfied. "Maybe you were right," he said. "That would be very funny: play cancelled because of a fight over a dishwasher. Did you see that in your crystal ball?"

"Why are you making fun of me?" I said. "Didn't what I feared come true?"

"One could hardly have known," he said.

"Do you think I have any good thoughts, or intuition, about anything?" I said.

He said nothing for a few seconds. Then he said: "Why on earth this should provoke a fight between us, I don't know. Please accept my apology for doubting you. It's just that you weren't too explicit about people fighting upstairs and your friend stalking offstage. Not that it's really a stage. But it's all very contemporary, I understand."

"You're being horrible," I said.

"Actually, until you began criticizing me, I was starting to enjoy myself."

"It's like *The Honeymooners,*" someone said. "Are you too young to remember Jackie Gleason in *The Honeymooners?*"

I looked around. Most people simply looked perturbed. A man a few seats away had closed his eyes and clasped his hands over his chest. Though I hated to admit it, Liam was right: a film of the audience's reaction would be very interesting. The woman next to the snoozing man was flipping through her daybook.

"Let's get dinner," another man said to the woman he was with. She nodded and got up, picking up her hat and coat. Outside, sirens wailed to a stop. The police had arrived. Everyone got up and rushed toward the windows. I followed Liam. Before I reached his side, though, Trenton took my wrist. "This is for you," he said. It was a note, with "Jean" written on the envelope. Trenton disappeared into the crowd as he pushed his way toward a window.

It had to be a note from Dara. I went into the hallway, where the elevator had disappeared, either to the ground or to the floor above. There were only a few people standing around talking. I leaned against the far wall, by the emergency exit, and opened the note. How had she written it so quickly?

*Dear Jean,*

*I've sent a couple of post cards you might not have gotten because I might have the wrong address. When Trenton told me he was going to Dara's play I figured you'd probably be there so I asked him to give this note to you.*

*I've been thinking about our encounter last fall and apologize if I in any way offended you. Trenton and I were talking one night and he said he always liked you but didn't know how to be friends with you. Not because Bob would have been jealous. It's more like neither of us could tell if you had any interest in being friends. When guys don't know they usually back off.*

*I'm actually writing you for four reasons. One is to apologize if I did anything that made you feel bad or in case you thought it was all meaningless to me. It wasn't. Also, I don't think you meant what you wrote to me last, so let's just forget it. I want to let you know that I've moved. My new address is 160 West Neck Drive, apt. 2. The last reason is that I've been going to meetings of ACOA. If you haven't heard of that it's Adult Children of Alcoholics. It's helped me a lot. I've also wondered about your aunt. Do you think she could have been a secret drinker? The things you told me about her make me wonder now that I know more.*

*My father is doing better but sometimes backsliding. I would like to see you again.*

> *Your friend,*
> *Derek*

I was afraid that Liam would see the note; that Derek was going to be harder to shake than I'd thought. He was a kid: What was this about? Why didn't he understand that I no longer wanted to see him? He had friends—why was it so important that I be his friend? I doubted that was what he really wanted. An image came to me of Derek, kneeling between my legs. It made my legs go weak. I had only done what I'd done because I'd been depressed and confused. I certainly didn't want to see him again. He must have told Trenton. Otherwise, why would he have given me the note when Liam wasn't around? From the minute he'd seen me in the elevator, he had been holding the note, waiting for the right minute to sneak it to me. That was proof that he knew what the contents were. I read the note again, hurriedly. I was embarrassed I had confided in Derek. Regardless of what he thought, we didn't have any common bond. Both he and Trenton had been correct. I hadn't wanted to be friends. I wanted to keep to myself. But with both of them, strangely, I had crossed my own boundaries. Just half an hour or so ago, I had resolved not to be drawn into conversation with Trenton, and a few minutes later, my thoughts were all of taking him aside and demanding to know what he knew. Why would the two of them have been talking about me? It aggravated me that I occupied space in their minds. It also embarrassed me that Trenton knew about something I had done privately. It was just like men to talk.

The performance never resumed. The host never arrived from the airport. His wife, though, continued to be hysterical. After the police had spoken to the people upstairs and left, loud music started, but it didn't really matter: there was no performance anyway. A woman who had gone into the kitchen—damn it! that was where I would have been, if Trenton hadn't given me Derek's note—said that Dara had disappeared down a back staircase, using the emergency exit. Two people said they had seen her go. She was not crying, according to them: she was furious. "Who exactly was that actress?" I heard one woman ask another.

The lavender programs were left behind on chairs. People soon began to talk about things other than the performance. Like people in the wake of any disaster, they stood around talking about what they had in common, trying to feel some connection to one another. They also talked about trivia and gossiped and laughed. Somewhere among them were the would-be patrons. Dara had told me the drama critic from the *Village Voice* would be there. Had he been? They were all strangers to me, except for the unmistakable Edward Quill. Except for Liam, who was talking animatedly to a pretty young woman who was laughing about something, and Trenton, whom I cold-shouldered.

People began to mill around, hoping for champagne anyway. The place became a blur of overheard conversations, a cluster of strangers—no place I fit in; no place I wanted to be. If the ripple of disapproval in New Hampshire had been discouraging for Dara, imagine how she must feel tonight. Yet I had the lingering suspicion that even if she had performed, she would have been performing for a very different audience.

T̲hat night, on the way back to Connecticut, I disliked the audience for being too sophisticated, just as I had once disliked the audience in New Hampshire for being unsophisticated. What didn't occur to me until we reached New Haven, and Liam began responding to my description of the text—my typing it; laughing over it with Dara and Tom; the absurd Edward Quill, whom Dara was hoodwinking—was that Dara was not so much a victim as a victimizer, who had gotten her comeuppance.

"In a way, the show Dara put on back in the barn in New Hampshire was analogous to a book published by a vanity press," Liam said. "But even there, you can assume the book is something the author cares about. But what's the virtue of acting so well you trick people into believing they're being offered something of quality, when they aren't?"

I understood what he was saying; there was something unsavory about Dara's having agreed to do the performance as an existential act. She had been exploiting Edward Quill, who was delusional. She had led him on, and she had had the hubris to think that her acting ability could convince people that a fatuous text was actually important. She hadn't been wrong about that—or, at least, she hadn't been entirely wrong, if she considered her audience. In the piece I had written for the New Hampshire paper, I had been under her spell; even though I had seen the magician put the rabbit in the hat, I had still been stunned when the magician pulled it out. We had both known, instantly, that Grace Aldridge's text was as ridiculous as Bob's Buddy Holly glasses. But now I saw that what Dara had done was even worse than my taking money to type a worthless text.

But then again, who was to blame if other people were desperate and foolish? Edward Quill was a grown man, and he had convinced himself Grace Aldridge's life meant something.

Or had he? Might he also have known that her life was inconsequential and vaguely pathetic? Even without the fight upstairs, the bubble would have had to burst eventually. Why had he put his trust in Dara, who was vain enough, in turn, to trust her ability to seduce even the smartest people?

"Say something," Liam said. "Don't start pouting just because you and I have different perspectives on something."

"I don't have a different perspective anymore," I said. "You're right. They're both contemptible."

"Foolish, perhaps," he said.

"Don't pretend to be moderate, Liam."

"I'm not pretending," he said. "I rather pity those caught up in self-deception."

"You never deceive yourself?"

He thought about it. "Depends on the day," he said. "Sometimes I pretend that I'm succeeding just because I've left England. That I'll write a great book one day. That you and I have a future together."

I was so surprised, I couldn't speak. I only looked at him.

"When I look at things rather grimly, I think we're stepping stones for each other," he said.

"What about when you're more optimistic?"

"I guess what I'm saying is that I really am not very optimistic any longer."

He was telling me goodbye. For whatever reason, that was what he was doing. Driving along on the highway, both of us tired and shaken up by the New York expedition, he had maneuvered the conversation to a point I hadn't anticipated. My ribs suddenly felt heavier, my head lighter. It was the odd, scary feeling of being lassoed: as if once his words tightened around me, those words would have the power to drag me out of the car, into the night air. I decided to see if I could speak.

"Is it something I did?" I said.

"No. Rather more that I don't think we're that well suited. Two moody people probably don't do one another much good, with one always catching the other's moods."

"Did you know you were going to say this tonight?" I said.

"Yes, I suppose I did. I shouldn't have said I'd go. I might have been thinking that we'd have a wonderful time and that would change my mind."


I didn't go to class. I asked Megan to walk the dog. I alternated between being furious at Liam for calling things off so precipitously and furious with myself for having put myself in a position where Dara's problems had become the backdrop for the end of my relationship. I was flooded with resentment, going back all the way to my aunt Elizabeth—I was not so crazy I blamed my parents for dying—and continuing through all the people in the recent past I thought had done me wrong, which was quite a long list. What had Bob meant, that we both deserved to be happier? He had meant that *he* deserved to be happier, which meant trips to Europe he would never have taken with me, and hiking in the woods with the guys. Out of sight, out of mind: When was the last time I had heard from Janey? I had been nothing but a diversion for Liam (wasn't that what Gail had warned me about?). I resented the way he had confronted me with his interpretation of Dara's insincerity. So my friends were imperfect; his were so much better? Because they lived in Stonington and went to parties at James Merrill's, they were superior people?

I walked the dog. I went out with no scarf, and with only one mitten in my jacket pocket. I had thrown away the other after the encounter with Derek. The encounter that probably every man in Dell now knew about.

The dog was annoying, trying to dig rocks out of the frozen ground. He ran to the ailing butterfly bush I always took care to chase him away from, raised his leg, and peed on it.

If Elizabeth hadn't gambled, I would have enough money to live in a beautiful house, alone.

If I had gone back to college earlier, instead of serving Bob and Bob's family, I would already have a career.

If, if. If I did, then what? Then I could be as unhappy as everybody else. As unhappy as Dara. She would love it if she could really insinuate herself so I would think of her incessantly. She had almost managed to bore into my brain permanently. What good luck it had been that I had moved away, gotten some distance. There was even one good thing about having been with Liam: he had helped me to see things differently. I thought of the countless times she'd asked for something and I'd responded, starting with the time I'd driven her home from the optometrist's, right through the night before, when Liam and I had set off in bad weather to see her perform in a farce masquerading as a drama.

The sky was white, the road I walked down already heaved up because of the winter's ice. The broken asphalt looked like giant black anthills, sent lopsided by some boy's well-aimed kick. The dog was being stupid, poking his nose in brambles and yelping, backing up, and tripping over his own hind legs. When I called him to my side and knelt and stroked him, it was an effort to be kind—to try to soothe him out of the anxious clumsiness he'd nervously fallen into, picking up my own anger and awkwardness as I mentally thrashed around. Nothing was going right for either of us, but while he sat and I stroked him and he became calmer, a fierce wind suddenly whipped my hair across my face, stinging as it lashed into my eye. What did it matter? I was crying anyway.

Just because I had returned the ring to Tom Van Sant didn't mean that Dara could keep my warm, comfortable alpaca jacket forever. Why hadn't she offered to give it back? It had been a loan, not a compensation prize. As I walked, hugging my arms around me, I lamented the loss of the coat. Though Bob had divided the money from our savings account and sent me half, he had not sent anything from the house. I had written him, asking for only a few things, all unbreakable, but he had made no response at all. Why not? Did a person have to emote like Dara to get attention?

Back at the house, there was one message on my answering machine. "Hello, this is Bob," the voice said. "Please call as soon as you get this message. Please," he said again, more emphatically. What did he want? I didn't soften when I heard his voice. What could I "please" do for him now?

I stretched out on the bed. The dog sensed not to jump up with me. He went over to his bed and curled into a little ball. I was fighting back tears. I was angry that I had let Liam matter so much to me—and that it had happened without my even realizing how much he had meant. Was I only capable of seeing something when the rug was pulled out from under me? I felt like some young novice, taking instruction about everything: the actual meaning of letters I received; needing to be told point-blank when someone no longer cared for me. It reinforced my worst fear: that I was so naive, so needy, that people had no choice but to overcome their own hesitancy and, for my own good, bluntly confront me with whatever it was I didn't know or needed to know.

When the phone rang ten or fifteen minutes later, I got up, in a total funk. It would no doubt be another call for my own good. Frozen with resignation, I picked up the phone.

That was when I found out one of the worst things I have ever had to hear. It took me longer than it should have to shake myself out of my own self-absorbed despair to realize that the voice that was trying to speak to me, chokingly saying my name so quietly, over and over again, was Bob. "I don't know how to tell you," he said. "All I can do is say it. Frank's dead."

The external temperature of my room dropped twenty degrees. I looked in the direction of the dog, without really seeing him. Eventually, as he came into better focus, I saw that he was looking at me with a strange expression on his face. He slapped his tail once or twice, then stopped. The sound seemed to be amplified. On the other end of the phone, Bob continued to cry. I found it very hard to follow what he was saying, and he must have known that, because as soon as he said something, he repeated it, trying to speak more distinctly. Eventually, his words began to come clear: Frank had died just before dawn, in his car, going at high speed. He had hit a stationary crane in a cordoned-off construction area on the highway, head-on. No one had seen it happen. They had had to cut open the car to get to him. He was dead at the scene.

I shook my head no, but I didn't say the word to Bob. I managed, instead, a flood of words that asked only the most inane question: What had Frank been doing on the highway before dawn?

This elicited an outpouring of information, though none of it answered my question. It answered the unasked question of whether he was drunk or sober. He was drunk. Very drunk.

"Janey—" I said.

"Janey's at Sandra's. What is she doing there? Those two can't stand each other," Bob said, then began to cry loudly. "My fucking sister," I thought I heard him say.

"Bob—"

"Yes?" he said. He choked back a sob. "Yes?" he said again.

All I could say was, "It can't be true."

He began to cry again. I heard him through a roar in my head that was almost like a white-noise machine; I heard him as I tried to choke back my own tears. So that was it: Frank was dead. I thought back to the time when Bob had told me what Frank had said about Dara's having wanted to check into a hotel, make love, then go over a bridge. Which she had denied. Which she had said simply was not so. Regardless of who had been telling the truth, now Frank was dead. I could hear Dara distinctly, the day we had taken the walk, saying: "Frank said *what?*"

In my mind, while there was only the sound of Bob's crying on the other end of the phone, I invented the gory crash scene, then tried to erase it. I pictured the highway empty of cars, the sun just coming up. It was so vivid, I felt I could reach out and touch it. What was I thinking of? Why would I even want to touch a highway?

"Bob," I said, "It's unbelievable."

"Listen," he said, "don't say anything about his carrying on with that bitch, nothing about—"

"No," I said.

"No is right," he said, sniffing deeply.

I looked around the room. I suppose I realized I wouldn't be in it much longer. I was already back in Dell. But what was I going to say to Janey? What was I ever going to say to her?

"I've got to go," he said. "You can imagine what pandemonium it is. Are you going to come up here?"

"Don't you want me to come?" I said.

"Of course I think you should be here, but I'll think of something to tell them if you can't do it right away."

"Come get me," I said.

There was a pause. I could feel Bob's surprise. Why was he surprised? My knees felt like rubber, and the white-noise machine was scrambling sound in my head. Did he think I didn't ever need him? Could it have been my mistake to have always seemed more self-sufficient than I was?

The news had focused my attention. Whatever happened with Liam didn't matter at all, in the long run. The ups and downs of relationships just didn't matter. What was important was being at Janey's side, and I was equally sure that the thing I most dreaded was seeing Janey.

"I need directions," Bob said to me. "I don't know where you live."

"J ean," Dara said to me on the phone when I had returned to Connecticut, "I thought you'd call."

She surprised me. First, because she'd used my first name. I think it was the first time I ever heard her address me that way. Second, because she was right: it was strange I hadn't called, but days after the cremation—which was what Frank had wanted, so Janey did it even though Barbara was horrified—days later, I would mean to do something and confuse that with having done it.

"Are you there?" she said.

"I'm here," I said. I forced myself to be calm. "It's really, really horrible. I don't know what to say."

"It was one of the worst moments of my life. How could you know what to say?"

A cold chill went up my spine and spread across my shoulders. She didn't know about Frank. She was talking about the play. She was calling to talk about her silly play.

"Edward was ridiculous, insisting the show must go on. I mean, the vibes were horrible before the people upstairs started fighting. Do you know that a lot of them were opera patrons? There was a whole contingent of them staying at the loft. Then there were other people involved in bringing art to New York from Caribbean islands. I don't know what Edward thought we were doing, performing for those people. He promised me the reviewer from the *Village Voice* was going to be there, which he apparently based on the man's having sent him a form letter saying he didn't attend performances on request. Sweetie, I have been dealing with someone with the brain power of a thistle. And I am so, so *embarrassed.*"

I couldn't tell her. All the time she had been rattling on, I had thought of various ways to bring it up. It was not going to be possible.

"I don't think you and he are a good team," I finally said.

"I assure you: I *completely* understand that."

Was it so disastrous that she had to break up a business relationship, when I had had the courage to leave my husband? When the first man I cared about since leaving Bob had summarily dismissed me?

"The icing on the cake was that he threw me out," she said. "I had to go to Bayonne that night and get my car. I couldn't face that garret in Portsmouth. I've made it to the bosom of my family, at least, here in Alaska." She paused for dramatic effect. "Provincetown," she said. "I'm with my sister and her family in frozen Provincetown."

I almost blurted out the bad news. I almost said the three words, but I just couldn't do it.

"I want you to know something, in case anything happens to me," she said. "I want you to trust me about this: Edward is a violent and dangerous man. Anything he might—." She broke off. "It's times like this when you can really, truly, hate men, isn't it?" she said. "Sweetie: I'll write you."

I sighed, but said nothing. I had become fatigued by everyone's demonizing everyone else. It was like the flu: everyone who lived, or had ever lived, in Dell eventually caught it. And furthermore, what did she intend to write me? Were there more letters from Chekhov that would seem appropriate? I bit my tongue. I remembered her so clearly, holding the cake box she had joked was a birdcage, standing in Tom Van Sant's kitchen. How interesting that she had been thinking in terms of traps, when she had returned to Dell to entrap us all. I had needed a friend so much—any friend, apparently—that I had ignored the mounting evidence that I was just a convenience for Dara. I also had reason to feel guilty, though: I had taken the easy way out and put another person on a pedestal instead of doing the hard work of putting my own life in order. One thing we had in common was that we had been complicitous.

"Dara—I'm sorry," I said. Meaning: about everything. I was sorry she wasn't famous. I was sorry Frank was dead. I was sorry for Janey. For everyone, myself included.

"I know you are," she said quietly. "But we have to go on, don't we? You're my shining example of that."

And do you know—my heart softened. Something loosened inside my chest like an internal sigh. I was flooded with the realization that everything was complicated, and that within that complication, she and I might still find a new footing for friendship. Chekhov himself had remarked on finding life tedious. If it was, even for someone as talented, as brilliant, as Chekhov, then surely I needed to cut myself some slack about having romanticized someone who was ordinary into someone who was extraordinary.

Her goodbye was so quiet, I didn't even have to respond.

I called Janey. Sandra answered the phone. "How are you, dear?" she said to me. She had called me dear every time I'd called since Frank's death. I was surprised she was still at Janey's, because Janey's brother had flown in from California, and he would be staying indefinitely to help her.

"The question is, how's Janey? How are the kids?"

"Well," Sandra said, "her brother is very—I don't know what you'd say. He's very hearty. He had Max out tossing the football in the backyard. Pete hangs around Janey like a two-year-old. He's started to suck his thumb again."

"How's Janey holding up?"

"You know Janey: she's trying to do the best she can so everybody else will keep it together. She put on her coat and went out and sat on the swing set, trying to look interested while the football tossing went on. It's worrying me that she doesn't eat."

"She has to eat," I said.

"Well, yes. Of course." There was a pause. "Maybe now that we've shooed Barbara and Dowell out, she'll feel a little more comfortable with . . . with, you know, just the younger members of the family around."

"Can she come to the phone?"

"She went into the bathroom to shower just before you called," Sandra said. "I hear the water running."

"Oh," I said, disappointed.

"Jean, Marie wants to say one brief thing to you," Sandra said.

Marie's voice: "Aunt Jean?"

"Hello, Marie," I said.

"Have you ever heard of the fashion designer Halston?"

"Yes," I said.

"Good," she said, "because I'm writing a paragraph about him for school. Halston always has all his friends that he dresses and goes to the disco with to his New York apartment for Thanksgiving, and he does the cooking himself. His real name is Roy Frowlick, and before he was a famous designer, he made hats."

"Put Sandra back on, Marie. You can tell me about Halston another time."

"Marie, let me have the phone now," Sandra said. There was a rustling sound. Sandra came back on.

"Bob's come for dinner," Sandra said. "I don't suppose you'd like to say hello?"

"No," I said. "No, I'll call another time."

When I hung up, I got my telephone book and looked for Elizabeth's number in Montana. I wanted to be angry at someone. I was irrationally angry at Sandra for moving in with Janey the way she had; I was angry that unless I called Janey's house, no one called to let me know how things were. If Bob could go to dinner there, why couldn't he call me? He knew how much I cared about Janey. He must have known that I'd like to know what was going on. Probably, like Elizabeth, he was ignoring me out of cowardice. Elizabeth also was trusting that I wouldn't call and press the point. So what if she had done many things for me when I was a child? She had also stolen from me. She had taken what by rights should be mine. I searched for her number with shaking hands.

Her husband answered the phone and was very matter-of-fact about what he told me when I asked to speak to her. He was neither pleasant nor unkind. He said that Elizabeth had been gone for many months. She had gone to get groceries and simply vanished. Her car was found at the airport with a grocery bag in the backseat. It was from a store where she never shopped. The police had tried to find her. He had no money to conduct a search of his own. He told me that to keep his sanity, he had stopped guessing about what might have happened to her. Before we hung up, he wished me "a very happy New Year."

There it was: the woman who had raised me, lost in space. Perhaps gone wherever my parents had gone. When the shock registered, I began to wonder whether I might be the next to mysteriously disappear. The fear of abandonment was obvious. Less obvious was the fragile foothold I suddenly thought I had on planet Earth. My long period of anxious, silent counting—touching inanimate objects over and over; putting the dog on a leash and fearing constantly that he would be run over anyway; awakening repeatedly at night when I did fall asleep, because I'd heard brakes squealing, seen the dog tumbling—those things began soon after my phone call to Elizabeth's husband, but gained on me slowly, exhausting me, making me question my sanity, while another shock broadsided me, proving that bad things always come in threes. For a while, after the phone call to Elizabeth's husband, whose name I couldn't even remember, I lay on the bed, looking at the ceiling. Then I turned on my side and looked across the room, to the empty fireplace. I stayed that way for some time. Then in an attempt to shake myself out of my sorrow, I called Liam and asked if I could see him. Exactly how much I was kissing the hand that slapped me, I had no way of knowing. I heard music in the background, but no voices. He asked what was the matter, as if seeing me was conditional on his judging my crisis worthy. I considered blurting out the news about Frank, but while I knew he would express sorrow, he hadn't known Frank. Frank would be just another sad story to Liam. And it wasn't because of Frank's death that I was calling. It wasn't even to report on my surprising call to Elizabeth's husband—though Liam had urged me many times to call if Elizabeth refused to respond to my letters. So why was I calling him? I must have sensed that there was more bad news to come and wanted it all, in a landslide. Instead of hanging up, as I should have, when I realized he wasn't particularly happy to hear from me, I simply stayed quiet, waiting for him to say something. "Please leave the dog at home," he said. "I've gotten myself a puppy, and I think it would cause too much commotion."

A dog? He had gotten a dog?

Obediently, I left Sparkle behind, pushing him back from the door gently with my knee. So many comings and goings, as Liam had once said, kidding me fondly. On the drive to his house, I felt, in some odd way, that Liam would always be on top of things because he arranged for replacements for losses, while I muddled through, accepting a dog I had co-opted as a sort of replacement for both husband and lover. And look at who I accepted as friends: Gail, holding on to a semblance of the life she wanted, surrounding herself with admirers, entertaining to distract herself; Megan—well: even in my sourest mood, I could not really criticize myself by pretending that I had cultivated Megan as a friend.

Liam was in jeans, bare chested, with a green satin robe I had never seen before tied at his waist. His hair was rumpled, as if he'd already gone to bed. The Irish setter puppy was adorable, small and clumsy, awakened from sleep by the sudden nighttime activity. Liam had turned the music off. The light was on only in the living room. He let me know by his remoteness that I was intruding, but still he would surely be shocked when I told him the news. But talking about Frank's death would be too much for me; I realized that I didn't want to say anything about that. It would be too difficult to give him a sense of who Frank was. Had been. I was even wondering myself who Frank had been. And if I was wondering, what thoughts must have been going through Janey's mind? She had not even known he wasn't in bed the night of the accident. When she had gone to bed, Frank had been beside her. What had made him get up in the middle of the night? Insomnia? The desire for a drink?

Liam listened to my story about the phone call to Montana. I had gotten up my courage to do something, and I had been so unprepared for the result. Of course, Elizabeth's disappearance was not something I could have anticipated. Yet the idea of existing without what little was left of my own family so soon after having severed myself from Bob and his family . . . it was all so abrupt. So painful, and perplexing. Liam had said—implied—that I was a competent person. Did he still feel that way? I could not have been more obvious about asking for reassurance. I didn't notice that he did not offer me anything to drink. I assumed— if I assumed anything—that the magnitude of what I had to say was probably perplexing him, making him think—wasn't it possible?—

about his own position, exiled from his family in England. Was I talking to him because we were similar, or dissimilar? Or was I talking to him just because we had once been close, and I was grasping at straws? I told him a disjointed version of what Elizabeth's husband had said to me, my story full of digressions and self-doubt. "When we hung up, he said to me, 'Have a very happy New Year,' " I said. "Do you think he was being sarcastic?"

"I don't think so. Probably trying to be unemotional. Trying to go on with his life."

I wished the puppy was in my lap, not Liam's. I wished the puppy could be on the floor, and I could be in Liam's arms. But the puppy stayed, and I sat where I had first seated myself when I came into the room: in a chair I'd always avoided because I'd never found it comfortable.

"I'm awfully sorry," he said. "She might be fine, of course. People disappear every day. There's still a chance you'll hear from her eventually. Since she was a gambler, this might just be another form of gambling. Gambling on a new life, I mean."

"But that doesn't excuse—"

"Oh, Jean, you're not a judge. You might not know what her life was like. You might agree with the decision she'd made if you did."

"You sound like you know all about it."

"I know exactly nothing. I realize that this was a big shock. But we don't know all the facts, either of us."

"That's just an easy way to dismiss the subject."

"I'm afraid any words I say would be inadequate. I can see that this would be shocking to you."

"Liam—what's made you so cold toward me? You were angry at me before we ever set out for New York to see Dara. What is this all about?"

He looked at me, his thumbs tucked under the sash of his robe. "Well, since it is inevitable that you mention her, maybe this would be an opportune time to tell you something I do know something about," he said. "I met her before we went to New York. She came here. I talked to her. But before you jump to conclusions, it's not what you think."

"You met her before that night? You're serious?"

"She arrived in the much-discussed Brown Bomb," he said. He

raised his hands and imitated the motion of a driver holding a wheel. "She even borrowed fifty dollars," he said. "I admit she tried to seduce me, but she settled for disturbing me. What started as a sort of game between us escalated to something quite contentious and upsetting. I can see that people would be taken in by her. But I'm afraid this is a case of unpleasant, but not expected, on my part, pathology: in the guise of caring deeply about you, she actually cares most deeply about gaining ground by disparaging you. She feels a great sense of entitlement, and she's quite jealous of what you have."

"When did all this happen?" I asked hollowly.

"I'll tell you the whole story if you promise me you'll do something more with the information than have a tantrum or be perverse and keep on just as you've kept on, forgiving her at every turn."

I couldn't say anything. I wanted to hear, but I couldn't speak. I knew—deep down, I knew—that whatever Liam had to say would be horrible. After a few seconds of silence, he began to speak, without any promises on my part: "Well, she rang me up, ostensibly quite worried about you, thinking you might go back to your husband."

I could hear it. I could hear the breathless voice; the tone of harried self-importance.

"I met her for a drink at the tavern in Ashford. How exactly that resulted in her going home with me, I'm still not sure, but at first I listened with interest because she was so keyed up. I thought perhaps you hadn't wanted to tell me, of all people, about your quandary, if you were torn between me and your husband. And in all the pregnant pauses—because I was listening, not talking—between her telling me what she'd come to tell me and our leaving the bar, we did get slightly tipsy, and that was when she suggested, rather obliquely, that you and she were lovers, of a sort. She explained that since taking up with me, you had given away her token of love and that furthermore you had decided to stonewall, pretending you had done the morally correct thing. What she told me was that although the love between the two of you was platonic, that only made it stronger; nothing, ultimately, could come between you. If you think this is easy to tell you, it isn't."

I listened, believing it at the same time it seemed incredible—which was so often my attitude: the only attitude anyone could have toward Dara, I was coming to think. He said that by the next morning, he began to sense her hidden agenda. While she said how much she cared for me, she was too heavy-handed in cueing him that I might not be everything he hoped. Increasingly, it seemed she wanted me to get back the diamond-and-ruby ring that had, as Liam put it, "such a history." He saw clearly that it was not the token she described. She seemed frankly materialistic, wanting to know whether he was renting his house or if he'd bought it, what salary he was paid at the university. In the light of day, he just didn't like her. He suspected her motives, and worried that she would not stop with him in her campaign to disparage me, but he was too embarrassed about what he'd done to come clean. It had been easier when he'd had it confirmed in New York that she wasn't a great actress. Until he saw her there, he had tried to convince himself that she might be mad, but brilliant. "She's got nothing left for the stage, if she ever had it," he said. "The truly great acting goes on every day, and she calls it a life. How can there be much of anything left over?"

"Why didn't you tell me at the time?"

"Because I had the distinct sense she was about to fall on her face, and I guess I thought you might hear it better if what I said followed your observing that. I wasn't sure she'd fall on her face onstage, so to speak, but however she did it, I sensed she was about to self-destruct."

"Are you lying about not sleeping with her, Liam? What did you two do?"

"Well, we started talking, and she somehow worked the conversation around to her wanting to perform for me. She was flirting, I admit, but since I wasn't interested, I thought I'd just let things play themselves out. She wanted to say some lines for me—performing for Daddy, no doubt. And appropriately enough, they were lines from *A Doll's House,* not from that travesty that we both know is absolute hogwash. Anyway: it was bitter cold, and we had a brandy back at my house, and when she did her little performance, she fixed her eyes on me and gave me what-for, as if I really was that egotistical man Nora was married to, and she his newly assertive wife. And I thought: Maybe she truly hates all men; maybe she is gay, and she's projecting onto Jean. Still, I wasn't completely and entirely sure: I thought there might be something between you; that it might even be sexual."

"You've changed your mind?" I managed.

"Yes. Certainly. The next morning everything was crystal clear. That night she was extremely interesting, if nothing else, and I realized almost immediately that what she intended was to get me to her level of excitement. I expect she thought sex might follow. I'm not saying she wasn't on the make. But she was clearly willing to settle for exciting me in any way she could. So she did her scene, and really—the drink did not explain why she simply could not act very well. She was passionate but awful: it was all about her, trying to stare through my eyes clear to the back of my head. And then something impish took over in me, because what she'd done from start to finish was embarrass herself, which she didn't know she had. I said: 'I should have this on tape. Let me get this on tape,' and she was flattered. She wanted to do it again and have it taped."

"If you think you're going to play it for me," I said, "I don't want to hear your goddamn tape."

"There isn't one. There never was. But I pretended I had a cassette in the machine, and then she did her scene and I made my pretend recording. I don't know exactly what I hoped to accomplish, because I admit it had been a long day, and some part of me simply wanted to be mean and go to sleep. But I pushed the record button and it was quite eerie: she was more convincing emoting for the machine. But when the time came to hit playback, there was nothing, of course. It was nasty of me, but when she was done, I cocked my head as if some infinitesimal sound on the tape meant it was about to begin, and then I frowned and looked very disappointed: my own best version of a disappointed person. I said to her, 'I guess all we have are the sounds of exquisite silence,' and she could tell from my expression it was no accident. And it discombobulated her. She was furious, but she turned the anger inward and seemed to get much drunker all of a sudden. She went into the bathroom, and I heard her puking, in fact. The water running. And I thought how much I had always hated it when I was a pawn. I thought that and felt very self-righteous and put-upon, but then I heard her vomit again and something made me go to the door, and when I did, I thought: Stay out of it. She can clean herself up and leave. Everything will be perfectly fine if you just don't open the door."

"Stop," I said. "I don't want to hear it."

"But I told you it's not what you might think. I didn't open it, but I was standing there when she came out, and for a second we both looked at each other without any defenses, I think, and she looked so guilty, and I must have too. There were the two of us, in the middle of the night, and it was sort of pathetic. But at the same time, I knew I couldn't embrace her because if I let down my defenses, she might make another move. Intoxicated as she was, she might relax just enough to try the next thing. And then she fell asleep in my bed. Clothed, as was I. She fell asleep, and in the morning she went away, trying to sound triumphant by saying that I'd been her ideal audience; that she'd appreciated the applause of one hand clapping."

"You slept in the same bed."

"Yes, well, as I tried to say: sympathy for her aside, I was thoroughly sick of being punished because I'd been caught up in someone else's problems. It's my bed. I sleep in it." He looked at me. "What do you want me to do? Deny that her energy is sexy? She's really out there. She *is* interesting. She just isn't what she thinks she is."

"That night . . . had you already written me off?"

"Jean, I entertained the thought that not only did she have designs on you, but that the feeling might be reciprocal," Liam said. "In that light, your revelation about Gail could have been deliberately concocted to throw me off track—that you hadn't known about Gail when everyone on campus knew. But you confused me later when you told me about her Chekhov letter. I could see you were genuinely distraught. So I thought that, well, maybe it was possible that you didn't understand what she wanted from you. And I was in something of an internal struggle myself. Yes: I'd begun to sense things weren't going to work out between us." He looked at me. "It also seemed possible that it was a ménage à trois she was after."

I could feel my face burning. Who cared what she wanted, or would settle for, or was determined to get?

"She showered in the morning. She undressed in the bathroom with the door open. She knows she has an attractive body. I'm not defending her. Quite the opposite."

"But you get to be the good boy because you didn't touch her."

"It did take some courage to confess. I'm not saying I'm blameless. I'm just saying that since you like facts so much, I didn't fuck your friend, who wanted me to fuck her. I'm telling you I was had. She made me desire her, at the same time I resented her because she was such a bad friend to you, and such an impostor. That's the word for what she is: she's an impostor, not an actress. But then I realized she was in bad shape. I picked up on her exhaustion, which was right under the surface. I thought that she should stay because she was tired. She was drunk. I realized the lateness of the hour." He let his words hang in the air. "I thought about the unreliability of her car," he added.

I cringed. It was too painful. I had intruded too long, cross-examined him when I should have realized that all he was capable of was rationalization. He continued, "What I realized with the light of day—you have to believe me—I believe she's a succubus, Jean. That's who I got involved with."

Not only did Dara cast a spell when she spoke—people who had come into contact with her, in describing her, also cast a spell. At the moment Liam told me what he thought, in his hushed voice, wincing, the rude laugh I felt sure I'd emit stuck in my throat. It could have sounded crazy—condescending to the person he was telling it to, and as crazy as any lie Dara ever thought up—but if you thought about it not on a literal level, but metaphorically. . . . In that sense she did, indeed, have supernatural powers. Liam was only attaching a specific word to what we already knew.

He got up and sat on the arm of my chair, slipping his arm around my shoulder. I threw it off, as if the tentacle of some monster had reached out to grab me.

"You know that women distrust you, don't you?" I said. "Can you understand why you've made another enemy? Are you even capable of understanding why I feel so deceived by what you've done?"

"Would it have been better to have fucked her? Then you could really indulge your self-righteousness. You and your friend aren't entirely dissimilar, you know. You both stand your ground, and you both want what you want, whatever that requires putting other people through."

I gave him the finger. It was the first time in my life I had ever used Frank's favorite gesture, and the simplicity of it, the saneness of it, gave me a moment of pure peace.

I woke up the day after seeing Liam remembering no particular bad dream—the dog had not died; I had not been sucked into infinity—but my surroundings looked strange, slightly tainted, as if onionskin paper had once covered things, and then been peeled back. That left me with a darkly dusty rug, a splintered bookcase, and a front window crisscrossed with masking tape that looked like an X ray of a patient who has suffered nerve damage. At the very least, I could find another, more attractive place to live, where I would stop being a shutaway; ultimately, closing myself up in one room had probably only been my déclassé version of imitating Dara.

I took a shower and washed my hair, dried my hair, walked the dog, and left a message on Liam's answering machine saying that, while he probably felt better for having confessed, it was my thought that he should rot in hell on a pitchfork. I referred him to his favorite Bosch print, hung in his bathroom. I went to class and listened to Gail lecture on *To the Lighthouse*. I ripped up my parking ticket. After class, I went to Gail's office. She was talking to a student, but I scribbled a note for Joyce, who was visiting on a winter vacation, asking her whether she felt like taking a spur-of-the-moment drive with me: I would drop her in Wellfleet to visit her parents, and then continue on to Provincetown. We could return in a day or two. I was proud of myself for remembering where Joyce's parents lived. It was also frustrating that I could retain trivia while I was oblivious to things transpiring in front of my eyes. I asked Joyce to go with me because I thought that having someone seated next to me who had no idea why I was really going to Provincetown would be empowering; I felt that I needed to deceive someone myself, rather than be the one who was always deceived, and my deception of Joyce would be harmless. Also—although I didn't really believe it possible—her presence would mean that I would not turn back.

Joyce called me that night, saying that it was a splendid idea. "Gail was slightly put out that you didn't invite her, but I pointed out that she shouldn't run out on a job she was trying to hold on to, and anyway, she gets more vacations than I do," Joyce said. She had already phoned her parents, and they were delighted. She tried to convince me to stay for dinner in Wellfleet, but family dinners were a part of my past.

The next day we hit the road, eating a picnic lunch as we drove, sharing it with the dog in the backseat. I was careful what I told Joyce about the reason for my trip to Provincetown. It seemed pleasingly ironic to describe what I was doing as "going to a party." I also told her about breaking up with Liam, because I had found out he was every bit the ladies' man Gail had described him as being. As I presented it, I had ended the relationship, not him. Since it might have been any woman I'd found out about his sleeping with, there was no reason to explain the fine points. No reason to mention that technically he had not had sex with her; no point in bringing up the painful double betrayal of his having chosen a close friend of mine.

"He's probably pathological," she said. "Beyond redemption."

It was a long drive, but once we'd passed Boston the cars stopped tailgating and passing on the left and right, fanning out around my car like stampeding animals avoiding another animal that was limping. At a service area, we got out to go to the bathroom and to walk the dog. What I was preoccupied with was whether Dara had slept with Bob. I watched the dog peeing on a tree and identified with the tree. I was not the first woman to be betrayed by her friend, but when had the betrayal started, and with whom, and what was the extent of it? Even if I was on to myself, I could imitate Liam and rationalize anyway, like slipping my toes into a too-small shoe to see how pretty my foot would look.

Joyce drove the last fifty miles to Wellfleet. It was dusk when we got to her parents' house. They were nice people—delighted to see their daughter, and they even pretended to be delighted to meet her friend—but I left as soon as I could, impelled by the increasing necessity of seeing Dara.

When I was back on the road, Sparkle came up front into the passenger seat. Soon, he curled up and went to sleep. His whimpering, and the jazz I listened to quietly on the radio, continued almost to Provincetown. I stopped at a convenience store and asked directions to Dara's sister's house. I was carrying an envelope Dara had sent me with her sister's return address. A haggard woman, sitting on a stool by the cash register, put the chicken leg she was eating down on top of a newspaper and, licking her fingers, showed me on a map where I wanted to go. She handed me a pen with her greasy fingers, and watched me write down what she said. "Most people going the opposite direction in this season," she said. "Hope you get some good beach weather."

Though I thought I had written down carefully what the woman had told me, I had trouble finding the street from her instructions. The side streets were steep, narrow, and icy. Either snow had just melted, or there had recently been sleet. Street signs were bent or missing. Very few lights were on, so it was difficult to read house numbers. I sensed I was driving in the wrong direction and made my way back to the main street. Very little was open, but I parked by the Atlantic House and went inside and asked again for directions.

Before driving in the direction the woman sent me, I went outside and crossed the street to look at the water. The air was so cold that I saw the water through a haze of tears. I stared until my head started to ache. It was as if my frozen nose were exerting force on my forehead. My nose felt too large, too heavy—my face was distorting. I had a horror-movie vision of my changing features. I would be ugly—terrifyingly ugly—when I saw Dara, and that pleased me. She should see that not only was she monstrous, but that her vileness had begun to transform everything around her. I didn't wipe away my tears. I stared at the ocean, thinking that in winter, it still had an odd, disquieting beauty, but that the water was not in any way inviting. People always romanticize the beach out of season: the strange, sculptural dunes; the choppy, inky water empty of everything but the sturdiest sea life. But what was so wonderful about the winter Atlantic? The sheer extent of it, its vastness, its putty blackness? When it could not be entered—when few boats sailed on it, and when no bodies swam in it—it could intimidate; that might be why people romanticized it. One way to feel less fearful was to ignore the fact that something was off-limits, unapproachable. I thought back to Gail's class, to her discussion of the lighthouse in Virginia Woolf's novel: that the characters were drawn to something that offered the possibility of transcending time because it remained a constant symbol. But a lighthouse seemed a rather grand symbol, something worthy of fixating on, while in my own life it had sometimes been inexplicably hard to look away from even the most ordinary things: the configuration of cracks in a windowpane; the impression made by the dog's body when he rose from his pallet. I sometimes stared at things almost in order to come to no conclusion, letting objects and the banal physical appearances of things relax me the way worry beads preoccupy, and thus absorb worry. Which might have been patterned behavior, more an imitation of Elizabeth watching the night sky than anything about my personality that carried deep significance. She might even be amused if she had died and gone to heaven—if the heaven she maintained she believed in really existed, and she had a clear view down to me—that I was standing and staring at the Atlantic, which symbolized so much, and ultimately meant so little.

How long had I been there, freezing? A minute? Ten?

I had once thought about marrying Liam. I had thought we were on the same wavelength. I had thought that because he was having sex with me, he didn't desire sex with other women. What was the lying way he had put it? That it was her energy he found sexy.

Her own excessiveness robbed other people of energy.

Dara had taken things from me.

Shivering, I went back to the car and began again to search for Dara's sister's house. This time I found it. The house was small and shabby, with two broken shutters leaning against the weathered clapboards and a rusted wheelbarrow by the front steps. It was also unlit and possibly unoccupied—something that had not occurred to me until I saw it, so silent and empty. Wouldn't that be just perfect? To drive all the way to Provincetown, only to find that I'd been lied to again: no one there; everyone gone. I got back in the car and double-checked the address. I saw a light on several houses down, started the ignition, and coasted in the direction of the house. I got out and knocked on the door. After a while, a man with a beard came to the door. "I'm looking for a friend at number forty-three," I said. "Do you know if people are living there?" He had on a nightshirt and a black vest. His cat ran out the door.

"Which one?" he said, peering around me. "The Feldstones' house?"

"The yellow house," I said.

"The Feldstones. I think there are people there. Were yesterday, anyway," he said. "Do you need a phone?"

I said no and thanked him, then returned to the bar of the Atlantic House to try to figure out what to do. She was not going to get away with this. I was going to confront Dara, and I was not going to let her off the hook. I ordered a hamburger and a brandy. That seemed odd, but what the hell. It tasted wonderful—warm and delicious. I hadn't realized until I ate real food how hungry I'd been. I looked around. Here I was in this unlikely place, at the start of my so-called party. There were a few men at the end of the bar, two standing and one sitting, though there were plenty of empty seats. There was a couple having coffee at one of the tables. There was very little business, so after serving me, the bartender sat at a table adjacent to the bar and opened a thick book and began to read. I ran through some possibilities: go back to the house and sit by the curb and wait; ask the bartender if there was any place open to spend the night, if that turned out to be necessary. There had to be someplace. Then all I would have to worry about would be whether they would take dogs. If I had to, I would wait until the next day to find her. I looked at a man sitting alone, drinking a beer and reading the paper. The crazy thought went through my head that I might pick up someone as a little adventure, as an oblique way of warming up for a fight—which is what I'd done once before, though I'd miscalculated because Derek had been too needy. That was when I looked up and saw Dara, red-faced and windblown, race into the bar out of the cold, and then I saw her in tandem with herself, just to the side of where she had first walked, moving slightly slower, red-faced and windblown, and her dual entrance scared me to death because I knew I was hallucinating.

Except that I wasn't. It was Dara and her twin sister, her identical twin, and I had no idea which was which. Of course, it didn't take Dara long to realize she was being stared at. Dara was the one who stood completely still, staring at me with her mouth open, as if the wind had caught up with her and frozen her. Her sister was fussing with her own parka, trying to unzip the stuck zipper. My alpaca jacket was some-where else; they wore the same dark blue parkas. They wore the same jeans. Only their shoes were different. Even their bright, windblown hair was identical.

Dara came toward me with her arms outstretched, but it was the slowest recovery I'd ever seen her make. She managed something, though. She got within a few feet of the bar stool before her expression changed and she stopped, putting her hands over her mouth. It was the oddest thing: on such a cold night, instead of wearing woolen mittens, she had on white cotton gloves, the gloves that ladies of our mothers' generation had worn, and my thoughts turned to static, so that I saw an image of my mother, dressed to go to the wedding, interrupted by an image of Dara, windblown but oh so proper, and then another unex-pected image: a photograph that had flashed on the TV screen at Liam's, weeks before, as the newscaster explained that a woman from Pomfret had been killed in her backyard, hanging out the wash, when a hunter had mistaken her white mittens for the flash of a deer's tail.

I have come back to that moment many times over the years. In fact, it is a recurrent nightmare. I realized simultaneously that a trigger-happy hunter might have shot at Dara, and I took the sound of quarters falling into the jukebox to be shots, looked at my own hands, and realized that I was capable of murder. I dropped my hands to my sides. Only Dara's arms were extended as she continued the last few paces of her slow walk toward me. Though there was absolute numbness in my arms—nothing, in that second, could have allowed me to lift them—it was not that I wanted to return her embrace. But that she touched me, when I could not touch her—that I registered her touch, but could experience only heaviness—made me feel totally helpless. And then she had whispered to me, "Oh, sweetie, now you know all my secrets."

But of course I didn't. I didn't know anything more than I'd ever known, except that she existed in duplicate. What did it mean? That everything she'd told me was a mishmash of her life and her twin's? Was I about to find out the truth about who'd run away, and who'd been hospitalized at McLean? Who'd had the baby—if either of them had? Was I now about to get full disclosure from someone I had decided, before coming to Provincetown, would no longer be a part of my life?

The other people at the Atlantic House were regulars. No one there was surprised to see Dara and her sister. Those who still looked our way were wondering about me: why I was gawking at the two of them; why I was standing like a martinet; what it was I couldn't seem to recover from. The sight of twins was not exactly the most remarkable sight in the world.

"Darcy," her sister said, "how about an introduction?" She had gotten her zipper unstuck. She seemed at once outgoing and shy—or it might have been reluctance. She could not have known what to expect either. Would she have any idea who I was, even if she heard my name?

"I'm Jean Warner," I said, extending my hand. I saw that my hand was trembling. Inside, I could feel my heart keeping time with my shaky hand. Of course, she shook it. She gave no sign of recognition, but neither did she seem confused. "I'm Franny Feldstone," she said. "What brings you to P'Town?"

"Do you know anything about me?" I said. If I couldn't find out anything from Dara, at least I might find out something from her sister.

"You're Darcy's friend from Dell," she said. "What do you mean?"

I could see her wariness. What I had wanted to ask was whether she knew about my life. If there was any possibility that I occupied a position in Dara's life similar to what Dara's position had been in mine. I wanted to find out if she had any idea how much—or whether—I mattered to Dara.

"Why are you looking at me like that?" Franny said.

"Sweetie, she knows that you are my *dearest* friend," Dara said.

She might have been speaking simply, and she might have been cueing Franny. I had no way of knowing, because Franny's expression remained neutral. Even her nod was neutral.

"Two Bloody Marys?" the bartender said. He had gotten up from his table almost as soon as they came in. He had been standing behind the bar, watching us, sensing that whatever we were saying to each other should not be interrupted right away.

"Henry, darling, you have read my mind," Dara said. "Though perhaps three will be necessary."

She looked at me. I didn't say anything. The bartender set to work.

"Dara," I said, "do you have any idea how shocking this is?"

Franny had walked away. She draped her parka over the back of a chair, then walked to the jukebox and stood far across the room, leaning forward to look at the selection, her back to us. The bartender began to pour ingredients into a cocktail shaker. Everything happening could have seemed ordinary, except for the fact that yet again Dara had fooled me, and every time she did, it seemed the world became a stranger, more unpredictable place.

"What would the difference have been if I'd told you?" Dara said. "Can't you believe that when I put together a life for myself, I wanted to be totally unique? It wasn't easy being a twin. When you're younger, you can't get used to the stares. Then you *pretend* to get used to them. It didn't make me think I was special. What it made me think was that I had to get away from her." Dara's face clouded over. "But I never can," she said. "We're always living vicariously through each other. When I'm down, she's up. She's down, I'm up. And I am very down, right now, sweetie. You saw me on one of the most embarrassing nights of my life."

"I don't know," I said. "I think the way you embarrassed yourself with Liam was worse."

She started to say something, then stopped. She sat at the table, still in her parka, sitting on Franny's chair, Franny's parka draped behind her.

"So I'm foolish," she said.

"You really are," I said. "I was your friend, and you did that. You won't stop at anything, will you?"

"Don't be angry," she said. "I was drunk. Nothing was going right in my life."

"You know who else got drunk recently and did something irreversible?" I said. It was cruel, but I couldn't resist. I was sure that if she hadn't said anything in all the time we'd been in the bar, it was because she didn't know. "Frank," I said. "Frank got drunk and drove into a stationary crane inside a construction area on I-95. Frank's dead."

She put her fingertips to her eyebrows, then slowly lowered her hands. I had made an impression on her. Something I'd said had surprised her as much as she'd surprised me. She was obviously stunned, but unlike me she wouldn't have to wonder whether she was hearing all the story, or if it really happened the way I said.

But much more must have happened. He was asleep in their bed. Asleep next to Janey. And then there was a head-on crash, on I-95, and he was dead. The image of Frank standing on the beach on Barbara's birthday came back to me: his holding the carp kite, as its big mouth swallowed air, heading toward the clouds. I had once stood beside Frank at the beach. The realization that I never would again made tears come to my eyes. Dara was already crying.

"His wife," she said. "All those little babies."

The bartender set two Bloody Marys in front of us and walked away. Franny was sitting at another table, talking to the man who had been reading a newspaper.

"Oh," Dara said, reaching for my hand, "now you see. Now you know that *he* was suicidal. It was never me. It was Frank."

"You know," I said, "I can't believe anything you say. That might be true, and it might not."

"You do believe I loved him, don't you?" she said, suddenly, brushing her hair off her cheek. "Because you did, too. We both loved him."

I didn't even think to ask what she meant. I looked at her for a long time, widening my eyes and slowly lowering them, trying as best I could to suggest an unphrased question. Some underlying question that existed between us, that would have to remain enigmatic, because it would be too painful, too powerful, to ever articulate. I couldn't see myself in a mirror, but I could sense that I'd learned well from her; I thought that I was doing a good job. And I was doing it just to do it. I was doing it—and therefore I wondered if Dara had ever done it—just for the hell of it.

The bartender took Franny her drink, but Franny never came back to the table. Dara seemed—but then all I could say was that she seemed—heartbroken and dejected. She tried again to take my hand, but I withdrew it. Neither did I meet her own wide-eyed stare. The days when I would fall under her spell were over. I had done what I'd set out to accomplish. When I stood, I put a five-dollar bill on the table, leaving Dara and the untouched drink behind. Though I would see her again, it wouldn't be for a very long time. And then when I did see her, I would always have the knowledge that that night in Provincetown I had effectively turned the tables. As much as if I had actually toppled the table—which for a little while I had been angry enough to do—I felt that the few things I said, and the way I refused to be drawn into her melodramas anymore, had finally registered, and altered the dynamic between us for all time.

It didn't occur to me until I went outside that I hadn't asked the bartender where I might spend the night. It was dark, and cold, and I was suddenly exhausted. When I got back to the car, I was grateful that the dog moved into the driver's seat and put his paws on me, and licked my face. For the sake of the dog, I would find a place to stay. Unlike Dara, I thought, I was a responsible person.

It would be difficult to explain why Dara and I went on to have a kind of friendship. It was a friendship—"relationship" is probably a better word, since the word "relationship" can mean almost anything, from people's fondness for their dogs to their over-the-counter chit-chat with the butcher—in which I listened in a desultory fashion and trusted absolutely nothing she said, and in which I considered anything involving Dara that transpired in front of my eyes to be entirely inconclusive.

You never really recover when a person's death comes as a total shock. I don't mean that the pain is less when you lose someone after a lingering illness—just that a startlingly unexpected death takes a different toll. I did believe Dara was horrified that Frank died. Whether she was right about Frank's having a death wish, I'll never know. But there were those few minutes in which I clearly had the upper hand, being the one to tell her about Frank's death, and her acknowledgment of that—her own vulnerability—sealed something between us. I knew then what Liam must have meant about the closed bathroom door. If you didn't know better—if you didn't know that Dara herself was always Pandora's box—the temptation would be simply to reach out and embrace her. I fought that urge in the bar, knowing by then that even letting her hold my hand, I could be subsumed in her cat's cradle of lies and deceptions and half-truths, all so very well acted that, in the moment, you would believe whatever she wanted you to believe. You were never really on equal footing with Dara in any situation; though it might have seemed that you had volition, or even power, ultimately you remained at her mercy. She was the most manipulative person I have ever met.

I decided, that night in the Atlantic House, that I would never know the truth about her background, and neither would I ever know the truth about the present. I had fallen into a peculiar trap. I had been drawn in by her, persuaded that we were really talking, simply because we did so much of it—though most of it was one-way talk, and time and again, all I had done was listen. The more we talked, the more she dissembled. Finally, I doubted that it mattered whether certain things were real, or only real to Dara. When she cast them so that they had an impact on your life—and she was very, very good at tailoring stories for different recipients—the impact retained all of its power, even if you later found out you had been deceived; it was irrelevant whether something had been based on fact or fiction. Though she seemed open to possibilities, and though she solicited your views, and certainly your sympathy, and though she turned her attention equally to you, and your life, and your problems, actually there was no openness to anything on her part. I think she always had the whole script in her head, memorized; whatever you came up with would only be an improvisation—a harmless digression, something amusing for her to consider. The closer the bond you felt with her, the freer she became. But she stayed around, pretending devotion. Letting you think that you were wise, kind, necessary. Dara never really cared about anyone but Dara—and even there, I wonder if that wasn't her most compelling role: to remain fixated on herself, when there was every chance she didn't know any more than the rest of us what she truly believed. At the same time, she was a delicate creature; though paradoxically, she was also a creature who could not be tampered with. However carefully you steam open a sealed envelope, it will still appear puckered when you reseal it; pour an inch of water into a bottle you've taken a secret nip from, and the connoisseur will immediately taste the dilution. Children, who think adults have supernatural powers, are reluctant to learn that lesson, but eventually they do. Unless you're very, very lucky—which, as everyone knows, we so rarely are when we really, truly need luck—those things we've done wrong will inevitably boomerang. With Dara, you could end up looking like the one who was unkind. Like the one who was the aggressor.

That night, in Provincetown, sitting at the bar before Dara and Dara came in, I had been wondering if Dara's attempt to seduce Liam might in any way have been retribution for something I had done. In some baroque, cosmic way, might Dara have done it because I had steamed open letters from Derek to see if he had anything new to say, and then resealed and returned them? Had I done something, way back when, to deserve Dara? Had I put out signals that I was a sad orphan, an easy mark, a vulnerable person she could subsume, gathering strength from another person's waning power? I had been so cautious about doing something that might offend my husband that the day I took the flask to Corolli's bakery, I had watered the rum, though missing liquor was clearly nothing Bob would ever have noticed, or cared about. But I had been so taken with my own adventurousness that I had imagined he would become furious. We all have our little fictions about people. We guess at their sex lives, become titillated by their friends' gossip about them, imagine what they look like doing something humbling, like puking out the night's alcohol. For a long time, I'd tried to do just what I'd done all through my childhood; I'd tried to do what Bob's family expected. But the people I'd selected had been the sort who would never accept me for who I really was. I'd selected people who'd retreated to their niche as quickly as animals in a zoo, burrowing into their phony caves, ducking behind their plastic foliage—people who were unadventurous, uncommunicative, unwilling. They weren't bad people. They were just trapped, small-town people. And we could only live harmoniously as long as I believed what they believed.

I'd tried, for a while. I registered the fact that the triangular sign with the emblem of the leaping deer was most certainly an indication that a deer might cross the road in that place. More personal signs? The greeting cards they sent certainly must mean that they cared for me as much as the card, with its store-bought sentiment, said they cared. But I couldn't sustain it. I couldn't settle for so little. It wasn't because of Dara that I stopped being willing to compromise; regardless of what Janey maintained, I had considered leaving before I met her. I had begun to feel constricted in my clothes. Isolated in bed, even if Bob and I had just made love. In fact, ironic as it would have been, that first day I met Tom Van Sant, I had considered flirting in return; taking him up on what he was offering. Letting the bushes sit there by the side of the road. Going off with someone just because he offered the possibility of excitement, just as Liam had thought about having sex with Dara because she offered the same possibility. Hearing about how that possibility nearly materialized, with Dara, hadn't been easy. It had made me wonder if I would ever partake of anything as exciting as scattering flower seeds and falling to the ground to make love, passionately, impulsively, unwisely. It was in my mind when I made the stupid mistake of having sex with Derek—the idea that I could catch up with something I'd missed.

Because that was the way I thought of my life. My life was the form of my days, not the content. My life was one in which I took my lead from other people: I followed after them; I stifled my personality, trying to absorb their ideas, their enthusiasms. I have a clear image of myself as a little girl, trailing after my aunt Elizabeth like a human pull toy. I became her shadow, bumping along behind her. Which was the same thing I had done when I fixated on Bob in college. I didn't need Bob the way I had been genuinely needy, as all children are, but I sensed that because I'd suffered such a blow, I had only so much energy in reserve—that time was running out, and that I should commit myself to someone and let him know I had by staying at his side. Bob had been flattered. He had thought I was a little too demonstrative, a bit excessive, but no woman before me had ever been so devoted. No one had ever professed great passion for Bob. It was a passionless family.

When Dara courted me, I underestimated how disturbed she was, but I eventually realized that in deciding on me, she was doing a random thing. I wasn't so silly as to be flattered, though I admit there were times I faltered, when I thought she might have genuinely understood the things I kept hidden, the things I repressed, the energy I forced myself to hold back. But she didn't, because the life I was living was my own masquerade, and she was too busy with her own performance. I was never really a compliant, conservative, good girl. I had carried that over from my timid childhood, marrying Bob because he wouldn't have the ability to see through me. I would have protective coloration forever. Those times I was almost persuaded to think that we might be soul mates, she and I, she always went too far. In my private conception of myself, I was wild but virtuous; in her private conception of herself, she knew that she was only desperate. It was desperation, and the best twist she could put on it was to make it appear to be devotion. I knew all about that. It was the way I had survived as a child. It was the path that had led me to Bob, and to Dell.

My mistake—and I flatter myself that it is not a mistake I would make as an older person—was in assuming I could have fun with Dara, learn from Dara, let Dara show them how women who believed in their talent and who felt a justifiable sense of entitlement acted, but still draw the line. There's no such thing as drawing the line with a person who is really crazy. That person will take the line and lift it up and use it as a whip. She'll laugh as she points out that your line was drawn with disappearing ink.

But my time with Dara wasn't wasted. It wasn't wasted because for the first time in my life, it made me think about what I wanted. If Janey thought that that resulted in the end of my marriage, then so be it. Like so many people, I had said many times what I didn't want, but until I met her, I had thought the best I could do would be to hide who I really was; to live on the defensive. What I learned from Dara was that you could go some distance by not being any one clearly defined person. That if people thought they understood you, it was time to move on. Because if you didn't move on, you would become a statue. You would stand in a park, and pigeons would shit on your head, and all the while the pigeons would be looking for new places to roost.

Dara might have wanted to give the impression that she knew someone by her ability to define them in one sentence, but she was actually only doing what was expedient for her; she wasn't really trumpeting the arrival of the other person. I caught on to that pretty quickly, but what did it matter if she defined me as the person who had gone to

England with a man the day after meeting him? That was true enough. Who doesn't understand that lives are lived in off moments, in outtakes, and in snapshots, as well as in public appearances? I look back now and see, more than I did then, that certain people in my life—Dara, among others—gave me the message that men (or relationships in general) were not to be taken overly seriously. Easier in theory than in fact, but still: something to temper ridiculous passions. From my friends at the time, I got positive reinforcement for what they saw as my justifiable skepticism toward men. Joyce, and particularly Gail, were well on their way to becoming strident feminists, and I got the benefit of their perspective. Janey, who moved to Albuquerque with the children after Frank's death and became increasingly spiritual—at least, that was how she presented herself in her letters; after the funeral, I never saw her again—used to write me that she had come to admire my lack of connectedness to worldly things, a category in which she included people. At the time I was doing it, it didn't occur to me that pulling the wool over the eyes of some Brit's aunt in order for him to get money from her for a nonexistent wedding might have been my version of retaliation against Liam, for what he'd done years before. But for whatever reason I'd done it, I did like the outcome. I liked my ten percent of the cash, and I liked the grudging respect it got me from the regulars at Cafe Central.

Years after leaving Bob, I met a man in New York. He was a hotel manager, and I met him when I went to a conference about near-death experiences. I went with a woman I did volunteer work with, who had almost died when an elevator she was in plunged five floors and killed the other occupants. I strung along just to have something to do that night and heard people recount stories about seeing lights at the end of tunnels as doctors did CPR; women who had been lifted from their wrecked automobiles by some enormous being with a kindly face, whose arms safely enveloped them. I hoped that had happened to Frank, because I believed them. At least, I believed that they believed what they said. The closest I could come was to remember what it had felt like to learn that my parents had both died in a plane crash, but that was my experience, not theirs, and frankly, what I remembered was my aunt Elizabeth sitting on the sofa, the big picture window behind her totally dark, weeping. Looking at her head and seeing dandruff. Thinking: Something terrible has happened, and she is crying, with dirty hair. I must have been in shock, and that shock must have lasted for a very long time. When I think about it, my life has been bracketed by that shock, and by the shock I felt when I first learned about Frank's death. Frank's death closed the parenthesis.

I met the man who was to become my husband as I stepped off an elevator. He was behind the front desk, and he looked at me as though he recognized me. It wasn't the perfunctory look he'd give hotel guests—Well attired? Yes, they belong here—it was the happily surprised look of an old friend, yet it was also the look of a person who wanted a relationship closer than friendship. How interesting that just when I'd realized that two terrible deaths had bracketed my life, the person who was going to be my way out locked his eyes with mine and stopped me before I left the hotel. My own version of the enormous being with a kindly face, no doubt. My big chance, and I wasn't going to blow it. I still think of him as my big chance. He's my chance to live a moderately eventful, often pleasurable life. My chance for a new start—because, to this day, every moment lived on the lam from Dell and its inhabitants seems a potential new start. I look at my husband's brother, suffering because of his wife's infidelity, embarrassed because he was duped, cynical because his wife committed adultery with their minister, of all people, and I think: Be glad you have a chance to float free. Be glad to be cut loose, whether you cut the string, or someone cut it for you. Although I suppose you could argue that I might not be empathic enough, having resolved never to be close to the brother of a husband again.

I lived with my husband-to-be, John, for a year before marrying him, during which time he was rotated to a new hotel in San Francisco. Then we returned to his home state, Connecticut—full circle; appropriate enough?—where he was given a job managing the golf resort he still runs today. The hotel has a reciprocal agreement with many other hotels, and we travel often. For a while after college, before going to New York, I taught at a community college, but the money was bad, and most of the students were trying to learn a trade and only suffering through my course because they were required to take it. A year was enough of going through the motions—especially when all around me I saw the most innovative teachers being asked to conform, and the brightest lecturers eventually deciding to keep quiet and take better-paying jobs in corporations. The year I graduated, Gail Jason took a job with Exxon. I don't suspect she had many occasions on the job to bring up her favorite Virginia Woolf novels. Back in England, Liam became a contributing editor to the English edition of *Esquire,* specializing in long, gory true-crime pieces. He sent me tear sheets of several of them, without comment, but when I didn't respond, they eventually stopped coming, though I have no doubt he continued to chronicle people who tortured and murdered one another. My husband says that when he first looked up and saw me, he was immediately attracted to me, but at the same time, because he knew that much of the crowd in the hotel was there for the "Near Death Experiences" seminar, he hoped that I wasn't among them; that I was—this is as much a favorite word of his as "dreamy" was Dara's—"normal." It wasn't that he disbelieved near-death experiences; it was just that he thought that anyone who had gone through such a thing must be hugely changed, and he is convinced that once subjected to such a trauma, a person will spend his or her whole life trying to regain equilibrium. He sympathizes in the abstract with people who have suffered something terrible and are trying to put their lives back together, but he doesn't want to be around those people. His brother, yes—of course he will extend himself to his brother. But he does not wish to know about people's suffering, for the simple reason that he doubts that there will be a good outcome. He thinks the world is wicked, and that it is not changing for the better. He believes that most often suffering leads to nothing—and that is one of the things I find most interesting about him. That while his own view of things is bleak, he is happier not to expound on it; similarly, he does not welcome other people's angst and well-articulated despair. I realized soon in our relationship that he didn't want me to dredge up every bit of unhappiness so he could turn it over and over in his hand, examining it like some strange shard found on an archaeological dig. He actively hoped I would be cheerful, and happy, and he believed that one way to accomplish this was not to dwell on the negative. It was that second thing that set him apart from Bob. I should probably give Bob credit for having good intentions, but in his reluctance to believe that happiness could be achieved, he backed off totally. He didn't plan pleasant moments together, or buy silly little presents, or tell me I was beautiful. Bob left me to myself, while John is—as he likes to put it—"always nudging." It is a standing joke between us: he pokes his elbow in my ribs if he thinks I might be sad, making his nudging literal.

In all the years of our marriage, I have spoken Dara's name only a few times, when she's part of a story I'm telling—a minor character. From England, Liam wrote me a letter, when he first left Connecticut, urging me to go into therapy to find out why I had such a fixation on Dara. He maintained that his involvement had been one of brief curiosity. But my own involvement . . . did I realize how focused I was on her? How she always seemed to have been part of our life, as real as if she stood in the room? Had she represented something that I embraced precisely because it was haunting? And if so, what exactly did she embody?

He was wrong about my being fixated. I was interested; I was in some odd way validated; I was sometimes titillated, I admired some of the things she did and was repelled by others. Ultimately, I was had, and things spun out of control, as they do when you're dealing with any volatile substance, but Liam had met me at a strange point in my life. I was never as fascinated with Dara as he thought. He was the one who apparently couldn't forget her, even miles away. He was the one who had written to reintroduce the subject, in the guise of helping me. It wouldn't have surprised me if they had gotten together. Which they might have, for all I know. Or perhaps, if she was more of a prankster than I thought, she could have sent her sister in her place. Dara always liked to see things through to their conclusion. It was just that she alone was the one who decided when they concluded.

A little less than a year ago, I got a letter from Dara. She had only an old address, but somehow the letter survived two forwardings. The mailman handed it to me on top of the pile, and I thought he might have put it there deliberately, because the handwriting was so interesting. It arrived at the golf club when I was alone in the house, for which I was grateful. As I opened it, I remembered the awful letter she had sent me when I returned the diamond-and-ruby ring, expressing her self-righteous anger in an attempt to hurt me more than I had hurt her. Dara always had to get even. First, she made everything into a competition; then she had to win, even if she was only the self-declared winner. Time had not changed her handwriting. It was as lavish as ever, nearly filling the envelope with sweeps of brown ink. I was amused to see that on an envelope, though not in life, she felt the need to spell everything out: no "Cir." for "Circle"; no abbreviation for the name of the state. The letter said:

*Dear Jean,*

*I hope this finds you well and happy. I think of you often and hope that you and your husband are still travelling and seeking the sun, when appropriate, and the moonlight whenever romance fills the heart. I still get the odd letter from Trenton, who passes on whatever news he has of you from Bob, who says that from time to time, people tell him if they've heard anything about you. It is wonderful that you have opted out of the workaday world, and it is equally wonderful that you've learned to golf. I'm sure it's wonderful fun. Do you ride in a cart, and if so, do you feel like the president? For a few astonishingly wonderful months I was involved with a man who made my heart leap, but his misery at having his young children living on the West Coast so far from him made him decide he must pull up stakes and return to Los Angeles. I suppose the way you felt about Dell, I have come to feel about L.A.—that it is an amorphous place that pretends to be a city. Well—maybe that is not pretending to so much, but I, at least, cannot pretend that it is where I belong. Though acting jobs have dwindled almost entirely, it would be stupid of me to think that I could go home again, either to L.A. or to New York. I was part of a book discussion group at the local library for a while, but so many of the people really wanted to talk about politics in the guise of talking about books that we never really seemed to discuss literature. I came upon your copy of* GODOT *a month or so ago, which I remember once having taken from your bookshelf. As though the world—as though even you—cared what my perceptions were! I was jealous that you were pursuing something I thought was the exact right thing for you, and I suspected that I did not have what it took to prevail as an actress over time. Not long ago I found one of my notes to you (I admit it freely; I was so vain that I kept carbons; I was that thrilled with my words!)— one of the many I "lifted" from Chekhov, as you told me so irately shortly after that long-ago, black, bleak night in Provincetown, and now I freely admit it, darling: I have eventually been able to see what you found so infuriating. Do you remember? The letter I found was (yes, it was wrong of me to omit attribution; yes, it was also unfair, not to quote the ending) Chekhov to S.N. Plescheyev, 1889. I have the carbon before me now, and I can see that the way I wanted to speak to you was too lofty—something that could not be successfully lifted from its context, though I'm afraid the attempt to transcend contexts has often been a personal failing. My affection for you was sincere, though. I hope you know that. Will I risk condemnation if I write the words again, if this time I quote them exactly? It has a tone that still brings back exactly how I felt, but my God! The youthful pomposity! Who was I, to think myself the equal of Chekhov, just because I, too, was skeptical about so much of mankind?* "Write me a letter, my dear. I love your writing; when I see it, I grow cheerful. Besides, I shall not hide it from you, my correspondence with you flatters me. Your letters and Suvorin's I treasure and shall bequeath to my grandchildren: let the sons of bitches read them and know what went on in times long past."

*Tell me that you still read voraciously and that you still love books. Or tell me something. Tell me about your life, tell me what to read, tell me a story that is distracting. There seems no way to state bad news except to be blunt: I recently saw a doctor, and it seems that my worst fears are confirmed, and that there is something seriously wrong. That's a euphemism, but I can't (won't) write the word. I am going to Sloan-Kettering for further tests, though I understand that the odds are not in my favor. However things turn out, I regret having been out of touch (which has been my doing, my envy, my inability to ask for help, those times I really needed it). For what it's worth, you have a piece of my heart, and whatever drugs or radiation might damage, that has already been sent to you. Long life, much love, and may all your cappuccinos be laced with rum.*

It was signed simply with her initial—the one abbreviation in the letter.

I finished reading it while sitting on the living room sofa. I got up and looked out the window, where I could distantly see a party of men putting on the green of the fifth hole. Two golf carts awaited them. When the last ball was putted into the cup, they would head for the carts, some jubilant, others discussing the quirks of fate that interfered with sinking their balls on the too-high, brushlike grass, or their bad luck—their simple bad luck—in ending up in the rough. Sometimes I made the rounds with my husband. I knew what the talk sounded like.

You could usually predict early in the game—as they teed up for the first drive actually—which people would be quick to blame themselves, and who would blame the world. More tended to blame themselves, which was the opposite of what I would have expected. Very rarely do you hear about the grass being too high, or about the stifled sneeze that ruined their swing. I amused John by calling golf one of the talking sports. Swimming was a silent sport.

I went to my bedroom and stretched out on the bed and read the letter a second time. There was nothing accusatory in the letter. I was glad that she was not trying to manipulate me, relieved that it was not one of those letters from years ago—something perverse that she had impulsively sent. Those letters had turned me against her, so that it was difficult to read the letter she had just sent with compassion, and I felt ashamed of myself—ashamed, but relieved that she didn't know my telephone number, glad that I would have time to compose a response.

In my head, I wrote several drafts of the letter I thought I would send, though I never did send it. In all of them, I told her how sorry I was to hear such bad news: in some, I feigned optimism; in others, I joked bleakly; in my final imaginary attempt, I simply asserted that in time, in spite of the ordeal she would have to go through, she would be fine. That, I felt sure, was a lie, since she had never been fine in her life. But perhaps that would have been the most appropriate response of all, because a liar could appreciate another liar. I scanned her letter a last time. What did she mean when she said that the world would not care about her opinion, let alone me? I had cared all too much about her opinions, and she certainly knew that. And the idea that she could not bring herself to ask for help . . . what did she think not giving her my new address meant? That I still welcomed her requests? Hadn't I done enough, with all the things I had given her?

I rubbed my hand idly on the bedspread. It was pretty: quilted, with a pattern of small autumn leaves swirling across the material. The resort provided everything: our linen; the bed covers; the soap. They were all of good quality. Every morning, new soap replaced the old. Each winter and summer the bedspreads were replaced. Finally, I got up. The golfers were gone. It was late afternoon—not the most popular time to be on the links. I watched for a while, but no one appeared. I turned on the stereo, which was tuned to the classical-music station. Something smooth and melodic was playing—music Dara would have called "dreamy." I listened for a few minutes, then folded the letter and put it in my night-table drawer. I didn't want John to see it. I had had enough discussions about Dara's letters in my lifetime, and even if my lifetime was very long (thank you, Dara) she was not going to be a subject in my marriage.

When I eventually read Dara's obituary, I decided to keep quiet about that, too. Because the truth was I couldn't imagine at what point I would begin describing Dara—which, at least, was an improvement, or at least less torturous, than all those years in which I had not known at what point to stop.

As for her last letter, perhaps she had been finally drained of energy, had simply run out of steam, because I wasn't enough of a friend, but I also wasn't enough of an adversary. Even without my presence that always gave her something solid to bounce off of, she might have had fleeting moments when she saw the present clearly, at the same time she saw the future darkly. And since she'd left nothing in her wake unharmed, it seemed appropriate that what remained was to curse the future. In her scattershot indictment of "the sons of bitches," Dara had found her perfect exit line.

A NOTE ON THE TYPE

The text of this book was set in Simoncini Garamond, a modern version by Francesco Simoncini of
the type attributed to the famous Parisian type cutter
Claude Garamond (ca. 1480–1561). Garamond was
a pupil of Geoffroy Tory and is believed to have
based his letters on the Venetian models, although he
introduced a number of important differences, and it
is to him we owe the letter that we know as old-style.
He gave to his letters a certain elegance and a feeling
of movement that won for their creator an immediate
reputation and the patronage of Francis I of France.

*Composed by ComCom,*
*an R. R. Donnelley & Sons Company,*
*Allentown, Pennsylvania*

*Printed and bound by Berryville Graphics,*
*Berryville, Virginia*

*Designed by Dorothy S. Baker*